THE WAY *to* BYZANTIUM

There and back - somehow!

THE WAY *to* BYZANTIUM

There and back - somehow!

PJE BAILEY

.

For my family, friends and the fabulous Istanbulluler

Contents

Preface

There is a novel in everyone, or so I am led to believe. Any person over the age of sixteen years must have a wealth of experiences locked up in their subconscious. But how to unlock them? Nobody has lived an uneventful life, it's just that those rich experiences which may have happened to us: enjoyable or traumatic, uplifting or horrifying, tend to get submerged beneath the routines of a monotonous existence.

We may be able to contemplate and savour those occurrences, or even dread their return in nightmares. All too often though, they lose their savour over the years. How can we encapsulate something special that happened, say, fifty years ago and still retain their unique flavour and poignancy? After all, surely, we were different persons then. Would we not, in the present time, see those experiences in the light of a more adult way of thinking?

Suppose our minds could somehow hold on to clear memories of past events, then recount them accurately to others. For example, we may wish to relate what was happening to us during those wild but formative years between adolescence and adulthood. We are at once faced with the problem of a time lapse between those events and the present day. Next, there is the organisation of narrative. Would each event be a short story, or a chapter, or section of an autobiography? Even those individuals with perfect recall cannot achieve concretion of experience. At best, it is mere duplication. I believe that it is in this way, a work of fiction, based on real events, is born, able to share the emotions, tensions, despair and the sheer joy or otherwise, of times remembered.

In the novel that follows this introduction, four graduates from a college of education decide to set off on a world tour. This kind of venture would later be categorised under "gap year" activities. In terms of period, it is set at the end of a decade often referred to as the "Swinging Sixties". The four young men, although they are not necessarily or directly influenced by the liberating aspects of this period, do not wish to settle into employment before experiencing, in a visceral sense, something of foreign parts. I say "visceral" because their modes of transport are to be strictly on the ground, among real people. They intend to hitch hike, and, where cheap enough, use buses or trains. They also take the trouble to book in advance three sea passages across the English Channel, the Adriatic, and The Mediterranean

So to the expedition itself. It is meticulously planned during their final weeks at college. The students are vaccinated against smallpox, typhoid, tetanus and yellow fever. They purchase tents, rucksacks and sleeping bags, along with small stoves, extra clothes and some food supplies. Each of them is equipped with a knife – for self protection and other general purposes – and one of the group has spent six weeks training them in martial arts.

Somehow, they have secured employment at a match factory in Khartoum, should they ever arrive in this city. Beyond that destination, plans for their further progress become rather more opaque, and somewhat bizarre. There is mention of crossing Somalia in a converted landing craft; avoiding Afghanistan by traversing Iran; finding work in an Indian public school, and then working their passage from Southeast Asia to San Francisco. Readers may conclude that this latter part of their so called itinerary would exist only in the realms of fantasy, consisting of an ill-conceived and vague set of ideas for such a serious venture.

This novel is concerned with the journey from London to Istanbul and its aftermath. Anyone who has read this introduction will not be too surprised at the expedition's outcome. For one member of the group, the real adventure has only just begun.

A guide to Turkish pronunciation

Letter	Example	Pronounced	As in...
a	kanal - canal	u	bus
c	cevap - answer	j	jug
ç	çorba - soup	ch	chop
ğ	oğul - son	(Lengthens vowel)	goal mile
i	bin - thousand	i	bin
ı	salı - Tuesday	(schwa)	jok<u>er</u> sudd<u>en</u>
j	makyaj – make up	French j	leisure
o	okul - school	o	orange
ö	öğretmen - teacher	er	Work pearl
s	sokak - street	s	summer
ş	şeker - sugar	sh	shop
u	bulut - cloud	oo	look
ü	hükümet - government	ugh	suit
v	savaş - battle	w	want

b, d, e, f, g, h, k, l, m, n, p, r, t, y, z are pronounced the same as in English.

The letters q, w, x do not appear in the Turkish alphabet.

Other long vowels: ar - are
                   ay – eye
                   ey – day
                   oy - boy

11

Istanbul Dreaming

Once I journeyed far away
To a city on seven hills
Where somehow I learned about
The foibles of love, and the art of life.

Now in my dreams I return some nights
To the stone steps of Pera,
Reaching down sea-facing slopes,
Along cobbled alleyways.
From where I can glimpse
The distant minarets
Of old Istanbul.

Ships on the Bosphorus
And far out in the Marmara
Haunt the night air,
Piercing the silent darkness
With their plaintive cries.
As if calling upon the sleeping city
To fetch them back
From the catastrophic clutches
Of those cruel waters
On which they have ventured.

I am floating in mid air
Towards the harbour,
Catching just a glimpse
Of Asia, across the windblown straits.

Light mists enshroud Leander's Tower,
Standing proud amid white flecked waves,
Guarding a tragic legend
Of long ago.

Haunted by the dream,
Once more I am drawn
To the ancient harbour,
Of Karaköy, where cargo ships
And cruisers make landfall
Amongst the mackerel boats.
I stroll past byways rank
With oil and fish heads.
Sewage gurgles just beneath me,
Below gutters strewn with
Fag ends and melon skins.
I know this place.

Again, I return to
A street of lighted shopfronts.
Behind each huge window
Are bevies of whores,
All of them curvy
You might say,
A few extra pounds.
You could fuck them for five lira
But I don't.
I never did.

In front of these emporia,
Dressed in grey jackets,
Soiled black trousers and
Backless, worn out shoes,
Crowds of men prowl,
Gazing upon the indifferent women.
Horny men with needs beyond their means,

Clutching their five lira notes.
And you'd better get it over quick!

All day they'd had to watch
The well to do
Parading through the city;
The suited men
In their German cars.
Their trophy wives, bedecked in finery.
Painted ladies with
Gold chains, dresses from Paris,
Trotting like tame gazelles
In their husbands' wake.

I cross the Golden Horn
And find myself in Sirkeci,
At the station.
Once more I've missed the westbound train.
So I walk, and soon
The benighted city
Becomes a distant vision
On a darkened horizon.

I am in open fields,
Floating again
Along country lanes,
Familiar somehow.
An aroma of new mown hay
Hangs in the air,
As if I am back in England,
With no end to my journey in sight,
Save for the gathering light
Of my reawakening.

PJE Bailey

My place is placeless, a trace of the traceless.......... and know, first, last, outer, inner, only that I breathe, a breathing human being.

Mevlana Rumi (1207 - 1273)

Part One

The Party

One thirty. One thirty am, or thereabouts. Returning home after a party but what a party! Who was that girl and what was her name? Suzie - Sexy Suzie, that's what the guys had called her. Now Pete was alone on a remote footpath in a grassy meadow, a mile or so from home, having accepted a ride back in Phil's van. Phil was an old schoolmate. Fancy him turning up at the party. His presence had certainly proved valuable in more ways than one. Now it was time to proceed homewards. To his left lay vistas of pinewood; marching conifers as far as the eye could discern in the half moonlit small hours of an early September morning. Dampness caused Pete to shiver, to raise the collar of his Levi's jacket in a futile attempt to stave off the creeping cold air now pervading the forest edge. He faced a mile and a half trudge back home across fields only too familiar in daylight. Why had he asked Phil to drop him off near here? Had he chosen deliberately to venture on one last patrol of his beloved home territory before departing on his eagerly awaited expedition around the world next day?

Next day......it already was next day! He was supposed to be getting up at seven. Only about five hours' potential shuteye. Or would mounting excitement drive away any thoughts of sleep? Excitement was what he had also been expecting at the party but not with Suzie as it happened.

Before the party, he had not even met her. Oh no, his hopes had been fixed on Emma; the virginal Emma whom he had bumped into in the High Street a few days before. As he set off along the narrow footpath towards the railway crossing, he recalled the scene.

*****

She had stood on the pavement in front of him. Shiny soft brown eyes peered up at Pete, slowly expressing recognition.

"I remember you, you're Pete."

"Er yeah, that's right err...."

"Emma. Don't say you've forgotten my name. I'm so upset." There was a glint of irony in her eyes – and was that some desire too? Her look prompted Pete to reply

"Sorry Emma, I don't think we knew each other at school."

"I was in your girlfriend's class. Oh well, see you around then."

"How about sooner than you think, like tonight for example. Are you free by any chance?"

"Might be. What have you got in mind?" Typically, Pete had no more in mind than a film, or a pleasant stroll – at least to begin with. She continued, cutting in on his thoughts.

"My, your hair needs cutting. I cut hair in my spare time and I could do yours if you like."

Pete thought he had struck while the proverbial iron had been reaching top temperature. However, this apparent forwardness on Emma's part had made his direct approach appear a mere feinting move. A few minutes later, as he saw her on to her bus, she handed him her telephone number written on an old bus ticket. Once on board, she called out,

"Call me and we'll arrange that haircut." She leaned off the rear deck common to buses of that era and they kissed each other farewell. Then she was off into the conduit of late afternoon traffic, made denser with joyous streams of workers cycling from the emptying factories. Swallowed up by the traffic, Emma's bus made its steady, ponderous way towards her home in the Dengie Marshes. Pete called her that same night.

And so it came to pass, the following evening, that after Emma had made more than a passable attempt to relieve Pete of his collar length locks, fallen tresses lying forlornly piled on newspaper under the improvised barber's chair, Pete found himself sitting beside the lovely Emma on his front room sofa. This was the unremarkable mustard coloured sofa where he had similarly reclined with a number of girlfriends, experiencing varying results and consequences. Now he was reminiscing with Emma about school days and generally catching up on the intervening three years' worth of events since they would have last had any contact. During the conversation, indeed, while she had been cutting his hair, there had been a kind of tenderness in her every movement; a deftness; a soft inviting archness in every nuance of her chatter which seemed to hold for Pete the promise of joys to come. He had begun really to admire this sweet girl and better still, she had even invited him to her party the following Saturday night.

Draping the obligatory arm confidently around her shoulder, he turned his face, and to his delight found hers turned towards him. Their first kiss was tender, luscious and mutually longed for and the following embraces lacked nothing in passion. This was so enjoyable. Pete's emotions were bounding along, seasoned with all the joys new love can bring. So why not?

Emma's voice, when she spoke, was gentle, friendly and reassuring in a way. She had shifted her position a few inches back on the couch; far enough back, however, to stop Pete in his tracks:

"I'm a virgin Pete and intend to stay that way until I am married. You're lovely and I loved the way you kissed me. ("So why stop?" mused Pete.) "But no further, please. This is our first time."

Pete duly made his way to Emma's party on the following Saturday night as arranged. It just so happened to coincide with the eve of his long awaited global expedition. With three friends, he was to set out the following morning with an uncertain future beckoning. Indeed, the only certainties about the whole enterprise were three sea ferry bookings: from Folkestone to Ostend, Brindisi to Patras and Beirut to Alexandria. They were to make their way to these destinations using any forms of transport at their disposal, but principally by hitch – hiking.

To reach the party, he had to catch a bus to town, then another which carried him through a late summer landscape of gold hued cereal crops and ripening apples. The green double decker rumbled up Danbury Hill with its views to the west of purple tinged clouds that heralded the impending dusk. Later, in the middle distance, Pete glimpsed the darkening river estuary and the marshland which was his destination. He boarded yet another bus which took him from the ancient Saxon town of Maldon and out to the marshes where Emma had told him she lived. There were no thoughts in Pete's mind of how he was going to get back. Would he even want to?

Later, on reflection, he could remember little about the house where the party had taken place. Perhaps it was a large two storey building, gabled, quite old and set in maybe half an acre of tree lined garden. Darkness had enveloped the property by the time he had arrived and the approach road was weakly illuminated by a pale moonlight. As he trudged along the lane leading to Emma's house, a muffled silence was punctuated at intervals by high pitched cries of marshland birds. He drew nearer, and he could hear loud music that was getting the party off to a lively start. Peering through the windows he could discern youthful bodies gyrating to a booming, amplified track from Free. He watched for a while, then entered the house, just as the Rolling Stones' "Sympathy for the Devil" was starting up.

He caught a glimpse of Emma, surrounded as expected by a host of young bloods. She managed to beam a slightly coquettish smile in Pete's direction before an unrelated comment from one of her admirers brought forth uproarious laughter and her words of welcome were submerged beneath a chorus of guffaws. He was also most surprised to see, emerging from the group, and old friend of his from school named Phil. He had driven over from Chelmsford in his white Transit van and was most willing to offer the rear of his vehicle to Pete, should he get lucky.

It was just then, as if by some magical incantation from Phil, that Suzy had appeared. She was a fairly short, round featured but attractive brunette. Her boyfriend, she said, had gone into the village to buy some more drink. Would Pete mind dancing with her until he got back, she wondered. Would he ever? A couple of callow youths, evidently on the verge of sixth form entry, somewhat furtively informed Pete that Suzy's boyfriend had actually left the party, accompanied by the eponymous "Julie Bunkup" and would be unlikely to return. This saddened him to realise that such cavalier behaviour was possible towards such an amiable, agreeable young girl. Nevertheless, intelligence of this nature was to be viewed with more than a little caution.

The local off licence must have been some distance away. Or maybe he had walked. On the other hand, could those smirking advisers have been just having him on? He looked over Suzy's shoulder during a slow very close dance and spotted the two boys nodding their encouragement in his direction. He and the girl had been grooving for the best part of half an hour and his alcohol intake was increasing in relation to his rising lust towards this gorgeous girl. He began toying with the notion that maybe he could supplant the errant boyfriend – at least for tonight. So much for caution. An hour later saw them in the back of Phil's van,

As they lay together, both glowing with the memory of what they had just experienced with each other, Pete became conscious of a soft tapping on the side of the van. Callow youth number one was whispering the dreaded news that Suzy's boyfriend had returned. He was suddenly reminded of lines from a Wilfred Owen poem, though in a massively different context, "an ecstasy of fumbling..." This was certainly the case as they hurriedly reclothed. The two lovers emerged from the van, heads lowered and looking to blend in with the other party goers as swiftly as possible. It was then that callow youth two sidled up to Pete and muttered, "had you goin' there mate!"

"You tossers!" barked Pete as he drew back his fist, then thought better of it. Joining in with the ribaldry instead.

"Reckon he's well away with Julia by now. In more ways than one."

"You might have waited before springing that one on us." Pete was, however, highly amused by now.

Suzy was being consoled by a group of friends as she had by now learned about the circumstances with regard to her boyfriend. Pete went up to her and she did not seem displeased by this.

"Sorry about the bastard going off like that, Suzy."

"Oh never mind Pete. I really liked meeting with you and I had a feeling he did not really love me."

Oh love was it? Well I never! Despite his scepticism regarding teenage relationships, Pete was happy. As far as he was concerned, things had panned out just right. Indeed, what a way to say farewell to England. At that moment, Suzy announced she was leaving. He took her phone number anyway, but what was the point? This time tomorrow he hoped to be in Ostend. But you never know

Memories in the dark

Two hours or so later, Pete was making his way between two tall hedgerows, having just crossed over the railway tracks. There were silent woods to his left and humming overhead electric cables to his right. A train of empty rolling stock whirred past on the embankment high above him. Then he was alone again with his thoughts, trudging through these oh so familiar woods at this unfamiliar, ungodly hour. As he progressed, his mind wandered once more back to the party. Yes, he had actually finished up with Emma but not in the way he had hoped for. However, it had been pleasant enough sitting on the floor with the remnants of the party guests, making out quite passionately with her, listening to her brother entertaining with vocals and guitar.

He remembered someone asking for a volunteer to finish off the revels with a song. It was Pete who took the guitar and gave his own rendition of Fleetwood Mac's "Man of the World". The lyrics flowed out:

"...there's nowhere I'd rather be but I don't want to be sad any more..."

*****

It was certainly a swansong for the first phase of his life in the UK. What would his next anthem be? Another conundrum was how to return home from this far flung region of East Essex. There was no chance of a bus at one am. But these were the carefree days of the late sixties. Something would turn up and sure enough it did. Phil, the old school chum who had earlier donated his van to the further enhancement of Pete's sex life, now offered him a lift. He would be able to take him as far as the footpath, just off the A12, from where Pete could proceed towards his rest. On the way they conversed about their memories of school, girls they had known, friends they had made, enemies they had clashed with. And then Pete informed Phil of his planned world tour.

"Tomorrow! Christ you're cutting it fine!" Phil felt quite astounded as he had never viewed Pete as the over adventurous type.

"I just had to go to Emma's party. A last farewell to this country and my old life or maybe I was having second thoughts about going. Even though we have planned ahead, it's a hell of a step to take."

"So you're doing the hippy thing then." Phil's tone was not altogether mocking. Maybe he was envious.

"No mate, as you can see, I'm no hippy. Can't even say I've met too many of them that I've actually liked or got on with all that well. Some at college but they were a mixed bag. After all they were being turned into teachers."

"Lots of hippies at the Isle of Wight last month, mostly peaceful friendly types," Pete continued, "but surprisingly enough, I sensed some aggression there too. They weren't averse to joining in when cans were being flung at the front row audience, which included George Harrison and Eric Clapton. Bob Dylan was on at the time and according to newspaper reports, the audience didn't like his performance. No chance; he was fantastic. It was just that those sods in the front rows were standing up and blocking everyone's view. Mostly press, I think. Ironic or what?"

"Still, throwing cans, and bottles. That's a bit extreme to say the least"

"Sometimes I reckon that so called hippies, based on the ones I have met, are just a bunch of pseudo revolutionaries who conform to the hegemony they so vigorously oppose the moment they find themselves a job." Pete had made these somewhat drink-fuelled generalisations but Phil's response was both pragmatic and sardonic.

"Well, I suppose we all need to work, So much for peace and

love. Up the revolution eh!" he rejoined. "Alright to drop you off here then?"

*****

As Pete progressed along the footpath, he left the woods and entered a large fallow field. The time had not yet reached that moment when all of nature seemed to fall still in anticipation of the dawn to come. Indeed, a half-moon hung to the west of a clear night sky and illuminated his surroundings. On his right, a hundred yards distant, stood the gargantuan structure of a railway arch which carried the London to Norwich line over a shallow river which Pete could now hear tinkling over its stony bed. By his left shoulder, a thorny hedge marked the borders of a golf course where he used to caddy on Sunday mornings. The thwacks of drivers had long since died away and ghostly putters inhabited the greens, still way over par.

The nearby river had, in a sense, defined his early adolescence. It flowed just past the foot of his garden, tempting him at last to set out on its surface in a variety of craft, with some degree of success; when they did not fall apart or spring major leaks. At one time, there had been a rowing boat which enabled Pete and his friend to travel a hundred yards maximum along the river, then a stop to empty out several litres of turgid water. No matter what substances they had used to seal the hull, the results were the same, bringing to mind that very vessel utilised by the owl and the pussycat on their wedding trip.

Rafts though, were a different proposition. The best one they ever had was made of birch poles and half a dozen five gallon oil drums. Pete and his friend Spam had worked tirelessly, securing the various parts, nailing the poles to planks and lashing the drums with his mother's old plastic washing line. The river at the bottom of his garden was comparatively deep and perfect flotation was achieved. But the raft was very heavy. Then it was off on the familiar voyage to the railway arch, one punting and the other steering. However, one time, after spring rains had raised the water levels they were able to push on under the arch into the notorious bomb hole on the other side, where the Germans had attempted to destroy the bridge during World War Two, but had only succeeded in creating a deep, wide pool about twenty yards in diameter. To their knowledge, no-one had yet negotiated this stretch but they sailed triumphantly across, then turned and made it back home to where anxious parents had been waiting by the side of the river bank.

"We thought ourselves invincible." Pete's involuntary outburst surprised him but who was there to listen? Maybe a badger or a fox had heard his utterance but it floated away, unanswered on the night air like the forgotten dreams of his childhood. Unfortunately, Pete and his friend had paid for their hubris not a month later. A challenge had been delivered by two snotty adolescent raft owners who needed taking down. The Great Raft Race, as they had called it, took place on a cool Sunday morning in May. The river banks were thickly shrouded in multiple tones of greenery and a translucent mist hung over clumps of stinging nettles and reeds, diffusing light from the weak early morning sun. They had carried the raft between them a mile up to the starting point which was a seventeenth century riverside mansion converted into apartments where one of their opponents lived. Victory, as far as Pete was concerned, was a foregone conclusion. They only had to turn up and start.

Sure enough, not long after a mutual friend had dropped the flag to start them off they had built up a lead of one hundred yards or so with their superior punting and steering techniques applied to maximum co-ordination and effect. However, when they reached the first set of shallows, disaster struck. Due to the sheer weight of their craft, they had to get out and push. On clambering back on to the raft, they tipped up the front end, and whereas Pete managed to keep his balance, the momentum was too much for his friend. The raft see - sawed back and deposited him unceremoniously into the cold brown water. Pete did not escape this law of Physics – the one that states what goes down must come up - and soon he himself was joining his comrade in two feet of reeking river. His friend quickly scrambled up on to the raft again but he again was forced to join whatever fish had been unwise enough not to swim away from this scene of carnage.

They had always dismissed the construction of their opponents raft as inferior. The words they used were less polite and included "crap" and "fucking shite". It consisted of a large wooden board mounted securely on an inflated paravane. This ex World War Two device, formerly filled with gas and positioned on car roofs, which Pete had thought would burst on contact with sharp underwater pebbles, had given them maximum flotation, once they reached the shallows, where Pete and his pal were demonstrating a singular lack of maritime skills. As they floated regally past the wallowing pair, the only danger they faced was that they could have fallen off their raft due to the uncontrollable fits of laughter from which they were suffering. Pete even tried to poke a hole in the paravane but to no avail. Very sporting of him.

Soaked through and deeply humbled, the "Invincibles" had made their way home. Sadder but probably not much wiser, they dried off and went to meet their conquerors who had completed the race and were returning. The only consolation was that the other pair had been too exhausted to take their raft home so it was left at Pete's mooring place at the bottom of his garden. They were able to enjoy many weeks of watery fun on that raft until its owners eventually turned up to collect it.

*****

With every stride he took through those silent small hours he was carried towards his bed. He would now have about four hours sleep, before rising and setting off to London and, as he imagined, the rest of the world. Despite the time of year being late September, the soft, grassy surface upon which he strode did not seem damp, due probably to a drier than usual end of summer this part of England was experiencing.

Again his mind wandered. Damp grass had certainly not been a factor when Pete had enjoyed full sex for the first time. For both he and Celia, it was the ultimate consummation of young love, in all its bittersweet splendour. He was only reminded of this because now, to his left, he was passing the very spot where the act had occurred. In a field; on the bank of a stream; twenty yards or so off the main footpath. Fortunately, Pete and his girlfriend had been hidden from prying eyes by a small clump of bushes and the long grass of June was soft enough for them to lie on.

He had been very much in love with Celia, as she was with him, and they had been seeing each other for almost a year. He was the envy of many of his Sixth Form colleagues, as Celia was a tall, beautiful honey blonde with a much admired figure. There were many subsequent such occasions to follow, mostly in his bed when his parents were out. The relationship itself had lasted over a year, until shortly after Pete had started at a college where the female students had outnumbered male students by a ratio of five to one. It was also true to say that Celia had been tempted to stray during Pete's absence. According to his best mate, Spam, "Absence makes the heart grow fonder – for someone else!" And he had been proved right. The serpent of temptation was a powerful destroyer of young love's ambitions, and Eve, in this case, never did get back with her errant Adam. This particular Paradise had been lost forever.

With a start, Pete realised that he had arrived home. He had been so absorbed with his memories of his first time, he could easily have taken a wrong path and walked into the river. Dear, sweet Celia.....

*****

There had been a strange sequel to this memorable event at the brook side which was brought back to Pete's mind as he entered the gates to his family's front garden (big, neatly cut striped lawn; marigolds in the border....). His best mate Spam, he of raft race fame, had somehow guessed what had happened. Was he psychic? Best friends seem so much into each other's minds and they are often able predict their next moves, even utterances, blurting them out simultaneously. Those adolescent mental signals, driven by minds typically obsessed with sex and pure love of smut, had somehow alerted Spam to a momentous event having taken place in Pete's life.

That same evening, after the event, Pete confirmed that he had at last fucked Celia. However, words alone were not enough for Spam – or for Pete as it happened. He demanded evidence. Only on production of the used condom would he finally believe what had happened. To this end, the twosome repaired to the meadow where not three hours before, Pete and Celia had consummated their mutual young love. Spam began to search the flattened grass.

"That's definite evidence of you two lying down here then mate…but wait, what's this?" Spam had switched his search to the weed filled banks of the nearby brook and was probing with a long stick. He brought it up and sure enough, hooked on the end, was the evidence he was seeking. A used condom.

" Congratulations Pierre you lucky sod."

The brief spark of triumph Pete had felt was soon dampened when he put his hands in his jeans pocket and fished out a torn foil wrapping. He could have produced it and saved all this rummaging around.

Had Pete been proving himself to his best mate? Had Celia provided him with a rite of passage to be later celebrated by the two cronies? The glance that had briefly passed between Spam and himself after the excitement had died down told him everything. He had crossed a personal Rubicon, aided and abetted by Celia who, in fact had achieved the same. Though he suspected that she would have dealt with it all in quite a different manner.

The zany, absurd, Goon Show inspired humour they had always practised on a daily basis provided a lens of sorts through which they had hitherto viewed and dealt with most life situations they found themselves in. Their world was a distorted mirror of their surroundings, in which absurd characters and events substituted for reality. However, this kind of situation felt somewhat different. It was neither funny nor titillating, but marked a celebration, of kinds, of a mutual commitment by Pete and

Celia. A time was to unfold for Pete and Celia of pure joy and heart rending jealousies that passed for going steady - or what their parents may have termed as "courting".

Spam flung the used condom from the end of his stick into the stream, where it floated off in a westerly direction to join the main river. Now who were their village team playing at cricket this weekend and had they both been selected?

Into Europe – unlike the UK

A thin sunshine was attempting to break through the light grey cloud cover that was hovering over the central Belgian countryside this September morning. Pete awoke to the distant sound of traffic on a main road half a kilometre to the north. Their last lift had been in a tiny Renault CV6 driven by a priest. Pete had been able to converse with him in French. He could not help noticing a heavy looking crucifix on a large rosary dangling from the rear view mirror. He hoped the priest would not notice the commando knife which hung in a sheath from the left side of his belt. The tent in which they had passed the previous night was briefly ruffled by a slight breeze. The heap beside him in the other sleeping bag dozed on; Martin, the college champion sleeper. No need to rouse him yet. Time to take a look around. Time to take stock.

Pete emerged from the tent flap, stood up and stretched himself. He looked across rolling meadows towards a huddled farmhouse beside derelict looking outbuildings. This was the same farmhouse where they had asked permission to camp the night before. A pretty brunette teenage girl had answered the door and informed them that her mother did not like foreigners and they were not allowed to camp there. In fact they were to make themselves scarce. Despite this, the girl had secretly led them to an adjoining field where they would be out of sight and beyond the range of her mother's malice.

Pete started up the small methylated spirits stove which, along with a set of steel pans and a khaki jacket, he had purchased from an army surplus store, and began to prepare some breakfast. It was now scarcely twenty four hours since the party of four had landed in Ostend. Pete placed tea bags and sugar in two tin mugs as the pan, filled from his water bottle, started to show some signs of boiling. He began musing on what had happened to them during the preceding day.

The chill of summer's end pervaded and a hint of rain drifted over the meadow, adding to Pete's anxiety regarding the progress he and Martin might make that day. Yesterday, unfortunately, they had taken a wrong turning twenty kilometres south of Marche-en-Famenne and would have to plot a new route to Luxembourg. In any case they were pursuing the old summer southwards and warmer climes were beckoning from behind the misty hedgerows. A sound behind him indicated that Martin was struggling out of the tent and was already fumbling for his first cigarette.

"Well old boy…." Martin began speaking in that early morning languid tone that had become all too well known to a number of college girls during the past three years… "We'll have to start thinking about how we get ourselves back on the road to Bastogne."

"Quite right," replied Pete. "Maybe after breakfast we can find something to write 'Bastogne' on, then stand by the road, maybe not looking quite so prattish as we did yesterday."

"Speak for yourself young man!" guffawed Martin as he stubbed out half a cigarette on the sole of his camel - brown desert boot.

Breakfast consisted of rashers of streaky bacon brought from England, and cups of tea. After washing up their pans, plates, mugs and cutlery, they dismantled the tent and packed up their gear. They then set off towards the nearest settlement in search of something that might be used as a hitch hiking placard. Just off the N89 and about half a mile from the farm where Pete and Martin had camped, nestled the small town of St Hubert. Ancient, neat grey houses on the outskirts of the town straddled a straight road which itself continued northwest across flat muddy farmland. But that was not the direction they wished to take. At the junction with the main road they came across a tumbledown barn behind a low stone wall. They picked their way through an untidy yard and peered inside. At first it appeared to be more of a storehouse for outdated junk; an Aladdin's cave to any dealer in second hand tat whose mouth would water at the sight of mouldering farm machinery, rusty implements and an assortment of strange rotting wooden boxes. A smattering of light rain assailed the building and began to drip down through ragged roof patches.

"Here's a bit of a board," shouted Martin, triumphantly holding up a flat piece of plywood about a foot square. This broke Pete's reverie concerning the content of those wooden boxes.

"Well done son, we'll tape some paper to it and write the word 'Bastogne' on there and we'll soon get a lift. And yes I have got some Sellotape."

Ten minutes later two intrepid English baby boomers were standing by the roadside on the outskirts of a Belgian country town. Fortunately, the rain had eased, thus lessening the risk of smudging the carefully written sign they had produced. It seemed that no-one particularly wished to travel to Bastogne that day but at last, after two hours, a grey Mercedes slowed down and after the driver had inspected them briefly, opened the window to speak:

"Je vais pres de Bastogne si vous voulez!"

"Merci beaucoup, monsieur," replied Pete. They loaded their packs into the car. Pete sat in the back and Martin parked himself confidently in the passenger seat. The driver happened to speak English and explained that he would be heading north to Tenneville and would drop them off by the N4 from where they could proceed south to their destination.

As they travelled through different stages of their journey and with various sympathetic drivers who had offered them lifts, they traversed the shadowlands of the southern Ardennes region with its multitudinous tall trees reaching for the daylight in dense forests. Sometimes, breath taking vistas of distant hills backed by azure skies smudged with puffs of white cumuli could be glimpsed through gaps between those trees. Their goal was Luxembourg City and another night under canvas. They were fortunate when their last lift of the day took them fifty kilometres across the border and into the capital. They had been given the address and location of a camp site and Pete, utilising his 'O' Level French, was able to get directions to its whereabouts. It was half way up a hill overlooking the city, about a kilometre distant, and only a ten minute walk from where they had been dropped.

One thing Pete soon noticed was the superior organisation of this camp site compared to the ones he had stayed at in England. Oh the joys of camping out during an English summer! He reflected with distaste on the muddy mediocrity of one particular site in Essex, where he had sojourned once or twice, with its single outside cold tap, mainly concrete green stained floors in the shower room and the kind of catering which stretched only to curly fish paste sandwiches and grey lukewarm tea. This Luxembourg site seemed more geared to the culture of camping in general, even to the firm state of the ground underfoot, toilet and washing facilities and its overall smart appearance. The café also served a variety of tasty meals, so he and Martin feasted on the local variety of sausage, salad and beer. There was also plum tart which they were unable to resist.

"I like this place!" Pete blurted out between mouthfuls. "Beer's not bad either." That night, however, as darkness crept slowly but surely across the city skyline and its lights began to twinkle in the summer twilight, an ominous rumbling started up in the distance.

Back in 1916, it was said that in the days before the Somme offensive made its ill - judged, ill-fated push towards the German defences, the roar of the British artillery could even be heard as far away as central Essex. It would almost certainly have been noted with some alarm in The Duchy of Luxembourg. Although the country had declared its neutrality at the outset, the Germans used Luxembourg's railway lines to prevent the French from doing the same. Now the sounds of this embryonic thunderstorm brewing from afar may well have brought back uncomfortable memories to those who had heard that ancient gunfire, and indeed to the hideous roaring of the various battles that were taking place on the killing grounds of France and Flanders. And so the rumblings continued for the next two hours or so; somewhere far away; someone else's storm.

It was around midnight when a tumultuous crash awoke the

sleeping pair. It was followed by a brilliant burst of ultra-bright lightning which seared Pete's eyeballs as he struggled to shake off the drowsiness of his rudely interrupted dreams. Amid the external chaos of son et lumiere that was breaking out, Pete was able to discern a pitter pattering on the canvas, as if someone was actually urinating on their tent. Suddenly, the pattering intensified until the deluge from the skies above hit home with the impact of a steam hammer. The intrepid pair, cowering inside their sleeping bags, were just waiting for the storm in all its fury to come bursting into their tent and wash them away. However, the guy ropes held, as the elements, with terrifying ferocity, pitched their forces against the land as if seeking to drive humanity back into the void whence it had emerged. Fortunately, their canvas fortress managed to withstand the assault. Within half an hour, the battle had ceased. Like a vast army withdrawing from its final failed attempt on the hillside, the forces arraigned against them dwindled to a distant rumour of conflict.

Next day, a couple of lifts south along the E31 saw Pete and Martin across the border and into France. The second lift was noteworthy as a blonde French lady, maybe in her forties, picked them up in a shiny mid blue Thunderbird. She informed Pete that she owned a carousel in a travelling fair but when Pete announced, *"nous sommes Anglais"*, she screeched the car to a halt, having travelled a mere two hundred metres and gave them both a look which in any language spelt "Get Out!" She did not deign to give any reason for her impulsive move but then changed her mind again and accelerated her powerful motor towards the main highway before the two friends had a chance to disembark. Strange!

To say that the pair were somewhat puzzled would be an understatement. However, they soon both settled in their seats to enjoy the ride, hoping it would not be curtailed again for some while. For most of the journey, the woman veered in her attitude between stony silence, making pleasant small talk about the weather and then pointing out the passing scenery. She even bid them "Au revoir" after she had dropped them close to the town of

Thionville. According to the map they were less than twenty miles from Metz now and hopefully some lunch.

The region of Alsace Lorraine has witnessed myriad changes over the centuries. This sleepy corner of Eastern France has seen fluctuations in populace; changes in language; even changes in ownership. The destructive juggernaut of war had constantly rolled back and forth over this area and a visitor might have been expected to be greeted by a broken landscape bearing permanent scars of past conflicts. All that can be perceived, however, is the rich mix of French and Germanic influence in a predominantly French population, as reflected in the architecture of many of its idyllic towns and villages.

One such sublime village is Delme, near Chateau-Salins and that is where Pete and Martin found themselves, by the roadside, close to the village hall, one sunny afternoon in mid-September. Beside the village hall was a sign pointing to a free camp site in a field to the rear of this somewhat utilitarian modern building. They made their way along a dusty footpath, overhung with stinging nettles, into a meadow of green and well mown yellowing grass where perhaps half a dozen tents were already pitched. It was the work of ten minutes to put up their tent, then the search was on for food and drink.

Across the road from the camp site they spied an ancient looking stone built hostelry in the solid style of the region. They were in Moselle and there were no *pan de bois* buildings here that one might have associated with Eastern France. Inside, the rough wooden dining tables were populated by a dozen or so working men dressed in dark blue or grey dungarees and wearing on their heads, the ubiquitous colourless cloth caps. From the general buzz of conversation, Pete found he could distinguish more words and phrases he understood than in other regions of France. The accent they spoke in was accessible to him and he felt confident that he could converse with some confidence. In his mind's eye he could picture his French friend Yvette, from his teenage years. She would have called this brogue "horrible" but then she was from Haut Savoie via Paris. She once described the way Pete spoke French as *"comme un Belge"*. Evidently, this had not been a compliment.

However, the Belgians came to play an unwitting but important part in the unfolding saga of Pete and Martin's journey south. As they seated themselves at one of the tables an ample French lady dressed in a long black skirt and white blouse with frills bustled towards them. They ordered a pint of Kronenbourg each and were delighted when the old fashioned bottle arrived containing the celebrated brew.

"Just like the old Corona bottles with metal flip tops! Brilliant!" Chuckled Pete.

"Have a look on the label, Pete. Bit more than a pint in here. Delightful, cheers."

They carefully poured the beer into tall glasses and took their first few gulps. Then the cheese rolls arrived.

Oh yes, cheese rolls would have brought to mind curly luncheon meat sarnies, sausage rolls and cups of grey tea which formed the mainstay of refreshments at cricket matches, fetes and garden parties back in England. Scraps of lettuce leaves, sliced cucumbers and squashy tomatoes were the usual accompaniment to this feast of delights which always enjoyed the distinction of being totally lacking in any kind of taste. Well, maybe the arctic rolls were acceptable as long as the ice cream had not melted too much. The Moselle version of cheese rolls, when they arrived, were yet another culinary culture shock. A long, thick baguette loaf had been cut in half and split down the middle. Various charcuterie had been inserted and the cheese seemed to resemble Brie; creamy in colour with a whitish rind. They had not ordered a dessert but once they had ravenously consumed their rolls, the rotund madame brought them rich sweet plum *compotes* wrapped in steaming *crepes*. She had evidently thought they still looked hungry. Not only that, but she also told them that the dessert was free of charge. Overall, the taste experience was very much to Pete's liking, as with most of the food on their journey to date, especially the seafood platters in Belgium.

It was when they came to settle the bill that a most bizarre situation arose. Pete and Martin both realised to their horror that they had no French money about their persons.

"Pardonez moi Madame, mais nous n'avons pas l'argent Francaise. Jus'qua les francs Belgique."

Whether the denizens of Delme suspected that this was a ploy on the part of les deux Anglais to get out of paying the bill, or whether they instinctively judged the young English men in a favourable light, Pete and Martin were never going to find out. It appeared that the locals were totally untroubled by what seemed to Pete an embarrassing predicament. One of the men grabbed a newspaper and turned to the financial section. A small group gathered behind him as they calmly searched through the various exchange rates. It was simple. All they had to do was to work out what was owed in Belgian francs and the bill could be settled.

The warmth and generosity of these far from affluent French villagers – not to mention their entrepreneurial skills - was not lost on the travelling companions. Thanking their hosts profusely, they wished the company a cheery farewell and repaired to their tent.

"That Kronenbourg was good, remarked Martin. We could have had a session there but I was pretty knackered after today's trek."

"Another time, Pete replied, "When we meet up with the boys in Rome perhaps."

Nevertheless, he was clearly moved by the friendly reception they had received in Delme, especially after some of the anti-English feeling that had been shown to them in other parts of France. Martin seemed to read his thoughts.

"These locals have the simplest and best approach to life – take as you find and bugger where people come from. We could learn a lot from them, I reckon."

"It did not bother them a lot that they would have to change that money into French francs. I can't imagine anything similar happening in England, though I'd like to imagine that it would. In my part of the world they'd probably think we were trying to get away without paying."

"Perhaps this lot did and came up with a very artful method of making sure we did pay. Anyway, the plum pancakes were fab to say the least."

The last comment was lost to Pete altogether but had he been listening instead of musing to himself he would certainly have agreed. After a brief but portentous silence, Pete spoke.

"Why is it that just about everything I have seen, every place I have visited seems so much better than in England? I was born and raised in the countryside; it was lovely and it was safe too. I also got to see lots of other areas such as the West Country, Wales and East Anglia for example. I'd swap it all, even for this village. It's great here and it was great in Brussels, Namur and Luxembourg."

"Ah well that's all quite laudable and I have to say," responded Martin. "I enjoyed passing through those places too. However, you are labouring under a misconception, if you don't mind my saying so, old sonner. There was this feller in my karate club who said that whenever he visited a new country he was possessed with an almost uncontrollable desire to settle down and live there. But it was the novelty you see and the longer he stayed, the more he yearned to get back to Blighty, as he put it. But he did visit lots of different countries and he concluded that if you can stay somewhere long enough, even endure some bad experiences and you still want to live there, then that's a fitting place to call home."

"Where's he now? Enquired Pete, obviously struck by Martin's exemplar.

"Last time I saw him, he was leaving for Japan and that was about three years ago."

They fell to listing the advantages and disadvantages of living in their own country as opposed to the rest of Europe. What did the continent have that the UK did not have and vice versa? However, tiredness overtook them both and they were soon asleep. Darkness enveloped them once more. Still the unknown beckoned them from the south and the east, while in Delme life would continue much the same as it had for several centuries before. Pete and Martin, transient dreamers, had crossed the paths of some of the villagers; may even have made a slight impression on them. But they were never to pass that way again.

After sleeping soundly through the night, undisturbed even by the barking of a few dogs and possibly a couple of foxes, in this idyllic area in an almost forgotten corner of France, they prepared to set off once more on their quest for kind hearted road users. Fortunately, later on in the day, they were picked up by the driver of a large red articulated lorry. They had never seen one as big as this; it was somewhat noisy and reeked of engine oil. However, the driver was bound for the outskirts of Strasbourg. Inside, as the journey progressed, the steady throb of the ageing machine under the bonnet continued throughout the eighty miles or so across Alsace. On some of the roads they were actually rattling around in the cab; they enjoyed pleasant exchanges with the driver, who managed to speak some English. At one point, Pete was even asked to take the steering wheel for a few minutes when a long straight road stretched before them. The irony was not lost on Martin as he was the qualified driver, not Pete. As the afternoon sun beat down on them, the ancient cab started to heat up. A raging thirst was upon them both, and Pete could not help reflecting on the glasses of chilled Kronenbourg they had consumed in Delme. Consequently, it did not help to be informed by the driver that there was only one industry in Alsace: the brewing of beer.

They were traversing another picturesque part of the world; a world totally unknown to them before today, except for the odd references in History lessons. Alsace was charming in every road that led off from the N55 into dark forests or over the grey-green plains; charming in every whitewashed, dark timbered farm building and field of hops which could be seen at frequent intervals along the highway. Suddenly, a roadside café appeared before them, oasis like with its promise of the kind of liquid refreshment required by all. The monster truck snorted as it drew into the forecourt and the driver slowed his machine to a halt. Once inside, Pete and Martin insisted on treating their hearty transporter to a meal but he politely turned them down, bid them farewell, making his way towards a group of his companions gathered round a table in the corner. It so happened that they were a mile or so from the suburbs of Strasbourg and they could glimpse the taller buildings in the distance. The far off metropolis hung in the afternoon haze like a mirage, symbolically beyond the reach, for now, of the British and their thwarted aspirations to join the Common Market.

Two young French men in a Volkswagen took them the rest of the way into the city. Happily, one of them was kind enough to take the travellers to his flat to feed them with a large loaf, some cheese and a lot of beer. He was an avid fan of Bob Dylan and was anxious to know, of all things, the lyrics to "Masters of War". Pete was able to oblige him as it had been the first song he had learned to play on guitar. E minor and open chord had sufficed for his limited skills at the time but he was now able to convey all the relevant chords and lyrics to a delighted young Frenchman. They were listening to the strains of "Blonde on blonde", and as the mighty Mr Zimmerman was purring out the words to "Just like a woman", black shadows were beginning to fade into dusk, outside the apartment .

From the corner of one eye, Pete could discern the sudden bright intrusion of a street light across the road. It was time to move on and strike out for the Rhine Bridge which would see them on the Franco-German border. Bidding their farewells to the young man whose name just happened to be Pierre, and noting his directions to the bridge, they proceeded through the still busy streets of Strasbourg. Walter's flat was just off the Rue Vaubans, close to the four hundred year old University Louis Pasteur where he was studying at that time. Pete and Martin were faced with a walk of about a mile, and soon The River Rhine was in view, illuminated by lights from numerous street lamps, buildings and ships. As they crossed the bridge on foot, with a chill breeze cutting across them, Pete became aware of a broad but apparently fast flowing river beneath them. This had been the region's main artery throughout eons of history and it now welcomed them to the Bundesrepublik.

Once they had crossed the bridge, a fortuitous long lift south along the autobahn found them in the company of a man at the wheel who was planning to turn his back on his own country. He spoke English fluently and opened a diatribe whereby he reflected on the current state of West German society which he felt was subsiding into a comfortable apathy. He spoke of attitudes to the last war with the older generation either feeling ashamed about all that had happened, or some who felt it had nothing to do with them. On the other hand, he believed, the younger generation were always trying to make up for the failings of their forebears who had submitted to an evil and destructive political force. At any rate, to his way of thinking, the West Germans were settling into a cosy bourgeois existence on the back of some sort of economic miracle that had occurred in the last decade or so. Consequently, he was planning to move to France, where, as far as he was concerned, the people knew how to live life to the full.

So what of British attitudes to the terrible conflict of 1939 – 1945? From the World War Two propagandists to his own generation, Pete thought that they had more or less been told what to think about such a remarkable victory for the forces of good. He seldom questioned his own parents' attitudes. Britain had won, Winston Churchill was next to God and that was all that counted. There was also the somewhat grudging admission that the Allies had received some help from the Americans who had joined in a bit later on after conning the UK by selling them old Liberty boats and dodgy aircraft.

It was obvious to Pete that this information smacked somewhat of hindsight, but he had never ventured an opinion in that direction. Remarkably, it was also evident that Great Britain had been swarming with GIs long before the halfway mark of World War Two and he himself had seen the horrendous figures for the U.S. dead from 1941 to 1945. Strangely enough, those statistics hardly bore out what his parents' generation had always been telling him about America's contribution to the last war.

Just as these uncomfortable thoughts were shifting through Pete's troubled mind, the Mercedes they were travelling in drew to a halt. Having crossed the Swiss border at Basle, they were being dropped at a camp site known to their driver near Le Landeron. As they stood at the entrance to the site, all was quiet around the dark tents of varying shapes and sizes. Even the crickets, late summer's nocturnal accompanists, were evidently not feeling energetic enough to stir their little legs in order to punctuate the silence of this balmy night. That was hardly surprising, as according to Martin's watch, it was one am and they could not check in, as the camp office was closed. Without further ado they pitched their tent, unrolled their sleeping bags and settled down to their fifth night away from home.

It had lately become a habit with Pete to awaken gradually from his slumber to thoughts of a new day with all its prospects and promises ahead of him. But in his semi - comatose state, his mind would then start to reflect deeply on past events and episodes. Now the events of the past few days had driven themselves to the forefront. It would make no difference if it was sunny when he awoke or utterly wet and cold, as the working of Pete's mind seemed held in a stasis of imagined time and space; almost as if he was half in and half out of a preceding dream. This time, a bright sunshine seemed to be illuminating the inside of the tent and his consciousness alike. In his head a clear vision of his present situation began to emerge. An overwhelming feeling was washing over him of utter despair, even remorse at leaving his home life, his family, friends and country in this way. Should he not now, at this moment be settling down to the routine of a teaching job somewhere?

This present time though should have been one of great excitement and exhilaration. He was on the threshold of a kind of metaphorical bridge between his studies at college and a future career. He was in fact entering a period of his life that would later come to be known among the over twenty ones as a gap year. One difference was, however, that Pete and his companions were meant to be away for two. How could it be then that their schemes for a world tour which had appeared so promising and discussed with such eager anticipation should take on a new and chilling aspect in one's waking moments; in the harsher light of a new day? What were they doing here and where were they heading? As the awakening process gradually took hold, an engulfing wave of misery ran through him. He now lay supine, just about to open his eyes. When he did open his eyes, he soon wished he hadn't.

Swiss Time

Framed by the tent flap and against a beige bivouac opposite, Pete could discern a dark blue, red striped trouser leg. Astonishment caused him to do a double take and he soon realised that a Swiss policeman was standing outside. It sounded like Martin was trying to make himself understood but without a great deal of success. As he struggled out of his sleeping bag and after managing to pull his jeans over his Y-fronts, Pete attempted to wake himself up and put a few phrases of explanation together. As he made his way towards the policeman, he called out,

"*Bonjour monsieur. Nous sommes arrives a une heur ce matin. Il n'y avait personne ici. S'il vous voulez nous avons l'argent pour le camping.*"

"Now I wished I could have said that," chuckled Martin. "Could have if he was Spanish!"

"Why didn't you wake me up then?" Moaned Pete in anticipation of the policeman's response to his perfectly plausible but perhaps not quite grammatically phrased reason for non-payment of camping fees.

"Didn't want to disturb your beauty sleep old chap." Evidently Martin was displaying a more flippant approach to the situation. "Mind you, sonner, looks like that's done the trick."

Pete was now standing outside the tent making up a trio with Martin and Monsieur le gendarme. Then they were joined by a scruffy little man wearing a grubby blue denim shirt and black shorts which had also seen better days and posteriors. He was the site manager and he was the one who had called the police. He exchanged a hurried but animated dialogue with the stalwart upholder of Swiss law and order who promptly withdrew along the rutted track on his black bicycle and without so much as an

Au revoir. As he pedalled off into the distance, no doubt reflecting indignantly on why his breakfast had been disturbed, Pete and Martin managed to settle their bill. The camp boss was also far from amused though, and Martin counselled an early departure from the site. Breakfast would be taken in a friendlier environment – hopefully.

Later that same evening, they arrived at a small public park near Lausanne. It had been a slow but relaxed journey with short hops between lifts and along some narrow roads which picked their way through some awe inspiring scenery. Lakes, mountains, picturesque towns: typical Swiss but unlike anything Pete had ever seen except on television and on postcards. There had been ample time to appreciate the scenery as they had had to wait four hours for a lift to Neuchatel. Consequently, if they had not been able to hurtle through the last stage at speeds of one hundred mph plus in an Alfa Romeo, they may not have been able to cover the one hundred and fifty kilometres which eventually found them next to Lac Leman. Hitch hiking in the dark would have been pointless, so they decided to sleep rough on park benches. Across the starlit expanse of Lac Leman the myriad lights of a large city sparkled in the clear, cool dusk. Then trailing across the carpet of night, somewhere out in the middle of the lake, a passenger cruiser was making its way back to its home port. Pete could judge the size of the craft by measuring with his eye the number of twinkling lights from fore to aft and top to bottom.

"Maybe that's the Swiss navy!" Quipped Martin.

Suddenly, about fifty yards away, another light appeared, swaying up and down and from side to side, making its way towards them. Progress was gradual and every so often it stopped. It was purposeful, however, and as it got closer a figure could be seen in silhouette behind it. The figure seemed to be bending down and digging things up.

"Hang on Martin we did pay for that last campsite." Now Pete was attempting to be humorous. "The cops can't still be after us!"

"Vorms," came a voice from the approaching stranger. "I am digging up zese vorms for fishing."

The man was much closer to them now and they could see he was tall, fair haired and dressed in an ex-military anorak style jacket, dark jeans and army boots. He carried in one hand a plastic bucket of fat wriggling earthworms and in the other hand a small digging fork.

"I am doing ze night fishing a bit furzer up ze lake. You can see vere I fish from." Sure enough another speck of brightness broke through the gloomy waterside approximately a hundred yards distant.

"Caught much tonight?"

"Oh I haf not yet started my friends but I hope to catch some brachsen - you call zem bream and some carpa."

"Good luck with that," remarked Martin with more than a hint of pity in his voice. Neither he nor Pete were great fans of angling.

"Look over there!" Pete suddenly spluttered, "There are fishing lights as far as you can see." And he was right. Pinpoints of light, ever decreasing in size were to be seen all along the lakeside." Going to be a lot of lonely women in town tonight."

"Ah but zere are ladies who enjoy ze fishing too."

There was no answer to that last riposte and they had warmed to this friendly character and his obviously popular and relaxing hobby. But at night? Living next to a river most of his life, Pete knew that fish tended to bite more frequently after dark. Surely though there were better things to do, such as sleep. This led him to ask,

"Do you think the park keeper would let us sleep on these benches?"

"Of course, I often do that myself when I am bored mit the fishing."

"Right," said Pete "thanks, but where can we find some drinking water?"

"In the fountains my friend." It's pure ice cold mountain water. Goodnight"

As the fisherman disappeared once more into the gloom, Pete and Martin decided to fill their bottles from the fountains as recommended, but also to add some purification tablets, just in case. They placed their sleeping bags on two park benches and spent a remarkably comfortable night in the silence which seemed to spread over the vast lake, broken only by the slight stirrings of cedar and pine trees in the park itself. There was an almost tangible presence of distant mountains across the water to the south, brought about perhaps by the light but chill breeze wafting across from their snow - capped peaks.

On first sighting those peaks the next morning, Pete would be reminded once more of approaching winter. Indeed, as they had progressed through north Europe and southern Germany, there had always been the sense that autumn was snapping at their heels. This became more apparent during each night spent under canvas – or in the open – with steadily intensifying periods of cold and damp. Mornings and day times had generally been sunny to date but it felt as though there was always this brooding presence of darkness in the background, steadily gathering in the streets, woods and hedgerows of the lands they had crossed and which Pete was always anxious to avoid. It was as if Nature itself was calling time on the young adults and reminding them that in reality what lay ahead of them was the more serious prospect of work, possible marriage and a lifetime of responsibility. And that short lease of life would eventually be snuffed out when their time was called. However, in the immediate future, it was sufficient for them to continue heading towards sunnier climes.

The following day found the pair in a Lausanne café consuming rolls and Swiss coffee, ready for the next stage of their odyssey. They had earlier been drinking the fountain water, left overnight after adding the purification tablets and were relieved to find themselves still alive. They managed to pick up lifts past Montreux and into the Alps, reaching the Swiss – Italian border at Brig around one thirty pm. Mighty mountain peaks surrounded the towns, Wasenhorn, Geisshorn, Nesthorn, Hegdorn among others. Predictably, it was cold and windy in the mountains but at least the sun was still shining. The snow clad conditions of the Swiss mountains served to demonstrate how the freezing climate could imprison whole regions in its cruel grip. In this region, life itself was a constant struggle against blizzards, icy roads and the threat of avalanches. At home, Pete hated the winter and as each yearly cycle swung into October there was always the chance of an Indian summer. For him, what inevitably followed that last, brief outpouring of a season's bounties, was little more than an annually occurring catastrophe.

They took the train through the Simplon Tunnel and arrived in a small town just across the border called Iselle. They had left behind them sparkling mountains and neat, tidy red-white villages. They had entered the darkness of Simplon and emerged into a landscape of misty slopes, untidy buildings, grimy garages, carelessly botched up shopfronts and cafes serving cheap vino. This was late 1960s Italy. Further contrasts with the country they had just left were all too apparent. Here in North Italy, the landscape seemed drier, with dusty roads crossing shallow, almost stagnant rivers. Despite the brackish appearance of these streams, Martin, whilst they were waiting by the roadside for a lift, suggested filling their water bottles from one of them which happened to be nearby. Pete was not convinced.

"Think I'll give it a miss. Too much of a risk, especially stinking like that."

"If we add some of our tablets that'll make a difference," argued Martin but he also sounded less than sure about this. Unfortunately, their water bottles were almost empty.

The unrelenting late afternoon sun seared them from between gloomy clouds above. Their thirst situation was starting to become more desperate, but help was on the way. A four wheel drive, the make of which neither of them could identify, stopped just a few metres past them. A short man with a weather beaten face opened the door, leaned out and said, "We're going to our village about an hour down the road. Any good to you?" They gratefully accepted and climbed into the car. This was a stroke of luck, as the realisation was beginning to dawn on them that in Italy most cars appeared to be very small Fiats of a type not yet so common in the UK. Furthermore, it was not always possible to cram themselves into these vehicles along with all their equipment. The men in this much larger car which turned out to be a Chevrolet Nova, correctly identified by Martin as a four wheel drive, had just returned from South Africa where they had been living for some years. They had now returned to settle in Italy and were touring the area around their home village.

An hour later, they reached a small town where a carnival was in progress. The scenes that met their gaze could accurately be described as general mayhem. Pete was reminded of the annual carnival held in his home town of Chelmsford. On carnival days, usually in mid July, sedate rows of onlookers would line the High Street pavements as bunting bedecked floats, assembled by local firms, colleges and scouting groups paraded in procession, accompanied by half a dozen bands. All of the latter would be playing different tunes and some floats would be blaring out recorded music. The resultant cacophony was the closest to any form of chaos that might have disrupted those orderly proceedings. The carnival always sparked excitement but there was never any hysteria. There would generally be a measure of ribaldry when members of the crowd spotted acquaintances in the procession and the participants would always look garish as people of all shapes and sizes took the opportunity to bedeck themselves in outlandish costumes. As always, John Bull would lead the carnival procession. A fair would follow that same evening in Central Park and run for several days.

Whatever joys and high spirited jinks may have been experienced by such a momentous occasion, they failed utterly to match the unbridled, ecstatic outpourings of loud music, maniacal singing and dancing plus a general sense of abandon that accompanied the carnival in this small Italian town. The fair contained, along with the usual rides and sideshows, a seething mass of humanity, young and not so young, all seemingly intent on outdoing each other in demonstrating their joy of being alive. Pete and Martin found themselves drawn into those scenes of pandemonium, eventually ending up inside a convenient café bar, on the fringes of the field where the fair was in progress. Here, they were treated by their new acquaintances from South Africa to multiple glasses of local wine, both red and white. Indeed, it appeared that their kindly drivers and the assembled company in the bar wished them to sample every variety of wine available – and there would be no spitting out. Later, they sobered up with a Spaghetti Bolognese in a small restaurant next door. Despite the enormous intake of alcohol which their livers had been subjected to, the resultant drowsiness usually experienced was notably absent. So thanking their hosts profusely, they bid farewell to the heaving Saturday night revels still taking place and pressed on with their journey towards Milan.

Viva Italia

The coffee stall looked oh so tempting. It was only just across the road from the flyover under which Pete and Martin had, of necessity, spent the previous night. They had reached Milan via several lifts from the festive village near to Domodossola. Then their luck had run out, as subsequent attempts at hitching on a slip road leading to the fabled Autostrada de la Sol proved fruitless. A decision was therefore made to spend the night on two nearby park benches close to what looked like some university buildings. Unfortunately, around one am, a fine but persistent rain forced the sleeping pair to shelter under a flyover next to a slip road. For the first (and last) time in his life, Pete was forced to sleep sitting on his rucksack to keep out the light from a few passing vehicles and the drizzle that was drifting in on a light wind. Martin had elected to continue his slumber on the concrete itself with his head nestling on his wrapped up sleeping bag. Indeed he was fast asleep when Pete underwent a most bizarre experience.

As if in some kind of crazy dream, he sensed that a car was speeding towards them over a distance of a few hundred yards. The engine noise seemed to grow louder and he was suddenly jerked awake as a feeling of intense foreboding shot through his brain. Even in his drowsy state, the crescendo of sound from the approaching car added to his deep seated sense of alarm. With seconds to spare, he instinctively reached down and managed to pull the supine Martin towards him, just as a Fiat 128 pulled into the space under the flyover and stopped abruptly with its front nearside tyre on the exact spot where Martin's head had been. The would-be recipient of a squashed cranium did nothing more than complain about his rude awakening. Pete decided that he should remain blissfully unaware of the incident; at least until the other two joined them and they could have a good laugh at Martin's expense. The wind ups would be bound to continue for some time after and therefore it was worth saving up this morsel of mockery for the time being. Additionally, "blissfully unaware" would describe the young driver who had hopped out of his car, locked the door and set off for the aforementioned coffee stall, where he joined a steadily growing queue.

They also joined the queue, which consisted mostly of male artisans, varying in age and appearance: boiler suits, cloth caps, the occasional jacket and tie. They were being served frothy coffee in strong white plastic cups which they bought together with sweet cake slices wrapped in white paper. Soon there was only one customer in front of them, then, to their astonishment, this customer turned round and handed them two cups and some cake. All he said was, "Cappuccino!" Pete and Martin could only chorus a "Graci signor" before their benefactor, with a broad smile displaying his pleasure at performing his good deed for the day, took off towards the distant city.

Unfortunately, in choosing this spot to spend the night, they had been in error concerning which motorway it was nearest to. Reaching the Autostrada de la Sol involved a long hike, according to the map they consulted. Milan Railway Station turned out to be very much nearer.

The next sequence of events which were to typify their progress across the Italian peninsula, involved what Pete had always described as "fiddling the trains". He had frequently resorted to this method of transporting himself across South East England, especially when returning from college for the weekend or at the start of vacations. It was not known whether he ever acknowledged this practice as a criminal activity, but he certainly enjoyed riding the railway system whilst paying as little as possible in fares.

One particular favourite ploy of his was to take a bus from his college in Reading to Hanger Lane in Middlesex, which was handy because it was by the North Circular and also on the Central line.

From Hanger Lane he would purchase a ticket to North Acton, the next station, then stay on the train until he reached Stratford in East London. A couple of steps across the platform that he alighted on would give him access to a Chelmsford train which needed to be non-stop to Shenfield. It was strange but most opportune that Central Line and British Railways trains should use opposite sides of the same platform. It was usually after the train had left Shenfield when an inspector caught up with Pete and he would pay the single fare from that station to Chelmsford. He would always allege that he had had to run for the train at Shenfield. This cheapskate abuse of the public transport system gradually became something of a pastime with Pete and differing varieties of his home route emerged over time. That was until he tried one variation too many.

He later remarked to anyone who cared to listen that the embarrassing incident that had occurred was compounded by the fact that he had been accompanied by a particularly beguiling young female fellow student, to whom he had expounded the advantages of his easy riding. She had been up for an adventure and cheerfully complied. All went to plan, especially as they were able to hitch hike to Hanger Lane, from where they planned to take a tube to Newbury Park, almost into Essex on the A127. However. Fate was about to deal a most extraordinary hand to him that day. As they had saved money by hitch hiking, they decided to purchase tickets to Newbury Park, legitimately this time. Although this had gone somewhat against the grain, it was almost as if Pete had had a premonition. From Newbury Park, a bus would take them to within a mile of Pete's house, where Pete was to alight and she would continue to Chelmsford railway station to catch a train to her home town in Suffolk.

However, at Newbury Park station, when the ticket collector asked for their tickets, Pete, who was supposed to be carrying both tickets was unable to locate them. He began to experience a creeping feeling of acute embarrassment, followed by panic stations! Quick as lightning, he realised that the Shenfield tactics had to be brought into play so he informed the collector they had boarded the train at Gants Hill which was the preceding station and he had somehow lost their tickets. To his immense surprise and chagrin he was immediately interrogated by the tube station employee.

"Tell me, are there stone steps at Gants Hill or escalators?" That was his opening question. He did not need any more.

Now Pete had used Gants Hill once or twice previously but for the life of him could not remember how the general public perambulated between the daylight and the nether regions of the Central Line at that particular station and so, suspecting a trick question, he made his gambit. The girl, to her credit, remained ice cool during this exchange but Pete felt she was somehow enjoying his discomfort. His reply, when it came, was delivered with utter conviction – top acting - but doomed to miserable failure.

"It's got stone steps." He asserted. His inquisitor's facial expression, which had shown signs of kindliness and tolerance beforehand, now turned to a more serious one.

"Nope, wrong answer. It's got escalators."

At this moment, Pete began fully to comprehended what people meant when wishing for a hole to open up in front of them. Unfortunately, there would be no such seismic escape route for him. However, as previously mentioned, Fate was in play, and on this occasion held the trump cards. The ticket collector suddenly made a grab for Pete's left arm and, almost choking on his words said,

"Hang on, a sec. What's this?"

To Pete's astonishment and some relief, he pulled two train tickets out of the cuff of his long sleeve polo shirt. Two aces, it would appear. Pete had not managed to recover his composure and merely muttered,

"Er sorry, I forgot they were there." Nevertheless, he could not help feeling squeaky clean with the sure knowledge that the tickets were, for a change, actually for the station in which he was standing.

"I could definitely have had you there, you know!" was the collector's parting remark, though his expression showed he was doing his best to suppress a mighty grin. Pete's female companion was also finding great difficulty in keeping a straight face, and Pete interpreted her look, as she turned away from his glance, as somewhat dismissive. He began to feel like a naughty child who had just been caught nicking another kid's sweets. Well, she was training to be a primary school teacher. However, Pete was quite wrong about this. Doubtless she had enjoyed his discomfort initially but she was also strangely impressed by the episode and she later showed her appreciation when, after hitch hiking as far as Pete's house, she went home with him instead of taking a bus to Chelmsford station. They only just managed to finish some very enjoyable activities in his bed before Pete's parents arrived home from work.

Pete was wrenched from his reverie by Martin who nudged him gently between the shoulder blades and exclaimed.

"Here we are ole sonner, at the ticket office. Let's go for it."

Accordingly, Pete and Martin purchased tickets to Piacenza which was the next large station down the line. Their intention was, with luck, to stay on the train until Firenze. If caught by a ticket inspector their excuse would be that they had missed their stop. This was never going to work and sure enough, they were thrown off the train at Piacenza just as it was about to pull out of the station.

The next phase, Martin's plan, was to wait until the last train to Rome had departed, then try to cadge a ride on a mail or freight train going south. Some of Pete's friends had achieved this in the past on early morning milk trains out of Liverpool Street. No one knows from which realms of fantasy this plan had emanated but they seriously intended to put it into practice. They were doomed to failure from the start. It was now approaching midnight and their earlier removal from the Rome train had attracted the attention of a railway policeman. He approached the pair and asked them, in passable English, if he could be of any assistance. He listened sympathetically to Martin's concocted story – which was delivered half in English and have in adapted Spanish – before informing him that there was one more train to Rome which was due to come through at just after one am. This kindly and supportive approach from the conscientious railway official proved to be their undoing, as he proceeded to take Martin in his car a few blocks away to wake up his local bank manager. Incredibly, the bank manager was able to exchange their travellers' cheques for Italian lire. Thanks to these selfless acts, two tickets for Rome were duly purchased. As far as acting was concerned, though, Pete and Martin's show of gratitude would certainly have won them Oscar nominations.

As their train sped through the Italian night, Pete could not shake the idea from his mind that their other two companions could already be in Rome impatiently awaiting their arrival. The concept of a reunion with them at their first rendezvous was becoming vitally important to him. They had bought third class tickets and they had not been prepared for the hard wooden seats on offer. Consequently, sleep was elusive, especially as the two men opposite had kept up a particularly croaky and deep voiced conversation all night, as well as scoffing a seemingly endless supply of salami rolls. Light began to break through the vista beyond the train windows and the rugged, hilly landscape of Tuscany began to take shape. Or was this a dream? Surely it was too early for the arrival of dawn, as the scenery gradually began to take on an idyllic golden hue, the like of which he had never witnessed before. All was gold; sky, hills, grass, trees, as if Midas himself had run wild and gone on the rampage, touching everything in sight. The vision seemed to last some minutes but then the urge for slumber overwhelmed him. He awoke as the train entered Rome station with his head on the shoulder of a very surprised member of the Italian military and much to Pete's embarrassment.

At Rome station, Pete and Martin consumed pizzas for breakfast which were available on the platform at very reasonable prices. They were square, flat, topped with cheese, tomato and herbs and with not a morsel of ham or pineapple in sight. Above all, their taste was a delight. They left the station feeling much refreshed after a ten lire wash and brush up in the men's cloakrooms. Ascending and descending two of Rome's seven hills, they felt the morning heat intensifying by the minute. At last there was sunshine which had mostly been absent since they had left Switzerland. After crossing the Ponti Garibaldi, they could at last make out the dome and spires of St Peter's and Vatican City. They passed Government House, then over another bridge until they could see at last, spread before them, the vast square of St Peter's, with the majestic, eponymous cathedral holding court form the top of its stone steps. Two parallel rows of pillars, four hundred metres in length, ushered visitors into the square which was traversed by a variety of automobiles at breakneck speed. Anxiously, they scanned the cathedral steps for signs of their friends.

Across Italy – the hard way

Sam and Bob had not beaten them to it. As this fact began to dawn on them, a mutual, barely subdued sense of triumph seemed to waft over the pair. Their obvious pleasure at making the rendezvous point and reaching it before the others was subsequently tempered by a measure of concern over Sam and Bob's present whereabouts. Hopefully, they were pointed in the right direction and heading for this very spot.

Entry to St Peter's Cathedral itself was free at that time so they decided to take a brief look round this renowned monument and -- besides Popish scholars' interpretations of Christ's teachings -- the very cornerstone of the Roman Catholic faith. It pleased Pete's aesthetic sensibility to observe, first hand, the devotional works of art hanging at appropriate holy places in the church. There were also ornate statues of myriad popes who had served over the centuries. Particularly awe inspiring was the magnificent ceiling work by Michelangelo whom, Pete was informed, began the paintings aged seventy seven and completed them when he was eighty eight. This, he mused, represented eleven years of total devotion to his art and his faith, but towards the end of what in those days must have amounted to a much extended lifetime. Indeed, during this era, the average inhabitant of medieval Europe was fortunate to reach the age of forty.

After deciding not to visit the treasury, due to what they considered to be exorbitant admission prices, they emerged once more into bright sunlight and sat down either side of the main entrance at the top of the steps. There, amid the bustling crowds of tourists pouring into and out of St Peter's, they both promptly fell asleep, resembling two vagrants after a hard morning's begging for alms, but at one of the world's holiest sites. Pete was awoken by the cathedral clock striking two. Predictably, Martin slept on until Pete prodded him a few minutes later.

"Time to get a coffee, I think and maybe a bite to eat," suggested Pete.

They selected a café with chairs and tables outside and from where there was a vantage point towards the cathedral steps. They consumed coffee and a very rich chocolate cake each for which they paid St Peter's Square prices. They also spent some time observing a group of Swiss Guards. In their red, blue and yellow, vertically striped, puff-sleeved sixteenth century costumes they would have comfortably outshone those splendid uniforms of the Tower of London beefeaters. They were not just fulfilling a ceremonial role, as Pete found out when he attempted to enter an interesting looking building just to the side of St Peter's. He was prevented from doing so by the Pontiff's dutiful guardians. Not to be thwarted in his determination to explore the building, Pete tried again, sneaking around one of the outer stone walls. These somewhat puerile antics annoyed the guards to such an extent that about half a dozen of them in modern battle fatigues, who had been sitting around a table behind their flashily dressed comrades, started to take an interest in him. Their looks said it all and as they moved towards him the historical building suddenly seemed to lose its appeal. He returned to the café. Memories of his A level History lessons were revived in Pete's mind, particularly the massacre of the Swiss Guards at the Tuileries Palace during the French Revolution.

"That lot are still defending anachronisms, I see," he remarked but Martin, in mid cigarette, merely chuckled.

It was now two thirty pm and peering through the gathering dusk, Pete could just make out the figures of Sam and Rob as they struggled towards them, obviously fatigued from carrying their rucksacks. They caught sight of Pete and Martin on the cathedral steps and simultaneously put on a spurt towards them, their unbridled joy and excitement plain to see. Some of the visitors milling around the square were astounded to see four seemingly crazy Englishmen engaged in hugging, back slapping and hand shaking. What had happened to the famous British sang froid?

It transpired that Sam's and Rob's fortunes had been similar to Pete's and Martin's. They had taken the main motorways, autobahns and autostradas, experienced warm welcomes wherever they went, spent a high proportion of their ready money and cashed half of their travellers' cheques. The bars and tobacconists en route would certainly have been the richer from their visits, mused Pete. Martin, by contrast, had cut down dramatically on his smoking. However, when they had stopped off to visit the Leaning Tower of Pisa, they had been washed out of their campsite by flash floods which had hit the area. They had been forced to head for the higher ground. In addition, they had met with similar difficulties in hitch hiking, after they had crossed into Italy, and were subsequently obliged to catch a train from Genoa to Rome.

As part of the pre arrangements of their expedition, Sam had managed to obtain the address of a campsite on the outskirts of Rome. Just outside the square, they got talking to a local man who had shown a friendly interest in the quartet, having witnessed first-hand their frenetic reunion. As a result of their conversation, conducted half in adapted Spanish and half in broken English, the worthy Roman citizen offered to drive them to their camp site. They never really learned whether the man was actually heading home or had gone out of his way for their benefit. As things turned out, this was to be their last lift anywhere.

All told, the Trans World Expedition party spent four days in Rome. They visited the customary tourist sites such as The Colosseum, the Spanish Steps, the Pantheon and the Vittoriano. The latter made quite an impression on Pete in its overall massiveness. Although the monumental building was established in the nineteenth century, with the rise of Fascism in 1922, the Vittoriano became the setting for the military parades of the Mussolini's authoritarian regime. He was ignorant of these facts at the time and mistakenly thought it was one of the edifices erected under the auspices of Imperial Rome. The gargantuan building did indeed stand out like the proverbial wedding cake or "la torta nuziale" amongst the other grey or brown stone relics. He also later learned that the ever inventive Roman citizens had invented other less than flattering nicknames for the gigantic monument, such as "la dentiera" -the dentures," macchina da scrivere" - the typewriter and, most amusingly, "la zuppa inglese" - English soup dessert, which referred to a trifle. Overall though, he he remarked to the others that it had certainly been worth visiting.

However, despite the obvious attractions awaiting their further inspection, they needed to reach Brindisi by the following Sunday as they had bought tickets to Patras in Greece in the weeks prior to their departure from the UK. Sam reasoned that it would be a waste of time trying to hitch hike there and it would work out cheaper to travel by train.

"A lot cheaper if my diabolical plan works out," he announced, grinning rather too smugly, even for him. Pete was actually concerned about their finances as were Martin and Rob. Roman restaurants were not the cheapest and one attempt to get away without paying the bill had been foiled when Pete realised he had left his camera in the restaurant. On returning the next day to retrieve the said camera, it was duly returned on settlement of their almost certainly inflated bill.

Then in a flash he realised the implications of the phrase "diabolical plan" and memories of his former exploits on the railways of South East England returned to him. But would those highly questionable methods work in Italy? They certainly hadn't so far and the prospect of Italian gaol time did not exactly appeal either, any more than did the ignominy of returning to England in some disgrace.

Friday morning dawned, and the quartet broke camp, proceeding by bus towards Rome railway station. It had become apparent to all of them that there were no ticket barriers at Italian stations. The system was that once on the train, passengers would have their tickets clipped by one of the inspectors on board. The first part of their plan was to purchase tickets for Valentina which was the next station along the line. They were to split into groups of two, keeping their baggage within easy reach for a quick escape.

From Naples, they would make their way across the east of Italy using the same method. The theory behind all this was, of course, flawless. The main problem was that it relied heavily on the actions of living breathing human beings. Not only those as yet unknown to them, but also themselves.

The plan, in theory, was watertight. It now required being put into some form of practical application. The central idea was to deceive railway officials on each stage of the route across Italy. In the actual execution of this plan, the participants would need to speak and act both individually and in concert according to circumstances as they arose. Obviously, they had no way of predicting its outcome and in their naïveté, failed to take account of how their adversaries – the inspectors and railway police – were going to react. Those worthy officials could not be expected to read the script. There was no script; only human discourse in all its fateful unpredictability.

Had they but realised the said plan was, in reality, ill conceived from its very inception, they would certainly have had second thoughts. But they did not. As it was to turn out, in terms of execution it would soon degenerate into the category of make-it-up-as-you-go-along. As a system of achieving free transportation, the plan was riddled with flaws that the architects themselves became painfully aware of only too soon. For example, they believed that the train toilets would be ideal hiding places for them, provided of course they were vacant. They also believed that their only adversaries would be the railway officials and in this respect they made the classic British error of underestimating the enemy. Another misconception was that the language barrier would be a factor working in their favour, allowing them to hide behind their lack of Italian which would get them the sympathy vote. The worst they thought could happen was that they would be ejected from the train at the next station after they were caught. At least they would have made some progress towards their ultimate goal. Rob, a celebrated and much experienced train dodger was the first to acclaim such an ingenious scheme. Pete also found himself agreeing and it was decided to put it into effect on the Friday. It was now twelve days since their expedition had begun.

At the appointed hour of midday Friday 19th September, the Transglobal Expedition assembled or rather slouched like a group of dropouts at Rome Central Station. After a meal of locally purchased bread, cheese and tomatoes washed down with Ruffino, they bought their train tickets to Valentina, ten minutes before the train was due to leave. They boarded separately, trying not to stand out, as being foreigners, they were bound to look conspicuous anyway. Sam and Martin went to the front of the train whilst Rob and Pete chose the rear.

The Naples train departed on time and soon they were heading south at speed. Pete stood watchfully in the corridor, ready to report on any movements by the inspectors and trying not to resemble a train fare dodger, whatever one of those was supposed to look like. To his mind, every glance from a native traveller seemed to be filled with suspicion. That group of nuns was obviously aware of what he was up to and the soldier looking up from his magazine towards the corridor knew exactly what Pete's next move was going to be. Gradually this paranoia began to be edged out by reason and the miles sped by. Tracing the route on a wall map in the corridor, Pete was able to measure their progress and little by little his confidence increased. Soon they had travelled one hundred kilometres for about ten pence.

Outside, the landscape had changed to a desolate wilderness of rocks and dried up rivers, dotted with occasional scrub and conifers. The warm lands of the south which the four of them were seeking so earnestly always paid the price for the amount of sunshine they received, in their general dryness and lack of visible populace. Indeed the ruggedness of this environment reminded Pete of the backdrops to so many Spaghetti westerns such as " A Fistful of Dollars" and "The Good the Bad and the Ugly."

Suddenly, at the moment he was least expecting it, possibly because he was so taken with the view outside the carriage, a ticket inspector of the Italian Railways appeared at the end of the corridor. Clad in an embellished grey uniform, topped off with a red banded peaked cap, he moved deftly towards the spot where Pete was standing. Pete immediately set off for his hiding place in the toilet. However, he also needed to warn Rob who was calmly ensconced in his compartment, lost no doubt in a world in which Clint Eastwood was mowing down gangs of Mexicans and blowing up bridges. At least, trance like was how he appeared, because try as he may, Pete could not attract his attention. He put up the prearranged two fingered V sign but without any luck. Instead he had to reach his arm through the sliding door and practically stick his fingers up Rob's nose. Unfortunately, just as he was turning round to make his exit, he came face to face with a very stern looking *ispettore del treno*.

Two words only spilled from the official's mouth: "Bigliotto signore!" With somewhat shaky hands, Pete presented his ticket for Valentina, complaining bitterly that some well-meaning but incompetent official had put him on the wrong train in Rome. This rather pathetic piece of improvisation presented in what could only be described in the kindest terms as pidgin Italian was never going to convince anyone. His passport was summarily confiscated and he was angrily instructed to sit in an empty compartment a few carriages further along.

However, he could not sit patiently in that compartment while his rucksack was still at the front of the train. He went to retrieve it, then trudged up and down the corridor, edging past priests, soldiers and whole families who seemed intent on placing themselves as obstacles to his progress. To make matters worse, Martin and Sam had also been caught. In that instance, the inspector had been more sympathetic and sorry for the inconvenience caused to them in missing their crucial stop. Nevertheless, it appeared that in this case, Anglo-Italian relations were unlikely to be enhanced if the inspector who had caught them were to discover that those idiots on the train without valid tickets were actually in a group together. A fact that would all too soon become apparent as soon as he happened to bump into his colleague who had apprehended Pete.

Pete had reached the unfortunate pair who informed him by speaking to him quietly but not looking in his direction that they were to be put out at the next station which happened to be a city called Aversa, just three miles north of Napoli. Pete eventually managed to reclaim his rucksack when the train stopped and he hurried to the end of the platform, where his inspector was waiting to return his passport. Although the afternoon was hot, it was not only the temperature which had caused his flushed cheeks, but also embarrassment and self-anger.

As they stood on the platform, still somewhat stunned by their experience, they realised that they could not be identified as friends. This called for some improvisation on their part, the execution of which would at least have impressed Pete's former drama lecturer. Their aim was to confuse the railway officials by not showing any recognition of each other. Pete went into the station bar where Martin and Sam were already seated at a table consuming half litres of Italian lager. Rob, with all the luck characteristic of his exploits on English trains, had managed to remain undetected and was lurking in a dingy corner near the bar itself. He was also busy with a large glass of beer. Thanks to his half Indian parentage, his skin was an olive hue and his hair was almost black. He could easily have been mistaken for an Italian. The ensuing drama unfolded thus:

Martin: (Aside to Pete) Don't show you know me.

Pete: (Gesturing to pretend that he supposed Martin to be Italian) Er sigaretta…er matches…er light for cigarette please.

Martin: Sorry old chap, I don't smoke.

Pete: Oh sorry, didn't realise you were English. (Aside) Any idea how we get out of this mess?

Martin: Yes, I am just here for a couple of weeks, then back to the U.K. (Aside) Sam is going to reconnoitre and give us the lowdown on our situation.

Sam: Scuse me chaps, are the bogs over there? Yep? Ta.

Pete: I need the bog myself. So how are you getting back? (Aside) Good scheme. (An animated dialogue continues but they run out of banter, and dry).

Sam: (re-emerging from the toilets) Aah, that's better! (Far too exaggerated)

(Aside|) The place is crawling with cops but we could try sneaking out one at a time.

Pete: Reckon I'll use the bogs now lads. Nice talking to you. Bon voyage.

As Pete proceeded to the toilets, Martin and Sam made their move towards the station exit. When Pete came out, relieved more by his escape from that chamber of foul odours and brown stained walls, he observed them in conversation with an Italian man close to the exit. What they had not bargained for was that the inspectors had informed the local railway police that there were three Englishmen on the station who desperately needed to get back to Valentina. These same police saw it as their duty to make sure that was exactly what was going to happen. This information was imparted *sotto voce* to Pete by Rob who had appeared at his side as if from nowhere. Apparently, the police had thought he also wanted to get back to Valentina but this he denied. Incredibly, they had not asked him for his ticket.

Just as calamity beckoned, there was another bizarre occurrence. When Pete looked towards the exit once more, Martin and Sam had vanished. The police seemed to be focused on him but when they too perceived that the other two *Inglese* had removed themselves, they were utterly confused so they consoled themselves by passing round cigarettes, shrugging their shoulders and generally trying to look unconcerned. It was now or never. Pete moved purposefully towards the exit and in no time had joined his colleagues on the opposite side of the street. They quickly put as much distance as possible between themselves and Aversa Station.

"That's the last we'll see of that dump. I shall miss it so much" muttered Pete, panting from the exertion of lugging his rucksack whilst walking at a very rapid pace.

They had reasoned that they needed to reach Naples by another means and chose to take the bus. Luckily, the local coach station was clearly sign posted. The coach fare was surprisingly cheap compared with the prices charged in England and they clambered on board. Approaching the city of Naples, they glimpsed in the distance the blue haze of the Mediterranean Sea. They progressed through a landscape of tree lined hills, ribbon development of dirty corrugated iron shacks, then the inevitable stretches of suburban outskirts. The blue haze earlier witnessed transformed into a rich blue sea, contrasting, on its horizon with a cloudless azure sky. A golden warming sun seemed to be beaming down approvingly on the travellers and their endeavours as they neared a part of the city characterised by utilitarian, almost industrial buildings of steel and glass. The area where they stopped and disembarked reminded Pete more of Basildon New Town in South East Essex.

When the bus reached Naples, it came to rest near the *Centrale* railway station in Piazza Garibaldi. Everywhere, Pete could see contrasts between age and modernity; affluence and poverty. Crumbling stone buildings, embellished by fading stucco, faced the gleaming modern station which had been renovated nine years previously. Its widely sweeping semi-circular entrance hosted a shop selling fashionable clothing, a delicatessen and an audio equipment store. This structure gave on to a large forecourt. Twenty five tracks provided starting points for any number of destinations throughout the Italian peninsula. Across the Piazza, old men carried sacks on their backs almost as large as themselves, while a young man in a white linen suit and Zeiss sunglasses strutted past them into the "Mexico" coffee shop to purchase his weekly requirements.

After unloading their packs from the bus, Pete and his two companions marched over to the station and there, standing nonchalantly by the ticket office was Rob. He had succeeded where his companions had failed, but there was no time to gloat, even if that had been his intention. In fact he was both delighted and relieved to see the others. He was smoking an Italian cigarette which one of the inspectors had given him and between puffs he welcomed his colleagues. They did not even ask him how he had effected his escape but were relieved to see him for all that.

"I knew you fellas wouldn't be too long. Anyway, the Brindisi train leaves in ten minutes," Evidently their train had terminated at Naples.

"Great stuff," chuckled Sam. "You always were a jammy sod. Remember those weekends he came to stay with us at college, fellas? Eventually, even the domestic bursar must have taken him for one of the students."

"And he's still got my sodding college scarf," observed Pete as they advanced towards their next train, though he was flushed with relief that their expedition was back on track – literally. The sense of elation felt by all at this moment in time, however, was short lived. Apparently their train was due to travel a few kilometres north before turning eastwards to Foggia, thence to Bari and on to Brindisi. As chance would have it, the next station along the line was none other than the infamous Aversa. The idea of returning to the place they had left in such haste filled them with a dread and a mutually felt temporary loss of morale. In reality, they were bumbling across Italy, and snapping at their heels was the all too realistic prospect of arrest and possible incarceration. This prompted them to consider a special course of action and after much discussion which truly demonstrated how much they had learned from their previous mistakes, they bought tickets for Aversa.

Once again, on this trip, it was vital for them not to attract attention. This, they had no chance of achieving as the train consisted of a mere half dozen carriages and was crowded practically to bursting point. Their packs were also going to take up a lot of space. Undaunted, they climbed on board. It seemed that even the train itself was conspiring to wreck their plans to keep their heads down and remain inconspicuous. A wheezing diesel locomotive coughed and chugged as it struggled out of the station. Its progress was stop start, stop start and it leaked pungent fumes into the carriages. Burdened as they were, the English travellers were bumped and bounced around like cattle in a farm truck, colliding frequently with the native passengers and setting off a domino effect along the corridor. To add to their problems, it was going to be well-nigh impossible to find any toilets to hide in.

Inevitably, a ticket inspector presented himself within five minutes of the train's departure. A seasoned professional, he was used to negotiating congested corridors while the train was in motion as this one was; just about. He plied his trade happily enough, giving cursory glances to tickets proffered to him from among the mass of sweating bodies and clipping one or two every so often. When he discovered the party of Englishmen in the corridor, he was moved to speak to them, in passable English punctuated with numerous swearwords.

"Bloody hell, how you like my English? Listen. Fuck off bastard! I learn this in Australia."

Stunned by this admittedly good natured verbal outburst, they all remained silent until Pete blurted out, "That's really impressive. Seems like a lot of Italian men have been to Australia."

"Oh yes, fuck me, I was in prisoner of war camp!"

There followed what seemed to be one of those awkward silences where the only discernible sounds were the muffled rhythmic clacking of the train over the tracks below. That is how it seemed to Pete, anyway. However, Martin cunningly chose this moment to offer up their four tickets but this conscientious servant of Italian Railways responded in a casual, good natured voice. "Later, later," he chirped, with an extravagant wave of his hand. Was that a slight Aussie accent Pete could detect? He left them alone and turned on his heel towards the rear of the train.

By this time, the said train was already approaching Aversa, so the party of travellers split up and sped towards their selected toilets to hide. Pete for one welcomed this opportunity as his stomach was starting to give him problems. His chosen toilet was vacant, much to his relief and he entered the white walled cubicle. Behind the obscured glass window, blurred images of Aversa station slid into vie. The train was gradually slowing down to the dreaded stop, and this instantly hastened Pete's bowel movements. Fortunately, he had managed to position himself over the pan and soon he was sitting in his small prison, confined and waiting. He did speculate that the odour emanating from this cell may deter anyone from wishing to have the door opened. Nevertheless, his inner senses began to long for the shrill guard's whistle to signal the train's departure from the Aversa district which seemed to be drawing them in like a magnet.

Another analogy occurred to him as he reached for the toilet paper hanging on a roll by the window. It was the wheel of fortune which he had always had lengthy discussions about in English lectures and which had appeared to have come full circle. Had the expedition party been guilty of *Hubris* and were about to meet their nemesis? The Furies, in their railway police uniforms would be delighted if Pete and co. could once again be delivered into their clutches. After what must have been the longest station stop in railway history, made tenser for Pete by periodic hammerings on the outside of his toilet door, the joyful blast of a guard's whistle rent the late summer air, eventually reaching a triumphant, crescendo, causing the train at last to drag itself away from Aversa.

Martin was waiting in the corridor by an open window. "Well, every step we make now is progress." He regarded Pete as he looked away from the detective thriller he happened to be reading. Pete was certain he had heard that statement somewhere before. For his part, he was content to watch the suburban landscape slide by, then give way to dry rocky hillsides sparsely shrouded at intervals by olive groves and cherry orchards. These eventually petered out to be replaced by mostly coniferous trees in a drier terrain.

"Beautiful day, Martin and it looks like there are mountains in the distance. We are in for some great scenery coming up. I'm starting to enjoy this."

At that precise moment, Sam appeared next to Martin. The somewhat melodramatic shift of his eyes and the serious set of his jaw did not bode well. "We were nabbed!" he announced. His words had the effect of a sudden cold autumn shower on a bright summer's day. As a further harbinger of doom, the radiant Italian sun, which had previously presided beatifically over their endeavours, now retreated behind some white puffy clouds.

"OK," responded Martin, "so what did you tell the inspectors?" It appeared that Sam had been unable to find a hiding place and when the inevitable check came for tickets, he could think of nothing more creative to do than to feign sleep. It did not help his cause that he was actually still standing upright. He was promptly shaken awake and had to explain away his ticketless status by claiming that a friend had it in their possession. This of course was perfectly true; a rare gem of veracity which sparkled in a screen of deception thrown up by the quartet of friends on their travels to date. The latest news he brought was that the said inspector was now searching the train for the holder of his missing ticket.

Rob soon joined them in the corridor then moved off with Sam towards the rear of the train. Out of the corner of one eye, Pete observed Martin placing the four train tickets inside his novel, then he closed it. A sudden pang of dread, tinged with very slightly raised hopes, sent a shudder through his entire body. He guessed what Martin was planning to do and it was both a desperate and reckless move on his part. A devious mind was at work and Martin was giving that squinting look which had always signalled that he was dreaming up a ruse of some sort. Casually, he leaned his right elbow on the base of the open carriage window. His right hand gripped the novel with the four tickets sticking out like a quartet of miniature book marks.

Minutes later, their two companions returned but this time Pete could just make out behind them a uniform, a peaked cap and a stern face. This inspector had clearly had his fill of these whining *Inglesi* with their ducking and diving and their utterly implausible excuses. Their time was up. However, before he could utter any dire threats that might have come into his mind, Martin announced loudly and confidently,

"Don't worry, I have our tickets."

"Ah at last. Please give me…." But even as he spoke, Martin, just as Pete had expected, opened his book and there, for all and sundry to see, were four tickets (to Foggia they would claim) fluttering away into the wide wastes of an Italian hillside.

Sam and Rob gasped with astonishment, tinged with more than a little admiration. Martin always presented himself as (and was known to be) a straightforward, upstanding individual who was also at times prone to off the wall behaviour. This had most definitely been an off the wall moment.

"That was a good move," muttered Sam, reverting to his

current favoured expression. Rob could only whisper, "Brilliant! When did you figure that one out?" Meanwhile, the inspector and Pete were exchanging glances of helpless disbelief. A disagreeable grimace stole across the Italian official's face. Any empathy he may have felt towards these travellers was now at an end. Pete began to realise that this was not about to go well for them.

"You 'ave to leave this train at Benevento." With that curt command, the inspector turned on his heel, no doubt to inform the railway police who would ensure his instruction would be carried out to the letter. Benevento, it transpired, was a large town in central Italy, not fifty kilometres from Foggia.

As dusk began furtively to shade in the nooks and crannies of the ancient streets and alleyways of Benevento; as tones of violet and ochre spread noiselessly through the surrounding forests and hillsides, four young Englishmen, having been unceremoniously evicted from the train now departing from Platform Two, stood disconsolately among their rucksacks on that very platform. In the gathering gloom, close to a dingy station lamp, they began to discuss their next move.

A decision was made to purchase tickets for Foggia and stay on the train until Bari on the east coast of Italy and the last major conurbation before their destination of Brindisi. Two of the party suggested that they may as well travel legally all the way to the port from where they were due to catch a ferry to Greece. However, a combination of foolhardiness and a thick skinned resilience appears to have prevailed. They seemed by all accounts to be quite prepared to put themselves through the same mental stress and humiliating encounters that had so typified their great railway odyssey to date. On the positive side, they would be making a hundred miles further progress towards their goal.

To their immense surprise and delight, the train they boarded turned out to be a brand new high speed express. As the sleek ten coach green and white multiple unit slid noiselessly into the station, Pete could not help noticing the plush seats discernible through the train windows. These were not even first class seats and would have put to shame most of the equivalent accommodation on British

Railways. He also recalled with distaste the wooden benches they had had to endure on one or two of the Italian trains. This one seemed to be designed like a modern passenger jet. Sam and Rob chose to seat themselves in the rear, and Martin, sitting opposite Pete was soon engrossed once again in his thriller. As the express took off on its journey eastwards, Pete began to meditate on how the next couple of hours might pan out.

As the *rapido* thrust its way through the surrounding darkness, Pete found himself wondering what scenery they would have been missing. After all, appreciation of landscapes, industrial and pastoral, formed a major part of his enjoyment of train journeys. It was still going to be dark by the time they reached Bari.

Soon he was deeply engrossed in remembrance of rail journeys from London to his home town. The main line passed right through the Wid Valley before reaching Chelmsford. First there was the build-up of anticipation as the train traversed flat meadowlands, then entered a cutting before revealing before his ecstatic gaze, a splendid panorama; a sylvan dream of green hills gently rolling upwards to two villages, tree lined with patchworks of geometrically arranged fields spreading towards distant horizons. A river meandered lazily through this landscape until it turned sharply westwards to flow under a mighty railway arch. This was a sight Pete always relished and never tired of it. One day, maybe in two years' time, this is the beloved location to which he would return. Then, without warning, the shadow of an intruder was cast across his idyll. He became aware of Sam leaning over him displaying a mischievous grin.

Pete knew the signs only too well. This meant more trouble. Sam seemed to delight in getting into all kinds of scrapes, usually of his own making. On one occasion, at college, he had enlisted Pete's help for a spying expedition on a girl who had dumped him after she had caught him in flagrante with a Fresher. Somehow he had heard that his now ex girlfriend had invited another male student to her room that evening. Sam was still entertaining ideas of a reconciliation, and this development seemed like a major blow. So just before dark, Pete had found himself with Sam on a spying mission, crouching under the girl's ground floor window. As far as they knew the male visitor had not yet arrived, so Sam had started pleading with her, still keeping below the line of her window. "Oh Cheryl, it's me. Please listen. I am so sorry about what happened. I can explain everything. I love you, not her…" Then a gruff female voice interrupted him.

"I think you'll find you are outside the wrong fucking hostel. Sod off!"

It had not helped of course that the pair had partaken of several pints at the college bar and evidently this had adversely affected their navigational skills. They shot off across the grass that separated the college buildings but Sam was determined to continue with the mission, eventually they managed to locate his ex-girlfriend's room.

"Have a peep inside and see what they are doing," whispered Sam. Pete slowly raised his head to look directly into Cheryl's room. It came as no surprise to him that the couple in the room were sitting, innocently chatting and drinking coffee, but Pete could not resist it. Lowering himself down again to Sam's level, he blurted out,

"Christ Sam, he's taking off her bra!" Sam's eyes widened with horror but worse was to come as a voice shouted out from about fifty yards away,

"Oi, what are you two up to? Hey, it's the peeping toms, folks!"

Unfortunately for them, the college had recently been plagued by intruders who turned out to be a couple of local perverts wanting to catch glimpses of young female students in their underwear. The girls on the ground floors had been terrified and the previous week one of the outsiders had even made it up to the first floor. To their immense chagrin, Sam and Pete realised that their silhouettes had been mistaken for the intruders or even worse, they themselves would be exposed as the peeping toms.

They had just had enough sense to run to the nearby woods then double back behind their own hostel. Luckily, the hue and cry had not as yet been raised and they were able to return to their rooms unobserved. Pete felt compelled to put Sam out of his misery by telling him that he had only been winding him up about what Cheryl and her visitor had been up to.. The shriek of "You bastard!" could be heard all over the campus. In the months to follow, they still found themselves laughing hysterically over that incident whenever it was mentioned.

So it was with more than a little trepidation that Pete looked up at Sam, pondering on what new catastrophe they had steered themselves into.

"Well men, we've really done it this time!" Before the familiar ice cold feelings of dread and foreboding had time to creep over him, he perceived that Sam had only paused briefly then he continued to roll out his report.

"Rob and I were wandering about at the back of the train when we heard this voice spouting English with an eyetie accent. It was only the bloody guard inviting us to sit with him, so we did. We had to, really. Thank Christ he didn't ask to see our tickets. Then a sodding railway policeman turned up and he introduced us. I tell you, we nearly crapped ourselves."

Sam then waited for a few seconds to let these tidings sink in. By now Martin was looking up from his novel and paying full attention. Sam continued,

"He asked us where we were heading for and Rob just blurted out that we were going to Bari."

"Good move," interrupted Martin.

"Well anyway, we've been having a rare old chat back there. I think he wants to practise his English."

"For fuck's sake be careful!" was Pete's philosophical advice. Martin joined the discussion.

"You're on to a potentially good thing there, as long as Pete and I stay here looking as inconspicuous as possible."

There could be no doubt that they were making good progress but the prospect still remained of discovery and being put down at some remote station – or worse. They were all unnerved, despite their outward show of bravado. Pete tried to sleep but always in his mind he could hear the click of a ticket punch and ominous footsteps in the gangway between the rows of seats.

The Italian night rushed past on either side. The train, like a surrealistic jet liner thrust its way through space and time, as if in a kind of suspended animation, and when it stopped at a town or a city, it conjoined with the lives of their citizens, yet it shared little of their hopes and dreams. Then once more the train would leave, carrying the hundreds on board towards their destinies, maybe never again to pass that way. The *rapido* pulled into Bari just after midnight and disgorged its passengers, including four very relieved Englishmen. Another one hundred kilometres and they would be in Brindisi. They purchased rail tickets for Monopoli, a mere twenty five kilometres from Bari.

No, they had not learned.

Part Two

Istanbul

"On the meeting point of two worlds, the ornament of Turkish homeland, the treasure of Turkish history."

(Mustafa Kemal Atatürk)

Daylight seeped into a small basement room, no more than three metres square, somewhere in Istanbul. Pete stirred from his fitful slumber. It was another awakening among so many other awakenings and to what? How many futures have dawned on helpless, unknowing humanity with their prospects clear and stark in the cold light of morning? All too often the outlook is so far at odds with what might conceivably be achieved during the next twenty four hours. So much optimism is raised at that time only to founder on subsequent events of the day.

Take for example this morning of all mornings. Bright sunlight was beginning to lance through gaps in the tatty blind covering a smut spotted window to his right and above his head. Now a single sunbeam teased at Pete's eyelids until, at length, his semi-comatose form rolled over to avoid the blinding pain. Rolled over on what? Good question. It was a three inch thick length of nylon covered foam barely a metre in width and less than six feet long. The makeshift mattress was grubby and somewhat malodorous too. It was a few seconds before realisation of his present, parlous situation came flooding in as his mind gradually cleared.

Twenty four hours ago he had awoken in his own tent some ten kilometres from central Istanbul. He had twenty pounds in his money belt and five pounds' worth of Turkish Lira in his jeans pocket. That had been the previous morning. What about this one? So much had happened since the events which had ultimately landed him in a back street basement flat in the district of Harbiye. The only clothes he possessed he was actually wearing and on checking his pockets he discovered a mere five pounds and a few lira. As if in a kind of trance, Pete started mentally to recall the events that had unfolded since their departure more than a month ago.

This was because the previous day, a chain of the most ludicrous errors, born of a naïve assumption that no matter what happened to him, everything would turn out just fine, had concluded catastrophically for Pete and for the expedition as a whole. In mitigation, it would be claimed and acknowledged that three of the group were virtually out of funds and that Pete was only trying to rectify the situation by changing up the money he had and sharing it out. Nevertheless in all seriousness, the group collectively did not have enough money to see them through the next couple of weeks. That is how long it was going to take them to reach Beirut from where they had booked passages on the ferry to Alexandria. Ironically, the nearer they had got to their destination, the further away from them their dream seemed to be receding. But what had gone wrong?

The journey to Istanbul had taken Pete and his companions a shade over four weeks. He and Martin had hitch hiked from Ostend, all the way through Belgium, via France, Germany and Switzerland to Rome. They had been the first to arrive at their pre-arranged meeting place on the steps of St. Peter's and the other two had struggled in a few hours later. They had proceeded through Italy by train, taken the ferry from Brindisi to Patras across a royal blue Adriatic, and traversed the whole of Greece by bus. On a warm dark autumn evening, they had triumphantly entered the teeming eastern metropolis that was late nineteen sixties Istanbul.

As far as accommodation was concerned, there was a campsite ten kilometres outside the city in Ataköy which had been recommended to them by Metin, a young Turkish boy whom they had met on the bus from Thessalonika. This was the boy whom Sam had insisted on calling a "little shit" as he had been persistently harassing the group during the journey, poking his nose into where they were going and why. He had also shown a certain amount of cheek when his questioning had gone unanswered. It became apparent that this was his way of making friends and trying to be helpful and when they eventually reached Taksim Square, it was Metin who had guided the intrepid four to the relevant bus stop.

The walk from Beyoğlu, where the bus had dropped them, to Taksim Square was unlike anything Pete had ever experienced before. True he had participated in the scrum like activity that frequently occurred around Oxford Street Station on a Saturday afternoon. By contrast, in a similarly crowded Omonia Square in Athens, the numerous parties of pedestrians seemed almost regimented. In Beyoglu, one of the first things a visitor would notice in those days was a maelstrom of sound, a continual cacophony of car and truck horns which assailed the ear drums of the swarms of citizens on the move through that wondrous street. In Athens, such sounds had been banned from the city centre by the Colonels – or the *Junta* as they were known. It seems they did get something right after all.

Here though, in Istiklal Caddesi – Independence Avenue – hundreds of Turks of all social backgrounds promenaded freely, in an autumn evening illuminated by multifarious lights of restaurants, headlights of honking taxis and radiant window displays of still open shops. Street vendors who haunted the pavements at intervals croaked and wailed, advertising their wares of boiled sweet corn, aromatic roast chestnuts, pickled vegetables, brightly coloured fabrics and fake luxury goods. Shoe shine boys were active, as were ragged men who crouched in shop doorways with domestic weighing scales in front of them, and water boys, weighed down by contraptions on their backs, hoped that their potential customers were feeling sufficiently thirsty that evening.

After about a twenty minute walk, dodging round the other pedestrians and trying to take in the multitudinous sights and sounds that they were experiencing for the first time, they finally reached the bus shelters of Taksim Square. The sheer acreage of this vast municipal epicentre was lost on the four at this point in time. They were focused on catching the bus, reaching their campsite and getting in some much needed sleep. At the Ataköy bus stop, around fifty people were standing in line awaiting the bus's arrival. As the red and cream single decker drew up alongside, any semblance of an orderly queue disappeared in a mad scramble to make it on board. Packed tightly at the front of the bus, among the throng of standing passengers, rocking and rolling with each curve of the streets and sudden stops, the quartet reached their destination in a fraction under half an hour. Strange how, when viewed from inside a bus or a car on the move, all towns seem to look the same at night. After registering with the camping officials, a couple of whom spoke a smattering of English, they pitched tents and settled down for the night.

However, as Pete reflected, that had all happened two days ago. The first morning they had spent an hour or so swimming in the warm blue Marmara Sea. Of course that was in the days when it was still possible to swim there, before that part of the Marmara became too polluted for people to even stand on the beach without gagging on the stench of freshly dumped effluent. On this bright autumn day, in the second week of October, Pete and his friends had been able to relax outdoors in bright sunshine and temperatures in the mid-twenties, as the limpid waters lapped lightly on fine white sands. Was it this seemingly timeless stretch of calm inactivity and pure aimless relaxation after their long trek from England that had lulled Pete into a false sense of security?

He could not help drawing comparisons between this pleasurable experience and the three days at the campsite near Brindisi. Despite the frequent and persistent droning of military aircraft taking off and landing at the nearby airbase, they had enjoyed a complete rest from their travels and were given a chance – not actually taken – to plan later phases of their journey. All along the route from Belgium, each situation generally had been safe, unthreatening and they had hit it off well with the locals in most of their stopping places. Pete, friendly and gregarious by nature, had ventured abroad before but never further south than Boulogne. He was naturally trusting, and most people he and the others had engaged with en route had, by their actions, only reinforced his trust in human nature. Subsequently, on their second day in Ataköy, the four companions decided to take in the sights of fabled Istanbul; Constantinople, and Byzantium of antiquity. It had been a much-anticipated visit, about which Martin had waxed lyrical concerning St. Sofia, the Blue Mosque, Topkapi Palace and the Grand Bazaar. Unfortunately, on that fateful day, these were sights that Pete was destined to miss, not only at great personal cost but also with a decisive effect on the whole enterprise.

On alighting from the Ataköy bus in Taksim Square, the company of four soon found themselves mingling with the mid-morning crowds of strollers and shoppers milling around, heading both towards and away from the main street, Istiklal Caddesi. Their steep learning curve as to how to survive in this mighty city was dramatically enhanced when they attempted to use a designated pedestrian crossing, complete with traffic lights suspended from above the road. These same lights might just as well have been hanging in the nearby Gezi Park for all the notice taken of them by maniacal drivers intent on slaughter in the streets. On seeing the green lights opposite, the English quartet set off across the black and white stripes of safety. After taking no more than a couple of steps they were back on the same pavement again, having narrowly escaped being flattened by a Desoto Adventurer backed up by a Chevrolet Impala, whose drivers seemed to be competing for their prey. Their actions were accompanied by a deafening blare of horns. Behind them, three taxi cabs were ready to clean up, in case they had missed – which of course they had, this time.

"Fucking sods!" Bellowed Sam and accompanied his assessment of their driving skills with a Churchillian gesture. "I'll tell you what fellas, in Britain that would be breaking the law." The would - be assassins were long gone but the street was still a dangerous place for a pedestrian to be. There was no way across but at that moment the lights changed again.

"When in Rome," chirped Martin and with that, he promptly took off across the road, dodging around the hooting swarms of traffic. Somewhat tentatively, the others followed and, to their immense relief, were soon on the other side of the street.

They had decided earlier in the day to try and locate the British Consulate, which they had been informed was situated in the district of Galatasaray at the end of Istiklal Caddesi. Once they had visited the consulate and gained the necessary information and advice for the journey onwards, they were to take a dolmuş or filled taxi across the Golden Horn to the old city. They had been advised by some friendly Turks at the campsite regarding public transport. According to them, the dolmuş was a very popular and cheap method of transportation in Turkish cities. Most of the cars used for this purpose were battered American models from the 1950s and early 60s. They were told they had to wait in a queue at the appropriate *durak* or stop, as all of these had designated destinations which covered the districts of central and suburban Istanbul. It was a simple enough process; you named your destination, took your seat in the car, waited for it to fill up with more passengers, then the driver would take his place and set off. People would alight and board the vehicle at different stops, official and not so official, along the way. The fares, apparently, were ridiculously cheap by European standards as long as you could endure being jammed in a hot car with up to six others, while the driver negotiated the seemingly endless traffic jams.

The British consulate was within walking distance so they started to stroll along Istiklal through the district of Beyoğlu. The scene took on a very different appearance from that of the night of their arrival, only two days ago. In the bright sunshine, there was, despite the heat, an energy exuding from the populace, whether they were engaged in serving in the smart clothing stores, restaurants, cafés or employed in the various businesses and banks. There was a buzz in the air and the streets were alive. Young girls thronged the pavements, wearing Italian style blouses with Levi jeans or plain coloured skirts which just dipped below the knee. By contrast, they saw a few older men clad in black jackets and black shalwar trousers. Some were even followed at respectful distances by their wives who were dressed from head to foot in black with white yashmaks covering their mouths. There was a mingling of the classes as the super-rich, having abandoned their Mercedes or BMWs, rubbed shoulders with the shabby poor, some of whom, might, one day get to build BMWs in Germany, as *gastarbeitern*.

Every hundred metres or so there were beggars. Rob found himself being moved to tears by the appearance of many of these unfortunates. Some exposed leg or arm stumps to public gaze. Others, with no legs at all, were rocking up and down on the bottoms of car tyres and were only able to move at all by pressing wooden blocks on the ground with their hands. There were also child beggars who pestered one and all in the streets, babbling pathetic but totally incomprehensible pleas for *kuruş* in exchange for tiny boxes of matches. This was too much for Rob. He had always struck Pete as being compassionate by nature. Behind that tough but good-humoured exterior lay a kind heart and a desire to do good in the world. He began to distribute some one lira coins and soon he was surrounded by a dozen children all with hands outstretched. This particular act of charity was very short lived as his group of admirers was soon dispersed by a couple of shouting police constables with truncheons drawn.

It was therefore ironic that the next building of note that they passed was the St. Antoine Roman Catholic church.

"Ah look there fellers, 'tis surely a sign!" Rob guffawed in a mock Irish accent. However, the spectacle he had witnessed with the beggars seemed to have affected him profoundly. The others marvelled \at the ornate church which also boasted a steeple, a large exterior and it would have graced any Christian European city.

"The Ottomans always permitted other religions to be practised in their empire. Tolerant lot, really, as long as you did as you were told and paid your taxes," Martin informed his colleagues.

They passed Galatasaray High School on their left, then looking across the street to the right, they could make out the palatial British Consulate, standing behind impressive high walls, amid extensive tree lined grounds. Pete experienced a brief frissant of patriotic pride as he and the others crossed over towards the majestic looking building that at one time served as the British Embassy.

Sam spoke up for the first time since his encounter with the Istanbul driving fraternity and announced,

"well, now we all know where the consulate is, we'd better go to a bank, get some cash and have a drink somewhere.

Even as he spoke, the rest of them became aware of a smartly turned out young man dressed in a dapper light grey suit, blue tie, along with a white striped shirt and highly polished black shoes. He had slipped into the middle of the party while they were halted on the pavement and he began speaking to them in friendly, welcoming tones.

"You guys English? I speak English very well. I can help you. Welcome to my city."

It was so easy for them to take to this very personable interloper. His manner was at once disarming and then again fairly assertive. He seemed to ooze warmth and positivity as he offered to show them round the city, then they could go back to his house for a meal later on. They could even stay over if they liked.

"That's very kind," said Martin. "What's your name?"

"It's Izzet, but you can call me Izzy."

They were soon all shaking hands and somewhat miraculously, as a neutral observer might have remarked, they appeared to be on intimate terms with this young man in a matter of minutes.

Had they known the true nature of this well-mannered, hospitable young Turk, they would have instantly turned away and set off for the British Consulate at a gallop. Indeed, they should have done. To begin with, his name was not Izzet; his English was limited to a few rote learned phrases picked up from films; his smart clothes were not in fact his and nor were his shoes. He was a confidence trickster and a thief who lived by his wits on the streets of Istanbul. On this particular day, he was targeting the area around the British Consulate. Rich pickings indeed.

His life story followed a pattern familiar to many millions of other Turkish males. At the age of eleven, with his father in prison and his mother eking a living out of taking in washing, plus the odd paying gentleman, he began haunting the streets of the Tarlabaşı district as a shoeshine boy. With his sparse array of cleaning materials, his customer base was practically non existent so his method was to deliberately splash mud or dust on to people's shoes then offer to clean them for a lira. Unfortunately, this led to him receiving several beatings at the hands of irate pedestrians. As a consequence, he soon learned to choose his victims more carefully. He also developed a very good turn of speed to escape his pursuers and, later on, the police.

Unsurprisingly, his activities led him into a life of petty crime ranging from what Shakespeare's Autolycus would describe as "a snapper up of unconsidered trifles" to shoplifting, then on to house breaking and burglary. He was, of course, apprehended by Istanbul's finest on a number of occasions and, owing to the fact that he lacked sufficient funds to bribe the arresting officers, he ultimately found himself as a guest at the notorious Sağmacilar Prison. Being slight in build, he had naturally been a target for the bullies – and worse. Not only was he brutalised by some of his fellow prisoners, whom he eventually learned to defend himself against, but also the prison guards. His introduction to the noble art, practised in Turkey, of *falaka* or bastinado would live long in his memory. As soon as he set eyes on the gorilla who was about to punish him and the cane he wielded, he unhesitatingly lay down on his back and presented the soles of his feet for beating. However, the heavily built prison officer, made him stand up again so he could have the satisfaction of wrestling him to the ground.

Unfortunately for him, this was not the last time he was to be incarcerated and beaten. However, on the day he acquainted himself with Pete and co., he had not seen the inside of a prison for about two years. Swindling tourists, using the change money routine, was practically the perfect crime. He would offer them exchange rates higher than the official ones, then abscond with their cash. His outrages was rarely reported. After all, his victims themselves were attempting to swindle the banks and gain a bit more money for themselves. Furthermore, these luckless travellers and holiday makers would not be staying in the city for more than a week or two. He would merely hide himself for a few days in another district. Should he ever be foolish enough to get caught doing this, he knew that a sentence of ten years beckoned, together with more doses of *falaka*.

His opening gambit with these English guys would be to offer them the best rates of exchange for their sterling. He needed to deal with just one of them, as they could easily overpower him if they began to suspect his motives. Then again, he did carry a six inch blade which would be enough of a deterrent. He did not know, of course, that that the four of them each possessed similar weaponry.

Pete was first to respond to his offer to change their money for them. "We have travellers' cheques and we don't intend staying in Istanbul all that long. We are actually making for Beirut and Alexandria."

"You have sterling then."

"Yes and we have tickets booked on the ferry from Beirut."

Just why Pete had to impart that somewhat irrelevant information was not initially very clear but may have indicated how well Izzet had been able to inveigle himself into the group's collective confidence. It was the travellers' cheques that most interested their new acquaintance.

"Listen my friends, when you travel to Anatolia and Middle East, best currency dollars." He was not lying, actually.

"I've heard that too," replied Martin. "We should try to get some before we continue our journey."

There was unanimous agreement with this suggestion but how were they to achieve this? Izzet had the solution, of course. "I can get you dollars at very good rates. I have a friend in Grand Bazaar with plenty foreign money. First you use travellers' cheques to get lira, then I exchange them for dollars at ten lira for a dollar."

Seriously, the young felon could not have scripted this meeting any better if he had tried. The Englishmen were playing right into

his hands – *bir aptal ve parasi hemen ayrıldı*; a fool and his money...
etc. There was a momentary stir of excitement, tempered
somewhat by the fact that Pete was the only one with sufficient
funds to carry out this procedure. If this came off, the continuation
of their journey looked to be possible and the others would be able
to arrange for money to be sent to banks en route. As it stood, Pete
had twenty pounds left in travellers' cheques, together with the
equivalent in lira of about five pounds in cash. He had also had
ten pounds transferred to Barclays in Khartoum. Sam had the
same amount of lira but was hoping his ex-girlfriend back home
might send him some finances. Martin and Rob had just under two
hundred lira between them but along with Sam, had been seriously
considering a return to Blighty.

Now there was a good chance of them continuing with the
world tour. Khartoum was certainly within reach, provided they
were careful regarding their expenditure. If Pete could manage to
procure the dollars with Izzet's help, entirely illegally of course,
they would soon be able to proceed eastwards. The plan was for
Pete, accompanied by Izzet, to exchange his cheques for lira, then
their Turkish financial adviser would exchange them for dollars at
a rate better than the banks were offering. Put like that, it would
mean lots of dollars at their disposal. Rob suggested that they
should all go with Pete and for a brief moment it looked like they
would do so, but Izzet told them that the whole transaction would
take about ten minutes or so and they could meet back at the bar
in front of the consulate where he would buy them all a drink.

Just off Istiklal was the Beyoğlu branch of Türkiye Iş Bankası
where Pete was able to exchange his cheques for Turkish lira.
He presented his passport, and a bundle of money, having been
carefully counted, was handed over to him. The next phase would
involve Izzet's so-called friend. Soon he was walking along a
crowded back street in the direction of Cihangir, accompanied by
Izzet. In a few minutes, they came out into an open cobblestoned
space where there were steep stone steps, possibly Byzantine in
origin, descending steeply down a slope, before crossing a canyon
of crumbling apartment blocks, then climbing up the other side.

There was no other person in sight, save a heavily laden porter struggling up the steps in the distance towards Sıra Selviler. It was going to be too easy for Izzet. He said to Pete,

"Give me the lira and I see my friend near here who will change to dollars. Then we go back to the street with the bank and your friends."

At that very point but rather too late, Pete was struck by a blinding flash of realisation. But this was no epiphany. Suddenly, the whole scene in front of him was spinning before his eyes and he found himself lying flat on the cobblestones. Izzet, clutching Pete's money, had already set off at a trot downwards before Pete could regain his balance. He was also quite certain that he had felt a slight push just as he was about to tell the thief that he had changed his mind and wanted his lira back. Unfortunately, by the time Pete had made it to a fully upright position, Izzet – or whatever his name was – was long gone, together with any hopes of making further progress with the expedition. At least for the time being.

Numbed by shock and with his head aching from its contact with the hard stone ground, he found himself aghast at the speed with which the robbery had been carried out. Only now was he beginning to grasp the full horror of his situation and indeed that of the others. He was trapped in a foreign city with no more than the equivalent of about five pounds in his pocket. What was he going to tell the others? Certain events from the past few weeks came flooding back unbidden into his mind. As he trudged sadly back along the narrow street, he could not help reminiscing on how they had interacted with people they had met along their route and how they had often put their trust in different persons in a range of differing situations. Their experiences in this respect had been positive. It seem seemed, almost, as if all of humanity was willing to give them a helping hand on their travels and in their quest for……well what? All too frequently they had taken these kindnesses for granted and in their often insensitive way had, in some cases, repaid their continental hosts with displays of dishonesty and selfishness.

Firstly, there was the whole business of the railway journey across Italy, deceiving staff who had genuinely believed that the young passengers were lost or on the wrong trains. They had left a restaurant in Rome without paying the bill and had repeated that transgression at the World Trade Fair in Thessalonika. Also in Thessalonica they had helped themselves to several litre bottles of water that had been left unattended in crates on a restaurant balcony. In Athens, Pete had stolen a packet of biscuits from a park kiosk and they had also skipped out of their campsite in Dafni without paying for their stay. In truth they found all of this a huge joke; minor indiscretions to relate to friends back home, eager to learn of their exploits. So was the disaster that had just befallen Pete a kind of nemesis or even karma? Retribution for what were, after all, minor felonies? Or viewed in a harsher light, was it merely that this bunch of middle class, inexperienced and naïve ex-students had finally got their comeuppance for tramping across Europe, displaying at times negative attitudes towards foreigners and looking to circumvent conventional modes of human interaction?

This is not to say that the young men were in any way disreputable, wicked characters. In truth, all of them were well liked back home and were regarded as having some integrity. They were known by friends and family as intelligent, respectful people who delighted in helping others. What had gone wrong? None of them had in the past committed any more serious crimes than those of the apple scrumping variety, fare dodging, trespassing on railway property to collect locomotive numbers, or fiddling overtime in vacation jobs. Nevertheless, as Pete approached the bar where his friends were enjoying a beer, he was in a sheer funk about how he was going to break the news to them of his stupid error of judgement.

As he related the events of the last twenty minutes or so, clutching a cold beer that had been saved for him, his friends' faces fell as one and mouths gaped. In essence, they displayed a mixture of sympathy for Pete and a disappointment that their journey into the sun was probably now at an end. Sam spoke first. "I knew we should have gone with him. If we had, this would never have happened."

"No, replied Martin. In fact, he would have taken off if he knew there was going to be four of us."

"You know, I never even thought about using my knife," mumbled Pete.

"Good thing you didn't or you would have been the one they slung in prison," sighed Sam, "even though you might have rid the world of a genuine piece of shit!"

Reality had still not hit home. How would they be able to afford to reach their next destination? As if losing his money had not been desperate enough, it now transpired there was more gloom to come. It was Martin who broke the news to Pete. He glanced round knowingly at the other two before imparting some newly received information. "Look mate, we bumped into a couple of American guys just now and they told us that Sudan has still not settled down properly after the coup that took place in May. The Marxist government has nationalised all businesses and because of factional fighting among revolutionary groups, the safety of foreigners can't be guaranteed."

"Not only that," added Sam, "they said they could not get visas for Syria which we were hoping to get from our consulate. Not much hope there, either."

Without passing through Syria, they would not be able to reach Beirut for the ferry to Alexandria. Furthermore, Martin had somehow arranged for the group to work in a match factory, of all places, in Khartoum, which they would undertake for a few months before proceeding further east to Iran and India. According to Martin, work permits were waiting for them, but now the situation in the Sudan had made their prospects of financing their further progress look extremely doubtful.

"So it looks like Khartoum is out of the question now and I had a tenner waiting for me in the Barclays branch there. Look I am really sorry, men, I've fucked up too, haven't I."

"Well, you did and you didn't," responded Martin. "But would you really have fancied travelling for hundreds of miles over endless scrubland and desert between here and Beirut"

Rob spoke up for the first time. After gulping a mouthful of ice cold lager, he announced that he would not actually have minded it even if that was the unpromising nature of the terrain.

"After all," he added, "there are hundreds of great sights to see on the way and perhaps we could find some work here for a month or two."

The suggestion did not meet with universal approval. However, Pete was beginning to recover his faculties and he acknowledged Rob's idea with,

"I'd be in favour of doing that. There are bound to be English language schools here requiring foreign assistants or something like that."

Sam and Martin nodded but without much enthusiasm. The discussion would have to be continued later, as it was now decided they should report the crime to the police. It so happened that when they asked directions to the police station, an English speaking Turk informed them that it was a hundred metres further along Istiklal then turn right.

On reaching the grim, forbidding exterior of the police station, they ascended the stone steps with a mood hanging over them that perfectly matched the dreariness of their surroundings. They pushed through the double doors at the entrance into a large shabby hallway which stank of carbolic and stale human sweat. They approached the front desk and Sam started to explain the situation. But no-one spoke English, apparently. The desk officer shrugged his shoulders and appeared almost Gallic as he announced, "Nous ne parlons pas Anglais ici." Apparently, the Turkish police service still used French as their second language, unlike most other institutions which had already converted or were converting to English. Pete, who had been able to use his French in all countries as far as Greece (excluding, of course, Germany and Italy), took up the verbal exchange.

"Un voleur a pris tout mon argent près d'ici il y a une demi-heure."

"Combien d'argent?"

"Vingt pounds sterling."

The officer managed to affect a sympathetic smile in Pete's direction, then enquired where they were staying. On being informed about their accommodation arrangements, he told them that they would have to report the crime to the camp police in Ataköy. Yes, there were police at the campsite, but how could they possibly investigate an incident that had taken place in central Istanbul? As Pete translated to the others, it became depressingly obvious that the green uniformed constabulary before them had no interest in pursuing this particular offence.

"Merci beaucoup," muttered Pete as they made for the exit.

"Yeah, thanks for nothing," Sam snapped angrily.

The obvious next port of call was the British Consulate where they were able to explain their parlous situation to an assistant consul. He was a Maltese who spoke English with no hint of an accent and who listened earnestly to Pete's story. It was clear that he recognised the gravity of their situation but was this because a UK subject had lost his money or because Pete had been party to committing an offence under Turkish finance laws? His initial response was to declare that it had not been the first time something like this had happened and would probably not be the last. It appeared that there was nothing he could do.

"You must be joking!" Stormed Sam. An Englishman has just had all his money stolen from him, the police don't wanna know and you're not going to tell them to hunt down the thief!"

"That's not in my power," responded the consular assistant. Sam was livid.

"I don't know what we pay you for if you can't be more helpful than that."

"I think we do need some sort of assistance in resolving this situation, especially as we are British subjects. I thought the consulate was here to help," added Martin

"Is there any work locally where we might be able to earn enough cash to at least get back to England," Pete asked, without much hope of a positive response."

"Not without work permits."

"How do we get those?"

"You ask around and see if there is anything going,"

Sam exploded. "Full fucking circle, in other words!" But he was not the only one losing his patience. The official had had enough of the demanding young men confronting him, even though Pete and Rob had been comparatively restrained. For his part, he had to deal with similar situations every day of his working life. Sam was of the school of thought that to get things done required the direct approach and an insistence underlined with more than a hint of aggression. Martin, whose father was a senior civil servant, always believed that he could use that kind of influence in such eventualities, together with the threat of official action. He spoke to Sam but loudly enough for the Maltese to be able to hear.

"Yes and when we get back, my father will be taking this up with the Foreign Office. Overhearing this, the official dismissed them with,

"As you wish sirs. There is always repatriation but you will have to surrender your passports to us."

They were bowed but unbeaten and defiantly determined to resolve this crisis. The prospect of repatriation began to take root and apart from losing their passports for a few weeks, at least they would be safely back home in a matter of days. However, they had told all and sundry that they would be away for around two years, not five weeks. As they reached the door leading to the consulate's grand entrance hall, the vice-consul they had been speaking to managed to catch Pete's eye and beckon him back.

"If you go to this address and ask for Mr Vefbi, he may be able to give you a job as an English language assistant at his private school."

The address was The European Languages School in Sıra Selviler which, as they discovered, was a street running parallel to Istiklal Caddesi. He thanked the consular official for his thoughtfulness then re-joined the others. After getting directions, they made for the address they had been given.

A parting of the ways

The European Languages School was situated on the first floor of one of a number of grey fronted office blocks in Sıra Selviler – in English, Cedars Row. A couple of crumbling concrete steps led up to the black and grey tiled hallway, then a flight of steep concrete stairs ascended in a slight curve to the school office. Students were taught in two large rooms, either side of this office. In addition to classroom teaching, there were correspondence courses in English and French which were sent to students throughout Turkey..

As Pete and his companions made their way to the school, they discovered that they could take a short cut though a narrow connecting street where they passed two restaurants, a teahouse, a magnificent Greek Orthodox cathedral and an Armenian school all of which presented an exemplar of cosmopolitan Istanbul, with more than a passing gesture towards the city's roots. As they approached the block where the language school was located, Pete noticed a somewhat stern looking personage seated in front of the main door. Perhaps he could help them find the right floor. The man was in his late fifties, whiskered and wearing a battered grey jacket, crumpled black trousers and a pair of lace up brown shoes which had seen better days. He regarded the group of Englishmen balefully from beneath a black beret. Pete made his request as politely as he was able.

"Could you please tell us where we can find Mr Vefbi?"

"Vefbi bey yukarda, birinci Kat." This gruff and somewhat curt reply was accompanied by an upward jerking motion of his right hand. Martin added a thank you to which the man nodded; his face now expressionless. Of course, they had not understood what the man had said, which was "up there on the first floor".

But they got the gist and proceeded up the stairs.

As they climbed the lead hued, concrete stairs, each of them was feeling some trepidation, even though by now, at least two of the group had already decided on what actions they were going to take after today. The cream coloured door at the entrance to the office was wide open and Pete could observe the scene inside as he set foot on the landing. A portly gentleman with a neat short grey haircut, tanned complexion and a Roman nose was conversing on the telephone at his desk. He was wearing a smart brown tweed jacket, white shirt, no tie. To his right sat an attractive but solemn looking secretary; a girl about twenty five years old. She had an angular face, almond shaped eyes and long brown hair streaked with blonde. She was the first to notice the visitors.

"Can I help you sirs?"

"Yes, answered Pete, "we would like to speak to Mr Vefbi if that is at all possible."

The portly man seated beside her looked up from the green telephone and clapping his hand over the mouthpiece addressed the foursome in front of him in very grave tones.

"Mr Vefbi? Oh no you do not want him; he is a very bad man."

The secretary and two male teachers in the room now burst out laughing. Pete and his friends were visibly stunned and this made the situation for the teachers all the more hilarious.

"This is Vefbi bey and he is joking with you," the secretary announced but they had by now worked this out anyway. Amidst much joviality, the four young Englishmen were invited to sit down on classroom chairs which were brought in for them by the two teachers, then Pete, as requested by Vefbi bey, poured out his story, not forgetting to mention at the end that they had been sent to him from the British Consulate. When he had finished, the school boss looked both sympathetic and thoughtful. The others spoke in Turkish to each other but it was clear they had been angered by the events Pete had related.

"I am sorry this animal has taken your money. Where were you planning to go after Istanbul?

Martin replied to this query. "We were making for Khartoum via Syria and the Lebanon but we have not got our Syrian visas yet and there has been trouble in Sudan."

"Oh I would not go there at present. Very dangerous places. Also Anatolia dangerous. It is full of bandits who hold up the buses. Anyway, most foreign travellers go to Afghanistan then on to Kathmandu."

All was silent in the office, with those present not only digesting the content of Pete's narrative, but also intent on what Vefbi bey had to say on the matter. He explained that he and his staff were now preparing for the new term which was to begin the following week. He needed one or two English conversation assistants to help with fluency, grammar and knowledge of English colloquialisms. He was prepared to pay them ten lira per day plus twenty for the weekend.

"Actually, we are qualified teachers," asserted Sam, to which the others nodded their agreement. This was not quite true as Rob was a chemist.

"In that case, I will pay one hundred lira a week if I can see your certificates."

As far as Pete was concerned, this sounded too tempting to resist. He would just need to send for a copy of his teaching certificate and that would entitle him to the higher salary. The others were less keen, it would appear, and were muted in their response. He detected some interest from Rob but even he was starting to waver. Vefbi added that he had already found two assistants, both clever lads but not qualified to teach.

"Anyway, soon I send one of them to Anatolia to give leaflets about our correspondence courses. He is Biology graduate but has been here a few months and knows some Turkish."

Martin felt that they needed to discuss their next move and Sam agreed. It weas crunch time. Should they continue the expedition in the spring after earning money in Istanbul? The issues, which were not discussed in that office or at that time were apparent. Should they still be intent on reaching Khartoum, or instead push on to India across Iran when the time came? Pete himself was all for accepting Vefbi's offer. After all, despite what had happened to him, he had told his friends, family and anyone else who had cared to listen that he was going to be away for two years and he was not about to fetch up in GB, pathetic and penniless, after only a couple of months. Rob put forward a proposal.

"If we want to stay here then we'll have to sort out accommodation. We can't stay at the campsite indefinitely."

Vefbi was seen to whisper something to his secretary who picked up her phone and began to dial.

"One minute, please." Vefbi accompanied this request with a gesture to the party to stay put, then they saw the girl speak on the phone. The behaviour of Vefbi and his staff so far had been welcoming and supportive which Pete found comforting. However, as far as the group was concerned, this turn of events was puzzling and pointed towards more problems to be faced. As the secretary spoke, they could make out the words "Kemal" and "Ingiliz" which were repeated several times. Then she put down the phone and nodded to her boss. He regarded all four of them then switched his gaze to Pete for some reason.

"Mr Peter, if you stay here, we can find you place to sleep tonight then your friends can come here tomorrow and tell us what they have decided."

Much relieved that the kindly Turk was genuinely trying to help them, the three others took their leave, promising to return the next day at around midday. Pete stayed seated after bidding them farewell. For him, everything was happening with such rapidity, he need to catch up with himself.

Outside, the grey clouds that had been gathering over the Bosphorus region started to disperse and a watery sun made its appearance, just visible to Pete through a dusty window across the left hand classroom. He began to think that he had been rendered totally impotent but he also felt tranquil. Somehow, he could not, at that moment, feel sad, happy, uncomfortable or even disappointed. Something inside him seemed to be telling him he should be feeling utterly devastated. But he was not. His reverie

101

was interrupted by the arrival of a young man called Osman dressed in a white catering jacket and holding a tray with glasses of black tea balanced precariously on it. Pete gratefully accepted his tea, with a sugar lump that took an age to dissolve, then he was formally introduced to the staff.

Shortly, another young man appeared in the office. He was dressed in a smart beige cotton jacket over a white sweatshirt and blue Levi jeans. He also wore light brown suede lace up shoes. He was introduced as Kemal, spoke excellent English and informed Pete most politely that he would be able to put him up at an apartment he was renting along with three other Europeans who were attached to the school. Vefbi also gave Pete ten lira on account and, taking their leave of the school staff, Pete and Kemal walked out into the noisy late afternoon to seek out something to eat. Kemal impressed Pete as a kindly, intelligent person who seemed to delight in helping others. What he did for a living was to remain a mystery to Pete for the rest of his time in Istanbul. That may have been because he never asked. Kemal told him he was a Greek citizen of Turkish ethnic origin and he had dual nationality.

Once they had found a sandwich bar, he treated Pete to a Turkish style hot dog – long roll, no onions, mild mustard - and a glass of ayran. The latter was basically a mixture of yogurt and water; a highly popular protein drink in Turkey, Kemal explained. As they stood at the side of the sandwich bar, with their refreshments on the shelves provided, Pete gave Kemal a brief summary of the expedition to date. Some of the Turks lounging on stools under the shelves could not help staring quizzically at the foreigner in their midst. Few of them would have been able to comprehend Pete's story. However, Kemal listened intently and when Pete had finished, nodded sagely and told him that he had met many foreigners who had lost their money in Istanbul and were trapped until their families could send them more money or they could be repatriated. He had even heard of some who were giving blood at the city hospitals to earn some much needed cash.

"That's what we did in Thessalonika," remarked Pete. "They actually paid quite well."

"Best not to do it here as some places are not clean. I saw a couple of hippies who went to give blood three days in a row. The third time the hospital did not accept as their blood pressure too low. So they both ran round the park next to hospital to put the pressure up. Very dangerous."

"That's pretty desperate. I wonder what happened to them."

"I even heard there are bad men who take all your blood and throw you in Bosphorus but I don't know if that's true. Also you can get hepatitis."

"I'd better warn the others in case they plan to do that."

Evening was already casting its shadows outside, signifying to Pete the foreboding that was creeping into his mind. The relief at finding gainful employment, for the time being, was tempered somewhat by the embarrassment he felt by getting into this situation in the first place. Kemal was reassuring.

"If we see this guy who took your money, we'll grab him and make him give it back to you. In my opinion, he probably thinks you have already left Istanbul by now and so he may still be in this area."

They left the sandwich bar and the dusk enshrouded them as they proceeded across Taksim Square along Harbiye Street. After a quarter of a mile, they dropped left into a cobbled back alley which took a right turn after a further hundred yards or so. They came to a halt outside a modern looking apartment block painted beige on the outside. It was handily placed opposite the local grocer's. Once inside, Pete was introduced to three other residents who were about to eat their dinner of bread, white cheese and Izmir grapes.

Walter was a pleasantly crazy German architect in his forties who, like Kemal, spoke English adeptly, though heavily accented.

"You should hear him do his Hitler impressions – hilarious!"

It was Brian, the Biology graduate who spoke as he, in turn shook hands with the new arrival. Sitting in a corner, huddled over his meal but smiling in agreement was Roger. He was a fair haired, six foot bearded ex-marine who was taking a furlough abroad while he tried to figure out what to do next in his life. Brian was slim and lanky by comparison, whilst Walter, a somewhat wizened little gnome of a man wore, in unguarded moments, that facial expression that looked as if all the problems of the world were weighing him down. Indeed, the dingy lighting the room afforded by a single forty watt pearl bulb may have been depressing were it not for the general joviality of its occupants. Even Pete's story, after he had introduced himself, failed to dampen their spirits. Autumn was close. The bitter Balkan winter would be setting in come December and they all had something in common. In that they were all looking to exist and eke out their separate lives without a single clue between them as to what the future might hold.

As for Pete, he had no set plan as such, save for the general notion that by next summer he would, barring accidents, have saved enough money either to return home or continue the expedition. He felt that the latter option could still be on, even if only one of his companions wished to join him. The prospect of taking control of his own destiny looked, for the time being, remote to say the least. Meanwhile, he was practically penniless and highly reliant on Vefbi's largesse, the tolerance of his new acquaintances, plus whatever circumstances would present themselves during the next few months.

So this is how Pete came to find himself waking up on a malodorous mattress in a dusty sunlit room somewhere in Istanbul. Under the present circumstances, he would struggle to see the situation he had landed himself in as an opportunity. That was a philosophical concept for which there was no room in Pete's subconscious. Indeed, as he lay on that mattress trying mentally to prepare himself for the day ahead, he could not shift the nagging feeling that at this moment in time, things looked utterly hopeless. Eventually, it was hunger that galvanised him to further action, and on rising, he made his way into an adjoining room to reacquaint himself with the two Englishmen and one German he had met only the previous afternoon.

The European
Languages School

On the first day of the rest of his life, Pete tucked into a breakfast consisting of freshly baked bread, rose flavoured jam and white cheese. Walter had made them all a pot of Turkish tea but there was no sugar. Very little was actually spoken. All were anticipating the day ahead and only Walter had any idea of what they would be doing.

"Ve vill spend zis day in preparing ze classrooms for next veek's lessons and ze school opening. All cleaning materials, I made ready and zere is paint for walls and doors." At least he seemed excited at the prospect, if no-one else did

About an hour later, Pete and the three others were standing drinking more Turkish tea and chocolate filled croissants called "ay" (as in eye) which like their French counterparts were crescent shaped but more substantial. Outside, the autumn sky over the city was washed with tints of grey. Rain was expected but was holding back for the present. The school secretary, whose name was Zeynep, was engaging them all in cheerful conversation, while brooms, cleaning cloths and floor cleaner stood idle in the right hand classroom. In addition, a stack of paints and brushes awaited the skilled artwork that the Europeans were about to perform with them. Eventually, Zeynep felt it incumbent upon her, in the absence of Vefbi Bey, to get the work started.

"Please only do the classrooms and front doors. You don't clean toilet. We have doorman to do that"

"Oh him," laughed Brian. "He's a cheerful chappie." Pete was equally amused.

"Yeah, he gave us a really friendly welcome yesterday."

"Oh he is stupid man. He is *Yobaz.*" Zeynep remarked, somewhat scathingly.

It was to be a few more weeks before Pete and Brian found out exactly the meaning of the word *yobaz*. By the tone of Zeynep's voice, it did not sound like a compliment

They all set to, scrubbing the wooden floors and painting the walls of each classroom a kind of beige colour. At midday, Martin, Sam and Rob turned up as promised. It fell upon Sam to reveal the somewhat alarming news that the camp at Ataköy was closing until next spring but rather fortuitously they had been offered accommodation for a couple of days in the neighbouring town of Bakirköy. Sam spoke first.

"You remember that young guy who kept hanging around and hassling us on the way here from Greece?"

"The one we finished up calling "little shit"?

"Yes, little shit of all people. We bumped into him again on the bus coming into town and he offered to put us up at his place for a few days."

"Coincidence or what!" Commented Rob.

"Very fortunate for us," added Martin.

However, it eventually emerged that the camp officials had missed Pete the previous night and were convinced that he was trying to do a runner. The others had been asked to pay up but they had not done so as yet and they had left their tents at the site to collect later. Apparently, they reckoned they had been overcharged for meals taken and for the use of camp facilities. It did not look too good for Pete either, as all his possessions were still at the campsite.

"The bastards!" Pete spluttered. Well I haven't got the spare cash to pay for four nights plus the other stuff!"

Martin had a suggestion. "Time for the Reading Amateur Dramatic Society to put on another show. We'll go back to the campsite, then you follow a bit later pretending to be a completely different person who is just visiting us. We have already taken down your tent and it's in your rucksack next to your holdall in Sam's tent. We'll spin them some tale to draw their attention away from you, then you grab your stuff and take off sharpish but generally in a cool and collected manner."

Sam was utterly astonished. Pure fantasy land. Did Martin really just come out with that? Then he thought about it. This was in the same league as his ruse with the train tickets. It was hell or bust.

"It might just work. It's that crazy!" The others, Pete's new acquaintances and fellow decorators, paused from their work and stood smiling in disbelief. Then Walter made a contribution.

"You pretend to be not English, maybe an American and make sure zey hear you speak."

Pete felt elated, excited even by the prospect of one more piece of deception. The prospect of failure and its potentially grim consequences did not even register with him.

"Good scheme fellas. I don't really want to cadge any more money off Vefbi Bey. I'll do it."

Unfortunately, the mood was soon dampened by sad news for Pete. His college pals had made up their minds to be repatriated. He tried to persuade them to change their minds but they had obviously come to a firm decision. Indeed, they attempted to prevail upon Pete to do likewise. They intended to go to the British Consulate the following day to make the necessary arrangements. Pete's negative response to their not entirely unexpected decision seemed to throw the others. After all, they were naturally concerned for his welfare, trapped as he was in a foreign city two thousand miles from home and all the other comforts afforded by the UK at that time. One disadvantage for them was that Sam and Martin would be unlikely to find teaching positions before January at the earliest. Rob was not overly concerned about his employment prospects. In the meantime, operation equipment retrieval needed to be put into action. Roger looked up from his paint pot and remarked,

"I'd just love to see this. Beginning to end."

Martin, Rob and Sam were to return to the campsite and place Pete's belongings behind the one remaining tent. Then Pete would arrive, pretending not to know them then make off with his possessions as quickly as he could.

And so it panned out that towards late afternoon, the campsite was visited by a young man wearing sunglasses, Walter's check jacket and Brian's baseball cap. He spoke in an exaggerated American accent to three very shifty looking Englishmen and appeared to be asking them for information.

"Say you guys, could you direct me to the bathroom?"

"Sure, it's just over there behind the office."

He rather ostentatiously followed their directions to the toilet and as he passed the office, he greeted the occupants with a "Hi guys". He was ignored. They certainly had not recognised him. A few minutes later, he strode back over to the other three who surreptitiously handed him his rucksack and holdall. There were muttered expressions of good luck all round and Pete walked out of the gate towards the nearest bus stop. Before he left, he just had to indulge in some more play acting which could well have been costly. Quite loudly, he said,

"Well thank you for that, guys. See ya around sometime." So loudly in fact that one of the guards looked up from the newspaper he was reading, then apathetically returned to his sports page without regarding Pete any further. Even then, Pete could not resist walking straight past the guards with a "Bye guys!" They merely nodded at him in disinterested acknowledgement. Thus the great camping fraud had been perpetrated and the site owners had been stung for around five pounds in fees and meal prices.

Before setting out for the campsite that day, Pete had enjoyed a lunch of stuffed tomatoes and peppers with pudding *helva*, all washed down with a bottle of Tuborg lager. It looked to him as if the local food was going to be a key positive aspect of remaining in Istanbul. Hopefully, the others would by now have finished the work and they could decide where to have dinner. When he arrived back at the school, he found that all the walls had been painted and only the doors now needed doing. His new companions had to chuckle at his afternoon's exploits, then they all made their way to what was affectionately termed by Roger and Brian as a

"Walter restaurant", where a good meal could be had for around twenty pence per head, as opposed to almost forty pence in most other establishments. These very popular restaurants served food of the home cooking variety, whereas the smarter eating houses mostly offered different kinds of kebab. However, Pete was to discover in time that nowhere he had ever visited had warranted the expression "variety is the spice of life" so much as the city of Istanbul with its myriad types of Turkish cuisine on offer. As for the "Walter restaurants", sadly, within twenty years, these small but thriving concerns had been replaced by fast food outlets, including Burger King, KFC and MacDonalds.

The next day, Friday, was spent in completing preparation for the school's opening, due to take place the following Monday. The walls had been painted in a dull white matt emulsion and the type of brown paint applied to the doors gave them an opaque effect. Both classrooms and the central office were spotlessly clean which is more than could be said for the cleaning staff. At midday, Vefbi called a halt to proceedings and stood surveying his workers' efforts with pride.

"You have done very good job. Now school is ready to start on Monday."

The workers regarded each other. It was by now clearly obvious that they had been labouring in dirty, dusty conditions. They were stained and sweaty and smelt overpoweringly of paint fumes. The next clean up job to be undertaken would be on themselves, and for this purpose Vefbi whisked them all off in a taxi to *Galatasaray Hamam*: the Galatasaray Turkish Baths. This particular *hamam*, however, was not the famous one visited by the cast of the motion picture "Topkapi" but the smaller premises which was virtually next door. They entered the somewhat drab grey building by walking down stone steps into a steam filled entrance hall. There they were greeted by a short grey haired man with obligatory moustache who was dressed in a white cotton shirt and black trousers. Evidently, he was the desk man and Vefbi paid him the entrance fee for four persons.

A pair of swing doors opened into a white world of steam and gurgling water. A strong aroma of olive scented soap pervaded the cavernous room. The four new entrants went into their cubicles to change. The desk man had given them the required accoutrements for their ablutions, namely a large white cloth with either red or blue check designs, a bar of beige coloured soap each and four pairs of sandals made of wood and rubber. Once changed, they emerged into the steamy room with the cloths covering them from the waist down. The walls and floors of this chamber were of a matching grey marble like material. Two burly attendants, dressed similarly to the other bathers, invited them to sit on wooden benches and drew their attention to blue plastic bowls. These measured about six or seven inches across and were to be used to wash themselves down with hot water which was pouring into large stone basins through bronze hued metal taps. Immediately above the proceedings was a large dome which must have protruded through the roof. At the top of this dome was a circular window resembling a huge eye – the eye of Allah gazing benevolently upon them in their efforts to restore the virtues of cleanliness to both body and soul.

A number of other men were in the Turkish bath, all wearing the same attire covering their nether regions. There was an air of calm relaxation that had settled over all the bathers in this otherwise hot and vapid environment. Pete, like the others, found himself reclining like half remembered pictures of Romans he had seen in similar poses. All that was lacking was the *vinus* and raven haired women in topless togas. In fact there were no women of any kind to be seen, unfortunately. He lay on the slimy marble, clad in his loincloth, absorbing the soft warming vapours into the pores of his body. For the next twenty minutes, all of his cares and concerns seemed to vanish. As he lathered himself luxuriantly, he seemed to be washing them away with each gush of tepid water that he poured over him continuously from his bowl. He then went back to the slab to allow more of the invigorating heat to course through him and begin the cycle once more. It became apparent to him that the Turkish bath could develop into a serious habit.

As he lay supine on the hot stone, his attention was drawn

again to the eye of God above him. At that very moment, the waning sun flashed briefly through the glass. His mind wandered. Random thoughts popped up, disappeared and returned to him. Above this dome was the sun that they had all been pursuing southwards; a rear-guard action on their part, in the wake of summer's retreat. Indeed, Sam, when selling the enterprise to Pete back at college, would always stress that the Mediterranean sun would be brighter and more intense than anything he had ever experienced before. And he was right. He thought of the "lucky old sun" of Wilfred Owen's war poem. What was the title? "Futility." Maybe "Futility" was a fitting label to apply to all of their efforts made on the expedition so far. An epitaph, even. It would take more than the prospect of sunnier climes to revive this expedition as he was certain the others would never come back out from England to rejoin him. If there was a God – and up to that time he had had no reason to believe otherwise - what might the divine opinion be of how he and his accomplices had behaved throughout their travels? He was beginning to feel remorseful under that ethereal gaze from the dome above him. Another notion crossed his mind; that of *Nemesis* which had manifested itself in the loss of his money. However, despite everything that had happened, here he was, luxuriating in a Turkish bath, in the company of new companions, with every chance of working through this and eventually returning safely to England. If only the future could be guaranteed to work out as simply as that.

In point of fact, this visit to the hamam was more than just a physical washdown. This was a spiritual cleansing for Pete, even though he would not have realised it at the time. He had read an English translation of the Koran but could remember very little of it, but suddenly, these word came to him:

"Allah loves those who are constantly repentant and loves those who purify themselves." (Koran 2.222)

Somehow this *ayat* was one of those that had stuck and was particularly apposite to his present situation. Could this really represent a spiritual cleansing? A washing away of past misdemeanours? Well, there were certainly going to be a lot more of those in the future, so why not? Had he studied the holy book of Islam more closely, he may have come across another relevant verse:

"Allah does not intend to make difficulty for you, but he intends to purify you and perfect his favour to you, so that you may give thanks." (Koran 5:6)

Shortly though, he would be heading back to his lowly accommodation, ready to pass the most austere weekend of his life, due to his lack of finances, then facing him was the first opportunity given to him of actually practising his chosen profession.

The following morning, after a long refreshing sleep, Pete was awoken by the sounds of a *muezzin* calling the faithful to prayer. Extreme fatigue, born of events which had catapulted him into changed circumstances during the past few days, plus the hard physical work, had finally caught up with him as soon as his head had made contact with the tent bag he now used as a pillow. Now the time was shortly after six am, just before sunrise, and the wind must have carried the wailing across sleeping streets from a nearby mosque.

This was the first time his sleep had been interrupted in such a way but it was not to be the last. For him, the sounds of the *salah* were a cause for some excitement, a reminder that he was residing in an exotic location, in quite a different milieu from the one he had grown accustomed to during the past twenty one years. Strictly speaking, he was no longer a tourist but was about to become a denizen of this fabled metropolis. If he had listened carefully from the bedroom window, he would have become aware of dozens of mosques issuing their reminders to all Moslems to kneel and face east or be welcomed at the holy venues themselves. The city's backdrop of sound was like a cacophony of plaintive songs, all starting at different times. Pete's feelings of elation were not tainted when he later discovered that, contrary to his belief, *muezzins* had long ago ceased to climb the minarets to call to prayers but actually stayed at ground level, chanting into a microphone. Two speakers at the top of each minaret served as tannoys.

He dozed for another couple of hours until the voices of the others could be heard in the adjoining room. The four of them breakfasted on black salted olives with white cheese and bread. In addition, and to his immense joy, Pete remembered that he still had some Nescafe left from the supply he had brought from England. There was enough left to share out and his colleagues gratefully accepted. Walter was especially pleased.

"Zere iss no Nescafe in ze shops in Istanbul. Kemal zumtimes brings a jar or two back viz him ven he goes to visit his family in Greece.

This was of course quite true. In those days, at the end of the nineteen sixties, Nescafe appeared on some of the Istanbul café menus at inflated prices. Meanwhile, the espresso sized servings of Turkish coffee which consisted of one third grounds, remained the most popular choice among the locals. However, in the mornings, the city populace tended to prefer their glasses of tea. Europeans generally avoided Turkish coffee, but Pete was prepared to give it a try. He discovered that if you drank it carefully enough, you could avoid the bitter sediment reaching your taste buds and destroying an otherwise pleasant culinary experience, especially if you ordered it as medium sweet. Those were two words in Turkish that he had learned so far, namely *orta şekerli*. Among the other words which had stuck so far were *ekmek* for bread, *beyaz peynir* for white cheese, *çay* for tea and he remembered to say *lütfen* which was please when requesting these items, although he did not hear the word in common usage in the city. The expression for thank you was a mouthful but he managed a fairly passable *"teşekkur ederim"* when he felt it was required. Most times, though, the French *Merci* was acceptable.

The tea drinking continued in the school office as Pete fiddled nervously with his croissant and almost scalded his lips by sipping the hot tea too soon. He had watched the students enter the two classrooms and he was due to commence his sessions with the younger age group which meant those aged from fifteen to eighteen. He would work alternate hours amounting to six a day on Mondays, Wednesdays and Fridays. The Tuesday and

Thursday sessions were for two hours in the morning only, giving him the whole afternoon and evening to do as he liked. Lessons were supposed to begin at nine am and with more than a little trepidation and very little idea of what he was actually going to do in the lesson, Pete entered the classroom accompanied by the head, Mr Vefbi, to be greeted by the buzzing of excited young voices.

Mr Vefbi called for silence then spoke in English to the assembled class of thirty five students. He introduced their new teacher as "Mr Peter from London." No mention was made, of course, as to how "Mr Peter" came to be in Istanbul, but according to Vefbi he had graduated from Cambridge University, well Oxford would have been closer to his alma mater, at least geographically. The school head then swiftly exited the room in order to introduce Roger to the other class, while Pete was left facing a mass of shiny expectant faces, eager to learn and improve on their grades in English.

At least that was theoretically the case. The desired ideal. However, as Pete surveyed his charges, reality started to dawn on him. Several girls in the front row were chatting animatedly and casting giggly sidelong glances at their new teacher. Further towards the middle of the room, one of the boys had produced a pack of cards and he with five others began to form a card school – or so they hoped. It was the activities at the rear that more seriously drew his attention. Incredibly, two boys had lit up and they began to smoke, as if they were in a tea house. Some of the girls had stationed themselves near these boys and were severally applying lipstick and checking their make up in compact mirrors. Meanwhile, approximately a dozen students elsewhere in the room were sitting in silence, waiting for Pete to begin.

It is conceivable that these young people could be excused for not having high expectations of their latest learning mentor, as this was probably not the first time a foreigner had been placed in front of them, only to disappear after a couple of weeks. Indeed, for some of the group, this was their second or third summer in the school. What none of the class realised was that this particular foreigner was actually a qualified teacher who was going nowhere,

114

at least until the early spring.

However, no amount of teaching practice and educational theory could have prepared him for this situation. The school itself was apparently well thought of. Its fees were fairly high but easily affordable by the more affluent families. Its correspondence courses were popular and the summer camps in England were legendary. However, the kind of behaviour that now confronted "Mr Peter" had been tolerated and indulged by any number of his predecessors, even if the Turkish staff were stricter. Although these lessons were meant to be purely for conversation practice, his pedagogical instincts which at that time were raw to say the least, drew him into expecting more from his class. His pride would not allow him to perform his functions amid what was tantamount to almost total anarchy. This aforementioned pride, tinged with a certain arrogance on his part, then took over.

"Well, thank you to Mr Vefbi for introducing me." A deafening silence hit the room. "Today I am going to ask you to tell me a little about yourselves, in English of course." Murmurs began to trickle around the class; the flow increased and the murmurs began growing gradually to whispers punctuated by the odd giggle. Pete pressed on doggedly with his introduction. "But before we do start, you boys at the back will stop smoking now! You lot can put those playing cards away too, then perhaps we can all pay attention." The tone of his voice did not leave any room for dissent.

His opening gambit and his attempts to stem the rising tide of disruption were met with the return of that uncanny silence and there were blank stares all round. The smokers and the card school took absolutely no notice and the girls recommenced their chattering. This was not only non-co-operation but he also considered it downright rude. He paused on the thunderbolt of actually shouting at them but did raise his voice, maybe a couple of decibels. "Right, if you are not going to listen, you can leave the classroom now."

The social members stared at Pete in utter disbelief. The smokers summarily removed themselves, walking past their bossy teacher, no doubt intending to continue their nicotine addiction in the street below. They were joined outside by two of the card players. Vefbi bey popped his head round the door to enquire if everything was alright and Pete was able to assure him that indeed everything was alright but in a manner that would have done credit to an Oscar nominee. He continued his address to the remaining students.

"Anyone else wish to leave? No? Alright, now someone can start things off by telling me their name and their interests. How about you." Vefbi's head disappeared behind the door and the lesson got under way.

To an independent observer, the rest of the lesson must have been something of an anti-climax, as most of the group were seemingly interested and willing to participate. Evidently, the class, on this occasion, were prepared to cut their teacher some slack – give him a chance. Whether the situation could continue in this fashion, only time would tell. Suffice it to say that he was to hear more from the smokers and the card school, and they were to be the bane of his existence for a few more lessons to come.

In the weeks following, Pete's sessions continued in a similar vein and the half term break seemed a distant but joyful prospect for students and teachers alike. He began to introduce more grammar and vocabulary work into his sessions and much to their chagrin, he set written tasks. His enthusiasm for these soon waned, however, when he found himself with an ever increasing marking load. That was something else his training had not exactly prepared him for. The smokers began to absent themselves with greater frequency and the card players threw in their hands. The chatterers soon came to realise that Pete's lessons were marginally less boring than their gossip. Clearly, very little of a scandalous nature was going on in the city at that time to cause a great deal of excitement. Nevertheless, the temptation to disrupt and waste time was irresistible to some of those present.

There was also an afternoon class that consisted mostly of housewives and young clerical workers on day release while the evening group consisted of about a dozen university students and older professionals honing up their skills in English. One member

116

of the evening class was a stocky, grey haired man in his seventies who had served as an officer in the Turkish army. In his youth, the Turkish language had been written in Arabic script, certainly since the Middle Ages. Pete was curious to know why he took down notes during lessons using the Arabic script and he replied that he used it as a kind of shorthand. More significantly though, he also privately informed Pete regarding the identity of a pasty faced young man in a cheap suit who spent each lesson sitting at the back of the room taking notes and saying nothing. Apparently, he was a member of the secret police who had been tasked by the authorities to monitor the lessons in case any dissident or anti government comments were made. In truth, his main object for observation was the teacher, who might be using these sessions to propagate socialist ideals and western notions of human rights. The old soldier informed Pete that he needed to be cautious.

"If he doesn't come next lesson, means he is satisfied you are not spreading anti Turkish propaganda or encouraging us to rebel against the government."

It would appear that Great Britain and The USA were fast becoming "degenerate countries", and any such ideology that threatened Turkish society were to be nipped in the bud by Mr Demirel's government at every opportunity.

There was no evening lesson on Thursdays so Pete had to wait a couple of days to see if he was off the hook as far as the secret police were concerned. Not so secret if his class was able to identify one of their agents so easily! To say he was on tenterhooks would have called into question the very origin of such an expression. There was, of course, the possibility that this was a prank. He had not really had time to latch on to the local sense of humour but according to Walter, hoaxes and pranks provided moments of uproarious entertainment in this part of the world. However, the sinister interloper was conspicuous by his absence from Friday's lesson. In fact he never appeared again. All very bizarre, as far as Pete was concerned. Although he took comfort from this turn of events, he would dearly like to have known what had been written about him. Was this evidence of a narcissistic streak in him? A touch of egotism? Inwardly, he felt that such a report, if it existed at all, was never likely to find its way on to his future testimonials.

Pete had to admit he enjoyed those evening lessons. Not only did the participants generally respond positively to him but what they had to say was at least mature and stimulating. Their conversational topics touched on history, culture, politics as well as issues regarding family life and travel. However, between them, they always managed to steer clear of the more controversial subject matter such as religion, the First World War and Greece. Somewhere deep in his psyche there lurked an instinct for survival, which was his way of proceeding through life. In any kind of discourse with his fellow human beings, a kind of early warning system usually kicked in to prevent him from treading on the metaphorical thin ice.

In this way, he narrowly escaped a very tricky situation. On discovering that one young man's surname ended in …*yan*, rather that the more general …*oğlu* (son), he was going to enquire why this was so, but something caused him to refrain from doing so, almost at the last minute. It was not until a few days later, when the same the young man, Hagop by name, invited him to his family home to dine - on pork chops no less - that Pete discovered he was an Armenian. The young man's family was most friendly and welcoming, the evening was highly convivial. But Pete learned to his utter astonishment and horror something of the events which had taken place in Turkey earlier in the century which had led to the deaths of more than a million Armenians. He had never noticed any hint of malice from or towards Hagop among members of his class. Indeed, it would not have been far from the truth to say that in the Turkey of the late sixties, his family, the other students, the Greeks, the Jews, the Kurds and all those domicile in the city had something in common. They were all Istanbulites.

In his free lessons, Pete took great delight in slipping out of the school for a brief stroll in and around Taksim Square and Istiklal. The latter provided a pleasing contrast to the drab grey tones of buildings in Sira Selviler. The district of Beyoğlu throbbed with a rhythm that was the very heartbeat of the city, although it was to be some months before the hustlers desisted from accosting him with offers of money changing, hashish, sheepskin coats; in fact, all three if that was what he wanted. On one such occasion, just two weeks into the new term, an incident occurred which could have led to far reaching consequences for Pete's future in Istanbul. He was in the act of crossing Sira Selviler, as he wanted to visit İnönü stadium which was at that time the home ground of Galatasaray Football club. Glancing to his left for no apparent reason, he suddenly caught sight of an all too familiar face.

It was Izzet.

He was standing idly on the opposite pavement close to a side street, no doubt scouting for more gullible tourists to defraud. He appeared to be reading a newspaper, but was actually leafing through the pages quite quickly, as if not particularly concentrating on the news items. If Pete could just reach him and engage him in conversation, then as long as he was not recognised, he would be bound to offer to change money. Surely, it was well worth the risk.

A plan began to take shape in amongst Pete's rather frenzied and muddled thoughts. Maybe he could somehow persuade Izzet to go with him into the school, then with some assistance from Vefbi and the others, he would grab him and demand his money back. Perhaps they would even be able to call the police and have him arrested. He calmly crossed the road and placed himself on the pavement a few feet away from the con man who did not disappoint. He clearly had not recognised the foreigner who now stood before him and who looked, to all intents and purposes, a complete stranger to this environment. Fresh meat; this was going to be too easy. With these predatory intentions in mind, he waved to catch Pete's attention.

"Hello, are you English? American? Alman?"

"I'm English," Pete replied, keeping his face turned slightly away from his intended victim. Ironically, looking at it from Izzet's point of view, the "intended victim" was Pete.

"I show you famous places in the city. You need to change money? Sterling, dollars, marks? I got sheepskin coat for you – or hashish."

119

Clearly, the business was expanding into other key areas of economic activity. It was a classic case of supply and demand.

"I may want to change some pounds I have for Turkish lira.." Crafty, Pete thought. Izzet's reply sounded so routine, delivered as it was in a monotone.

"I get you best exchange rates." Now Pete saw his chance.

"Trouble is, I have left my money in that building over there. If you come with me, we can go inside and do the deal."

In all honesty, Pete had to admit to himself that what he had just said sounded rather lame but it was the best he could do at that moment in time. The pounding of his heartbeat was accelerating with nervous tension and anticipation. It reverberated in his head and even drowned out the roar of traffic in the street. Would this bastard take the bait?

"Ok I come with you....."

Hook line and sinker! Then just as Pete turned to cross back over the street, his impatience got the better of him. In his anxiety and the thrill of realising his plan was working, he made a gesture as if to grasp Izzet's arm and hurry him over to the other side. Unfortunately, Izzet seemed to sniff the air like the feral beast he was and his instincts warned him of impending danger. A momentary flash of panic was discernible in his face and he bleated,

"Oh I just remember, my girlfriend, she is waiting me. I have to see her."

In that instant, he turned on his heel, just as he had done in his first encounter with Pete. He swiftly trotted out of the reach of his would be captor and down the nearest side street. Within seconds, he had vanished and a despairing Pete abandoned any hope of pursuing and catching him. Had he been recognised at the vital moment? One thing was certain, his plan had failed miserably. If only there had been another person with him, but as before, and to his immense chagrin, there had been no-one. Now it was back to lessons; back to the grind; back to England next spring.

As he trudged dejectedly towards the school, he tried to console himself. Since that disastrous loss of his money, he had, after all, made some good friends in a relatively short space of time. He was living in very humble accommodation, but it was rent free. Furthermore, it was far from squalid by the standards of many dwellings in this city. He enjoyed free lunches every working day, which generally consisted of soup and kebabs, and he was able to afford to feed himself at other times. When evidence of his teaching qualifications arrived, he would soon get a pay rise, which would enable him to save enough money to return home.

He was most certainly not an optimist and he always considered that bright prospects would inevitably be clouded at a moment's notice by yet another catastrophe caused by humans or other means and just waiting to happen. Something he never considered was that life had an intriguing way of compensating the victims unfortunate enough to be living it, with a fleeting taste of pure pleasure; the opportunity to reach out for the bowl of cherries placed before them and help themselves to a few sweet fruits of joy. In point of fact, a metaphorical bowl of cherries was soon to be placed in front of him and much closer to his person than he had ever dared to dream of.

Hanife

If anyone asks you
how the perfect satisfaction
of all our sexual wanting
will look, lift your face
and say,
Like this.

(Mevlana Rumi)

Vefbi Bey, who ran the European Languages school, had a most affable but highly disreputable cousin by the name of Hasan. They were both probably about the same age but Hasan's portlier build displayed more of the outward signs of *keyf.* His chubby face was more likely to break into lascivious lines of lecherous intent at the mere sound of a woman's voice or the click of high heels on stone steps – or even wooden floors. One of his favourite expressions was, "I fuck her with my eyes!" and it was oft repeated. Hassan habitually wandered into his cousin's school and as a former student at Galatasaray Lise and Istanbul University, he was known to teach some English lessons, especially to classes where he could come into contact with the more attractive females. He was a familiar and welcome sight at the school where he generally succeeded in raising everyone's spirits, with his convivial chatter and risqué humour.

Hassan bey possessed a door key, a Yale key which was hung on a nail on the office wall of the European Languages School, just by the coat hooks. This happened to be a spare key to the flat that Pete shared with Kemal, Walter, Roger and Brian. It was often observed to be missing from its spot especially on Wednesdays and

Fridays, notably after Hasan had materialised in the office, usually with a young woman in tow. Pete had conversed with Hasan on a few occasions, though his mercurial comings and goings were a constant source of fascination to him.

On one occasion, in the middle of lunch at the Antalya Restaurant, to which he was treating the Englishmen, he had remarked to Pete;

"In this city never be in big hurry to fall in love. You will have many chances. There are plenty sexy women. Plenty sweet pussy."

On reflection, Pete was inclined to dismiss such a statement, emanating as it did from the fevered mind of a self-confessed sex maniac. That was because in the short time he had been in Istanbul, he had learned that any attempt at intimacy with a nubile Turkish girl would bring him into contact with what could at times be a hostile, repressive society, in which a girl's family would naturally see themselves as guardians of her virginity. Even a hopeful local lad could expect his intended to be chaperoned on a date by a maiden aunt, or worse still, the girl's brother. As a Westerner, he could perceive no "chances" coming his way from any women of this city. However, he was soon to learn that such preconceptions were flawed, to say the least.

On a particularly fine afternoon in late October, when the skies over the city seemed washed with a cloudless blue, Pete strolled nonchalantly along Sıra Selviler, among dappled shadows cast by rows of ancient grey buildings, interspersed with narrow alleyways leading deeper into the district of Cihangir. Passing the Selvi Lokanta, with the sun streaming across the pavement into the restaurant window, he remembered with much relish his first lunch in that hallowed eatery. Yes, it had been giant sweet peppers and tomatoes stuffed with spiced minced lamb. As if that was not enough to cause him gastronomic ecstasy, the dessert had been pudding helva with pine kernels.

As he neared the European Languages School, his spirits were lifted somewhat and even as he recalled the circumstances surrounding his enforced sojourn in this city, it failed to break his mood. It was his afternoon off, but he was calling in to check if any mail had arrived from home and to pick up the key to his flat. Vefbi bey was not in the office but instead Hasan was sitting at his cousin's desk, picking his nails with a paper knife. Pete was puzzled by the fact that the flat key was missing from its usual spot and that Hassan was visiting the office without the usual woman in tow. Maybe she was in the loo. Perhaps not, mused Pete with much inward disgust, the water would still be cut off at this time of day.

"Ah Mr Peter, *nasılsın?*"

"*İyiyim, merci.*" Pete replied, using the French for thank you, as he was still unable to twist his tongue around the Turkish word..

"*Şimdi,*" he continued, "I was hoping you would come or I look for you at the *apartman.* Listen, I make a telephone call, you go home now, pull all curtains, and then a little surprise will come to you."

Pete was puzzled but did not question these instructions. He had quickly discovered that Hasan shared his cousin's ability to make things happen through a series of genial commands, usually over the telephone. He set off back to Harbiye clutching the flat key. He was calm enough as he made his way home and at the back of his mind, there was the merest suspicion of what might be happening a little later. Inwardly, he began to tremble in anticipation. Was he going to get laid? No, this was Istanbul. This was Turkey. But what was going to happen? He dodged the traffic in Taksim Square; always a risky business, strode past the shoeshine boys outside the post office, and imbibed the aromas of hot chestnuts and roasting sweet corn. Finally he was plunging down the steeply sloping cobbled street leading to his apartment block. He slid the key into the lock and the door gave easily, for a change.

Once inside, he drew the Walter designed hessian curtains to block out a dingy light that was emanating from the scruffy back yard. Pete pondered briefly on Hasan's last statement; "a little surprise." Was he being unnecessarily naïve? Knowing Hasan as he did, the answer could only be yes. But who? What would she be like? Maybe he had persuaded one of the hippie girls from Sultan Ahmet to spread some peace and love with him. Oh God, could it be one of the prostitutes from the brothel area that Walter was always going on about? He sauntered into the bathroom and as casually as he could, he rinsed himself with the last trickles of cold water that burbled sporadically out of creaking taps. Next, he applied the last of his "Denim" deodorant to strategic areas of his body. Then picking up an old seven string Russian guitar he had borrowed from one of his students, proceeded to strum a few chords, balancing himself apprehensively on the corner of the bed. He sat in the darkness with the warm mid-autumn sunshine seeping through ragged gaps in the curtains. He strummed rhythmically, absent - mindedly and with half expectations of pleasure to come. He became aware of a gnawing in the pit of his stomach which induced a need to rush to the toilet, but the sharp drilling sound of the doorbell jolted him out of his reverie.

He crossed the darkened hall to the front door, opened it, and there, confronting him in the half-light offered by the street door above, was a very comely Turkish woman, maybe about forty years of age. The silhouette effect of the hallway in which she was standing showed her to have a voluptuous figure and, to complement this, a pleasant smile radiated from her face which was clear and had an olive complexion. She was made up tastefully, Pete thought, with eye liner, mascara and dark red lipstick. Her deep brown almond eyes showed some wrinkling at the sides but her hair, chestnut in colour and parted in the middle, coursed past he shoulders, ending he knew not where. Suddenly she was inside the flat and closing the door behind her. She took Pete's hands in hers. Her tone to begin with was formal but cordial. She could almost have been a prospective private student. Perhaps she was.

When she spoke, her English had an exotic tang, similar to the way he had heard some Asian girls speak back home. She might almost have lived for a time in an English speaking community. There was also a sexy hint of the USA in her voice.

"Hello, my name is Hanife. How are you, Peter?"

"I am very well thank you and pleased to meet you. Call me Pete."

"I like Pete, it is a sexy name."

"Ok, Hanife, would you like to come through?"

125

The private student theory had been well and truly shot down in flames. What next? They walked together into the bedroom and she sat on the bed crossing her legs seductively. Her skirt was tight but barely covered her knees, with the result that when she was sitting thus, a tantalising vision of her light brown bare thighs was presented. She was sitting beside the guitar. (Why oh why did he leave it there?) Picking it up, he became painfully conscious that he was not going to find anywhere else to put it so he held on to it and joined Hanife on the bed.

"It's quite warm in here," she said after a pause, "is there anywhere I can hang this jacket?"

She had removed a black cropped leather jacket under which she was wearing a thin white satin blouse. Beneath that, a black bra was visible. A genial smile played across her face which seemed less rounded than many women he had seen about the city. Perhaps she originated from further east – a Tartar or Kirgiz. Pete was totally entranced, as if in some dream. This was reality, though, and he was still clutching at ways to proceed from here.

"Whereabouts do you live, Hanife?"

"On the other side of the Bosphorus. You must come there one day."

"I'd be glad to. You're lovely."

Had he said that too early? He certainly meant it.

There was a brief silence. Somewhere across the sprawl of Harbiye two muezzins in separate mosques began their calls. The Arabic chants wailed nasally, from tannoys protruding from the tops of minarets. It was the time of *Dhuhr*; the afternoon prayer. The sounds blended with the closer hooting of car horns as traffic processed ceaselessly along the boulevard past the Hilton Hotel, just a few blocks away. Outside in the street above them, a rag and bone man intoned in a high pitched, throaty Anatolian accent, "*Eskici! Eskici!*" Pete looked fully into Hanife's delicious and inviting face. Desire shone in her eyes; her smile radiated invitingly and when at last she spoke, there was no mistaking how she wanted Pete to respond.

"Do you like me then?" Her tone was purposeful now, her

actions sensual as she kissed him lightly on the lips, keeping her face close to his.

"Y-yes I do." Pete's desire to make love with this enticingly beautiful woman had by now set a conflagration raging almost out of control in his body and mind. She sensed his nervous excitement and responded calmly.

"Do you want me?"

Oh yes, he wanted her.

Some while later, lying in bed, staring up at the yellowed ceiling, Pete and Hanife, wrapped up in each other's arms, were conversing in dulcet tones. She was asking him if he had a current girlfriend and he replied that he had been seeing a couple of girls but had to part from them as he was going abroad and was likely to be away for a couple of years.

"Were you making love with them both?" She asked, with a hint of mischief in her voice. She was inwardly amused by Pete's reply.

"Only one of them. The other may have let me if I wasn't intending to leave the country."

His mind strayed back to previous sexual experiences in England. The times he had made love with his fiancée Cathy were those he had treasured most, as they were very much in love. The sex was wonderful and she was more than willing to give herself to him as often as they wished. But in the end, she had broken his heart. Hanife's soft tones broke in on his reflections.

They tell me English girls are very sexy?"

"I would say they are but a lot of them don't want to go all the way. They are scared of getting pregnant or VD and for my part I am scared of getting them pregnant or catching the clap."

Pete was soon to realise that was now in Istanbul, legendary home of the School of Love, which was said to have dated back to Ottoman times. He was here to learn, and his first lesson had just drawn to a beautiful conclusion. As for Hanife, she was now well relaxed and in conversational mode.

"So you have two girlfriends in England, then." Naughty. Do they know about each other?"

"No they don't but it probably wouldn't matter."

"Oh it would. They would be so jealous if they learned. And you have made love with one of them."

"Yes, as I said, I never really got the chance with the other one."

"But you have had a few girls. I can tell that"

"Yes with a few" Very few in fact, thought Pete, but he did not say so.

"Did you enjoy with me?"

"Yes, very much." Yes he certainly had enjoyed this first encounter as he had never before made love with such a sexy, voluptuous, mature human being.

The arrival of a third party put paid to further passion for the time being. Glancing at the doorway, Pete perceived Hassan Bey's grinning face peeping at them. He was grinning approvingly How long had he been there? With Hassan's presence in the room, Pete quickly grabbed a nearby sheet to establish some form of modesty.

"*Naber, Hanife, nasıl oldu? İyi miydi?* Enquired Hassan, little realising that Pete had listened in to enough conversations in Turkish to have a good idea of what he was saying. Hanife seemed to perceive this and shot Hassan a reproving glance.

"We had a nice time, did we not *tatlım.*"

"We certainly did."

Hassan continued, "Your friend has to go now but you can see her again if you wish, *değil mi*, Hanife?"

Pete's new lover had slipped deftly out of bed and was dressed in a couple of minutes. Pete scrambled into his clothes and, at Hassan's request, he indulged in a suitably passionate farewell kiss with Hanife. Pleasurable as this was, Pete suddenly recalled that Hassan had told him he was an expert photographer and liked making films. Disturbingly, he could almost hear the cameras clicking or whirring in the dark recesses of Hassan's lecherous mind. He hoped not. Hassan and Hanife departed, but this was to be the first of a number of such assignations.

Alone in the room, he realised, with some alarm, he had lost all track of time. Then again, he had nowhere in particular to go, but the afternoon's activities had made him feel famished.

Now where was the nearest eating place? As he sat considering this minor problem, the room itself remained in silence and even outside sounds seemed muffled. Shafts of sunlight were streaming through curtain holes in the west facing windows and they seemed to be stirring up myriad dust motes which spiralled to the grey tiled floor. Gradually, external sounds began to catch his attention; children playing and neighbours engaged in animated chatter. Pete stood up, grabbed his jacket and made his way up to street level. Then, as if at a given signal, the hot, lazy, languid afternoon spontaneously burst into life before him. Traffic sounds intensified, as did the cries of shoe shine boys, near the hotel as well as newspaper sellers and *Milli Piyango* (National Lottery) touts outside the post office. The street traders' volume increased along with their optimism as office workers, bank clerks, shop assistants - all potential customers - ground homewards across the city streets and out to the teeming suburbs, taking the multifarious forms of transport available to the great Istanbul public. Anyone for a shoe shine? A lottery ticket? The latest news?

Not for Pete. He was on his way to the *Selvi Lokanta* (Cedar Restaurant) for some kebap or maybe a fish stew, or stuffed peppers. His feelings of near starvation gave wings to his feet as he approached Taksim Square. However, his progress was hindered somewhat, as at this same hour in the late afternoon, columns of pedestrians, three or four deep converged on the city centre, diminishing here and there as some of them entered the many bars, restaurants, shops and tea houses that lined their route. At length, he reached his chosen restaurant, sat down at one of the plain wooden tables and was ready to order his long awaited evening meal. The waiters were cheerful and busy. By now, they seemed to recognise him as a regular diner and he was afforded due respect, which guaranteed him prompt service. After breaking into and hungrily consuming some of the fresh bread that had been laid before him, he settled in his seat in delicious anticipation of the fish stew which had become a speciality of this restaurant. A bottle of Tuborg lager would suffice to accompany his meal and what better to finish off with than the local plum compote?

The Fishing Trip

Autumn had crept in on the city almost unnoticed, with the bittersweet aroma of wood smoke which had drifted in during the previous week, at first hinting subtly to the nostrils but now seeming to permeate each street and cobbled alleyway. By night, the scent of wood fires mingled with that of charcoal grilled sweet corn emanating from a number of stalls which had materialised along Istiklal Caddesi, Taksim Square and the road to Harbiye. A stiffening breeze bore the two fragrances lightly across every district west of the Golden Horn and beyond, as if nudging the population with a reminder that summer really had come to an end and the nights were now about to grow colder.

However, as Pete ambled homeward from the Selvi Lokanta, he could scarcely believe how warm the days had been. He remembered swimming in the Marmara Sea from the beach at Ataköy less than three weeks ago and over a month after their failed expedition had started out. In England, at this time of year, clocks would have gone back and people would be starting to shiver under grey clouds in anticipation of winter's misery. He sniffed the cooling evening air, enjoying the autumnal odours. Kebab restaurants now added their own contributions of frying onions, peppers and grilling meat, and these were further enhanced to by the wafting of home cooking from hundreds of nearby dwellings. Pete could not remember ever enjoying an atmosphere comparable to the one that now pervaded the city streets. Strangely, for one in his situation, it gave him a feeling of real safety and security. He felt welcome and wanted somehow, even if he had to share a basement flat with five others and was obliged to sleep on piles of camping foam. His rucksack contained all of his worldly possessions. Not once had he felt threatened. It was as if the city itself had opened its arms, holding him in a protective embrace, in recompense for the traumas he had suffered during the first few days within its environs.

However, from the point of view of his working life, it was true to say that all was not going too well in his teaching activities, as some of the students had decided to give him a hard time. It was true to say, nevertheless, that most seemed to appreciate his efforts in encouraging them to work at their skills in English, in order that they may matriculate at some point later in the academic year. This was preferable, he believed, to presenting himself as an English speaking time waster, standing uselessly in front of a group of chattering, smoking, card playing adolescents for a few lira, free lunches and free accommodation. After all, he was a trained teacher and this was his first post. He had even sent to his college for his Certificate of Education so he could earn the promised one hundred and fifty lira a week rather than the ten lira a day expenses earned by the others. That very certificate, or at least a copy, had arrived a few days ago, along with a surprisingly praise-filled testimonial from the vice principal. This astonished him somewhat, bearing in mind the raucous times he had spent in that excellent institution, especially during his second year. Still, he had sailed through his main subject, then passing the Education exams and all three teaching practices.

Vefbi, on receiving the documents, had not hesitated in giving him a pay rise - but not back dated. Nevertheless, Pete had made a decision to be confrontational in his approach to his classes, putting a stop to the smoking, confiscating the cards and insisting on the students actually listening to him while he was trying to conduct a lesson. Some of the older lads had not taken kindly to this and he had found himself in a couple of situations where two of the more aggressively inclined fellows had actually squared up to him. As it turned out, by facing them down he had caused them to walk out of the school,, never to darken its doorstep again. His boss at first lamented the loss of revenue, but tolerated the actions of his fiery young teacher for the time being. In addition, even though these were rich spoilt kids, there was never any comeback from the parents.

Among the more positively minded students in the class was a young lady named Lale. She was a short sixteen year old with a figure that might be described as fairly rotund without actually being fat. She had a fresh, innocent enough face and a very friendly manner. Even though she spoke English reasonably well, she had somehow failed her exam the previous year. Nerves, Pete concluded; lack of confidence under exam conditions. After one particularly stormy lesson, where Pete had just hung on to his temper after some abuse — in Turkish — from a would-be smoker, she had approached him afterwards and invited him to spend the next Sunday afternoon with her family and friends in Sarıyer, a small town on the Bosphorus, north of Istanbul. Although this was actually an example of the hospitality for which the Turkish people were justly renowned, a few of the other students, who had overheard this invitation, had other ideas. A trio of very pretty girls sniggered amongst themselves, but this did not deter him from accepting the invitation and he was even looking forward to the outing.

Later, after he had paid three or four visits to her family's home, Pete learned that the pretty girls were saying that he and Lale had become an item. Luckily, the adults in the school regarded this as mere gossip. After all, she was barely sixteen and he was no longer the randy teenage student on teaching practice. Furthermore, Lale had a boyfriend, or at least there was Kaya, a handsome Turkish lad who always called for her at the school and was to be ever present, with other young people, whenever Pete visited Sarıyer.

On the Sunday of his first jaunt to Sarıyer, Pete set off from his Harbiye basement at midday. Kemal's washing lady had just returned some clothes he had given her to clean so he picked out the light khaki ex-army surplus jacket with the breast pockets to wear over a lilac coloured grandad shirt. The temperatures outside were still warm enough during the day not to have to wear thicker clothing. He also wore his Levi jeans and beige chukka boots. In his hand he carried the written instructions from Kaya on how to reach his destination from Taksim Square. He was to board the Sarıyer minibus, pay the fare and look out for Kaya when he reached the town centre.

The day was bright and sunny but a few ominous white clouds had gathered over the Bosphorus. The minibus only took a few minutes to fill up, mostly with chattering families on a day out. It departed on time and, as was the custom, a young boy, this one aged around twelve years, came round to each passenger and collected the fares in a wooden box. In those days the minibus would take the coast road through Beşiktaş, Bebek and Yeniköy which was a distance of about twelve kilometres.

At length, after battling through traffic jams and the obligatory ignoring of several sets of lights, the somewhat battered minibus managed to clear the city's main sprawl, along decent roads which tracked through some dried out desolate scrublands, sporting desolate factory buildings and piles of rubbish by the roadside. There were also shanty towns of wood and canvas buildings which were populated by more traditionally dressed Turks. The men were in baggy black shalvar trousers with loose fitting check shirts and many of them wore white or multi coloured prayer caps. The women seemed more colourful in a way, as they were dressed in embroidered cream or maroon dresses with waistcoats topped with either hijabs or headscarves. Some of the older women were clad from head to foot in black and Pete was sure he observed some of them wearing the forbidden white yashmaks.

It had been explained to Pete, mostly by Walter, the German, that hundreds of peasants were arriving in Istanbul from Anatolia on a daily basis. Apparently, they believed the streets to be paved with gold and they would find well paid jobs. Pete had very little idea of what kind of lives they had left behind, but they must have been pretty dire to swap them for the new lives they had found here. He had also been informed that the shacks they lived in were called *"gecekondu"*, meaning put up in the night. Apparently, under Turkish law, if a habitable building could be erected before dawn and in one night, they could not be moved from the site. Twenty or thirty so called habitable buildings were blotting the landscape to his left which together with the piles of rubbish were not exactly enhancing the idyllic Balkan scenery. A few years later, he was to learn that almost all of the *gecekondu* settlements had been destroyed by army bulldozers when the military took over in 1971. The minibus sped onwards.

The road had veered away from the coast, and for about twenty minutes the minibus had been passing through a wooded area of large conifers. Then a slash of blue appeared on the horizon to the right and the Bosphorus came back into view. As they descended the timber lined slopes it was even possible for the passengers to make out the Black Sea in the far distance. Ten more minutes and they were entering the streets of central Sarıyer and heading towards the bus station. Pete had worked this out from a road sign which pointed out the way to the *"Otogar"*. Very French sounding, actually.

As he dismounted from the minibus at around one pm, he caught sight of Kaya waiting for him amongst the bustling crowds. They greeted each other with handshakes, and Kaya led Pete off on foot towards Lale's family home. This turned out to be a two storey wooden dwelling in the old Ottoman style, sitting snugly in a narrow cobbled street. Of course, "Ottoman" is a name Europeans insist on using to describe matters relating to that period of empire, instead of the Turkish *Osmanlı*. Looking at the house, Pete was fascinated by its construction. It was not the only such house in the street, indeed each one he saw seemed to possess its own individual character. The one he was about to enter was fairly compact in size, not like the *konak* or mansion style he had been shown in the old city. Its outer walls consisted of creosoted planks, windows with six small panes in them and in the top windows were faded wooden French style shutters. On entering, the first aroma that greeted his nostrils was that of the toilet, combining pine disinfectant with the smell left by its last user. Pete was to find out more about that particular convenience later on.

Lale and her family greeted him warmly. Out of respect for Turkish custom he removed his shoes before the introductions, of which there were several; mother, father and Lale's two elder brothers. There was another guest present, Lale's friend Nuran, a seventeen-year-old Turkish girl modestly dressed in a beige shalwar kameez but with no hijab or headscarf. The mother and father openly displayed their pleasure at receiving a foreign visitor and the brothers were able to speak to Pete in passable English. Everyone was anxious to find out more about Pete's home, family situation and interests. Kaya translated. Lale brought round the tea.

After drinking three glasses of tea, Pete definitely needed to take a pee. He discreetly mentioned this to Kaya who ushered him to the toilet. He entered what turned out to be a large white tiled cubicle, but unlike at Vefbi's school or at Pete's home, there was no pedestal, and consequently no seat or lid. Instead there was a hole roughly six inches in diameter sunk into in the middle of a square, which was a ceramic tray or shallow sink. The whole arrangement was at floor level. Set into this bathroom furniture, at the front, were two foot shaped indents facing outwards roughly twelve inches apart. Pete gingerly placed his feet in these and took aim towards the gaping, brown stained hole. The stench which rose to his nostrils was far from pleasant but considering what lay at the bottom of the hole it could have been a lot worse. Fortunately, there was a roll of soft toilet paper with which Pete was able to wipe himself. However, he had already thrown the paper down the hole before noticing the waste bin into which he should have placed it. Force of habit. Never mind.

He reached for the chain to flush the toilet but no water came out; in fact, no water was likely to be available until the next morning. That would account for the odour which had pervaded the toilet. As he washed his hands with a bar of olive scented soap, sparingly using a handily placed water bottle, he resolved not to visit this toilet for any other purpose. Definitely not crapping in here, were his thoughts as he dried his hands on a tasselled white towel. But would he be able to hold on? Stepping out of the toilet, he almost collided with Kaya who must have heard the clank of the cistern. He very kindly guided Pete back to the parlour where the family were sat, conversing quietly and waiting for lunch.

It was not long before lunch appeared. It was homemade lentil soup, which was consumed, as was the custom, lukewarm with squeezed lemon. The accompanying bread was fresh and crusty; then the main course appeared. It was called *pide* (pea day), an open Black Sea pasty consisting of spiced minced lamb, onions, tomato and a lethal long green pepper right in the middle. Lale's mother had prepared the ingredients that morning, wrapped them in the pastry and had taken them to be cooked in the local bakery. It was accompanied by a huge salad. Turkish coffee and small round sweet pastries were brought in after the main course. Pete, though feeling quite bloated, could not refuse the several delights that were offered him. It was time now to relax but Lale's brothers had other plans for the afternoon.

"Do you like fish?" asked Osman, the elder brother.

"Oh yes, I like fish." Replied Pete, anticipating a real treat awaiting him at dinner time.

"Then we go and catch some!"

Pete's digestive tract was still hard at work, as the quartet of young men made their way on foot down to Sarıyer harbour. There, they boarded a rowing boat, painted white, into which they just about managed to fit amongst all the fishing gear which lay on the floor of the boat, together with a couple of wooden crates. After settling on to his wooden seat, and before he had time to take stock, they had cast off and the two brothers were rowing energetically out to sea.

Now the Bosphorus may be a comparatively narrow strip of sea separating Europe from Asia, but the point at which the fishing expedition had set out was very close to where this channel met the Black Sea. Consequently, it could be somewhat more turbulent than it tended to be further south. The small vessel started to rock in the swell like a swing boat in a fairground. Pete had never been partial to white knuckle rides and for him, swing boats were definitely in that category. However, he never got seasick as a rule, and once he had been able to keep himself stable on the narrow seat, he started to experience, with some pleasure, a real sense of the boat's erratic motions. It was men against the elements, and they were winning. Or so he thought, until Kaya announced,

"Sea is calmer today. We'll catch plenty of fish." So much for defeating the elements.

"What kind of fish do you usually catch?"

"Uskumru." Replied Kaya. "The English is mackerel, big ones. There are also smaller mackerel who live deeper in Bosfor and taste very good. Osman says sometimes they get sea bass too."

"Levrek, levrek çok güzel!" (sea bass, sea bass, very good) chirped the younger brother.

Pete asked if he could take over a share of the rowing, as he was beginning to feel something of a spare part. He was now enjoying this fishing trip so much but he did not wish to be pampered. Kaya put this to Osman whose reply was pleasant but firm.

"Yok canım, sen bizim misafirimizsin. Çok ayip," (No. You are our guest. That would be shameful)

The boys all laughed at this but Pete understood. He was getting used to some of the Turkish customs which tended to be rigidly adhered to, especially the conventions concerning guests. He was, after all, a guest. It would be an insult to him if his hosts let him row. They now started to drop lines into the water, still buffeted by tall waves which seemed intent on tipping them over. Pete was now charged with helping Kaya to hold the boat steady. Within a few minutes, the wooden boxes started to fill up with wriggling, fat, tiger striped mackerel. Then disaster struck.

The first Pete knew of any trouble occurring on the boat, was that for some inexplicable reason, the three Turks were yelling to each other and also to him. Why? They appeared to be trying to dodge something that was writhing on the floor of the boat. Such was the panic and tumult that not only were they in danger of losing their catch but at any second their vessel could capsize, plunging them all into the grey icy depths. And the Bosphorus was known to be very cold and very deep. Pete then saw what was causing the mayhem; it was a large pinkish grey fish about twice the size of a mackerel. What alarmed him most though was that its huge dorsal fin displayed at least a dozen sharp spines and it not only occurred to him that the others were desperately trying to avoid these, but it might be a good idea if he did likewise. They were yelling

"Dikkat, be careful, Skorpid!" Kaya most considerately gave a breathless translation.

"Scorpion fish! Very poisonous!"

Although this was a situation fraught with danger, which could end extremely badly, the chaotic events appeared to Pete to be happening in slow motion. Strange, he had not touched any alcohol all day. He had never seen or heard of such a creature and the fish, for its part, did not seem too happy at making Pete's acquaintance. Also strange, and somewhat ominous, was that with every writhing motion, the monster seemed to be edging closer to him and its fishy frown seemed to match the venomous anger it was unleashing. Suddenly it was all over. He saw a short oar brought down on the skorpid's head, again and again. Splat... splat... squelch! Then it was scooped up and cast back into the sea. End of fishing trip. The terror caused by the piscatorial invader now subsided first to that of relief, then a general outpouring of youthful merriment. The two brothers began to turn their attention to counting the afternoon's catch.

"On üç tane," announced the younger brother and Pete who had been learning Turkish numbers responded with,

"Thirteen, that's pretty impressive."

"Aferin, Türkçe öğreniyorsun," (Well done, you are learning Turkish), laughed Kaya.

"I have only learned numbers up to twenty. Mind you, thirteen is an unlucky number, isn't it?"

"Oh no," replied Kaya, "in Turkey it is lucky number because in 1453 Sultan Mehmet took Istanbul from Bizants. If you add those numbers together comes to thirteen."

Pete's thoughts on that remained unspoken and he wondered what twisted mind had dreamt up that statistic. His beaming smile in Kaya's direction reflected his gratitude for the information. They reached the harbour without further incident and Pete could not help musing on the danger they had been in for a short while, out there in the middle of that deceptively inviting seaway.

A good fifty years after these events took place, as an example of the minor ironies that life tends to produce from time to time, Pete found himself comfortably ensconced in a charming seaside restaurant with a female companion on the Greek island of Leros. On the menu was Scorpion Fish, which triggered memories of that frenzied bedlam that had taken place on a small boat in the middle of the Bosphorus. They decided to order this delicacy, and the bill for the two of them came to two hundred euros – wine included of course. The waiter told them it was a Class A fish. Yes, thought Pete and he could tell them why.

Once they had moored up, the fishing party made their way to the still bustling fish market where Osman sold six of their catch to a fishmonger at an open stall, who in turn managed to dispose of them all before closing that evening. The fishmonger also gutted the remaining seven mackerel for them. One neat cut under the gills; one cut under the part where the body joins the tail, then use the point of the knife to pull out the innards.

Pete had not been back in the quaint wooden house more than ten minutes when he realised that the dreaded moment had arrived. It was the moment that he had been trying to postpone since the end of lunch. He was in desperate need to empty his bowels, but following his earlier visit to the family convenience, he was most reluctant to perform this essential function in what amounted to a squatting position. Indeed, he was sitting in a comfortable enough chair, but inner comfort was distinctly lacking. Even when he tried to take his mind off the subject, he could not help his thoughts drifting back to an incident that had happened about a week ago.

Whilst sitting in an empty classroom at Vefbi Bey's school, reading a battered copy of De Sade's "Justine", that, to his amazement, he had discovered in one of the office cupboards, he experienced his first virulent visit of the "Turkey trots". Amid much aching in the lower abdomen and a desperate clenching of buttocks, he rushed to the office toilet only to find it stinking and the pedestal full to the brim with floaters which would not flush away due to an empty cistern. Having fought off the first seizure, he started to relax and work out what to do next. Another attack was certainly imminent. Decisively, he legged it out of the school, hurried along Sıra Selviler and in ten minutes he had reached his apartment. His bowels, in eager anticipation of the relief to follow, began loosening. Unfortunately, and to his horror he realised he had forgotten to pick up the front door key. There was no one to let him in, as the flat was empty so he made his way as swiftly as possible back to the school. The Hilton Hotel was en route. Should he dodge in there? No, he would never get past security. He tore into the school office, after battling through crowds on Taksim Square – he was sure they had not been there earlier! However, the key was not on its hook. Who had taken it?

There was another surge from below, beaten back by world class sphincter control. The pain was immense but soon passed. Nevertheless, this evacuation could not be put off for much longer. He made the arduous journey back to the flat with a plan to knock on the door of the apartment above his. The students who lived there may allow him to climb over their balcony to land in the back garden and let himself in through the unlocked rear door. Luckily, two of the students were in. They spoke English and may not even have noticed the pained expression on Pete's face. He gingerly lowered himself into the back yard, almost losing his grip on the vital area between his bottom cheeks. The door opened easily enough and on reaching the toilet he barely had time to drop his jeans and Y Fronts. The relief of Constantinople never arrived for the Byzantines back in 1453 but it certainly came rather belatedly in that WC in a Harbiye back street. Had that small lavatory ever experienced such a storm? No chance, thought Pete as he pulled on the chain. Of course, nothing happened. No water in the cistern.

Now he needed to go once more. The cold Bosphorus winds over the open sea had probably given him a chill which would not have helped. He excused himself and made his way once more to the *zero zero*, as the Turks called it. Once inside, he bared his bottom, placed his feet in the foot marks and bopped over the central abyss. Twice he almost lost his balance but accomplished his task satisfactorily. A white, blue trimmed enamel mug had been placed on a shelf near to his right hand and he supposed this to be in lieu of a bidet while the water was off. No, he was not going to splash his bum with cold water. A couple of passes with the toilet paper sufficed. He placed the tissues in the bin this time, washed his hands as before and once again parted company with this room of torment. Now he was hungry again.

Dinner, naturally, was always going to be grilled mackerel. Pete felt it was the most enjoyable fish meal he had ever consumed, simply served with another salad. Nuran, one of the guests from earlier, was missing as she was dining at home with her family. However, she made a reappearance later on, just as tea and baklava were being brought round. Indeed, she helped Lale to serve out the goodies. Pete observed that she had applied light foundation to her face, also some kohl, mascara and pink lipstick. Very presentable. She re-joined Kaya and Lale who were sitting on a low backed sofa, known as a divan, with typically Turkish embroidered covers on the seat and cushions. Pete really admired the bright red and blue geometric tulip designs, against a cream background. Lale whispered something to Nuran and her mother overheard. She responded excitedly,

"Tabi, tabi. Haydi Nuran şekerim. Misafirimiz için güzel dans et. Söyle Kaya, anlat."

"Lale's mother says Nuran is a very good dancer and would like to do Turkish dance for us." Kaya translated for Pete's benefit.

Suddenly the rhythmic thudding of Turkish drums emanated from a record player on the sideboard. Then the nasal quartertones of a kind of flute and the soulful trilling of a violin threaded their way into the pattern of tunes to transform into a haunting and exotic piece of music. Pete had always loved eastern music anyway, since a troupe of Indian musicians, who had played on two Beatles albums, had performed at his college. His favourite Beatles tracks were the George Harrison sitar numbers on Revolver and Sergeant Pepper. What he was listening to was wilder somehow: a true presentation of the oriental soul, he felt. Then Nuran stood up and began to sway with the music. Pete was expecting some rustic folk dancing, similar to what he had seen performed in a square near Karaköy.

The dance certainly started like this; knees bent and waving arms above the head, but as the music intensified, he found himself witnessing a belly dance, with all its gyrating and snaking of limbs in what for him was a series of exhilarating and stimulating movements across the room. He was unaware at the time that most Turkish girls learned or knew this dance innately as it was part of their culture, rather than as a way of displaying their sexual wares to potential lovers. At least that was probably true in most cases. Nuran moved deftly and daintily towards him, twirling her arms then swinging her ample hips from side to side, almost touching his face. This plainly attired young girl had for him become beautiful and seductive. The next time he saw Hanife, he would definitely ask her to dance like this for him, before commencing the usual activities.

When the dance ended, Pete joined in with the family's enthusiastic applause. He was careful not to over compliment the dancer in case this was misinterpreted. He did not know this for sure, but his instincts, for once, were guiding him correctly. Many Turkish girls had elder brothers or cousins. These guys would be only too willing to deal violently with overzealous suitors who were not prepared to go through the customary channels in order to court their precious family member. That kind of deterrent did not stop Pete from wanting to get off with Nuran at some point – but not today. Back home, he would have asked the girl for a date without any hesitation.

It was late in the evening and time for him to take his leave. He bade everyone farewell, thanking the family for their food and hospitality. He also thanked Nuran for her fabulous dancing. To his surprise, he found himself exchanging kisses with her on both cheeks but then he did the same with Lale, her mother, father, brother and Kaya.

"Bye bye," they all chorused. "Seni bekleriz. We wait you. Come again."

Pete made his way back to the bus station, accompanied by

Kaya. As he boarded the minibus, he turned to Kaya and said, quite emotionally, "Please tell everyone again what an enjoyable day I've had." Kaya replied, "They enjoyed having you. Anyway, see you on Wednesday." It was half term the following week and Kaya had promised to take Pete round the old city.

Half Term

Monday of half term was spent idling about the flat writing letters to family and friends, then taking the five-minute walk to Taksim post office in order to send them off. Posting letters was always a complicated business, as Pete had discovered during the few weeks he had been in the city. At the root of the problem were Turkish stamps which were intended to stick on envelopes but not actually made that way. True, the stamps were sticky on the back but after being licked they stubbornly refused to stay stuck down. However, the ever-resourceful post office staff had solved the problem, as prominently displayed on the shelves lining the sides of the post office, were small pots of white adhesive paste, with applicator brushes. These would certainly ensure that stamps would not fall off en route. The second complication was queuing for the paste pots, and then you had to make sure the paste did not get on your clothing. Sometimes the pot you were waiting for became empty. And so on .However, as there were fewer customers today, Pete was able to complete the task in a few minutes .

Later he was joined by Walter who took him to one of the restaurants he had become famous for. This was not because he was a renowned gourmet, but he had actually discovered a number of restaurants where a good lunch could be had for three and a half lira per person. This came to about twenty pence in sterling. The furnishings were obviously quite spartan with narrow Formica topped tables for the food and rickety stools to sit on. Nevertheless, the restaurant was clean, the service good and the food very tasty. After lunch, they stopped into a tea house or *kiraathane* full of men smoking cheap Turkish cigarettes and playing backgammon. The atmosphere was macho but pleasant. The two Europeans felt that they were welcome, and a friendly waiter brought them glasses of black tea. Pete found that by listening to the men's chatter he could pick up the odd word here and there and maybe learn some of the language. There seemed to be a great use of words like *"choc"* and *"yok"*, together with something that sounded like *"gazelle"*. Prominent in the mix of discourse were *çay* and *kahve*, naturally enough and *şeker*: tea, coffee, sugar. Listening in like this was proving quite difficult today as Walter continued to regale him, between sips of hot tea, with stories of how he and his family had to survive in the bombed-out Berlin of 1945. Harrowing, but intriguing, nevertheless.

"I waz having to push zis hand cart through ze ruins of Berlin streets, looking in ze rubble for bits and pieces zat we might need at home. Ven I saw a food queue, I had to join it and vait for hours for bread."

So, Walter was around during the last war. Pete could never imagine him as a Nazi sympathiser. Clearly, as he was now in his early forties, he would have been a teenager during hostilities, enduring round the clock bombing raids by the allies, not to mention the presence of thousands of ferocious Russian soldiers intent on vengeance for the rape and murder of their own nationals. He wondered how anyone could possibly have survived that hellish time, and surely those who did must be severely traumatised. Walter was certainly quite mad. What was a chartered accountant doing hanging out in a third world city in crude accommodation with an assortment of young dropouts? In the evenings he would keep the flatmates in hysterics with his exaggerated impressions of Hitler, and Goebbels in full flight at the Nuremberg rallies. As a young person in 1940s Germany, he had actually witnessed these performers for himself, but on film, of course.

The following day, Pete decided to go into the school, as long as it was open, to collect any mail that may have arrived. Brian had the same idea so together they set off through the back streets of Elmadağ towards the city centre and Sıra Selviler – the street of cedars (though Pete had never seen any of those trees in that vicinity).

"We'll be able to get in if that retard of a *kapıcı* is not around."

Brian, who had been learning Turkish since his arrival a few months ago, was referring to the concierge of the building and he pronounced the word correctly as Kap - ı- jı. The dotless i in Turkish is pronounced as the e in *the;* in other words, it is a schwa. Pete had seen this man before. He lived in the basement with his family. Every apartment or office block in the city had a *kapıcı* and they were usually men or women from Anatolian villages. This doorkeeper could usually be found seated imperiously in an old wooden chair outside the building, or in the hallway by the stairs. According to Walter, these individuals were all members of a kind of mafia which controlled them and placed them in situ, after the exchange of the obligatory bribes. The same went for the myriad porters who could be seen around the city. These men used specially designed but traditional saddles, which were passed down the generations, to carry loads on their backs which in many cases weighed more than they did. Their life expectancy was not the greatest.

This keeper of the door had also been described by Walter as "*yobaz*". This term described a group of Moslem extremists who would roam the streets of Istanbul looking for non-believers to beat up. By all accounts, they were everyone's enemies, but they reserved their particular hatred for left wing students and hippies. All of them were bearded and sported black berets on their heads. Pete knew he needed to tread carefully when this concierge was around. However, there was no sign of him as they mounted the stairs and went up to the school on the first floor.

There was an air of quiet in the office and the aroma that usually emanated from the toilet was absent today. On the secretary's desk was an assortment of mail; one letter for Pete and two for Brian, all from England. Pete picked up his airmail letter and was in the act of turning round to say something to Brian. As he did so, to his consternation, standing in the doorway, hands on hips and looking fit to explode with hatred and anger was the dreaded kapıcı. In his right hand he was brandishing a large pair of scissors and looked as though he was poised to attack.

146

Now this was Pete's first time in Turkey and from what he had seen, Turks, like the English, came in all shapes and sizes. There was that beautiful Tartar girl in one of the classes, tall and with almond eyes, then there were others with round faces and dark complexions. The individual facing him now more closely resembled a *Selçuk* warrior whose general had just issued a demand for a besieged city's surrender. Without warning, the kapıcı charged across the office straight at Pete, striking him in the chest with the point of the scissors. This apparently motiveless assault was an affront to Pete's normally placid nature. Besides, his chest was starting to hurt. Without further ado, he grabbed the weapon from his opponent and flung it on the floor. Then seizing him by his grubby lapels, he threw him across the office into a classroom where he crash landed on some desks and sprawled on the floor. As he struggled to his feet, he appeared somewhat more cowed as Pete moved in to land a punch in his stupid bigoted face. He was prevented from performing this coup de grace by Brian who stepped in between them urgently whispering, "watch out his son is here."

A young man dressed in sweatshirt and blue jeans, about the same age as Pete, stepped into the office. He had seen his father being manhandled by the Englishman and looked far from pleased about it. He said something to Brian who translated.

"He says we'd better not make any more trouble as he is in the Turkish army doing military service."

Pete, still furious replied, "I don't care which fucking army he is in. If his dad touches me again, I'll beat the shit out of him!"

Somehow, Brian did not need to translate. The young soldier had got the gist. He took his father by the arm and led him back downstairs. He spoke to him respectfully but with some insistence.

"Haydi gidelim babacığım." (come on, let's go, my dear father). As he left, he turned round to Pete and Brian. "Sorry, he is very nervous man."

Brian explained that "nervous" was a translation from "*sinirli*" which also meant temperamental.

"Too right there, the bastard. What did I do to him?"

147

He would normally have felt some remorse for his own actions, but not this time, somehow. Later, when Vefbi bey enquired into the matter, the kapıcı had tried to excuse himself by declaring that he had thought the foreigners were stealing items from the office. Vefbi's response to that was to pronounce,

"He is foolish man, I kick him away!"

However, the following week and for the foreseeable future this clearly unbalanced personage remained in post. Every time he saw Pete after that episode, he would regard him with murderous glances – from a safe distance.

****

The next few days, passed uneventfully, apart from an excursion Pete took to the harbour district of Karaköy, on the Thursday evening, in the company of Walter and Brian. Situated at the confluence of the Bosphorus and the Golden Horn, Karaköy is the city's main port. In any one day, ships of numerous nationalities, sailing under a variety of flags, could be seen anchored at the dockside. In the latter part of the nineteenth century, a funicular railway had been built to connect Beyoğlu with Karaköy which was still operating up until 1968. Now it was closed for renovation, not to be opened again for a couple more years. According to Walter, early in the twentieth century, the cable which operated the train snapped, resulting in multiple casualties, as the train smashed through the station wall at the bottom and into the street. As this pleasant little history was being related, Pete felt grateful he was travelling in the marginally safer mode of transport provided by the *dolmuş* taxi.

They alighted at the taxi rank which happened to be opposite the old funicular railway station, now utterly desolate with boarded up windows. There was something about the dun colours and general dreariness of the surrounding buildings that caused Pete's spirits to sink, momentarily. After all, where was he and what was he doing here? It was almost surreal, yet the facts of his present location and life situation were beyond doubt. He had ditched the comparatively mundane, to wit a teaching post in Essex or Berkshire, for a chance to see the world outside the confines of his cosy existence. At home in Essex, he would be anticipating Guy Fawkes Night, Christmas and yet here he was somewhere in the middle of this antique city, coping with unfamiliar customs and an alien culture. What was it that had guided him into this daunting set of circumstances? Malign and implacable forces that had it in for people like him? Not a chance! A series of catastrophic errors had paved the way to his fatal entrance into Istanbul. Perhaps the grossest of those errors was for him to accept the invitation to join that Fred Karno's of an expedition in the first place. At the back of his mind, something was telling him that those thoughts were unjustified. After all, if the expedition was "Fred Karno's", he had played an equal part in its organisation – for want of a better word. He would have to wait and see.

The party of three had been standing in the fading light, peering at the old station building, and from where they stood, they could make out the Galata Bridge in the distance, carrying traffic over the Golden Horn into an even more ancient metropolis. There was movement from Walter as he beckoned them towards some dingy alleyways, and soon they were making their way through a maze of narrow back streets, until they came upon a passage which broadened out into a main street and they were able to glimpse the harbour in the background. There, a truly spectacular sight met their gaze. The whole street was filled with men strolling in pairs and in groups. Pete noticed that these men were mainly drawn to a row of shop-like buildings which stretched along the whole length of the street. These buildings provided the only illumination so there were plenty of dark corners where certain individuals were choosing to lurk.

On closer inspection, these dwellings all appeared to be fronted by shop windows with adjoining glass, wood framed doors. The three Europeans attracted very little or no attention from the thronging masculinity. They were practically invisible, like ghostly observers, experiencing yet not participating in events that were unfolding before them. They stopped outside one of the "shops" and behind a large window, their presence illuminated by a few dingy bulbs, were two rotund women, possibly in their forties or fifties. Both were seated and dressed in mid length see through green nightdresses and somewhat incongruously, grey ankle socks. All around the shop, testosterone levels were off the scale, as men crowded round, buzzing not only with excitement but also amusement, and in some cases, anticipation of needs about to be fulfilled.

Pete and Brian were so stunned, they caught each other gaping like naïve adolescents. They were astounded by the sights these women presented - and there were about a dozen more such establishments in the street. They became   more aware of the electric atmosphere, the multifarious odours pervading the street which were a heady mix of sweat, lemon eau de Cologne. There were also various food stalls plying their trade, consisting of blue wooden covered barrows glazed on all four sides, some containing *köfte kebabs* with mounds of white rice, others stuffed with jars of pickled vegetables or sheep's intestines on spits, known as *kokoreç*. In addition, there were open stalls selling peanuts, hazelnuts and pistachios. Two bands of musicians, in different parts of the street, were performing heady, wild, oriental sounds with finger drums, saz and violins, all playing pulsing the quarter tones so typical of eastern music. The exotic, one might even say erotic nature of this music was in sad contrast to the activities in progress between some of the men and women within those pitiful shops in that Karaköy back street.

Walter seemed to have disappeared momentarily, but then emerged from the crush of frustrated masculinity clutching a bag of Turkish salted peanuts roasted in their skins which he promptly shared out with the other two. He seemed to feel he ought to explain.

"Zis is known as government brothel area. All perfectly legal and the women they cost five lira per time."

As they strolled past each shopfront, they noticed that some of the women were sat posed on wickerwork chairs and others were standing beside them. No attempt was being made to appear alluring or inviting. Occasionally a customer would enter and one of the women would accompany him, unsmilingly to a room at the rear. Walter continued.

"Many of zese men haf come into the city from Anatolia villages. Sometimes they don't even see a woman for ze purposes of sex for months. Turkish girls haf to be virgins ven zey marry."

Neither of the Englishmen had ever witnessed such sights before. Despite the fact that there were red light districts in most English cities, prostitution, as they understood it, was still regarded as a criminal offence. Until he was sixteen or so, Pete had been convinced, as were most of his school contemporaries, that women in black mini skirts wearing gold ankle chains round black stockings were all on the game. Here, in this eastern metropolis and indeed, nationwide for all he knew, the openness of the trade was very much taken for granted. One aspect of the surroundings that Pete did find utterly captivating was a trio of blind musicians ensconced on the crumbling pavement, pouring out their strangely intoxicating melodies. They would have gone down brilliantly at the Isle of Wight or Cambridge festivals and would have stood up well against the wonderful Third Ear band or the Incredible String Band. The music continued to weave its oriental magic which had the effect of inducing Pete momentarily into a near trance.

It all happened in a few seconds. Without warning there was a noisy stirring of the crowd; a trampling of feet in a general rush towards one of the mid street brothels. If they had not moved with the mass of mobile bodies they would surely have been crushed underfoot. They managed somehow to edge their way towards the fringes then on to an empty roadside. Walter was breathless, like the other two, but he had begun listening to the hubbub of voices that had accompanied the surge. He was able to inform them that there had been reports of two new girls who had just arrived and who were apparently only in their early twenties. They were clearly going to be in great demand. But not from Pete, even though he confessed to himself that he would like to have caught a glimpse of them to see how they compared with Hanife – well at least as far as looks were concerned. They could not hope to be as sexy as her, he mused.

At last they managed to extricate themselves form the thronging masculinity and make their way towards Galata Bridge. They were famished. The fish restaurants there tended to be expensive but they did manage to find a small eatery selling *lahmacun*. In the midst of consuming these spicy Arab pancakes and drinking glasses of a yoghurt drink called *ayran*, Walter told his companions that most of the men only went to the government brothel area as an evening out and a chance to stare at the women.

"God, they must be desperate," scoffed Pete. "Never seen anything like it. They are all middle aged, fat and ugly but I suppose it's needs must etc."

"Wouldn't catch me using their services," added Brian

"But what would you catch if you did?" At least Pete thought his remark was quite funny.

"Oh no," Walter intervened, "Zere are regular medical checks on the women and all is kept very clean." He felt he had to explain the circumstances faced by most Turkish men at that time. "It's all part of the culture of zis city and has been zo since Constantine. It is difficult to find a woman for sex unless she is a prostitute. You often see teenage boys at zese place too. Zose who can afford it go to high class bordellos in hotels. It's much easier to get sex with European girls, I think."

"Don't you believe it," Pete replied ruefully. "Most of them prefer to keep knickers on and legs closed, but at least I have never had to pay for it. There are some sluts about, though."

"It's ironic," chipped in Brian, "that the girls who do it on the first date are regarded as sluts and the blokes who put it about get called studs. Double standards or what?"

Walter listened to the other two, fascinated by their views and marvelling to himself that maybe this evening's little excursion had made a difference to the way they would henceforth regard what he felt was an important aspect of their existence. Of course, he and the others had no idea of Pete's recent good fortune regarding sexual fulfilment. Indeed, he could find himself pleasantly set up for some time to come. What's more, despite the fact that what he had seen today had repulsed him, he felt that another visit from

Hanife in the next few days would do him very nicely thank you.

The next day, the promised excursion to the old city with Kaya took place. Pete found Sultanahmet and its environs nothing short of awe inspiring. Two mighty megastructures sat facing each other across the acres of trackways and multifarious shrubs like two great hosts about to do battle. Thus the sacred, legendary religious bastions of Aya Sofia and the Blue Mosque confront each other as in the olden days of Byzantine v Turk. The one bristling with minarets and domes like spears and helmets, the other, squat and defiant with little more than its intrinsic beauty and an ancient history on its side. The four minarets had been placed around Aya Sofia after the Turks had captured the city.

On that fateful day in 1453, history, it transpired, was to be of no benefit to the Byzantines, and the city of Constantinople fell, followed by great slaughter of the populace. The killing continued until the victorious Turkish leader, Sultan Mehmet, personally intervened to bring it to a halt. Aya Sofia was soon converted to a mosque and many centuries later it became a museum. on the orders of Mustafa Kemal Atatürk. The victors who captured the city declined to destroy this Christian edifice, instead placing large green discs which prominently displayed passages from the Koran written in gold leaf. So many of the stunning mosaics depicting biblical scenes, saints and past emperors had been damaged in one way or the other, mostly by marauding Crusaders centuries earlier. It was pleasing for Pete to note that work had recently commenced in restoring these.

What Pete struggled to understand, or even imagine, as he tried to take in his surroundings, was how it had been possible, more than one thousand five hundred years ago, to construct a dome of such a size that to follow it with his eyes to the top was enough to give him a kind of ground level vertigo. He was saddened by the damage to the mosaics which he guessed was down to the Islamic conquerors, as many of the subjects had their heads missing. Moslems did not permit the representation of human faces in any art form. In extreme cases, pictorial art itself was proscribed, along with music, dancing and many other aspects of life that tended to make people happy. There were also many bare sconces on the walls which would have held gold candlesticks, crucifixes or valuable icons, all conspicuous by their absence. However, on enquiry, Pete learned that the cathedral had been looted and vandalised by crusaders in the thirteenth century, supposedly on their way to liberate Christian territories in Palestine.

It can be said that the Turks took their ideas for domed mosques from the imposing Aya Sofia, which was already more than a thousand years old before the blue Mosque was built. It was Sultan Ahmet who commanded his chief architect, Mehmet Ağa, a student of the great Mimar Sinan, to construct a building which would supplant Justinian's former cathedral as the principal mosque of the Osmanlı Empire. Whereas the aesthetic qualities of Aya Sofia, with its old world honey and rose hued exterior, were immediately apparent to Pete on his first visit, the beauty of the Blue Mosque, apart from its sprawling grey majesty, lay inside the cavernous seventeenth century structure. Here, the walls were covered with twenty thousand ceramic tiles depicting flowers, fruit and cypresses. and a serene haze of blue paint adorned the upper reaches. Vast chandeliers were hanging from the ceilings, as prayers, offered by the faithful, kneeling on seemingly acres of pomegranate red and rich blue carpeting, found their way to their God through a massive dome above them which was encrusted with yet more tiles, sumptuously decorated in the ubiquitous tulip patterns.

Later, standing outside the mosque in the arena formerly known as the Hippodrome, Pete was imagining the chariot races that once took place here with their primordial roar of fiercely opposing sets of supporters, the cracking of whips, the whinnying of the horses, the shouts of the drivers. The Hippodrome had fallen into disuse long before the Turks arrived, but these days the site was regularly packed, not only with visitors to the old city but also picnicking peasants from Anatolia and vendors' stalls hawking *simit*, sweet corn and Coca Cola, along with post cards and other cheap touristic souvenirs. A tall obelisk at the far end caught his eye. On closer inspection it turned out to be the twin of Cleopatra's Needle which was sited by the River Thames on London's Embankment. Through the heat haze generated by a warm autumn sun, Topkapi Palace could just be observed, perched on its private slope in the middle distance, hugging the Golden Horn shoreline, seeming to gaze imperiously across glittering wavelets at the Galata Tower opposite. Unfortunately, part of the former sultan's palace, the harem as it turned out, was closed to the general public for the time being, as restoration work was being carried out. They would give this palace a miss today, as time was marching on and they had yet to visit *Kapalı Çarşı* – The Grand Bazaar.

Pete's thoughts returned to the two venues he had visited during the morning. In the Blue Mosque, he seemed to feel a wholesomeness that somehow permeated every crevice of stone and ceramic surface; every thread of the carpeting. All was in harmony and in peaceful accord with the common cause; that of communion with Allah, with total submission being expressed by the kneeling participants to the master of every Moslem's existence. However, inside Aya Sofia, and perhaps in keeping with the age of the building, there existed for him something older, even sinister, as if God had long ago deserted the place and left behind only the vestiges of evil thoughts and deeds, lurking in dark corners and much in evidence with the representation of so called angels on walls in the upper levels. These supposedly divine creatures bore more of a resemblance to huge, ragged bats or demons hovering over characters in the other holy scenes so lovingly depicted.

Later, beneath the alleys and archways of the Grand Bazaar, the vigilance of Kaya managed to prevent Pete from paying over the odds for what amounted to tourist tat. Despite its exotic setting and world renown, the outer sections of this gigantic ancient retail area were home mostly to numerous stalls selling cheap souvenirs and fake designer clothing. Some of the less expensive, smellier leather goods were also on sale there. The centre of the covered bazaar was in marked contrast and worth the extra slog through the narrow alleyways. It was truly a centre of light with its hosts of carpet shops displaying their wares from as far afield as Eastern Anatolia, Azerbaijan and Iran. There were other establishments selling expensive and exotic ceramic pots, plates and tiles, historic weapons, copper and brass goods, jewellery and sheepskin coats. Each customer would be offered a seat and a welcoming glass of tea. Purchasing these merchandises was an experience Pete would be forced to forego until another time, on account of his financial situation. For now he could only stand and observe the buying procedures, which tended to be quite long and drawn out. Hard bargaining would take place in a multitude of languages, despite notices prominently displayed by Istanbul City Council which read *"Satılık Yasaktır"* – "bargaining forbidden". In truth, no-one ever paid the asking price. Pete eventually purchased a small gold puzzle ring which cost him two pounds.

Türkiye Güzeli
(Turkish Beauty)

"…when it gets dark softly in Istanbul
I love you
Like thanking God that we live."

Nazim Hikmet

The second half of the autumn term began once more in earnest with half a dozen more students enrolling for the morning classes. Pete felt that this mere fact was a vindication of his approach to classroom management that some may have described as Gung Ho. Vefbi's fears that numbers would drop if Pete continued his hard nosed tactics appeared to be unfounded, after all. The students may even have considered that by participating in lessons they were actually learning something. It was also announced by the school secretary that the current Miss Turkey would be attending classes, presumably to brush up on her English, prior to taking part in the Miss World competition. The rebellious rumblings that were being heard across the western world concerning the eponymous contest being a humiliating parade of exploited femininity, had clearly not reached the Turkish Republic. Not that the protest movement had, to date, had much effect in the UK either. Although he was as keen as the next male on admiring the female form, Pete had never expressed any interest in Miss whatever country you care to name, and could never understand the appeal of such parades of young girls, always declaring to the judges, in a multitude of accents, that they wanted to see the world, meet people and work with children, and so on. However, Pete felt a frisson of anticipation at the prospect of teaching a beautiful celebrity. The feeling was dampened, however, by the news that she would be placed in Roger's group as his own class was full.

An innovation for the rest of the year was to be the Friday morning singing sessions. Vefbi was a great believer in the power of song in improving language usage. Now Pete had heard some of the summer camp songs, rendered to him by teaching and admin. staff, and if they were anything to go by, with choruses such as "…roll me over lay me down and do it again…" then this was a feature that he would be delighted to avoid. As far as he was concerned, Vefbi could do the singing lessons.

Pete looked up momentarily from his lesson notes for the day. Standing about two metres away and facing towards him was probably the most beautiful girl he had ever seen in his life. She was a little over five feet in height, dressed in a slim white roll neck jumper and a black A line skirt which was worn slightly above the knee. Her hair was a lustrous dark brown of a shade referred to in Turkish as *esmer*. But it was her eyes that he was drawn to. They were perfection; they were wide and clear and held him stunned in her gaze; they were a shade of brown that matched her hair. Her face was expertly made up, not overstated with excessive use of kohl like some of her compatriots. Of course, this had to be Miss Turkey. He found himself beaming a smile in her direction. He was definitely blushing. She returned his smile – confidently – as he perceived, then turned away somewhat dismissively to continue a conversation with two other girls and some boys. They were around the same age. He guessed she would have been about seventeen or eighteen years old.

The office and both classrooms were now becoming much busier and more crowded, as the students gathered for their lessons. Pete became aware of some excited movement just inside the doorway He glanced towards the hubbub, and there stood an attractive, almost European looking girl, quite tall too, with an elfin face and with long tresses of light brown hair which tumbled over her shoulders. It was clear she was trying to make her entrance into the office as unobtrusive as possible, but as soon as she was recognised there was a stir among the crowd.

"That's Miss Turkey," whispered Vefbi bey in Pete's right ear. Then he started to shepherd everyone into their respective classes.

Standing in front of his class, preparing to start his lesson, Pete searched in vain among the rows of young people for the subject of his earlier vision of beauty. No, along with Miss Turkey, she was also in Roger's group. Oh well, on with the show! Fortunately and to his great satisfaction, there had been a sea change in the way that members of his group now approached his efforts to teach them. They were, for the main part, attentive and rather more keen to learn than previously. He could not help feeling that in most cases their Spoken English was pretty good anyway. What on earth did the high schools expect of them? Then again, not all of them were taking reparation exams.

Two days later - one of the long days as Pete labelled it – he experienced a rare brainwave. A mental breakthrough arising from a desperate need to somehow dodge having to take the Friday singsong, or at least in the format that Vefbi had visualised. The end of the lesson was approaching, one in which he had been learning about Turkish history with its Sky Turks and the lake that dried up somewhere in the Caucasus. Other subjects covered were Turkish geography, namely The Black Sea area; Turkish culture, featuring shadow puppets; and Turkish rock music, highlighting a band called *Tatarlar* or The Tartars, for whom one of his class was road manager. All accounts were related in English which was variable in clarity, accuracy and required some help from him regarding syntax, grammar and vocabulary. He then put forward his question to the group.

"Does anyone here own a guitar?" Several hands shot towards the ceiling.

"Who would be willing to bring one in on Friday?" One raised hand remained. It was Fırat, the road manager.

"Thank you Fırat. Are you sure you don't mind. I can actually play a bit so I'll be especially careful."

"Of course Mr Peter, replied Fırat. I bring the guitar on Friday."

Pete had worked out a way of transforming what he considered a mundane, irritating and embarrassing chore into an activity he would actually enjoy. People that he had come into contact with would often put this down to his lack of maturity, which was true to an extent. He would always wish to do things his own way, especially if that involved fun and frivolity. Close friends would put it all down to his need not to take himself and life too seriously. He hoped that ultimately his charges would also be able to share his enthusiasm for performing songs of his choice. Furthermore, as he would be choosing the numbers, he would have control over the content of these singing sessions and that meant he could avoid the crass ditties that might have been suggested by others. That was not to say he would turn down all requests, just the campfire stuff really.

At break time, students from both classes were able to mingle and earnestly discuss what they had learned during the preceding hour. Meanwhile, back in the real world, they actually gathered together in small groups chattering excitedly about the latest news concerning prominent Turkish film stars, such as Türkan Şoray or Ediz Hun, and current popular singers like Ajda Pekkan and Cem Karaca. Some were conducting an animated discussion about the prospects of Istanbul's leading football teams. All of this was totally incomprehensible to Pete as he was yet to be introduced fully to these particular subjects. Naturally, some names had been mentioned to him but the only one he could recall was that of Türkan Şoray whose likeness he had observed on film posters in Beyoğlu. To say he was utterly captivated by her dazzling, doe eyed, oriental looks would be an understatement.

He also saw that one group of teenagers was engaged in particularly animated chatter and there was the pretty chestnut haired girl again. Now she did somewhat resemble a younger version of the eponymous Miss Şoray. Briefly, (or did he imagine this?) her eyes seemed to shine in his direction but her face remained expressionless for a few seconds until, turning towards her friends, she responded hysterically to what one of them had just said. At this stage, he was more fascinated than desirous. One thing Pete did notice, as by now he was fixated on the girl and her movements, was that whenever she wanted to contribute to the banter, she would always use the same introductory words. These sounded like "Back neddy jam!" delivered in a high sing song voice. This actually meant "Listen to what I am going to say" used as a kind of idiolectic discourse starter, but Pete was not to know this. After hearing it repeated several times during the discussion, he began to ponder on what words of wisdom she was uttering afterwards. Very few, he imagined, but her vocal tones were as attractive as she was.

Just then, Ekrem, the tea boy arrived, swinging his circular tea tray to and fro on which he balanced at least eight glasses of scalding clear brown liquid. In the middle of this tray was a glass dish containing misshapen sugar lumps of varying sizes. These lumps were so hard that if you waited for them to dissolve, your tea would become tepid at best. Pete had evolved a technique of taking two small lumps and attacking them with his spoon until they had fully dissolved. As he consumed his tea, alternating sips with chasing a few small lumps around the glass, he felt a presence quite close to him. He caught the faint aroma of a light citrus like perfume, and there was the pretty girl standing right in front of him. He looked up from where he was seated, just behind Vefbi bey's desk and became aware that the girl was speaking to him, smiling faintly.

"You like Istanbul?" She stressed the second syllable "...stan" in common with every other Turk he had spoken to but her voice was of a rich, quite low tone, sounding somewhat sexier than when she was chattering with her companions.

"Yes it's a fantastic city with lots to see. Oh and the weather's still fine, which is great for the time of year."

"Ha ha, they say the English people always like to talk about weather."

"You seem to be very well informed. May I ask you your name?" Pete could not really conceive any better answer to this stereotyping. Besides, it occurred to him that she might just be teasing. Why oh why did he need to ask her name and in such a lame matter?

161

"It's Selma."

"Selmer, thank you. Nice name."

"No it's Sel-ma."

"Ok I'll try and get it right." What was it that made him feel that she already had the upper hand?

"It's Ok. I am not in your class anyway."

Pete thought rather ruefully, "I am not in her class either."

Whether intended or not, she had him under a spell. She possessed a beauty and a dignity beyond her years, or that is how she appeared at this present moment. Would he attempt to ask her out some time? How was he placed to do that? Secret meetings with an older woman for sex were one thing, but Selma was definitely not for the taking; at least not in this life. He imagined that her usual suitors would come from a somewhat more affluent background than anything he could offer.

She threw him a wistful "Bye" as she returned to her classroom. Although their conversation had been brief and far from profound, he could perceive that behind that confident façade, there was a shyness that reflected a genuine enough nature. However, this had not been the first such exchange he had shared with young female students, or young male students come to that. He just had that nagging feeling that on this occasion he had been flirted with, and at that moment in time, he could think of no reasons on earth to object to that. It was just that he was in no position to flirt back and in case he ever considered doing so, outside the confines of the school, he had been amply warned about how a girl's brother or male cousin might respond to that.

Now there seemed to exist at the time, among many people in this city a kind of respect for all things English – they never referred to the "British" – based, in part, on a somewhat outdated concept of the nation's past status in the world. In other words, England, like Turkey, was a former colonial power, but where all males were "gentil-men" with stiff upper lips, cold personalities and a rigid sense of fair play. At least this was the impression Pete had formed from his many conversations to date. Then, of course there was the cultural renaissance that had burst into bloom in the UK, mostly centred on pop/rock music and fashion. This had seemed to elevate the standing of the English as "cool" and not just in Turkey. To anyone else, including the British themselves, this must have seemed like a new golden age.

Just to add to the high regard directed towards all things English was the fact that its national football team were the current world champions. One factor that the Turks had raised, regarding the World Cup final, was the so-called contentious third goal. It seemed that many of them supported Germany and claimed to have seen footage that clearly showed the ball had not crossed the line on that auspicious day. Pete's response had always been that he had seen that clip dozens of times and the ball had clearly crossed the line. "Roger Hunt was right behind it. If it was not in, why did he turn and celebrate when his natural instinct would have been to bang the ball into the roof of the net?" The protagonists did, to be fair, leave Pete with the last word on that one.

Although Pete was only too happy to take the plaudits offered to himself and others of his nation, he felt he had little to offer in returning those compliments. He had clearly not yet learned enough about Mustafa Kemal Atatürk. Selma had been the only person to talk to him that break time. The other members of staff seemed too busy. However, just as he was preparing to return to his classroom, two teenage lads approached and addressed him loudly. *"Geçmiş olsun Manchester City!"* All that Pete knew was that *geçmiş olsun* meant get well soon. It transpired that Fenerbaçhe – the current top Istanbul football team, had recently knocked Manchester City out of the European Cup.

"Well done to them," Pete replied, "but I couldn't care less. I live more than two hundred miles from Manchester and they are rubbish anyway." This reply was, nevertheless, not emphatic enough to prevent at least a fortnight of good natured ribbing from the boys. Indeed their silence after that time may well have coincided with Fenerbaçhe's exit from that competition.

Sweet Music

"If you miss this train I'm on
You will know that I am gone.
You can hear the whistle blow a hundred miles.
A hundred miles, a hundred miles,
A hundred miles, a hundred miles.
You can hear the whistle blow a hundred miles."

Not a shirt upon my back
Not a penny to my name.
Lord I can't go back home this a way.
This a way, this a way. this a way. this a way.
Lord I can't go back home this a way.

It was the second week of the music sessions, and Firat had been as good as his word in bringing in his guitar. This particular song, "A Hundred Miles" had proved very popular the previous week, so it was getting a well warranted reprise. The students were by now well acquainted with the repetitive choruses and repetition was, Pete had been told, key to the teaching of English as a foreign language. As the second chorus rang out, Pete's mind wandered. As he did so, he gazed at the assembled choir in front of him and there, seated in the front row was one girl he did not recognise as a regular member. The eyes gave her away. It was Selma, and she was looking straight at him. The sudden shock caused him to miss a chord and break off singing for a few seconds but no-one seemed to notice. What was she doing here? She belonged to the other group.

The question now arose. Was she interested in this lesson or the teacher? Pete dismissed the second alternative for reasons he had given himself after their first encounter. However, as the well known platitude put it, there was no accounting for taste. Selma was beautiful. Of that there was no doubt, even to the most objective of opinions on what passed for aesthetically pleasing female looks. But he knew nothing about her or her background.

In fact, she was generally held by those who were closest to her to be pleasing to the eye, agreeable towards most people, haughty with the likes of waiters, shop assistants and taxi drivers but gregarious towards those she regarded as her equals. Young, handsome men with impeccable family backgrounds, would pursue her relentlessly, only to be rebuffed, then to drive away crestfallen in their Mercedes and Mustangs. Her favourite method of rejecting these potential suitors would be to take their telephone numbers and promise to call them. Of course she never had any intention of doing so. On other occasions, if she chose, she could just simply be rude to them.

There was, however, a current beau in her life. One who had somehow managed to penetrate those harsh defences (even though he had not as yet been able to penetrate her!) to find that sweet-as-*lokum* nature hidden beneath. The fact that he very closely resembled a young Omar Sharif may have made a significant contribution to winning Selma's heart, but then such a comparison would have made her appear somewhat shallow, which she was not. She admired intelligent young men who might exist outside of the mainstream of typical Turkish youth, and their obsessions with sport, cars and chasing girls. Hamid Reza was a twenty year old Iranian student attending Istanbul University and who could speak Turkish. Unlike the majority of her other admirers he did not own a car, preferring to perambulate across the city by taxi. He hailed from Teheran where his parents had high expectations of him and they also knew he had met a Turkish girl. From the point of view of political or religious views, he was inclined more to Shah than Ayatollah. On the other hand, he had informed Selma that when they were married and moved to Iran, she could dress as she wished in their marital home, but whenever they went out, she

165

would have to wear traditional long clothing and the *hijab*.

Unfortunately, he had kept that particular bombshell to himself until he and Selma had become more serious, and this may well have contributed to the eventual decline of their relationship. Up to that point, both young persons believed they were in love with each other and if appearances were anything to go by, they were well matched. As far as meeting and going out together were concerned, they were only able to see each other in the afternoons, early evenings and sometimes at weekends. Not only was her father a devout Moslem who prayed five times a day, attended mosque regularly and always fasted during *Ramazan* but he also kept a strict eye on his teenage daughter. Of course, if Hamid Reza were eventually to pass muster, having formally proposed, they would be free to see each other as an engaged couple at any time - and without a chaperone.

Selma's attendance at the European Languages school was the result of the dressing down she had received from her father following her high school examination results. These had been mediocre at best. She had not gained a pass mark in English and had failed to matriculate. She was therefore required to take a reparation exam in the subject during the following spring. Needless to say, she had used much of the time socialising with her friends or with Hamid when she should have been in class. Who was to know?

One thing Pete was fascinated to know was how she had managed to wheedle her way into his group for the musical lesson. He made a mental note to square this with Roger later, but it was unlikely that he would be particularly troubled. Perhaps she enjoyed singing, she had certainly heard that the musical sessions were fun. One glance in her direction told him she was clearly miming. In the meantime, the song was coming to an end and there would doubtless be another reprise at the end of the lesson. Three more songs would see him through the next half an hour. One of the students had handed him the words to Peter Sarstedt's "Where do you go to my lovely?" which had topped the charts in several countries, including the UK. Pete was able to perform the number straight off due to the easy chords and he could remember the tune. Next, he gave the class the Searchers' "Sweets for my sweet" which may not have been exactly up to date but had a marvellous chorus for them to join in. He finished off with a rendition of Joan Baez's "There but for fortune" which was originally written by Phil Ochs but hers was the version Pete had learned at college. He knew that he had to be cautious with regard to political content of songs. After all, this was not England. However, as far as he was concerned, this number was hauntingly beautiful and fairly understated in that respect.

As Pete had mentally predicted, there was another run through of "A Hundred Miles" but the lesson came to an end before he could oblige his captive audience with a repeat of Mr Sarstedt's hit. It was lunch time, and he was on his way across the office floor to speak to Roger, when he found his progress impeded by a glamorous young woman with blonde hair, heavily made up face, black silk blouse, cropped black leather jacket and the tightest pair of blue jeans he had ever laid eyes on. These were tucked into calf hugging black high heeled boots. An imitation leopard skin Italian design handbag was slung across her left shoulder. She spoke directly to Pete.

"Hello, my name is Aylin. I am thinking joining a class here. I believe you are one of the teachers."

" Er yes, well, good to meet you. Your English is pretty good. You will enjoy the lessons.

"Oh yes, I heard the singing."

"We only do that on Friday mornings."

Pete was aware of a blushing sensation that he always seemed to experience when introduced to charismatic and attractive women. Nothing he could do about it and he reasoned that so far, to the best of his knowledge, it had not adversely affected his love life. Thus, a brief conversation ensued which culminated in Aylin suggesting that Pete might like to go with her to a disco. During this dialogue, Pete's eyes had been continually drawn to a thick black patent belt which hugged an insectivorous waist. This potential new student was sex on legs and possibly almost ten years his senior. He hesitated with his follow up comment, as he did not quite know how to pitch his answer and play it cool at the same time. Then it was too late. She was turning on her four inch heels.

"Well hopefully see you on Monday and maybe we go to disco some time too."

"Yes that sounds great. I can't make it this weekend but maybe next week."

Why had Pete lied? He had absolutely nothing planned for Friday night all the way through to Sunday night. They bid each other farewell and with that she breezed out of the office leaving a haze of heady perfume in her wake. Her shapely bottom, like a large juicy apple, briefly framed the doorway, then swayed jauntily as she disappeared on to the landing and down the stairs. Vefbi could not help grinning in Pete's direction and Hassan, who happened to be visiting his cousin that day, remarked to Pete.

"I could fuck her with my eyes!"

However, other eyes were now fixed on Pete and reflected in them were obvious signs of disapproval. It was Selma, and perhaps she had heard Hassan. Despite the gnawing hunger and his desire for a good lunch, Pete felt her gaze upon him and turned slightly to his right to face her.

"You want to go to disco with her?" She spoke these words quietly. Clearly no-one else in the office was able to hear her.

"Oh well I might," replied Pete, wondering why she should take such an interest in his affairs. Her answer was stark and to the point.

"Oh no, you must be careful. She is woman and she is big flirt."

He found her slightly indignant tone, along with her imperfect English, both fascinating and more than a little alluring. Surely she could not be jealous; just concerned for his well being perhaps. By using the term "woman", she meant, in a Turkish context, that Aylin was not a virgin. That was not a problem for Pete .He had been with promiscuous girls before and had emerged unscathed. But on reflection, the voluptuous Aylin did seem somewhat out of his league. Time to step up, maybe? Why was Selma making her out to be a slut? How did she know? What he did not realise at the time was that some of the more expensive Turkish prostitutes were dying their hair blonde. But it was also the case that a number of Turkish film actresses, singers and rich wives were doing the same. It was natural, then, for fashion conscious young women to follow the trend.

"If you want to go to disco it is better if you go with me and some of my friends. Do you want?"

Pete considered this as a very agreeable and friendly suggestion and no more than that. Besides, it could be fun. He accepted her invitation and arranged to meet her party outside the "Hydromel" Diskotek on Saturday afternoon at two thirty. He was delighted to learn that this venue was on the Harbiye main street just about five minutes from where he lived. He was, nevertheless, intrigued as to why Selma had tried to warn him off with regard to Aylin. Did she have his moral welfare at heart? A bit late for that. Anyway, he felt instinctively that Aylin was certainly not a prostitute. Another possibility was that this Selma might actually fancy him. He dismissed this notion out of hand, as she would almost certainly be accompanied by her boyfriend at the disco, who would later whisk her off into the night in whichever example of German or American automotive engineering his parents had bought for him.

On Saturday morning, Pete visited a chemist's shop in Istiklal Caddesi. He was accompanied by Ahmet, a friend from the school who was to translate for him, so he could hopefully purchase some toiletries. He had by this time used up all the deodorants and after shaves he had brought with him. In the *Eczane*, buying the soap and shampoo were not a problem but the shop assistant spoke no English and Ahmet's ability as translator was limited at best. When he asked for deodorant, after much confused dialogue between Ahmet and the assistant, they eventually managed to produce some odourless talcum powder and a box of French chalk.

By now, somewhat exasperated, Pete surveyed the shelves which were packed with the usual products and he was able to recognise some of the names he was familiar with back home. Then on the men's toiletries aisle he spotted a small green bottle with the label "Mennen" boldly standing out in white. He had not come across this make before, but when he opened the bottle and sniffed, the aroma was most agreeable. A few notches up from Brut, he pondered. Then he read the word "*deodoran*" which he guessed was the Turkish for what he was after, so he immediately added it to the other items by the till. Five minutes later, he was sitting in the Atlantic Pastahane enjoying a *börek* and a glass of cold *ayran*. Ahmet had also relished the shopping trip and was clearly delighted to have been of service. He also settled the restaurant bill. After all, Pete was a *misafir* - a guest - in his country, and as a Turk he could not allow him to pay for his own lunch.

Saturday afternoon duly arrived and Pete had collected his laundry, all clean, freshly ironed and well worth the five lira he had paid the woman upstairs on the second floor. His blue Levi jeans and lilac coloured cotton grandad shirt were ready for action. He also donned his suede jacket that Vefbi bey's friend, Remzi the tailor, had made for him. This would keep out the cold later in the day. He set off from his accommodation, quite excited by the prospect of an afternoon's fun, and he wondered what a Turkish disco would be like. Probably the same as an English one, he thought. He stepped out into the narrow street which was lit by a pale afternoon sun. Although November was upon the city, the air was pleasantly cool and the summer aromas of diesel tinged with rotting garbage had long since been replaced by a heady scent of wood smoke from residences and sweet corn boiling in the numerous roadside stalls.

Despite the fine late autumn weather and the prospect of a highly entertaining afternoon, a feeling of melancholy seemed to creep inside him as if from nowhere as he paused for a moment, alone in a deserted street. Surely he could not be the only person feeling this way, at this moment in time on this unusually empty street in a small district of a vast oriental metropolis. The gloom in his very soul began to intensify. To Pete's mind, the city's grey and ochre conurbation made up of wooden shacks, gerry built apartment blocks (such as the one he lived in), expensive looking condos and grand but bland public buildings, exuded a kind of melancholy which hung over everyone, forever trapping them in its dreary grasp. This was a strange sensation, though now he came to recognise it, the mood seemed to be echoed and taken up by the city's inhabitants, in the woeful cries of street vendors, in the faces of men huddled together in tea houses, in the expressionless countenances of women staring endlessly out of windows on to the streets below, and even in the doleful music that rang out from dowdy shopfronts.

The author, Orhan Pamuk, resident of this very city, was to describe this feeling as *"hüzün"*[1] or "black mood"[2] which is not just felt by one person but was mutually shared by millions of people and was, he believed, unique to Istanbul. What Pete was yet to grasp, due to the comparatively short amount of time he had spent in the city to date, was that this "general melancholy"[3] was of a kind that had come to bind a community together. At the same time, he had realised something else. It was almost as if the inhabitants of this city had sensed, as a body, the difficult times he was facing and they were sharing his burden in a way that he could not explain, but found it comforting, nonetheless. Contrarily, he was still being approached almost on a daily basis, by shady characters offering him the whole deal of change money, sheepskin coats or hashish.

As he resumed his journey along the cracked pavement and up the hill towards Harbiye Street, more of the Elmadağ denizens were now in evidence, standing outside their homes engaged in loud conversations or merely strolling and enjoying a leisurely Saturday afternoon. On the way along the street, he was greeted at intervals by grave nods in his direction or the odd "Merhaba" delivered with pale but earnest smiles from people who were, after all, his fellow citizens.

Soon the monotonous thrumming of traffic became more defined, so that the spluttering diesel engines of buses began to contrast with the choking sounds of ancient American taxis.

1. In "Istanbul, Memories of a City" Faber and Faber 2005
2. Op.cit.
3. ibid

Occasionally, the more agreeable buzz of a well tuned Mercedes or BMW could be heard. This constant stream of noise was accompanied as always by the manic hoots of car horns, as each driver took a turn to air their own protests at the funereal progress they were making along the main street. Waiting for one of the frequent traffic jams to form, Pete crossed over between the narrow spaces afforded between front and rear bumpers, towards the smart apartment and office blocks close to the Istanbul Hilton. He spotted the exterior of the Parizyen Bar Restaurant and strolled through the welcoming open glass doors.

Inside, seated or standing around a couple of square shaped metal tables, on the parquet flooring, he could discern Selma and her friends, some of whom he had not previously met. She was dressed in a white silky blouse with frills at the collar and on the cuffs of long sleeves. This tasteful top was set off by a navy blue embroidered linen mix waistcoat and matching pencil skirt, the latter of which just rested on her knees. She also wore sheer black tights with blue-white high heels.

In the centre of this group was Ahmet, looking most dapper in an Italian style tailored white shirt and crimson flares. He was engaged in a hushed dialogue with Selma. Was he the boyfriend? He spotted Pete and shouted in his direction, "Hey Mr Peter, do you want Coca Cola?" Pete replied in the affirmative, as he was feeling parched after his walk up the hill. He reached for his wallet.

"No it's all paid for," added Ahmet, "You don't pay." Pete supposed the group had started what was referred to in the UK as a tab. However, he was not permitted to contribute. As his drink arrived, he noticed something else by idly browsing one of the menus on his table. In this venue, a glass of Coke came to five lira. This was for a drink that could be bought in most shops for seventy five kuruş. The ice and lemon that floated in the glass, plus the service were expensive extras, evidently. Nevertheless, Pete did insist on paying his entrance fee, when at last the group shuffled into the disco. He shelled out ten lira and reflected that a sizeable number of Istanbul's population would be unable to afford this price, and neither, for that matter, the Coca Cola he had just finished drinking. "Keep the riff raff out?" He mused. It was not quite like that on Eel Pie Island as he recalled.

It seemed to him decades since his very first venture into a hall of dance. It was certainly before the advent of the discotheque. He was a mere fifteen year old youth at the time, and was accompanied on that occasion by the voluptuous Louise, a French girl, about his age who was on an exchange visit with one of his neighbours. A local band, who happened also to be charting at the time, provided the live music. They were called "The Fairies" and their style, as he remembered, was similar to the "Rolling Stones" and "Pretty Things". Rhythm and Blues it was called and the sound for Pete was truly awesome, as until then, he had only listened to records, as in LPs, EPs and singles.

The thumping, throbbing sound of Motown over the enormous speakers inside the Hydromel Disco almost broke into Pete's reminiscences. He was no stranger to loud music though, and had stood in close proximity to many a band's PA during the past five years. However, he had begun to squirm inwardly when the name of Louise popped back into his memory in a most unwelcome manner. He was standing in the darkness at the side of the dance floor clutching a complimentary vodka and fruit juice cocktail that had been thrust into his hand. Pete sensed in it a strong alcoholic content. Good thing too! At intervals, the probing coloured spotlight picked him out, as if to show him he could not hide from his recollections of that wretched but lovely French girl. The associated embarrassments would not dissipate as he recalled how initially he had been introduced to her by Mary, who lived next door but one to him.

He had immediately been drawn in both by her striking looks and her friendly nature. What else could he do but suggest a walk with her over the nearby fields which surrounded the road in which he lived? She readily agreed. Mary had left them both to it, not wishing to play gooseberry, so they duly set off along the grassy footpath. By the time they had reached the end of the first field they were holding hands. So far so good, and in addition, her English was passable; certainly better than his French, and this had certainly eased any communication issues – or so he thought. Eventually, they reached the river and Pete found himself sitting beside her on the bank, among the buttercups and cow parsley, staring down at rushes and lily pads swaying lazily in the gentle summer current. He was wondering what might happen next.

If it had been possible, even plausible for him to have gazed into a crystal ball, he may have acted differently. However, given his close proximity to this foreign beauty, he could do nothing more than reach round her belted slim waist and attempt to kiss her. Her response was immediate and took him by surprise, albeit pleasantly. She flung her arms around his neck and they both began kissing with steadily increasing intensity. After a few minutes of this divine intimacy, including, for the first time, a girl's tongue in his mouth, he found that his right arm was now around her shoulder. But what he could not quite grasp – and here, "grasp" was certainly the key word - was that she was continually trying to pull his hand down towards her right breast. Eventually, he caught on and he began to fondle her, but he did not unbutton her blouse. To say he was feeling well disposed towards this *jolie fille* would have been an understatement, but exactly why he blurted out to her, "Je vous aime," he would never really know as long as he lived.

She gently extricated herself from his grasp and replied, "but we have only known each other for short time." Pete was puzzled by this. What was she going on about? He only meant to say, "I like you." He was later to find out from his best friend Spam just what kind of *faux pas* he had unintentionally committed. Of course it must have been Mary who had informed his friend. How delighted she must have been telling him that Louise now regarded Pete as the "stupidest boy she had ever met". Perhaps she was the stupid one, thinking he could say something as unlikely as "I love you" on a first date. That was his first reaction to Spam's news, but the fire of his embarrassment had been lit and expressed itself in his glowing face. The whole neighbourhood would soon be sniggering about his foolishness.

"How could she think I was in love with her!"

"Well **I** know what you meant, mate," responded the loyal

Spam, but in truth he was he was just about managing to hold off a veritable spasm of giggles.

Unfortunately, Pete's humiliation, as he reflected, was far from over. The following evening, he, Louise, Spam and Mary attended the aforementioned dance at the "Saturday Scene" in the nearby town. He was dressed in a grey and black, small - check suit, courtesy of Mr Burton and his dad's cheque book. He wore a white button down shirt and a navy blue crimple flat ended tie. Sad to relate, he did not possess a fashionable pair of shoes, so his black, round toed TUFs had to suffice.

One hour or so in and the dance was going reasonably well. The dance floor was littered with hand bags and bodies gyrating around them. The young revellers were still twisting like they did last summer, and the summer before that, as well as performing other dances in vogue at the time. Pete was trying to dance as close as possible to Louise, almost as if to express ownership, but her response conveyed very little of that famed Gallic warmth, and considering their passions of the previous day, he was becoming somewhat deflated. Then to make matters worse, when the live music warmed up, Pete, who was loving this band, decided to jump up and down like a demented kangaroo with the end of his tie in his mouth. When the number ended, Louise was nowhere to be seen.

"Reckon you lost her there," remarked Spam who had sidled up to him from the side of the hall, where he had been standing among the onlookers. For once, he was sounding less than sympathetic, concerned more, in fact.

"Well at least I was trying to dance, instead of standing on the side as if I was attending a cattle market," was Pete's fairly waspish reply.

Perhaps "trying" was the correct word but more aptly expressed in its adjectival form. The ending of this mental anecdote was even more pathetic. As they left the dance hall at around eleven pm, Pete, who was waiting on the pavement outside for a lift home, glanced up and there, making her way down the stone steps was Louise, encased in the right arm of a tall young man who must have been in his early twenties. The way they both ambled past him, he might just as well been invisible. It was definitely the stuff of hit songs currently being churned out by sundry northern bands, as Pete's mortification and the loss of his French girlfriend were now complete. In the event, it was Spam who was later to inform Pete of the "stupidest boy" comment. He tried to explain but his best friend appeared to be unconvinced. After all, the original story was that much funnier. As far as he was concerned, it had been a minor incident, soon forgotten. And he was right.

It is to the eternal chagrin of all human beings that we cannot revisit our more shameful moments and replay them in ways that might show us in a better light, or take corrective actions. Pete's humiliation may have dented his reputation locally – though in point of fact, the incident was never mentioned again – but now, here he was, years later, standing in the Hydromel Diskotek, sipping his vodka cocktail and still smarting from hurt pride. In the great scheme of things, in the annals of world history and even in Pete's lifetime, the episode mattered not one jot, except perhaps to teach him to be a little more guarded in his discourse with the opposite sex. This could indeed have rendered him more inhibited in such circumstances - but it didn't. Besides, Louise would probably have ditched him at the dance, regardless.

Pete now became aware of a perfume he recognised which hung lightly on the air not a yard away from him.

"You don't dance," was Selma's first remark to him of the afternoon. "Come on."

Just at that moment, The Plastic Ono band's "Cold Turkey" started up. This was the first time Pete had heard the record and to him, the song's refrain came across as " Coz Turkey has got me on the run...!" It was months before he was advised of his error and the concept of cold turkey as not getting your fix of heroin was also revealed to him for the first time – by Roger. Meanwhile, the insistent beat and rhythm got inside him once again and he responded, but not in the way he had done so at the Corn Exchange. Although he had attended numerous dances since then and had developed his own technique, depending on the number, he chose to mimic the minimalistic movements of those around him and Selma seemed to approve. The next record on the DJ's turntable was Chicago's extended version of "I'm a man" which had a similar rhythm but, after about five minutes, Selma declared herself tired, and repaired to a nearby table to sit down. Pete joined her.

Thus, the afternoon continued in this pleasant and vibrant atmosphere which was to be punctuated temporarily by a brief but puzzling incident. During a pause in the music, a tall, swarthy but striking young man crossed the dance floor quite purposefully, and accompanied by a veritable fusillade of multi coloured flashing lights, he approached Selma, and the two of them seemed to engage in a brief, animated exchange of dialogue. At one point he took her hand as if to pull her away from the disco. Presumably, whatever he wanted from the girl he was unable to obtain, but he still managed a forced smile in her direction as he left her side, following their brief confrontation. The smile was made even more comically inappropriate by the ultra violet light which was flickering on and off exaggerating the whiteness of his teeth against his olive skin. He was clearly displeased as he strode past Pete who had been standing next to Selma, completely ignoring him and rendering him invisible. He nevertheless made a dignified exit from the disco.

Despite this occurrence, which in truth amounted to little more than a disregarded sideshow during the afternoon's proceedings, the group of friends continued to respond to the music, displaying their youthful energy and irrepressible zest for life. Indeed, there was a pleasing disconnect between the atmosphere in the disco and the communal melancholy which seemed, at that time, to be dominating the streets and the very residences of the city they inhabited. Young couples danced closely, chatted happily and canoodled in dark corners, avoiding the camera flashes of the club's photographer. All in all, they exuded a new found freedom afforded to them in a modern day venue set within a traditional and restrictive society.

It was well known, during the late nineteen sixties, that the youth of Western Europe were in revolt The promised world revolution, manifest in such cataclysmic events as the Paris student riots; the anti Vietnam War movement; the summer of love and the Prague Spring, had, quite frankly, failed to materialise. A sizeable number of young people in the western nations, together with their older mentors, had firmly believed that they could change the world, release the oppressed from the shackles of the old order, and replace it with a global society based on equality and love. However, it was less a case of "Something in the Air" and more a case of "We won't get fooled again" in which two years after Thunderclap Newman's classic, Roger Daltrey et al seemed to draw the curtain down on the promised Revolution. Despite the cries of "Organise!" this attempt to unite the world in a Marxist Utopia was beginning to lose its way, even as the youth of Turkey were themselves starting to dance to a new tune.

Thus, as the year of nineteen sixty nine drew to a close, American soldiers remained in Vietnam in their tens of thousands, Communist Russia had crushed the Czechs, in fact the Establishment in most countries of the globe continued to enjoy the benefits that centuries of being in power had bestowed upon them.

Meanwhile, at the Hydromel Diskotek, the privileged youth of Istanbul continued to boogie to the Beatles' "Revolution". The lyrics rang out, "....if you go waving your pictures of Chairman Mao, you ain't gonna make it with anyone anyhow." This strongly implied that the youth of China had taken a direction that Lennon and McCartney hoped the rest of the world would avoid. Their hope was in vain, as posters bearing Chairman Mao's likeness were clearly to be seen at just about every demonstration in the so called "free world".

And as for the youth of Turkey? Despite their affluent backgrounds, youngsters like those in the Hydromel were slowly beginning to attempt to eradicate the staleness that persisted in so many aspects of their daily lives. They believed that they were pushing back the gloom and letting in the light, at least until the boys were ready to take over their fathers' businesses or the girls could be married off to those who possessed sufficient dowries. The so called revolution was yet to reach Turkey. Unfortunately, its eventual arrival during the following year was to result in a decade of conflict, bloodshed and despair. The reaction to this upheaval would lead to periods of political instability, martial law and near financial ruin for the country.

All over the world, the impetus of ideological change was slowing down while the Establishment and monied interests attempted to regain what they would see as the moral high ground. However, it was debatable whether or not they had ever lost the high ground, moral or otherwise. According to Pete's politics, the revolution remained to him something quite whimsical and preached, to a large extent, by people he personally could not stand. And that was especially true of the pseudo Marxists in his college. In addition, free love, he felt was a sixties myth which on occasions, he was actually able to buy into. Nevertheless, the music that seemed to be heralding the imminent fall of capitalism, replacing it with a new world order, had hitherto provided him with the most massively inspiring soundtrack to his adolescent years.

The DJ in the club where he was now dancing with Selma and her friends seemed to favour Western rock music, and the next song to be played took Pete back to the eponymous Summer of Love of 1967. It was Procol Harum's "Whiter Shade of Pale". In one impulsive movement, he took Selma's hand and led her to the dance floor. He wrapped his arms around her waist and to his delight, she placed her hands on his shoulders. Together they shuffled in time with the slow tempo. Allowing the mellifluous tune to wash over them. Life for Pete, for those few rapturous minutes, took on a much sweeter aspect.

The number drew to an end with Gary Brooker & co's legendary keyboard solo and the faded out chorus known by this time to millions across the world. For some reason best known to himself, Pete continued to hold on to the young Turkish girl in his arms, imbibing her sweet aroma, her bodily warmth and the astonishing beauty of those deep brown eyes. Instinctively, he kissed her forehead. A look of surprise crossed her face which was swiftly dowsed by a kindly smile. No boy of her own nationality would have dared, nor would she have displayed any pleasure she surely would have felt, as this would have amounted to what Turks referred to as "giving face". Thus the progression from boy meets girl to boyfriend and girlfriend was a somewhat slower process than might generally take place in England, for example. There, a coupling could be on the cards within five minutes of two people becoming acquainted. Although as far as Pete and most of his friends were concerned, make that five hours/days/months.... delete as applicable.

By way of contrast, "Bad Moon Rising" leapt on to the turntable to end Pete's reverie. He removed his hands from Selma's waist, then attempted another kiss, this time on the lips as he had clearly fallen under her spell. But this was not the college dance, or even the church social. She jerked herself away from him but much to his amazement, took his hand and led him back to the group's table. The others appeared oblivious to Pete's brazen act and the hand holding was viewed as merely friendly. She turned to look Pete in the eye and spoke softly in tones just about audible above the dance music.

"I must leave now. I have to be home by six o' clock." Pete consulted his watch and noticed it was only five fifteen. She continued, very softly, "Will you walk to Taksim with me? We can pass through Gezi Park." Pete retrieved his jacket and Selma's long black coat from the cloakroom. They bade farewell to the others and made their way through the exit and along the path which lead to Gezi Park.

The aforementioned park was one of the last remaining areas of greenery alongside the avenue that runs between Taksim and Şişli via Harbiye. In former times, this avenue would have been lined with mulberry trees, domains of the silk worm. In spring time they would bear clumps of luscious berries. During the nineteen sixties, axes were wielded and bulldozers moved in, along with power cranes and construction workers, to create mundane apartment buildings, described by Orhan Pamuk as being in the "international style" and with "huge windows and walls covered with ugly mosaic tiles."[4]

In the streets outside, some dimly glowing municipal lamps were attempting in vain to push back the encroaching darkness of late afternoon. Traffic whirred and hooted along the busy street in both directions as Pete and Selma crossed over the road leading to Beşiktaş, past the Hilton Hotel. They then entered the dingy pathways of Gezi Park which were illumined every fifty yards or so by pools of light from low set lamps on each side. Silhouettes of ragged vegetation were also discernible, bordering a maze of concrete footpaths. By day, the park was frequented by portly, middle aged men seeking a blow job from young gipsy girls, some no more than eleven years of age and who charged one lira a time. At this time of day, even with the dusk providing an excellent screen for those uglier aspects of Gezi Park, the girls and their clients were conspicuous by their absence. Now, the almost full but luminescent moon and accompanying stars provided a romantic backdrop, as they had always done, long before the advent of Hollywood movies. There were, however, some troublesome clouds that insisted on shrouding the moonshine every so often, blown across by a gentle breeze on a damp but warmer than usual winter evening.

Pete took Selma's hand as they progressed through a sylvan oasis and there was no sign of dissent from her. On the contrary, she drew her body closer to him as they walked. Soon, a very conveniently placed park bench came into view just off the path to their right and below a tall, bare limbed tree of a variety indistinguishable in the darkness.

"Shall we sit down for a little while? Or perhaps you may not be able to get home from here by six."

Why was Pete answering his own questions? He never believed that this beauty would consent to sit by him unchaperoned in a park at night. His last few words revealed a voice trembling somewhat with a mixture of doubt and anticipation. What did he

4. Op cit.

think was going to happen in the next few minutes?

"Yes I have time."

Selma sat herself daintily on the bench and Pete joined her, positioning himself against her thighs and gently placing an arm round her shoulder. Would he dare? Impulsively he kissed her full on the lips and she held him there, drawing him into a long embrace and sucking his lower lip, much as Hanife had done. The moment turned into a perfect stasis. It was as if the whole world around them had come to a standstill, born of a young couple whose arms, eyes and lips were for no-one but themselves. The kisses became more searching, more sensual with the sheer joy of them discovering a mutual passion for each other.

"I didn't know English boys were so passionate!" Pete disengaged himself momentarily. God, she had tasted so sweet.

Pete was very pleasantly surprised at the effect he was obviously having on her, and was about to kiss her once more, when just as suddenly she shocked him with a harsh whisper.

"Oh no, stop! That man over there, he is looking at us!"

Her eyes were wide open with anger, disgust and fright. He followed the direction in which Selma was staring. There, not twenty metres distant was the scarcely discernible shape of a man, more wraith like than of this earth. He was sitting on another park bench across the patchy grass and appeared to have his right hand inside the top of his trousers. With his next glance towards the lovers, instead of gaining inspiration for his self congress, he realised that the game was up. Then just as if he really was a ghost, rather than a mere mortal of flesh and blood, he disappeared into the night without a sound.

"Dirty bastard! Pete spluttered. You know in England we call them Peeping Toms."

"Pipping toms," she repeated, giggling and looking clearly relieved that the mystery masturbater had not tried to engage with them. Apparently, snogging in public was not allowed in Turkey, but then neither was what he was doing.

He had to take this beautiful, friendly young girl with her sweet kisses in his arms once more and after more embraces, the couple continued their walk through Gezi Park. Pete became concerned that Selma would be late, as they found themselves stopping every twenty paces or so for more mouth to mouth contact. It was as if their passion needed constant topping up and they were relishing every minute together. When they reached Taksim Square, they hurried into the real world of noisy traffic, shouting vendors and a certain father awaiting his teenage daughter at home, ready to dispense rough justice should she arrive back late. Fortunately, her home in Gümüşsuyu was a minute's quick paced walk from Taksim, and Selma was not late this time. They said their goodbyes and Selma soon disappeared into the cobbled street that led to her parents' apartment block. Pete, ached with a yearning to see her again, then he realised, he was actually feeling quite hungry. He headed in the direction of the many cafés and sandwich bars on Taksim Square.

He knew that the emptiness that was growing inside him was not just hunger and he as missing Selma already. How would things pan out. To use an expression he often heard and now understood, what was their *kismet*? Was she now his girlfriend? What would be the reaction of the local populace when they would be seen out together. That was if they were to go out together again. In addition, how should they conduct themselves at the school? One consolation was that at least she was not in his teaching group. She was seventeen, the school was private so perhaps he would not be accused of professional misconduct. An earlier than hoped for return to England was the last thing he required.

The following Tuesday afternoon there were, as usual, no classes. In a certain basement flat in Harbiye, Selma was to be found lying in Pete's arms on the bed that only a fortnight ago had been put to similar use by Pete and Hanife during another of their Hassan-approved trysts. The previous Saturday, Selma had managed to arrive home virtually on the dot of six pm, thus avoiding any punitive actions from her father. She had, earlier that day, accepted Pete's invitation to go back with him to the flat for a glass of tea and hopefully to carry on where they had left off in Gezi Park after the disco.

Within the confines of this love nest, Pete sensed that something beautiful was about to commence in his life. Something even more delightful than sex with Hanife, which to be honest had become somewhat routine of late. It had always been enjoyable but meaningless and he had accepted that situation. Fortunately for Pete, Ekrem, the tea boy from the school who lived in that room, had secured employment on one of the Bosphorus ferries. This meant that he was away for most of the daytime and it was his bed that provided the venue for Pete's amorous activities.

Selma, a respectable young daughter of a reputable Turkish family, did not seem particularly phased by the drab and dusty appearance of the room they were in. After all, the bed was clean. Coincidentally, it was the same room that Pete had woken up in all those weeks ago, broken in spirit and with an uncertain future. Pete, for his part, would like to have to read the girl's thoughts at this point in time. In truth, though, he did not even attempt to do so. If she was at all nervous about this meeting, she certainly did not show it. They were able to resume the passionate embraces from Saturday, this time without an audience.

Pete was falling in love and he suspected that she was beginning to feel the same way about him. However, just in case he had any thoughts of easing Selma of her virginity, he was soon apprised of the utmost importance for a Turkish girl to retain her maidenhood until her wedding night. On such an auspicious occasion, many families even went so far as to place a white cloth under the girl, when the couple went to bed on their wedding night, so her father would, the following morning, be able to see for himself the bloodstains from her broken hymen.

Pudding Shop

Three weeks after his return to work, Pete received some papers in a brown envelope, together with a note from PTT – the Turkish Post Office. He was informed that he had a parcel from England waiting for him at the city's main post office. Kemal happened to be visiting Vefbi bey that day and offered to show Pete how to get to the main *"postane"* . He also suggested that they should combine the trip with an afternoon out in the old city and a visit to a café restaurant near the Blue Mosque which was always packed with Europeans. The plan was for them to proceed to the post office afterwards.

"Most of them are hippies on their way to Afghanistan and Nepal." Kemal was in tourist guide mode.

"Strange choice of destinations. We had hoped to reach India at some point but meant to avoid Afghanistan. Nepal would seem a step too far."

"They go to Nepal for the Buddhism and Afghanistan for the *esrar - hash hash*," added Kemal sagely.

They journeyed by dolmuş, descending through cobbled roads to Karaköy, then across Galata Bridge into Eminönü. There, Kemal was kind enough to point out some of the sights Pete had missed before such as Yeni Cami, or New Mosque, so named as it was built in the late seventeenth century. Just beyond it was the Egyptian or Spice Market, long and narrow, receding into the distance under its ancient, tiled roof cover. Ten minutes later, due to lighter traffic that day, their dolmuş drew up within sight of the Blue Mosque. They alighted and walked past a row of snack bars and kebab houses until they reached the Lale Restaurant, better known to all as The Pudding Shop.

185

The first thing Pete noticed was the small groups of young European women, flitting in and out of the restaurant and crossing to the other side of the street. They each seemed to display an air of nervous anticipation, impatience even. They were mostly dressed in cotton tee shirts with large band logos on the front or tie dyed in vivid colours. Some were wearing calico blouses tied in a knot at the midriff, sheepskin jackets, and some were in long paisley pattern skirts. There were even those in very short denim skirts that few Turkish girls would ever be seen wearing. None of them looked as if they were particularly enjoying life at this moment in time.

Just as Pete and Kemal were about to enter the Pudding Shop, the usual traffic sounds in the street were supplanted by the roar of a motor cycle. It pulled up next to one of the hippie girls and she promptly climbed on to the pillion seat behind the rider. Pete noticed that the girl seem agitated, willing the rider to move off as she bounced her ample bottom up and down on the pillion seat. The man in front of her was Turkish, aged around thirty, and he spoke to the girl in German. After kicking a few revs from the engine, he lifted his right foot on to the machine and the pair took off along the busy street in the direction of Beyazit.

Pete joined Kemal, who had already entered the restaurant, and as he closed the door behind him. He noticed another motor cycle drawing up across the street and yet another girl climbing on to the back. He had to ask. Perhaps Kemal could enlighten him. But not just now. Inside the Pudding Shop, crowds of hippies and other travellers were seated either in large booths or on couches similar to the ones he had seen in the house in Sarıyer. To Pete's delight, Jimi Hendrix was audible over the somewhat scratchy sound system, though he could not recall the last time he had heard "Voodoo Chile" played so quietly. Perhaps it was because there were alternative sounds, notably from the far end of the restaurant where a young girl with blonde hair down her back, a dead ringer for Joni Mitchell, sat singing a folksy tune, accompanying herself on a battered nylon string guitar.

The laid back mood engendered by the live music briefly reminded him of his visits to the Chelmsford Arts Lab earlier that summer. This was where a motley assortment of teenagers and twenty somethings met in a large above-ground air raid shelter in Galleywood to recite their poetry, sing some songs, many of which were their own work. They would also attempt to put the world to rights. Pete himself had performed two numbers from the album "The Rock Machine Turns You On" during his first visit. He was well received but when he sang the final lines of Roy Harper's "You Don't Need Money" which were:

"... except of course for scoring on a sunny day",

there was a second's awkward silence, then loud laughter all round, followed by applause. The reason for this response soon became clear when he was informed that the Arts Lab had been raided by police the previous week and – surprise, surprise - quantities of cannabis resin and a few sugar cubes had been seized from some of the members.

No such problems at the Pudding Shop, it would appear, as Pete was unable to detect one sniff of hash. The Çolpan brothers who ran the Pudding Shop, may have been tolerant towards their customers, but there were limits, he supposed. Pete and Kemal approached the food counter. This was a lengthy expanse of glass, encasing an impressive array of pastries and desserts, not to mention the brightly coloured meat and vegetable dishes on view further along. It was not quite the chocolate heaven Pete had visited with the others in Thessalonika (and on which they spent spent many of their drachmas.), but he was by now familiar enough with such culinary delights as *baklava* –nut and syrup infused pastries, *tel kadayif* - the shredded wheat- like dish drenched in syrup; *sütlaç* or creamy cold rice pudding; and *supangles* – chocolate pudding. But then he noticed a white pudding in a four inch wide glass dish topped with cinnamon. It resembled a blancmange.

"What's that one, Kemal?"

"Oh that is called *tavuk göğsü*. It is minced chicken breasts with rice, flour and milk."

"I'll have that."

Once they were seated, a young fair haired male hippie came

and joined them. He was wearing a cotton grandad shirt like Pete's but black not purple. He also wore blue denim jeans, matching denim jacket and light brown sandals. Without so much as a "mind if I join you", he began speaking in good English with a German accent, but less guttural than Walter's.

"Hi guys, I am Johan from Austria. How's it all going?"

Kemal had always come across as a friendly, self effacing fellow with a benevolent nature. These qualities allowed him to accept new experiences and acquaintances of any nationality with apparent ease. In this instance, he became a fascinated listener as Pete and Johan seemed to hit it off virtually straight away. They spent the next few minutes, sharing edited highlights of their travels to date. It transpired that Johan had caught a bus from Vienna to Istanbul and planned to stay in the city a month or so before moving on to Afghanistan and exploring the Silk Road. At the same time, Pete found a way of unwrapping the whole unvarnished saga of their ill-starred world tour, to which the young Austrian nodded in a sage, non judgemental manner.

"It's all good experience – even the negatives – which you learn from and grow to know yourself."

It sounded like a kind of platitude: a platitude from outer space from a not so angry young man. Ultimately, it was hard to disagree with Johan. Perhaps more importantly, as hunger was gnawing at him, Pete decided to order the *tavuk göğsü* and he would accompany that with some Turkish coffee, *orta şerkerli* or medium sweet. Kemal ordered, and the food duly arrived after a few minutes. The dessert, when he started on it, had the consistency of a blancmange with only the faintest hint of chicken breast. It was also very sweet to the taste but he found it an enjoyable culinary adventure, nonetheless. To Pete's surprise, Johan took his coffee in a larger cup and with milk. Considering the Turks blended their roasted coffee with cardamom, this surely was not the best idea. However, Johan seemed to like it. He regarded his beverage on the table in front of him.

"You know it was the Turks who first brought coffee to Vienna when they besieged our capital city and failed to capture it."

He pronounced that last piece of information with some relish but Kemal refused to be drawn in. He let out a hearty laugh.

"It's true we did not succeed in taking your city but it looks like we did some good. Did you know most of our coffee now comes from Brazil?" He added.

During this hiatus in the conversation, Pete considered that this would be an excellent opportunity to ask the question which had been nagging at the back of his mind from the moment they had arrived.

"What's going on across the street there with those girls and the motor bikes?

"Oh that." An amused expression crept across Kemal's face. He held the pose for a few seconds longer for maximum impact. Johan knew the answer but left the floor to Kemal who continued,

"You know a lot of the young people coming from west, when they get to Istanbul they get short of money. Sometimes they run out."

"Seems a common problem," interjected Pete somewhat ruefully. Kemal continued.

"If they want, they can give their blood to hospital for fifty lira a half litre."

Both Pete and Johan went to interrupt him here as both had given blood; in Pete's case, in Thessalonika, and along with his three companions. However, simultaneously, they decided not to impart that information and let Kemal continue.

"Well someone got the idea that these girls could fuck with the Turkish men for money and they would have enough to stay here for a while and maybe continue on their way, or maybe go back home. The restaurant owners will have nothing to do with it and that's why it's across the street. I hear it is mostly American, German and French girls."

"I guess that's true," interjected Pete, "if I know British girls, they'd be too busy giving it away. They probably depend on their boyfriends to get them out of the shit." Johan grinned wickedly.

"Of course, not in same way." Kemal was in on the joke. "But some men here do like fair haired European boys."

The discomfort with which Pete and Johan regarded each other following that remark, was tangible. But both ended up chortling loudly, which drew some attention from the other Pudding shop customers. Meanwhile, across the road, business continued, but in the restaurant there was a sense of camaraderie among the hippies, tourists, locals and staff alike. A pleasing air of non animosity had settled over the establishment as if this is how things had always been in that place. On the restaurant wall, just inside the entrance was a noticeboard where travellers could post personal messages, information and news of their whereabouts or intended destinations. Cards pinned to the board advertised cheap accommodation and camp sites.

Perhaps it was this very noticeboard that reminded him, but suddenly Pete remembered with a jolt about the parcel he was supposed to have collected from the main post office. Kemal had somewhere else to go now, as it was late in the day, so he started to give Pete directions to the post office. However, Johan knew of its location and offered to go with him. Evidently, he had been obliged to collect some packages sent to him from Austria the previous week.

"I should make my address the Pudding Shop. I am here often enough. I shall take you to the post office. It is a very interesting place. You will see."

They settled the bill and departed from the Pudding Shop, as the background twanging of a guitar and the warbling of a flute played them out and into the sunlit afternoon of the old city. Pete and Johan bid farewell to Kemal and they squeezed themselves on to the back seat of a *dolmuş* which was to take them to the district of Sirkeci.

Johan had not been exaggerating about the Istanbul head post office or *Büyük Postane* as it was known. Situated close to the Sirkeci Railway Station, which was the terminus for trains from Europe, it had evidently been designed in the grand style at the turn of the century. Architecturally, its cut stone and marble construction resembled one of the larger palaces, and it had a mosque attached to it. The frontage was characterised by a row of Islamic style arches, slightly pointed at the top. Pete and Johan mounted the stone stairway and entered a sizeable but musty smelling atrium, and on producing the documents he had received, Pete was ushered towards the rear of the building to the department which dealt with foreign parcels. Johan took a seat in the reception area and waited.

Once he had reached the relevant department, Pete found himself standing in front of a long, highly polished wooden counter, behind which was a scene of less than feverish activity as clerks and officials moved back and forth, none too rapidly, with packages, cardboard boxes and large brown or buff envelopes. The member of staff who attended to him had a head of short black wiry hair, an olive skin face, shaded by short stubble and the obligatory straight moustache between upper lip and nose. Stocky and slightly shorter than Pete, he addressed the Englishman politely, in halting English, and scrutinised the letters that in all probability he had himself sent. He retired to a rear office to retrieve Pete's parcel, and in his absence, Pete glanced at the shelves behind the serving area. He could not help noticing how many packages had somehow broken open and their contents spilled out. Among the items, there was a bizarre collection of packets of Indian tea, jars of Nescafé and cartons of Betty Crocker cake mix. People all over the city were expecting these. Well they were going to be disappointed. Evidently, the packages had been broken in transit and any claimants would almost certainly have to pay import taxes. That is if they ever got to receive news regarding the whereabouts of their goods.

The friendly clerk reappeared with Pete's parcel; intact thank the lord. It had been sent by his parents and apparently there was nothing to pay today. Pete returned to Johan in the atrium, feeling in himself a mixture of anticipation and puzzlement. He hadn't a clue as to the parcel's contents, so he found himself sitting on the bench beside Johan and opening it. He immediately wished he had waited. From inside the wrapping paper he pulled out two pairs of "St Michael" underpants which were styled as large briefs with a colour scheme of deckchair pattern red, blue and yellow. His face visibly reddened but his companion remained expressionless, inscrutable in fact.

"Looks like they sent you a fine jumper too. That's good because they tell me the winters here can be very cold."

He was right. In addition to the underwear was a thick cable knit beige pullover of the kind his mother had specialised in turning out almost every year since his childhood. Two pairs of medium thickness blue socks were also visible inside the package, along with a two page letter. Very thoughtful, he mused. In point of fact, it was pleasing to receive these items from home and to read of news regarding his family, friends and of course his football team. He thanked Johan for his invaluable assistance, and they made arrangements to meet up again for a drink.

"There is another café popular with westerners near the Pudding Shop called Yener's. We could get some kebab and some beer maybe next week."

As it turned out, more than two weeks were to pass before the two were able to meet again. It was now mid December and already the winds, which were slicing their way across the winter city, all the way from the Russian Steppes, were causing temperatures to plummet during the day, but especially at night. As the days began to grow darker sooner, events were unfolding in Pete's daily existence which were to impact on the rest of his life, even though he could not have been aware of this at the time. Indeed, he had once again become obsessed lately with what he felt had been detrimental occurrences not just in the present period but also in his past.

Up until the time of his enforced sojourn in this fabled Turkish city, he had found that somehow he could not shake off feelings of great anger and resentment towards certain individuals in his past whom he considered had not only disrespected him but seemed determined to cause discomfort to his very existence. Each morning as he woke up, he was in the habit of mentally running through some of the issues and negative situations that he had been dragging around like baggage for far too long. It appeared that his demons had been eagerly awaiting those moments when his mind had been at its lowest ebb. To wit, the moment of awakening. Worse still, his imagination would re-enact these issues and events, where he was mentally solving each problem, by telling him what he should have said, or actions he should have taken at the time. The latter illusory episodes would often end in imaginary, violent retribution against the perpetrators. More recently, however, just as soon as the offending memories had popped into his mind, a new hidden voice seemed to dismiss them all with some contempt. This had not been very helpful in itself, but perhaps he was evolving a kind of coping mechanism.

So what were these problems and was he the only person on God's earth experiencing them? Certainly, as a boy he had been bullied by the older kids in and out of school. But who hadn't been bullied by the older kids in and out of school? In adolescence, he had been let down and betrayed by male and female acquaintances alike, often with accompanying cruel taunts and remarks. Nothing uncommon there. At senior school, some of his peers had shown open hostility towards him, ganging up on him at playtimes and making his second year a living hell. But in that case, maybe he should not have been such a bully himself, or, indeed, constantly attempting to take over the role of class clown and failing even at that.

Then there was also the question of the school he attended. Educational snobbery was rife in his town as the local boys' grammar school and the girls' high school considered themselves superior to his institute, simply because its title bore the word "technical". Get over it! Murmured the hidden voice. Anyway, as even those bigots should have been aware, you still had to pass the eleven plus to earn a place at his school.

However, regarding more recent events, the fact that he had been so easily relieved of his money on that fateful day in an Istanbul alleyway had, for a while, filled him with a need for the cruellest vengeance. He lost count of the times he had relived that scenario, and at the crucial point had managed to extricate himself with money and pride intact. But he had not, had he? More importantly though, over time, his hostile thoughts towards the perpetrator had all but dissipated. After all, the outrage had hardly left him begging on the streets. His comparatively spartan existence that the crime had led him to may even have been helping to put his priorities in place. Nevertheless, he often kept an eye open for Izzet, in case he bumped into him somewhere. And there would be a reckoning, to be sure!

In the smoky but relaxed atmosphere of a Taksim *meyhane* – or Turkish pub, Pete surveyed his pint of Tekel lager, which was a beer brewed in a government facility, cheap in price and somewhat better than bland in taste. The drink had slurped over the sides of the glass on to a rickety round table of metal and Formica. The *meyhane* was thick with tobacco smoke and the air heavy with the odour of sweat and Turkish cigarettes. The pint of Tekel was gold, cold and got you drunk, eventually. Was it the haunting presence of those matters in his mind that was causing him to shiver in this draughty bar? He knew it was not the drink, as he was by now used to chilled lager. After a couple of rounds, as conversation began to flow between the two, Pete found that he was able to confide in Johan who turned out to be a kindly and sympathetic listener. Johan got to listen to something more like edited highlights of Pete's concerns, both past and present, to include the way he had been treated by some of his students at Vefbi bey's school and his blossoming relationship with Selma. When he had finished, Pete added the caveat that in recent months his anger and resentment appeared to be abating and he was beginning to feel less like one of life's victims. Johan regarded him intently.

"All this anger has been very negative and made you feel bad. Your time in this city has allowed you to take a step back and have a more balanced view of things. You have become more philosophical towards those things which troubled you. It is a sign you are growing up."

That was Johan's take on Pete's diatribe. He was perhaps no more than a year older than his English acquaintance but seemed to be wiser and with more of a handle on life. Perhaps his recent experiences and his travels had helped to bring this about.

"Shall I order another beer for us? Listen, I have been asked to do some people a favour and perhaps you can help me. I have been speaking with some hippies at the Pudding shop. Many of them are going to be here over Christmas and they would very much like to have a tree in the place. Think about it" And with that. Johan went off to order more drinks.

"Nice idea but where are we going to find one of those." Pete asked, as soon as Johan had returned. He was not only relieved by the change of subject but was also feeling distinctly more relaxed now.

"There are some Armenians and Greeks living in the city and lots of other Christians. They celebrate Christmas here. We must ask them where they buy their Christmas trees. There are many Christians in Cihangir and Gümüşsuyu.

A sweet pain jabbed him in the abdomen at the mention of Gümüşsuyu, as he was reminded of Selma. He wondered what she was doing at that moment. Probably at home with her parents, or listening to some music on the radio. Then in an instant but inexplicable flash of memory, a picture appeared in Pete's mind of the road to Sarıyer. Why had he suddenly thought of his visits to Lale and her family? Was it because Selma had teased him about her? That was obviously the connection. But now it was the Sarıyer road itself he remembered. About halfway between suburban Istanbul and the Black Sea, it ran between two high grassy banks and on one side there was a plantation of fir trees; proper spruces. Clearly this was one of the places that supplied Christian Turks with their Christmas trees.

"I've got it!" Pete almost shouted this and Johan very nearly knocked over his beer. Pete continued, oblivious. "We'll need to catch a mini bus going to Sarıyer then keep our eyes peeled for a fir tree plantation. On the right, I think."

"It's getting darker. It will be difficult to see but lets do this."

"Better still, I noticed that quite a lot of smaller trees were growing on the bank just outside the fence. If we can remove one of those, unseen, then we won't have to pay for it will we?"

Before they could depart on their mission, Pete suggested they should collect his commando knife from the flat. It was a five minute walk to his abode and once inside, he fished his knife out from his rucksack. Strange that he should choose such a lethal instrument when the others in the expedition group had all opted for sheath knives.

"We're not doing an armed robbery," he joked, " but we can use this to dig the tree out of the ground."

Johan grabbed a newspaper that he had seen lying on the table.

"We will wrap the tree in this to make it look like we bought it."

Fortunately, minibuses heading for Sarıyer were fairly frequent at that time of day and were filling up quickly enough to make for a prompt departure. Progress out of the city centre was as slow as ever, but in less than half an hour they were passing between the grassy banks Pete had recalled. Sure enough, they were able to discern the small silhouettes of spruce trees which stood out against the evening skies at various points along the bank. They disembarked from the minibus at a point roughly a hundred yards beyond the plantation. It was dark enough for them to make their way unseen to a slight ridge halfway up the bank, where a few small spruces had somehow escaped from the main crop, put down roots and were clinging to the hard earth under tussocky grass which grew to a height of about six inches or so. Despite the gloom, they were able to select a likely looking tree which had grown to a height of three feet with a two foot spread tapering at the top, as all good spruces should. A real Christmas tree!

Both Pete and Johan were forced to lie flat on the dampening grass as the road below them was still busy. Fortunately, the traffic was moving past them fairly quickly. Nevertheless, they were both wary of being caught in the headlights whilst carrying out their felonious activities. As he carved away at the tree roots with his commando knife, Pete looked out into the night skies. It was tedious work as he had to cut near the base of the tree, where the roots were thickest, otherwise their prize would have been too bulky to carry back with them. He paused in his work for a brief rest and Johan took over.

Lying on his back now but still keeping low, Pete was able to observe the masses of stars above him, so dense and numerous, they resembled skeins on a puddle of cracked ice. These heavenly phenomena were quite unlike those back home but he was, after all, a long way further south. People would often accuse him of having his head in the clouds but in truth he was more of a stargazer. Ever since he was a young child, living in green belt countryside, he had marvelled at the numerous shiny pinpoints of light in the uninterrupted blackness of a night sky. It was so dark then, you could lose yourself on the river bank, cross a cornfield unobserved and snog your girlfriend - equally unobserved - in shadowy woodlands. It was a pure darkness, almost indigo in hue, with the only other light being provided by a familiar moon in its various phases. Then in the late sixties, a sports complex had been built about a mile away at the top of the Wid Valley. As well as playing fields, a set of tennis courts had been established which were illuminated by powerful floodlights each night until about ten pm. The resultant light pollution had eliminated all but a few stars from view until after they had been switched off. Somehow, even though at that time he was only spending his college vacations at home, the beloved area of his upbringing seemed to lose some of its charm.

The spectacle above him presented the same firmament but with some different stars on show. Whole galaxies, it seemed, were massed against a darkened backdrop and then he caught sight of a tiny red speck in the heavens, like a small garnet on black silk. To his utter joy, he realised this must be the planet Mars and he was actually viewing it for the first time in his life. How he wished for a telescope or binoculars. Then suddenly, immediately in front of him he saw Johan stiffen where he lay and put his finger to his mouth. Then he uttered a curt "Sh" and flattened himself even lower against the ground. Turning his head to look back along the bank, Pete could just make out a swaying yellow light just fifty yards distant, which certainly did not look as though it had anything to do with movements of astral bodies. Turning on to his front, he also flattened himself behind an adjacent tree.

197

Soon, a human shape carrying a large torch or lamp could be seen ambling in a leisurely gait along the path below. He was wearing a brown uniform with a matching peaked cap, and Pete recognised him as a *Bekçi* or night watchman. He was a member of the lowest paid unit in the city's feared police force. Most of them were aged fifty years or over. The situation was, nevertheless, a dangerous one. If he spotted them, they would have to be quick on their toes. If they were caught, they would certainly be handed over to the green uniformed crime police, who were notorious for beating the soles of your feet first and asking the questions later. The watchman plodded ever onwards and the glow of his cigarette could be discerned in the darkness. He drew level with the would be tree snafflers and stopped. As he did so, he drew a whistle out of his pocket, removed his cigarette and blew a single ear shattering blast. The game was up.

The tree robbers' situation was hardly improved when the brown uniformed officer of the law began a sweep of the bank above him with his torch. However, as the beam travelled to and fro, it failed to pick out two sets of foreign heads and legs protruding from two sets of errant firs. This was probably due to the long grass and partly perhaps to the Bekçi's poor eyesight which must surely not have been A1. Another blast on his whistle and he was ready to continue his patrol of the municipality of Emirgan's crime ridden slopes. He must also been hearing impaired, as his ears definitely failed to pick up two heavy sighs of relief from just above his head.

As the speck of yellow light gradually faded into the distance, like a mischievous sprite returning to his dark lair before the onset of dawn, Pete retrieved his knife and once more set to work on the roots. Within a few minutes, he was able to twist and manoeuvre his prize out of the earth. Johan proceeded to wrap the tree in the newspaper he had brought, then they slithered down the bank and struck out along the footpath which ran parallel to the road in the direction of Istanbul. They hailed a passing minibus and set off on their return journey. The passengers seemed highly amused at the sight of two young foreigners struggling with their awkward, somewhat bulky package.

As they clambered aboard, Pete could not help but notice a young lady seated near the front of the minibus about whom terms such as "glamorous", "stunningly attractive" and "doe eyed beauty" may comfortably have been applied without seeming clichéd. He was utterly fascinated by her. He sat himself down two places behind the girl and was joined by his companion. Neither could take their eyes off her and neither could resist commenting.

"Now that's what I call gorgeous." Pete actually shocked himself momentarily with his opening remark, as he recalled that was exactly how Sam would have put it. He remembered Sam as being just like Alfie in the eponymous film, referring to females as "it" and "that". What was that all about?

"Lovely hair colour and so pretty face," replied Johan. " But I expect she has a boyfriend."

"Or maybe more than one. She'll be popular alright, but most of these girls pretend to play hard to get." Pete was aware that he may have been giving a little too much away concerning his relationship with Selma.

"Because she is so beautiful, I expect she can take her pick."

"She won't let any bloke get his leg over her yet. She'll wait until she is married."

"I wonder how far she goes now."

Pete felt he knew the possible answer to his friend's speculative query, but stopped short of giving a response, as the afternoons spent with Selma bounced joyfully back into his mind. Best to say nothing. Instead, the most thoughtful and intelligent reply he could muster was:

"Bet she'll be great when she does eventually get it on."

Their discussion of the virtues of Turkish femininity was entirely brazen and conducted without the slightest fear of them being understood, due to the language barrier inside that minibus. They soon tired of talking about the girl in front of them and both seemed to fall into a fatigue brought on by their exertions and near apprehension at the fir tree plantation. None of their fellow passengers paid any more heed to them, or even the bulky package they had brought with them with newspaper wrapped around its roots. They were two Christians in a cosmopolitan city purchasing a Christmas tree in December. Nothing unusual about that.

Eventually, their transport drew up in a dimly lit Istanbul side street that Pete did not recognise. He realised, in some panic, that they had reached their destination, as the driver and all the passengers were clambering out. But this was certainly not Taksim Square. The driver shouted out "Tarlabaşı!" and stepped down on to the pavement. Pete and Johan also made their exit and then stood in the street staring at one another and their body language almost screamed, "Where the hell are we?" Pete broke the silence. Rather louder than he intended, he voiced his concern:

"Oh fuck! How do we get to Taksim from here?"

In that instant, the attractive girl, who had been the subject of their discourse during the return journey, turned to them, and in perfectly phrased English, with the hint of an accent, declaimed,

"You must walk along that street for two hundred metres. Turn left and after a hundred metres turn right and you will see Taksim Square in front of you."

Her facial expression was deadpan. She did not wait for them to thank her. She just turned on her heels and took off in the opposite direction to the one they had to take. Meanwhile, the two young Europeans looked down towards the ground, as if mentally urging it to open up in front of them. She must have understood every word they had spoken about her. Five minutes later, they were back in the *meyhane* where, for a little while longer, they drank their beers in silence.

An Istanbul Winter

Christmas arrived in Istanbul; more as a date in the calendar than a festive occasion enjoyed by all. However, in a country where little or no importance was attached to Christmas and its festivities, Pete was astonished to see some decorative lights appearing in various parts of the city. Though rather less surprisingly, they were in evidence around the Roman Catholic and Greek Orthodox churches. Ironically, St Nicholas, the model for the modern Santa Claus, hailed from a district about seventy five miles to the south east. He was, Pete was informed, from the city of Nicea, nowadays known as Iznik. However, that was long before the Islamic Turks appeared in Asia Minor.

He was also informed that some Turkish families also celebrated Christmas but how they did so remained a mystery to him, except for the fact that in many areas of Istanbul Christians and Moslems coexisted peacefully together and shared some of each other's festivals. Suffice it to say that Jesus was regarded as a prophet of Islam and the date of his birth, however erroneous, would have been seen as an important event. Unfortunately, there had been rumblings and dark references from some of the populace about creeping westernisation, of which this was just another example.

For Pete, the usual celebrations would not of course be possible this year. In fact, this was a truly strange sensation for him. He could not work out why he was not feeling more profoundly nostalgic on his first ever Christmas away from his family. After all, it was always a joyous occasion, eagerly looked forward to. Certainly during his childhood years, it did finally dawn on him from the age of two and a half, that his stock of toys and sweets seemed to increase massively in one fell swoop – but only on one particular day of the year. Once the secret got out that a certain rotund white bearded gentleman in red, propelling a reindeer hauled sleigh through space and time, loaded with presents, lovingly and decoratively wrapped, was actually going to land on his rooftop, shimmy down his chimney and drop off a number of those presents, then sleep for the little boy became well nigh impossible.

There was also the indescribable thrill of waking up at six pm and finding it difficult to move one's feet. And why? Because they were weighed down by a football sock stuffed with small gifts. Breakfast always seemed to consist of cold meats and pickles on those special mornings. He and his sister would sit down next to two enormous white paper sacks bearing pictures of Santa Claus – who must surely have been back in Greenland by then. They were surrounded by family members with their own smaller piles of gifts on the table, all eager to see the joy on the kids' faces as they unwrapped their presents, taking their turns as patiently as they were able to manage, given the thrill of this occasion. As he matured from childhood into adolescence, his pile of presents also became smaller, and the three days on which the family Christmas was centred usually became lost to him in an alcoholic haze, together with food consumption of titanic proportions.

On his first Christmas Day in Istanbul, Pete and Brian had for some reason decided to visit a hamam in Galatasaray. Also, they had somehow managed to smuggle in a bottle of Thracian white wine which they consumed whilst perched on steaming slabs of marble dressed in Turkish towels. Later, the Harbiye household did mange to go out for an evening meal, accompanied by Kemal. However, they were unable to find a restaurant that served roast Turkey. This of course was another irony, as that well known guest of so many Christmas lunch tables was comparatively rare in the country from which it had taken its name. Indeed the Turkish for this creature was Hindi Kuş or Indian bird. The party made do with kebabs.

Christmas was followed by two weeks of freezing weather

that presented the city with an entirely new white coverlet. This cold snap brought with it a change to the urban landscape both in appearance and atmosphere. Perhaps it was a kind of reminder to the majority of the city's inhabitants of their historic origins in the Steppes, east of the Caucasus Mountains. A kind of stoicism set in, with people struggling through blizzards and thick snow across the city's hilltops. All vehicles were required by law to have chains attached to their tyres and the cobbled thoroughfares soon became coated in filthy grey slush.

One morning in mid January, Pete woke up to prepare himself for another day's work at the languages school. It was early in the new term and the daily walk to Sira Selviler had, for the past fortnight been miserable, tricky and indeed dangerous at times. To make matters worse, he had been unable to see Selma during this time, as she had been kept at home after school hours away from the snow. Furthermore, she was always collected by one of her sisters. As he drew back the curtains to glance at the familiar scene of apartment blocks and the *bakkal* across the street, he noticed that something was missing. The snow. It had disappeared overnight and all that was left was a wet covering of pavements and cobblestones which reflected a meagre sunshine on a mild winter's morning. The melted snow was now dribbling along gutters on both sides of the street towards the nearest drains which fortunately for all had not as yet become blocked.

Halfway through his breakfast, a flash of memory caught Pete off guard and he suddenly burst out with, "Oh fuck!" The others looked up from their bread, white cheese and black olives and Roger, almost choking with mirth exclaimed, "My oh my, such language from one so young. Most unbecoming!"

"I've just remembered, I'm in charge from today. I'd better get down there."

Roger's expression of merriment quickly changed to a frown. Yes, it was certainly the case that Pete had been elevated to the position of temporary headmaster. Vefbi would be going into hospital and Pete had been asked to run the school, much to Roger's annoyance. Although he claimed that he generally eschewed responsibility, he felt that as the eldest of the two, he should have been given the role. This delegation which would turn out to be purely symbolic, helped to compound Roger's resentment of Pete who was earning substantially more wages than him due to his teaching qualifications. To most, it seemed logical that Pete should run things for a couple of weeks. Pete failed to notice Roger's malevolent glance in his direction, as he was too busy gulping down his tea and grabbing a few last mouthfuls before setting off for work in more than the usual haste.

It was a known fact that Vefbi had asked Pete to take over the day to day running of the school while he was in hospital for an operation on his gall bladder. Apparently, gallstones was the most prevalent health issue among Turkish people. To be frank, this was not to be an onerous task, as all the young teacher had to do, in addition to his teaching duties, was to make sure lessons were running smoothly and interviewing prospective students. The secretary and her assistant would continue to handle the administrative tasks.

Another responsibility had also been handed to him, which gave him more cause for concern. This one came courtesy of Vefbi's cousin Hassan, who would be visiting family in Anatolia during the following two weeks or so. Sadly, Hanife would be left without her usual "nourishment" as Hassan had put it. In a hushed conversation in the deserted office, during the previous week, Hassan had wondered if Pete would be so kind as to visit his house when their son was out and make sure his lovely wife was satisfied. She was to call him at the school to arrange the first visit. An awkward scenario was unfolding before him. Although he had continued to meet Hanife, even after commencing his romance with Selma, this had only happened on three occasions recently and he was beginning to wrestle with his conscience about the developing situation. Suffice it to say that if Selma ever discovered he was seeing another woman, let alone his boss's cousin-in-law, their embryonic love affair would be brought to a swift end. On the other hand, he did not wish to let Hassan down.

These thoughts and concerns coursed their way through Pete's mind as he made his way to work. Meanwhile, he had a school to run. The other teachers at the European languages school, who were in fact Turkish, had abandoned some of their tried and tested methods of learning by rote and repetition. Although Pete would not admit it, he had a feeling that they had taken their lead from him in adopting a stricter approach and making their lessons more rigorous and detailed. For instance, they had abandoned the practice of making their classes mechanically repeat nonsensical sentences such as, "Ali cut Ayşe with a sharp knife." The subject, object, verb syntax was correct, and there was a useful adjective in "sharp" but he had felt it necessary to point out to the teacher concerned that the verb needed to be "stabbed" not "cut". He had not cared to ponder too long on the sinister ramifications of that all too brief narrative.

A new decade had begun, but to Pete it felt no different from the last one. He continued to be domicile at the basement flat but with only two others; Roger and Brian. Walter had gone to stay at Vefbi's home to work on some architectural designs for refurbishing the house. With Vefbi in hospital, he could get on with the job he had been asked to do in peace, away from the great man fussing over some outrageous ideas for replacing the façade, for example. Once Vefbi had returned from hospital, he could approve the plans and work would commence in early spring.

In this way, life continued, much as it had in the closing months of 1969. Pete obviously took his added responsibilities seriously but actually did not have to make one executive decision. Nor did he have the opportunity to interview any prospective students. He was also in the process of learning Turkish and found that the best way to do so was in listening to people having conversations, especially in the tea houses. In that way he was able to put certain familiar words and phrases together and attempt to use the language in shops and in taxis.

He was greatly assisted in polishing his use of the language by studying Yusuf Mardin's "Colloquial Turkish", a tome he had discovered in one of the school's store cupboards. He also immersed himself in learning about the nation's culture and

205

customs. For example there were always set statements for different occasions, such as *"Geçmiş olsun"* when someone was unwell or *"Güle güle giyim"* if a person had bought a new item of clothing. If someone was setting off on their travels, one would say *"İyi yolculuklar"*, which would be the equivalent in French of *"Bon Voyage"*. There were Turkish traditions and superstitions, such as the belief that black cats were unlucky, and putting a knife down on the table instead of handing it directly to another, as it might promote enmity between them. When people departed to travel somewhere, water was always thrown after them to ensure their safe passage and return.

However, there was one quaint custom that Pete had, since his arrival in Turkey, dismissed as superstitious nonsense. The custom was called *"fal"* and it involved fortune telling by reading the coffee grounds left in the cup after drinking. One mid morning break, he was drinking coffee, for once. He usually drank tea having not yet got used to Turkish coffee with its one third of dregs in a tiny cup. In any case, he had unintentionally washed his cup out and the secretary, who could read the grounds, mildly scolded him, as she was unable to do so on this occasion. Perhaps if he had acquiesced, she may have read something in the grounds. Then he may have been prepared for the changes that were coming; changes in fact that were very much in the air and with implications for his future. Equally, the reading may have been a more favourable one, thus proving the futility of fortune telling per se.

Walter, for example, never returned to the school. He went back to Germany, no doubt inspired by his work for Vefbi bey to resume his architectural career there. A vacancy now existed at the flat and Kemal needed to make up the shortfall in rent, so a certain Masood was introduced into the household. Exactly where Kemal had found Masood – or perhaps Masood had found Kemal, - was never explained, but a back alley near Kapalıçarşı was a strong contender. One thing was certain; he was trouble. In actual fact, he hailed from Aleppo in Syria and spoke what Brian considered to be fairly good but halting Turkish. Nothing was known about his background, but he was about twenty five years old, five and a half feet tall, olive skinned , wore his black hair down to his shoulders and did not appear to have any gainful employment. However, he seemed to possess a charming nature, could speak English and had fitted in with the others in just a few days, especially, and somewhat significantly, with Roger. This bonhomie was not to last, however, although later Roger was quick to excuse Masood's actions which were about to unfold.

The first incident involving the Syrian occurred one night in early February, when he appeared at the flat with two American hippies in tow. They were husband and wife and looked to be in their mid twenties. In common with so many before them, they had run into financial difficulties in Istanbul on their way to Afghanistan. Eschewing the methods Pete had previously witnessed near the Pudding Shop, they had decided to try and sell their car. That is where Masood came in. Apparently he had contacts who could do just that on their behalf, for a small commission of course. However, a somewhat unfortunate situation had developed, and it was fairly apparent that Masood's popularity with the couple had taken a nosedive. Masood had taken the car, and according to his account, he had handed it over to his friend, but there had been no news for a couple of days. Neither of the two Americans could be considered as shrinking violets, as they were quick to make themselves at home in the flat. They were vociferous in proclaiming their opinions on Vietnam, Turkish officialdom, the awfulness of Turkish food ("Can't get a decent hot dog around here!") and the lack of hygiene in Istanbul.

They had hardly been in the room for more than half an hour but they were well into their verbal stride about how superior the U.S.A was to anywhere else in the world, then contradicting themselves by saying the troops were "gonna be pulled outa Vietnam pretty soon" and that big changes were on the way. Also assembled in the room and unable to carry on with their own business, as they were constantly being harangued by the American couple, were Brian, a very embarrassed Kemal, Pete, and one of his mature students - a short portly man in his forties called Aladdin, who happened to be visiting.. It so happened, that

207

Aladdin had applied for a job at an establishment in Grimsby, UK, known as The Railway Hotel.

"I am cooker," he told Pete on first making his acquaintance. "I get up early in morning and go round to six restaurants and cook their food, then return in afternoon and do the same for evening."

Pete was helping him with his CV and application forms and was optimistic about his protegé landing the job. Of course, he had his qualms about a lively but naïve Turkish bachelor moving to and working in an English city which at the time truly lived up to its name.

"I think you will find British cuisine somewhat different and it can get really cold in that part of the world," Pete had warned. "Mind you, they love their fish, and just like all over England they fry it in batter and serve it with chips."

"I introduce them to Turkish cooking," was Aladdin's confident response. But was East Lincolnshire quite ready for such a gingering up of its communal taste buds? Pete had begun to visualise kebab shops sprouting up all over England. A totally inconceivable prospect, surely.

Due to the loud Americans, they had been reduced to *sotto voce* discussions regarding Aladdin's application for a work permit. Pete was trying to explain some of the intricacies of British income tax and National Insurance to the best of his ability, when suddenly the male hippie shouted out, "Hey look at this picture on the wall. Every damn bar, café, shop, wherever you go into has one of these – and framed as well. What the hell?"

Aladdin spoke first, and Pete could see that he was holding his anger in check. From his seated position he quietly informed the hippie that it was a portrait of Mustafa Kemal Atatürk, revered war hero and founder of modern Turkey. A picture or bust of Atatürk was supposed to be displayed in all Turkish buildings.

"Well don't that just beat all! Big brother is watching you! Well he ain't watchin' us!" And so saying the sheepskin clad American took the framed photo and contemptuously turned it around with that famous face to the wall. "Damn dictator, that's all. Worse than Nixon."

Kemal was quick to react to this desecration, although he could only mumble that such an act was illegal in Turkey.

"So what's gonna happen?" was the reply. His similarly attired wife joined him in his dismissive comments.

"He was just a tool of the establishment. A stool pigeon and ass licker of the west."

Unbeknown to the rest of the group, Aladdin had furtively crept out of the room. Inside him was a veritable *Erciyas[5] of hot resentment, ready to erupt. His seat was notably vacant and avoiding comments about magic and disappearing acts, Pete looked towards the Americans, who by this time had calmed down after a laughing fit. Masood looked clearly uncomfortable but then it would have been in his interest to hang on with these two for just a while longer. In fact he was the very person they turned to next.*

"Now Masood, what's the latest with our automobile?"

"I have my friend look at it and he say it is nice Studebaker but old and he may not get good price for it."

Now it was Pete's turn to feel uneasy. He could distinctly smell a rat here and it exuded the odour of one Izzet. There would certainly be a host of Izzets all over the city and the Americans could be walking into a well organised sting – or not. Perhaps Masood and friend were on the level after all. Suddenly he remembered that he needed to go out and buy some pasteurised milk which was not available at the bakkal opposite. His source was a sandwich bar on Taksim square, where a kindly server slipped him the occasional bottle for a few lira. Anyway, this was none of his business. Excusing himself, he left the flat to the strains of

"…listen you Arab creep ass, you promised to get that sorted for us today!"

Half an hour later, after consuming a hot dog at the sandwich bar and collecting his milk, Pete returned to the flat. His knock on the door was greeted by a grim faced Brian and he could sense an unsettled atmosphere, but above all, an all pervading silence. It was as if a gang of kidnappers had broken in and run off with hostages, and in a way something similar to that had just happened. Three persons were missing from the room; the Americans and Masood. It transpired that Aladdin, on leaving the

5.   Mount Erciyas, a volcanic mountain in Cappadocia, Central Turkey

flat had made his way to the nearest police station and reported the hippies for gross misconduct towards Atatürk. No one had thought to turn the picture the right way round again and when the police arrived, the evidence of this misdemeanour was in front of them. The pair had been summarily arrested and taken to the police cells. Masood, on seeing the two law officers at the door, promptly made for the toilet, opened the window on to the back yard, and made good his escape. Fortunately for him, he had not been spotted.

The married couple spent the night as guests of honour in a police cell and, in all probability, in no way chastised by their experience. Very little else was heard of them again, but the same could not be said of their car. Eventually, according to Kemal who seemed to have his finger on the pulse of everything that moved in the city, the said vehicle was recovered and returned. Masood's accomplice was arrested for illicit trading in second hand cars. It seemed that a government licence was required which he and Masood had somehow neglected to obtain. Very careless of them. Masood was also now a wanted man. The Americans were repatriated by their consulate but not before being given a warning about their disrespectful act towards the picture. They were, however, deemed to be entirely innocent of offences with regard to the attempted sale of their car. This lenient treatment did not prevent them from making disparaging comments about "fascist Turkish pigs!"

As for Masood, he pulled off a disappearing act that would have put Houdini in the shade. If only Pete had known that this was neither the first nor last of the many crimes he had been able to wriggle out of. He seemed to have vanished off the face of the earth. Despite this, a few days later, Roger reported that he had made contact with him, though naturally he was loathe to reveal his whereabouts. This may also have had something to do with a chemical project the two of them had been involved in, which was a process to extract opium from certain medications that were available for purchase in any pharmacist shop. Far fetched as this may have seemed, especially to Brian, the activities made perfect sense when linked to Roger's claims of being a "dope fiend" back in London" He had also claimed to be part of the West End gay scene without actually being gay. At least that aspect of his past had provided a host of hilarious anecdotes which kept the others amused. Nevertheless, Masood was proving a somewhat dangerous person to know, and maybe it was best that he had gone. Unfortunately, that was not the last they were to hear of him. There was some good news, though. At least Aladdin managed to get the job in Grimsby.

Nightmare in Beyoğlu

The next major blow to be struck from the strange and distant realms where Kısmet had its dwelling place landed on the Harbiye crew at the end of February. This particular turn of the wheel of fortune would result in the most serious ramifications for all concerned. Indeed, what was about to happen could be called a pivotal moment in all of their lives. The landlady of the flat Kemal was renting had decided that, especially after that last episode with the hippie couple, she wanted Ekrem the tea boy and his friend Osman to be her sole tenants. They would have the whole of the residence to themselves, even though they were often away for two days at a time. Indeed, Ekrem slept in the room that Pete had woken up in the morning after the change money disaster. The same bed had also served Pete well in other, more pleasurable ways. This decision, the worthy *hanım effendi* reasoned, made for a quieter life as far as she was concerned. What with regular employment on the Bosphorus ferries, serving tea and coffee in twelve hour shifts, plus the tips they received, the two young men would easily be able to afford the rent.

However, Fate or Kısmet, or whatever one wished to call it, is notoriously skittish, as discovered by countless generations of those who throughout history were willing to push their luck. The inescapable fact was that Pete and his colleagues would need to look elsewhere for alternative accommodation. As luck would have it, Kemal soon received news of a property in Beyoğlu which would be adequate for their needs. At that time it was being occupied by some Greek waiters who worked in one of the tripe restaurants in Istiklal Caddesi. They worked until one in the morning and some of them would continue to live at the premises while their new accommodation in Cihangir was being made ready.

This meant that in addition to Pete, Roger, Brian and Kemal, three waiters would also be sleeping there from one thirty am onwards. The said property - their new home - was on the first floor of a dowdy grey building on the corner of an alleyway just off Istiklal. The wooden stairs were rickety, creaking and wobbled with each step. A shabby brown painted door opened onto the room they were to live in. This room was about forty feet in length and possibly five or six yards wide. Another scruffy door led to a cramped, musty hallway where a crouch toilet was located. There were also hand washing facilities in a crude, tiny kitchen next to the hallway.

The new home that Kemal had found for them was an old building but would hardly have warranted a Grade Two listing. In fact it may have been kinder to bring in the wrecking ball. However, they needed to make the best of things. After all, they were situated right in the centre of Beyoğlu's main thoroughfare. Beyoğlu, the all day humming centre of an ancient metropolis; the retail and restaurant hub of the modern part of the city, which probably only dated back to the Middle ages, unlike its antique partner across the Golden Horn.

At the end of the day, after six, the frantic activity in and around the main street seemed to die down and the constant flow of human lives which paraded up and down Istiklal dwindled to a mere trickle. Then, gradually, darkness would take its hold on the neighbourhood, and phoenix - like, the streets would be reborn in realms of fiery, multi-coloured neon signs. Gleaming lights were like the sparkling eyes of a thousand temptresses lurking in back streets plying their trade, or haunting the clubs, the bars, the restaurants of Beyoğlu. In those days it was said that all waitresses in the city were in fact prostitutes, importuning for clients who knew exactly which restaurants to visit. Amidst this nocturnal radiance the crowds were back, and once more striking out along congested pavements. As if in acoustic accompaniment, cars streamed in an all night procession, hooting their way through the hours of dusk, until even they grew weary at around three am. To many, the bright lights of Istiklal represented beacons of hope in escaping for a while from the humdrum existence that for them constituted life in this city. They were drawn in on the promise of a good time, only for the pleasure palaces to spit them out hours later into an unforgiving dawn.

With much trepidation, on a Tuesday afternoon, the young refugees from Harbiye packed up their meagre belongings and walked the half mile or so to their new abode. On reaching it, one glance at the wooden floor of this drab chamber, with its faded yellow curtains, barely covering tall brown framed windows, was enough to dampen their spirits profoundly. It had certainly not helped that during their trek to Beyoğlu there had been a downpour of cloying, penetrating rain. Wet through and utterly depressed with their situation, they did not even argue about where they were going to sleep. On a more positive note, they would still be sleeping on their thin mattresses but which were now to be doubled up on iron framed beds. At least, that was going to be more comfortable than in their previous residence. Pete would still require his faithful sleeping bag which up to now had served him so well.

During these times of comparative adversity, adjustments were made and a settling in process ensued. To begin with, their collective guilt at the notion of Kemal paying the rent dissipated when they learned that Vefbi bey was generously footing the bill. In addition, they were now slightly closer to their place of work than previously and there were dozens of cheap eating places within easy reach. On the distaff side, not only did the external din from the street make it difficult to sleep, but every morning they were woken up at one thirty by noisy tripe restaurant waiters, who insisted on chatting loudly in Greek before settling down themselves. It was fine for them, as they would rarely rise before nine.

Then there were the toilet facilities.

At least there was a door. This opened outwards to reveal an odiferous cubby hole that displayed just about everything that was revolting to European and Turk alike about this type of toilet. There were no hand grips either, so you just had to half crouch before letting go. There was no water if you pulled on the rusty chain during the hours of daylight, or tried to use the crude bottom washing water spout. Consequently, there was an accumulation of dumps from previous users which were taking their time to sink down through an open black hole in the stained porcelain. Furthermore there was no toilet paper.

Something that most Northern Europeans could not get into their heads was that the Istanbul sewage system and drainage likely dated from the times of the Osmanlı Empire. To make matters worse, there was no paper in sight. This commodity was on sale in most shops but was not supposed to be put down the toilet – even the modern ones. Indeed, your Delsey or Andrex was and still is utilised traditionally not to wipe but to dry your bottom after washing your left hand which would be used to clean yourself with. This would then be placed in a waste bin next to the pedestal or foot holes. The better off families tended to have bidets installed, but in some houses these were just copper pipes sticking out of the pedestal in line with your poo stained bumhole. However, in this part of the city the water was cut off until the next morning, and no-one in the newly arrived group had thought to bring tissues with them.

The only paper immediately available in their new residence consisted of old European language School leaflets. These yellowing A5 sheets printed on the cheapest pulp paper had been brought from the school by Brian, who, like Pete, could not break the habit of putting paper down the toilet after wiping. Also, they eschewed the custom of using their left hands for cleaning. The leaflets, however, had not been designed to break up in any sanitary system in the world, let alone a huge middle eastern city. But what else could they use in the meantime? Even though they poured bottled water down the hole, this merely moved the noisome mess further along the pipes, until eventually they became blocked. Although within a few days they had actually acquired some conventional toilet paper, it still went in the same direction. This promised to be a disaster waiting to happen, especially as the foundations for this coming catastrophe had been laid with use of the thicker leaflets. Sure enough, before the month was out, disaster did indeed strike.

The day of the great kazi calamity began as soon as Pete and company awoke. In fact their very awakening was probably caused by the stench that pervaded their living quarters, diffusing a stink which must have emanated from the very depths of hell. On opening the toilet door, they beheld a revolting image of excrement and chewed up paper afloat on a rising pool of filthy brown liquid. It was payback time for the school leaflets. For too long they had lain mouldering in a dusty cupboard, abandoned before they had a chance to venture out into the world to proclaim the wonders of the European Languages School. Now it was their turn to exact revenge for not being allowed to serve their purpose, as they penetrated into the heart of the uncaring humans' waste disposal system. They had gradually accumulated and built up until neither liquid nor solid was able to get past their barrier. Ironically though, it was the humans who got their own back as the foul smelling fluid was now starting to ooze over the top of the white ceramic base and on to the living room floor.

Fortunately, one of the waiters was able to summon the building's *kapıcı* who ambled in, armed with a very large rubber sucker on the end of a sawn off broomstick. The gurgling mess drained away by degrees but the same could not be said of the smell and vestigial remains of three weeks' bowel and bladder movements. The occupants of the room were forced to use the public toilets near Taksim Square, which were little better, but for twenty five *kuruş* a guy in a cubicle would squirt lemon scented cologne on your hands from a large yellow plastic bottle. By the time Pete returned in the evening, the unfortunate kapıcı had cleaned up the mess and thanks to his efforts, the toilet looked and smelled clean and presentable. It was to be wipe-the-bum-and-dispose-in-a-bin from now on . This made sense, after all. However, Roger was complacent and gloating over the whole unsavoury event, as he had adopted Turkish toileting habits some time ago. He claimed that he had warned this would happen but had been

216

ignored. He was probably telling the truth

Regarding Roger though, there was growing concern for him among the others of late, as his behaviour seemed to be growing steadily more erratic. Age wise, he was the senior member of the group whose sometimes sage offerings of advice had been noted, even if not necessarily acted upon. The most worrying factor was his increasingly aggressive reactions to even the most minor issues. For example, when he saw a small gypsy girl being manhandled by council police in the street and the bird seed she was selling scattered over the pavement, he took off along Istiklal and shoulder barged every Turkish man he came into contact with. Pete followed in his wake, shrugging his shoulders apologetically to the startled victims, and, miraculously, his rampage did not seem draw any retaliation Bearing in mind his military training, this aggression spelled potential danger. Worse still, he seemed to be directing much of his ire towards Pete, mainly because his earnings were less, due to his lack of teaching qualifications. He wanted a pay rise, indeed parity with Pete's wages, but despite the fact that Roger had asked for his support, Pete remained stubborn and refused to participate in proposed strike action against Vefbi bey.

"Just put it to Vefbi bey and ask for more money." Was Pete's advice.

"Already done that and it's no dice. Therefore I shall use my right to withdraw my labour."

"All very well but this is not England."

"Don't patronise me you complacent tosser! I see you're comfortably off." And Roger stressed "you're" with savage irony.

Indeed, there were worrying rumours that Roger had been secretly meeting up with Masood and that the young Syrian had been hiding in their accommodation during the day. Furthermore, Roger had become inconsistent in his attendance at his teaching post, or was quite often late. He would disappear for a couple of days, then suddenly turn up at the apartment in Beyoğlu. One only had to look into Roger's glazed eyes to realise that his narcotic experiments with Masood had been successful. As for exercising his rights to withdraw his labour, it was all very well to attempt

217

that in the UK, at a car factory, a mine, the railways or school, for example, but this was a small private educational establishment in Turkey. He had no chance of success. As much chance, in fact, as a large group of men in Taksim Square Pete had witnessed about a week ago. They had carried signs which read *"Boykot"* and *"Grev"*, the latter meanings strike. The demonstration had been brutally broken up by riot stick wielding militia.

It was around this time that another participant strode on to the stage set of Pete's existence. He was an American from New Mexico in his late twenties, called Henry. He owned a chain of motor cycle stores across the state. He was in Istanbul on the lookout for a manufacturer of leather jackets, who might be able to supply him with high quality goods at knock down prices. He had certainly come to the right place, even though the locals sere renowned for driving hard bargains. He had bumped into none other than Kemal at the Pudding Shop during the previous week. Thanks to Kemal's entrepreneurial skills, he was able to meet Vefbi's cousin Hassan, who was acquainted with one Fikret bey, a leather merchant who lived across the Bosphorus, and who would welcome the possibility of exporting his wares to the USA.

For the past fortnight, he had been Fikret's guest at his well appointed detached house close to Erenköy railway station. Henry would spend most days with Fikret at his factory carrying out quality checks and selecting designs for the leather clothing he wished to purchase. At other times, he would be sightseeing in the old city. As it stood, they were yet to strike a deal because Henry had submitted some designs that Fikret's employees were struggling to perfect. In the meantime, Henry was quite content to be living at the merchant's home, as he was spending some valuable rest and relaxation time away from his parents, with whom he had recently experienced a colossal falling out.

Henry loved nothing more than consuming vast quantities of the local beer whenever the opportunity arose. He had called in at the school with Hassan, and was introduced to the staff just as lessons were finishing for the morning. Pete took a liking to this rumbustious, crazy yank, but Roger was not so keen. After all,

Henry was thickset, punchy, conservative in his demeanour, and – as Pete soon discovered – in his politics. One look at him and you would be confident that if it ever came to a scrap, he would be more than a match for Roger. He joined the others for lunch, but not until after an incident at the school office when, on spotting Selma wafting out of her classroom, he had picked her up in both arms, whirled her around then placed her gently back on her feet. Her only response whilst in mid air was a very sarcastic *"Ne güzel!"* (How lovely!) To which all her friends burst into fits of giggles.

"My but you're cute, honey!" However, Selma rejoined her friends and they all walked past Henry to the exit as if he was not even there. Pete, however, felt that some quiet response to this was needed, so he muttered to the American, "Yes she is, Henry and she happens to be my girlfriend, if you don't mind, mate."

Henry was highly amused. "Hey it's the li'l green monster. Lemme buy y' a beer!" So saying, he enwrapped Pete in a giant bear hug and lifted him up. Pete was the second person to be swept off his feet by Henry that day. On landing, Pete felt he had to continue.

"It's all very well but we don't do that to the local girls. They might have brothers who carry knives, or even guns."

Henry, for a few seconds, actually appeared to be chastised, but Hassan broke the mood. This had all been a huge joke to him and he knew exactly what had been going on between Pete and Selma for the past few weeks.

"What about that drink, Henry? *Haydi*, let us all go to lunch."

Henry became a familiar figure around the school during the next few days and he managed to stay clear of Selma and her friends. Also, he seemed to be overstaying his welcome at Fikret's and Pete wondered if all was well on the business front with those two. He and Henry became sometime drinking partners at local bars during the late winter evenings and they were often joined by Brian who had just returned from another leaflet distribution trip to Anatolia. He had only been gone a week but this time, for some reason, he had had fewer leaflets to deliver. One evening, after a consuming several litres of Efes Pilsen draft, the three of them returned to the Beyoğlu residence. Henry found a chair and

219

the other two were sitting on their beds. He looked up at the two Englishmen and confided to them the reason he had been hanging on in Istanbul and why he was in less than a joyful state of mind.

"My folks are thinking of moving over the border to Mexico," he moaned. "That's the most uncivilised shitty nation on this planet and I've told them so. Naturally, they don't exactly agree."

Just at that moment, Roger came into the room and immediately started haranguing the others about his pay dispute with Vefbi. Brian was puzzled by this, as he had been away since the dispute had started. He was paid the same as Roger but did not seem to mind, especially as he was also receiving expenses for his leaflet trips. Nevertheless, Roger was determined to recruit Brian to his cause.

"Don't you think we should be getting the same money as him for doing the same job?"

Pete felt nettled by this. "We don't exactly do the same job, do we? Anyway, you have not helped your cause by being absent or late on some days."

Henry butted in. "Look, I'll leave you ladies to it. I gotta letter to write to my old man and it ain't gonna be pleasant. Adios." So saying, he strode purposefully from the room. Meanwhile, Pete's riposte had obviously hit the mark with Roger. Indeed, if he had been totally sober, he may not even have made those remarks.

"I've been unwell," muttered Roger. Then he rose angrily to his feet. "You make me sick, you selfish little shit, with your coward's knife!"

Pete looked up, and to his horror, noticed that his commando knife had been removed from his rucksack and stuck into the wooden wall at the far end of the room. However, that was the least of his problems. A nasty situation now seemed to be developing. He turned and saw Roger approaching him, eyes wide and staring with pent up anger. With one movement, he had grasped Pete round the throat and thrown him violently down on his bed. He then leapt on top of him and started to squeeze Pete's neck with both hands whilst pressing down either side of his Adam's apple. Gasping for breath, Pete surprised Roger, and himself, by prising his attacker's hands from his throat and pushing him on to the floor. He clambered to his feet, only to see Roger on the opposite side of the bed, glowering at him and obviously preparing another attack.

Multiple potential outcomes, resulting from this confrontation, coursed through Pete's mind in those few seconds before Roger made his move. They were mostly unpleasant ones, concerning the treatment his assailant may have meted out in the past to unfortunate Malaysian terrorists; then there were the allusions Roger had made to his bouts of mental illness. Such traits did not bode well for Pete's continued existence on this planet.

Then in an instant, the whole situation changed. Brian, on witnessing the first assault, had rushed out of the room and intercepted Henry in the street outside. The American had rushed up the stairs into the room and in seconds had Roger in a head lock which, struggle as he might, he could not free himself from. Henry made a sensible suggestion.

"Better make yourself scarce while I calm this one down."

Pete and Brian left the room.

An hour or so later, Henry joined them at their usual bar in the *Çiçek Pasaj* [6] and chuckled when he saw them, both obviously still shaken from the unpleasant incident that had just taken place.

"I guessed you two would be in here. Pete, you still look pretty shook up."

"I'll be Ok," mumbled Pete who was still reflecting on his more than adequate response to the first strike. Pretty good the way he had thrown him off. "Thanks for what you did there Henry. I don't know how things would have gone if you hadn't intervened."

"He'd probably a killed ya – just kiddin'", laughed Henry. He could see Pete was still shaking not only from the trauma but he was also feeling a great deal of anger.

"He says he didn't mean to kick off like that and is really quite ashamed 'a his actions."

---

6.   Flower Passage – an area in Galatasary, famous for its bars and restaurants. It derived its name from Russian women who had fled to Istanbul from the Soviet Union, and had set up flower stalls in the passage.

This latter information seemed to settle the other two. However, no apology had been forthcoming from the assailant. Pete suddenly recalled the time, a few weeks ago, when Roger remarked to him about mosquito bites. Pete had said how he enjoyed squashing every mosquito he saw that buzzed within his range. He had always taken this to be normal human behaviour, especially as he had often been kept awake at nights suffering that infernal itching resulting from the attentions of those marauding pests. Roger was appalled by such comments and countered with,

"I consider the small drop of blood it takes from me as my gift to the mosquito."

Pete had actually been impressed by this, but on the other hand, in a discussion about the Arab/Israeli conflict, Roger had made it very clear that he would be quite prepared to fight for the Palestinians. Something that definitely went against the grain as far as Pete was concerned. Beneath a lean, tall and craggy exterior, there stirred a veritable magma of rage and resentment against the so-called system. In those times, some people personified the system as "The Man". In his better moments,

Roger could be caring and softly spoken. Perhaps some of the resentment he felt towards Pete stemmed from the fact that he had also taken a fancy to Selma soon after she had appeared at the school. To be fair, she had been friendly towards him and even liked him, despite the fact that she believed him to be totally "med", as she put it, pointing to the side of her head.

Brian declared that he was tired and left for home. Henry informed them that Roger had decided to stay elsewhere for a couple of days to get his head together, so the night of discomfort Pete had anticipated never materialised. Once Brian had departed, Henry's face took on an altogether more solemn appearance. Pete thought he was about to hear another stream of invective from the American against his parents' proposed move to Mexico. However, he turned to Pete and in confidential tones began to sound a warning.

"Look Pete, ole buddy, you need to get outa that place. Something's brewing, I know it. I smell trouble, big time and it aint necessarily about you an' Roger but somethin' pretty bad's about to happen. If you like, come and stay with me till you get yourself fixed elsewhere."

A stunned silence followed. Who was this guy? A soothsayer? A fortune teller? How had Pete missed all the subterfuge and skullduggery that had been going on under his very nose? If that's what had really been happening. The answer of course lay in the fact that Henry had the benefit of being on the outside looking in. He had obviously learned something from Hassan about Masood's activities and the misfortunes of two of his own compatriots. This, together with the involvement of the police and Roger's erratic behaviour, created a web of intrigue from which Henry, with nothing much better to think about, was able to make his hypothesis. He seemed very earnest in his entreaty to Pete to join him at Fikret's, over in Asia Minor.

"Er thanks for that Henry. Um yeah. Maybe we'll speak again tomorrow. Sounds like it could be fun as I'll be living in Asia and working in Europe. I hate that fucking place anyway. It'll be good to get away from it and that stinking shithouse"

"Okay, well don't chew on it for too long. Gotta feelin' there ain't a lot of time before it hits the fan. I won't be around for a coupla days. So what's today? Wednesday. See ya on Friday then. You better be packed an' ready."

Roger did not return on Thursday, so that night there were only Pete, Brian and Kemal using the beds, plus two of the waiters who were yet to move out. Pete was particularly tired after a morning's teaching session followed by an afternoon of pure bliss with Selma. Furthermore, he could not stop giggling to himself about that girl's wicked sense of humour. Every time they left the bedroom, she would remark, "Thank you Ekrem," to the absent but so obliging tenant, with her full smile and wide sparkling eyes. Indeed, Pete felt he could not stand to be without her.

Back at the flat, at around eleven that night, Pete wriggled into his sleeping bag, and, looking around him, saw that the faded curtains were now fully closed. Darkness filled the room and held sway in every dusty nook and cranny. The constant hooting of traffic outside in the street no longer disturbed the inhabitants. The noisy return of the waiters, just after one am, was so routine by now, it interrupted sleep for no more than a minute. The darkness of a late winter night now enshrouded the human forms slumbering peacefully, and dead to the world outside. It also perfectly suited Pete's sleeping habits; indeed, he had been so comfortable in this environment that on one Sunday, he had slept in until two in the afternoon. Then again, so had all the others.

Before retiring that evening, he had considered Henry's words very carefully. What could possibly happen? They were all reasonably comfortable in the flat. Although he still hated the toilet there, he often used the facilities at the nearby Bab Kafeteria which were clean and modern. Besides, the food in the Bab Kafeteria was the best he had tasted in the city so far, even though it was somewhat more pricey than elsewhere. As his mind drifted, he started to consider another problem. He did not wish to appear a coward by getting away from Roger. Indeed, he had never wanted to run away from any kind of confrontation in the past. However, this guy could prove to be truly dangerous. What if he attacked him in his sleep, when he would be at his most vulnerable? In the end, tiredness overtook him and chased away these worrisome thoughts. Shakespeare was so right when he wrote that sleep was the "balm of hurt minds".

It was no more than three hours later when Pete's nourishing slumber was very rudely interrupted. The perfect darkness that had always ensured for him an uninterrupted night's sleep was suddenly prised open. His eyes blinked briefly but immediately he had to slam them shut. On opening them again, he perceived a broad beam of torchlight shining directly on to his face. As he tried to focus, a most alarming apparition met his gaze. The severe, moustachioed visage of a Turkish policeman, complete with green peaked cap was staring intently down on him. A trick of the yellow light was making his face appear a great deal more sinister and threatening. However, after what seemed an eternity, but was probably no longer than twenty seconds, the face vanished and there was a trampling of feet as the policeman and his two colleagues made their way across the floor towards the door. They were mumbling to each other and Pete could just make out the words *"yok"* and *"burada değil."* Then the room was once more plunged into silence and darkness. He knew those words meant "no" and "not here" but to whom or what had they been referring? Henry had been right. He had to get out of there.

What had just happened was reality, not some nightmare. No comments were forthcoming from the others, who were probably just as cowed as he was, and they seemed to be nodding off again. Then with a shudder, he remembered that his visa had expired almost two months ago. What would have happened if the police officer had asked to see his passport? He had heard from a number of sources the terrible fate that befell those unfortunates who had found themselves in the clutches of the local police. A Turkish police station was not called a *"karakol"* or "black arm" for nothing.

Once more, a drowsiness overcame him and sleep was restored. What could be lurking in the darkness waiting to spring its unpleasant surprises on a by now quite vulnerable Englishman? It is often the case, however, that what might seem a catastrophe the night before, somehow diminishes in importance in the light of day, as if nothing so serious had even existed beforehand.

Although Pete was not fully aware of the fact, the solution to his problem lay in the not inconsiderable shape of Henry, who called into the school at lunchtime the next day. No mention had been made of the police raid. It was almost like a conspiracy of silence which none of the group seemed willing to break. The truth was, nobody knew exactly what to say about it, at least not in the constructive sense, so the whole matter was shelved, at least for the time being. In any case, Pete's mind was definitely made up about leaving the apartment, even though accommodation wise he faced an uncertain future.

"You packed an' ready limey?" Henry chuckled.

"It's all in my rucksack, yank," replied Pete, trying not to sound too offensive. He always found difficulty in responding to humorous insults with suitable ripostes. No matter, because his reply totally bounced off Henry anyway.

The last lesson of the day ended as usual at nine pm. At nine thirty, Pete and Henry were aboard an aging Scottish steamship which was one of several providing the ferry boat service between Europe and Asia Minor. They disembarked at Kadıköy which was the ferry's destination port, and Henry collected his jeep from a nearby car park. They set off along still crowded roads, lit only by shops and houses either side, and headed towards the village of Bostancı. It was now ten fifteen, on a clear starlit night in early spring. The temperature was chilly, as was usual in Western Turkey at this time of year.

Back at the flat in Beyoğlu, at ten twenty pm, a fully armed squad of Turkish constabulary burst in through the main door and arrested four occupants, who happened to be in the room at the time. They were Brian, Roger, Kemal and Masood. They were allowed to collect their outside clothing, then they found themselves being bundled into a waiting police truck. Fortunately they went easy on Brian, Roger and Kemal, but not on Masood who, as it turned out, had been the actual target of both of their raids. Apart from the Syrian, all three were released the following morning. Roger and Brian had been sensible enough to renew their visas by travelling to Komotini in Greece and back, shortly after Christmas, but it was pointed out that they had only a few weeks left on them.

They had been given a cell all to themselves. A cell to share with several cockroaches, a couple of mice, a lizard, and Brian swore blind he had spotted a scorpion scurrying across the floor during the night. A filthy bucket served for them to perform their ablutions, but Roger was heard to remark,

"We had it a fucking sight worse than this in Malaysia!"

The luckless Masood was detained on charges of attempting to trade a second hand foreign car without a government permit. Actually, his biggest mistake was to get caught doing it. Nonetheless, Pete, on hearing the news of his flatmates' ordeal, found himself feeling relieved but also remorseful that he had left them to their fate. But then, how could he have predicted something as extreme to him as a raid by armed police? He also felt sorry for Masood, as he had found him an affable soul and friendly to a fault. However, within a week Pete was to regret ever meeting him.

The following morning, at Fikret's house, which was situated in the affluent suburban village of Bostancı, Pete was introduced to the leather merchant with whom Henry was engaged in business. Also domicile in the Fikret residence was his younger sister, Selim. (Strange, thought Pete, that's a male name!). As he regarded the eponymous young lady, he could not help noticing her half smile of greeting between high cheek bones, her prominent nose, narrow eyes and lank dark brown collar length hair. She wore no make up and was dressed in a man's white shirt with grey and white pin stripe slacks. Distinctly masculine looking black shoes enclosed her large feet. Both she and her brother spoke English fluently, so Henry, wary of being overheard, waited until later when he had a moment alone with Pete before confiding,

"She likes girls! That's not her real name but she loves being called Selim."

Pete received this information with some interest. So she was not only a lesbian but everyone's stereotype of a lesbian. He had met a few at college and had even dated one; at least he believed she was. He had never been particularly bothered about people who presented homosexual traits and had always adopted a live and let live approach. He could not really claim to having had any gay friends. On the other hand, although he eschewed the negative attitude adopted by some of his contemporaries, he was not above retelling jokes he had heard about gay men and women. Henry interrupted his train of thought.

"Y'know she was takin' a bath a coupla days ago an' I went into the bathroom, grabbed her tits and stuck my hand right on her pussy. Know what she did? She just laughed it off as if we was a coupla guys havin' a locker room ruckus." He chuckled to himself at the memory.

The Nomad

With the weekend over, another five days of work began again on Monday morning.. Pete was now faced with the commute from Bostancı to Taksim, a journey that would take about one hour if train and ferry times were favourable. At just before eight, on a sunny March morning in Asia Minor, Pete and Selim were strolling towards the *Banliyö* station, along a pleasant tree lined avenue. Every twenty yards or so they passed by *Erguvan* or Judas trees, minus their splendid purple flowers, but ready to herald the season of spring, initially with spectacular displays of white blossom. According to Christian beliefs, this colour transformation occurs due to the shame felt by the tree as a result of Judas using it to hang himself, after betraying Jesus. It was also a fact that the variety of purple dye obtained from the erguvan was so rare that only persons of great importance had ever been able to wear clothes of that colour. As for betrayal? That was very far from Pete's mind at this juncture. After all, he had not betrayed his mates had he? However, one of them had already betrayed him, as he was later to discover.

Then something occurred that he found both absurd and highly amusing. Selim had spied two pretty teenage girls walking along on the other side of the road in the opposite direction. When they reached a point immediately across the road from Pete and Selim, the androgynous Selim remarked,

"They were looking at us. I think they like us. I'll keep my eyes open for them in future."

Pete did not answer, but merely nodded in response, as his thoughts were massively preoccupied with concerns about his future living arrangements. He was carrying his rucksack with him as he would be sleeping somewhere else until Thursday, when he would once more be Fikret's guest. His friend Costa who was a Turkish national with Greek ethnicity had offered to put him up at his parents' house for three days a week. Costa was a student at the language school and he was also a musician, so he and Pete had much in common when it came to conversation and interests. Pete was only too pleased to accept his invitation, as not only did it provide a temporary solution for him, but Costa's parents tolerated their son using a large room in their house as a band rehearsal studio. In fact, his band had just come third in the national "Golden Microphone" competition. Some achievement that, as this nationwide competition had been won the previous year by none other than the seminal Turkish rock band, the *Tartarlar*. Pete had enjoyed a long jam session with them before Christmas, thanks to his ties with Fırat, their road manager. He had even become a temporary roadie for them at two major venues, as they were not only beginning to attract huge audiences, but also the attention of European record producers and venue managers.

Whilst the Tartarlar had been more of a psychedelic folk rock band, who fused the technical aspects of rock with the melodies of Anatolian folk music, Costa's band played Jimi Hendrix and Cream numbers, so Pete could not wait to start jamming with them. The bass guitarist was ethnic Greek, as was the vocalist, and the drummer was of mixed Turkish-Greek descent. Pete was not in those days so adept on electric guitar, even though he had helped the Tartarlar to learn "Pinball Wizard" and "Sugar Sugar" (as they were obliged to perform western numbers in the first half of their shows!). However, he had been noted back in England as pretty hot on the blues harmonica. Therefore, he eagerly anticipated the proposed weekly sessions, although he realised only too well that the underlying problem regarding his nomadic existence could not possibly continue indefinitely.

Meanwhile, as the ferry approached Karaköy docks, after making its way across a millpond calm Bosphorus, Pete noticed half a dozen dinghies moored alongside a jetty adjacent to the ferryboat landing stage. A light grey smoke was rising from each of

229

these craft, and wafting over towards him was the tempting aroma of grilled fish and onions. As Selim took her leave and struck out for Galata, home of Istanbul's business and finance community, Pete made a bee line for the small boats moored just below the concrete jetty in which each occupant was frying mackerel and onions, seasoned with sea salt, and serving them enclosed in hunks of bread to passing customers. A second breakfast beckoned.

He found a wooden bench to sit on close to a row of fish restaurants that had not as yet opened for business. As he eagerly consumed his grilled mackerel and onion roll, he began to consider the changes which had crept into his life, rudely nudging aside the complacent lifestyle he had hitherto been leading back in the UK. For him they represented a reality check. The reality was that he remained stranded in a foreign city, and despite the positive relationships he had managed to form, the kindness that had been shown to him by most, and the amount of money he had been able to save, he was still in a kind of limbo. Furthermore, he believed he was no nearer to returning home.

He had managed to save about forty dollars but that would not as yet be sufficient to get him on a flight home. He had dollars, thanks once again to Kemal who had introduced him to "a dealer in all trades", as he had described himself, named Mo, short for Mohamed. Mo worked in *Kapalıçarşı*, the vast ancient Covered Bazaar, situated in the old city. The bazaar was awash with dollars, thanks to myriad tourists who flocked to this fascinating and exotic centre. Thus, he was able to obtain American currency and exchange it with Pete for his lira. He was an entrepreneur, fluent in several languages, and a real mover and shaker, or high roller to use the term more commonly used in the early 1970s. In all honesty, he was another Izzet who had moved on a few grades and attained some respectability. As far as Pete was concerned, his exchange rates were reasonable, if totally illegal. He calculated that he would need at least another thirty dollars to cover the flight home. He kept his savings in a money belt stowed away deep inside his rucksack which he kept under his bed in the Beyoğlu apartment.

As soon as he had finished his second breakfast, he climbed into a waiting dolmuş for his journey up the hill to Taksim. His thoughts were now on another aspect of his enforced move to Beyoğlu. The disruption to his love life. He and Selma had continued to meet in The Parisiennes and other patisseries around Taksim Square. Her father never went into any of these, so she knew they would be safe. However, in terms of the physical side of their relationship, they found they had no access to any location where they could be completely alone together. The apartment was clearly unsuitable for this purpose as any of half a dozen personages could potentially walk in on them at any given moment.

In the event, Fate had intervened on their behalf. A few days after moving out of the flat in Harbiye, Pete needed to return to collect some laundry which he had deposited with the lady upstairs prior to departing. She had washed his clothing as before and had left it in the living room for him. He had borrowed Hassan's key, which was still hanging on its familiar hook in the school office, and had set off for his flat just after lunch. As he turned the key in the lock, he seemed to sense a presence inside the flat, then the unmistakable hum of male voices reached his ears.

The first rush of adrenalin subsided; his hackles rose, more from pure fright than a readiness to attack. It could not possibly be Ekrem the tea boy, as at that moment he would have been performing his balancing act with a tea tray on a ferry boat half way across the Bosphorus. A movement in Ekrem's bedroom to his left attracted his attention and there, before his gaze, two young males were locked in each other's arms and rolling on the bed. Had he stumbled upon a romantic scene? A play fight? Two guys just horsing around, tickling each other? To be fair, both men were still fully clothed. As soon as they saw Pete, they both rolled off the bed and Ekrem, as he faced Pete, was

visibly blushing. Pete for his part was relieved that he had not disturbed intruders and greeted Ekrem in Turkish and asking him if he had no work that day.

"Merhaba Ekrem. Nasılsın? Bugün işin yokmu?" (Hello Ekrem. How are you? No work today?). My how he had improved!

231

"Hello   Mr Peter. I am good. This Mehmet, my friend," replied Ekrem as he introduced his companion, whose expressionless face failed to conceal his inner feelings of discomfort. After a few more pleasantries, Pete departed with his laundry and a broad smile on his face. A potential solution to his vexed love nest situation had been duly presented to him, but he would need to see Ekrem again alone, and quite soon.

Pete remained tight lipped about this encounter and intended to keep it so until an opportunity presented itself. Sure enough, at the end of the week Ekrem happened to call into the school for a visit. It also happened that the office area was practically empty, and the idea that had occurred to Pete a few days ago could now be put into action. Initially, Ekrem avoided eye contact with Pete, who in turn felt that a friendly smile and greeting would be the order of the day, and these were duly exchanged. At this stage, Pete's command of Turkish was marginally better than Ekrem's English so he attempted to put forward his plan. He beckoned Ekrem into an empty classroom.

Ekrem Dostum, senden bir şey sormak istiyorum. "

Literally, he had said "Ekrem my friend I want to ask something from you." He did not know the Turkish word for "favour". He hoped that would work. Ekrem for his part seemed more relaxed now.

"Tarzanca" was the term Turks use for discourse in which two or more people communicate utilising a mixture of Turkish and another language, plus hand and facial gestures. Evidently, this would have been the language form that Tarzan used when engaging with his simian colleagues. A nonsensical notion maybe, but in practicality, this method of discourse seemed to work. Consequently, through this medium, Pete managed to negotiate the use of Ekrem's room for meeting Selma on Tuesday and Thursday afternoons.

Was this not a particularly shameful form of blackmail? Pete's sense of guilt was allayed because that congenial scene he had witnessed at the Harbiye flat could well have been entirely innocent. Besides, Ekrem was a kind hearted young man who was sympathetic to Pete's cause. Thus, his sexuality certainly did not warrant speculation. Although Ekrem was not responsible himself for Pete having to move out, he still felt compelled to make it up to him in some way. The Englishman's quest for a love nest provided the perfect opportunity.

In this way, his relationship with Selma could continue in its fullest sense, given the limitations imposed by her family and her desire to remain a virgin. It was a fact that Pete's new sleeping arrangements would make no difference to them. Regarding their feelings for each other, he felt that he was in love and for her part, whilst in the throes of passion, she had whispered *"seni seviyorum"* - "I love you" - to him but did she really feel the same way as he did? Were either of them fully aware of what changes could be brought about once that oft misused four letter word had been uttered? What did they know of the implications for them or the sacrifices that would have to be made?

Long term commitment, including the prospect of marriage, seemed remote and absent from their discourse at the moment. Certainly, they were living for the present and a very agreeable present it was turning out to be. They were a couple in every sense of the word: holding hands in the street; going for drinks and snacks at The Parisiennes and other restaurants; pleasuring each other in private, when possible. However, the risks involved were manifold. Supposing they were spotted by a member of the family or a family friend. So far their luck had held. In truth, they presented as a normal couple. Normal, that would be until six pm when Selma would have what Pete described as her "Cinderella moment", except of course she did not turn into a girl in rags or even into a pumpkin. She just had to disappear from view down the same sloping alleyway into the depths of Gümüşsuyu and temporarily out of his life.

To all intents and purposes then, they were lovers. Nevertheless, strong human emotions such as love tend to turn up with other emotions in tow, like a semantic package of conflicting feelings, delicately balanced, and prone to the slightly mistaken word or action which would destroy an otherwise steady partnership, scattering it to the four winds. Buried near the surface of a loving relationship are seemingly contrasting human traits such as joy, ecstasy, longing, day dreaming, over sensitivity, paranoia, insecurity and jealousy. And that is without the intervention of exterior agencies such as so called friends, jilted exes, family, busybodies and predators, to name but a few. True love is often defined as being devoid of the more negative traits, but those who have undertaken that journey and returned as changed individuals, will declare that is just not the case. So, just as certain as a luxury liner cruising out to sea in calm waters is bound sooner or later to be assailed by a storm, Pete and Selma's love affair was about to encounter somewhat rougher weather conditions within a very short space of time.

All was going so well. There was the arrangement with Ekrem, the furtive dating, added to which only a few trusted friends knew anything about their relationship. However, it was by no means idyllic, owing to the manifold risks involved. In addition, they had drawn some stares and muttered comments like *"O Türk değil..."* (he's not Turkish) from some of Selma's contemporaries. They were, nevertheless, ecstatic in each other's company. The twin pleasures of a romance and a firm friendship were in blossom and as full of potential as the budding blossom of the hazelnut trees which grew in proliferation around the city. But blossoms are constantly prone to the elements.

One morning in early March, Kemal brought his friend Kezban into the school. She was a young Turkish woman who had been minded to enrol in one of the courses on offer and was due to speak with Vefbi bey. He had returned from hospital during the previous month, thus ending Pete's tenure of office as head teacher. Kezban was about twenty years of age; pretty, with a round face and light brown hair, which made her look more Western European than Turkish. She was however of similar height to Selma, at just over five foot three. It transpired that she worked in a smart clothing store in Istiklal Caddesi which stocked men's and women's apparel designed in Italy and manufactured in Turkey. Pete had actually visited the shop. It was three storeys high and would not have looked out of place in Bond Street. The quality of the merchandise was of the highest order – and so were the prices.

Vefbi deliberately addressed Kezban in English as he announced, "This is one of my English teachers from London, Mr Peter." She shook Pete's hand.

"Pleased to meet you." She spoke quietly with a strong accent. "I learned English at school but need to practise my grammar skills."

"Nice to meet you too," was Pete's reply. He found himself quite smitten by her looks; confident demeanour and honey toned voice. His body language may have given him away, and he felt himself blushing. A hint of a smile crossed the girl's face.

"I work in Vakko, you may know, the clothes shop in Istiklal."

"I've been in there. It's great. You must work long hours though, as it's open until quite late." Pete never quite worked out his reasons for saying this. It was quite a lame conversation piece, to say the least.

"Oh I usually finish by six o'clock."

Pete thought nothing more about her last remark which had probably been made in all innocence, rather like his utterance beforehand. Kezban turned back to Vefbi who was anxious to continue discussing the school's curriculum with her, then she left the building accompanied by Ahmet.

It so happened that the next Saturday evening at around six thirty, Pete was strolling along Istiklal Caddesi towards Galata, where his friend Costa lived. He was deep in thought about the music they were planning to play that evening. He happened to glance across the street and saw that he was now opposite Vakko, the very shop where Kezban had told him she worked. Standing in the entrance, between two large display windows was Kezban herself, another woman and a young man. Pete instinctively smiled in her direction and waved. She totally ignored him, and Pete walked on feeling somewhat slighted, but then again she probably had not recognised him.

The following Monday morning in school found Pete in conversation with Selma and two of her friends. Lessons were about to start. Ahmet appeared in the office doorway and when he saw Pete he addressed him with,

"Kezban says she is sorry she did not speak with you on Saturday, but she was with her brother."

Pete replied with a casual, absent minded

"Oh thanks."

However, he failed to notice the darkening of Selma's facial expression. In addition, her eyes flashed briefly with suppressed rage; a danger signal he had clearly missed.

Nothing more was spoken on the subject of Kezban which was more of a non subject as far as Pete was concerned. Despite this, Selma remained somewhat quieter for the rest of the morning and left the school at lunch time without the usual farewell to her lover. Something her lover had also not noticed was that she had been in hushed conversation with Ahmet during the mid morning break. Only the two of them were privy to that particular dialogue.

More puzzling was Selma's non appearance in school the following morning, but Pete had previously arranged to meet with her in the Parisiennes at two in the afternoon. Lessons finished, and Pete soon found himself at the main entrance of that teashop of the affluent. As he made his way into the serving area, he observed the usual bustle of rich Istanbulites consuming over priced Coca Cola or drinking large glasses of tea, whilst holding court on the fashion sense of the other customers. He felt a little put out because Selma had not been outside to meet him, so he went back through the exit on to the pavement in the hope she might have been there by now. There was no sign of her, but as he happened to glance through the large front windows of the café , he observed his girlfriend ensconced at table and engaged in conversation with another young man, who turned out to be Turkish.

Approaching the table and feeling a pang of disquiet, he noticed Selma looking up at him with glazed, disinterested eyes. She then turned away from him to continue the conversation she was having with her companion. Perturbed by this obvious, theatrical snub, Pete found a chair and sat himself between the two of them. Selma spoke first.

"Oh hello. This is Orhan."

"Pleased to meet you Orhan."

"Pleasure"

After this briefest of introductions, Selma, instead of talking to Pete, resumed her discourse with Orhan, leaving the young Englishman feeling like a spare part, the uninvited guest or a gooseberry as the expression goes. Orhan looked most ill at ease, as it was a Turkish custom to greet a guest more warmly. Pete, for his part, definitely felt slighted and Orhan sensed this. Selma seemed unconcerned by this breech of etiquette. Eventually, and rather brusquely, given his usual mannered self, he interrupted them both with

"I believe we are supposed to be meeting this afternoon. If you'll excuse us Orhan."

So saying, he grabbed his erring partner by the arm and in no time had whisked her out of the exit. Initially, Orhan had made as if to intervene, but evidently had a change of heart.. After all, and still unbeknown to Pete, she had made her point, or so she believed. Pete was fuming all the way to the flat in Harbiye, a venue they had usually approached in a completely contrasting but no less passionate frame of mind. Why was she sitting with that boy? Was she blatantly two timing him? It certainly looked that way. Why did he ever trust such a lovely but flirty young girl. This was a violation of his finer feelings, surely! Then, just as the front door was closing behind them, Selma dropped her bombshell.

"Why you try to meet that Kezban after she finish her work?"

To say that Pete was astounded would have been an understatement. Her obvious anger was a hammer blow to his confident demeanour. He had suddenly lost the high ground. He thought he had caught Selma cheating on him, and now she had turned the tables. Her accusations continued.

"You tried to flirt with her and she is stupid girl! She works in shop and you want her!"

Her snobbery, it seemed was undiminished by her bitter emotions. What she was saying was all very plausible, as Pete had asked Kezban what time she finished at work, then lo and behold, there he had been, outside her shop ready to chat her up. In his defence though, not only had he been on the other side of the street, but it was also half an hour after the time she had given him for the end of her working day. By rights she should not have been anywhere near the shop at six thirty. Perhaps in a court of law this may have been sufficient evidence; proof of his innocence. But not in the court of Selma's law.

"So you wait for her for thirty minutes, you poor boy!" Her tone had now become mocking.

"As if I would do that. It's pathetic. I was not trying to meet her and I am not interested in her. Now what about you and Orhan then?"

"Oh he is old boyfriend. He never even kiss me but he wants me back again." She must have noticed the look of abject misery that crept across Pete's features. She could have turned the knife here but instead added casually. "I am not interested in him. We finish last year."

Then the truth of the matter began to dawn on Pete. She had used the young Turk to show how easily he could be replaced if he chose to stray. Was this now the end of their relationship? Selma seemed totally unwilling to accept Pete's story which seemed to be growing more implausible by the minute anyway. However, he did consider that if she really loved him, then surely the notion of trust was a crucial element of their feelings for each other. Put more simply, perhaps she did not really love him after all. They spent the rest of the afternoon in heart rending debate, toing and froing over both incidents. Ultimately, Pete was happy to accept Selma's version of her apparent indiscretion but as far as her acquiescence to Pete's explanation was concerned, the jury remained in deadlock.

Inevitably, the time ticked round to that moment which, if delayed any further would result in Selma arriving home late and vulnerable to searching questions from her father. They were about to leave, but Selma remained seated on the bed as Pete rose to his feet. He happened to glance down towards her, taking special delight in seeing her skirt raised a few inches above her knees. This proved to be yet another twist of fate, as to his horror, there on her left thigh and plainly visible were two bite marks; unmistakably human bite marks.

"Looks like you went a bit further with Orhan than you were telling me." The pain he felt was unbearable and his lashed out response reflected this. Had he not suffered enough shocks for one afternoon?

An expression of panic spread across Selma's face: a gazelle at bay, cornered by an angry puma. How was she going to explain this palpable evidence of intimate contact, even though she was very clear in her mind there had been none. Her reply to Pete' accusation was, on reflection, ill advised to say the least.

"It was not Orhan. It was Hamid." This was much worse. Mortifying, in fact. Pete was struggling to contain his jealous outrage and failing miserably. He attempted to put on a brave face with similar success.

"The one you told me about? The Persian guy? Your ex boyfriend!"

"Yes, he bit my leg. He is *manyak!*"

Then in perfectly even tones, with little or no recognition of her boyfriend's shattered feelings, she proceeded to explain herself as he stood in the bedroom doorway, aghast. Apparently Hamid had wanted to meet up with her before he left for Teheran. She had thought this a reasonable request which had been discreetly conveyed to her by one of her friends. According to her account, they had met in the Parisiennes and had been chatting cordially enough. Then without warning, he had proposed to her. It was a last ditch effort on his part and she had refused. His next actions were equally impulsive and unexpected. He had leaned to one side, ducked his head under the table at which they were sitting and sunk his teeth into her thigh. Whereupon, she had stomped out of the café vowing never to see him or even speak to him again.

As far as Pete was concerned, the plausibility of Selma's narrative was not in doubt. Perhaps because the alternative was too painful for him to conceive. Her account of the events regarding the bite marks was very convincing as this action from her ex boyfriend seemed entirely consistent with his unstable personality, certainly from what she had told him and from what he had observed that afternoon in the disco. Later, however, the doubts began to creep in. How could he be sure the bite marks were not a result of bedroom activity? Had Hamid taken her virginity? Reassuringly, she had made no attempts to conceal the damning evidence. Or was that all part of some sort of game she was playing? The sham jealousy over Kezban; Orhan in the Parisiennes; Hamid and the bite marks. These considerations all added up in his troubled mind. They tormented him like demons created by Fate or maybe just human fallibility. For her part, Selma was still smarting from what she considered an attempt by Pete to two time her. She would continue to feel that way for some time to come.

Now believers in the existence and power of Kismet might well wonder what further setbacks awaited Pete along the path of life he was following, during a sunny early spring in a foreign city brim full of opportunities but laden with pitfalls. It was not long before he found out for himself. He was shortly to be reminded that he was living in a country which, although it was attempting to modernise with a view to joining the European Union at some point, the general public still clung on to customs that would be considered outdated in the west. One such custom which has already been mentioned was for marriages to be arranged between families, rather than as a result of girls and boys dating. In her desire to live as a free spirit, Selma had not even entertained the idea of a young man's father visiting their household in order to ask her father for her hand in marriage to his son. Only one of her sisters had been matched to her future husband in this way. The middle sister had married a millionaire she had happened to fancy.

A few days after the temporary nadir of their affections for each other, Pete and Selma were to be found strolling in Taksim Square. All seemed mended, all doubts apparently allayed and love's domain restored. Pete had been trying to practice his Turkish by ordering two lemonades in a sandwich bar. Whenever he did attempt to speak the language, Selma had to restrain a fit of giggling, caused more by nervousness than her lover's comical pronunciation and accent. Far from taking offence, he regarded her responses as "sweet" and even quite sexy.

A warming spring sunshine helped to brighten up the square's blandness with its statue of Ataturk in the centre and steps leading up to Gezi Park. All was grey and characterless but teeming with life, like an ants' nest, as scores of the city's denizens encroached on the square, buzzing around the perimeters, crossing the roads, or queueing for buses. The couple paused outside a cinema to check on which films would be showing.

Suddenly, and without warning, Pete found himself staring into the face of a highly agitated young man; a face which in the next instant was turned in anger towards Selma.

Kiz, ne yapıyorsun? Bu adam kimdir?" This, the young man fairly rasped out.

"Sen ne diyorsun be!" Karişma, Allahalla!" was Selma's waspish response.

Pete was able to understand what was said in this exchange. The interloper had shouted, "What are you doing, girl? Who is this boy?" To which Selma replied "What are you saying? Don't interfere, for God's sake!" He could not then make out the torrent of invective that gushed from Selma's mouth, leaving the young man in no doubt as to her opinion of his impeding their progress along the street. Maybe in doing this, she had gone too far, and Pete began to realise that Selma must know this person as more than a passing acquaintance.

Her tormentor now began to speak in more menacing tones. *"Babana söyleyeceğim, Selma kızım."*

This threat by the young man to tell her father had a calming effect on Selma.

Then removing his Levi's denim jacket with clearly aggressive intent, their ambusher spoke to Pete in English. "What do you think you are doing with her. She is promised to me."

Pete was fairly nettled by such arrogance, and more than a little shocked by yet another revelation regarding his girlfriend's apparent appeal to the opposite sex.

"You're wrong there son. She's mine. Fuck off!"

This was an injudicious riposte. "Fuck off" may be an Anglo-Saxon expression, but thanks to the widening reach of Hollywood, speakers of all languages knew exactly what it meant. In this instance, its use only brought Pete a punch in the mouth and it stung. He did not wait to remove his own identical denim jacket. He just struck back. He was not a south paw or even much of a scrapper, but whenever he found himself in these situations, he always lashed out with a right handed haymaker. The left jab followed instinctively. He was now eyeball to eyeball with the bruised face of his attacker. Testosterone flowed like magma. His split lip was sore and Selma was apoplectic. A crowd had gathered to enjoy the spectacle, but strangely, nobody was taking sides. Selma stepped between the contestants......

......Or rather that was what happened in Pete's imagination later that day when he recalled his strange encounter with a very aggressive young Kurd. The exchange of punches never actually took place but as Pete lay in his bed trying to sleep, repeatedly reliving the incident, the combat that never took place became more violent with each rehashed version. He could just not stop himself cogitating on what actions he could have taken.

Instead, before they had started knocking bits out of each other, it was Selma who had acted decisively. She had thrust herself between the two combatants who at that stage had started a mutual venomous staring match, like a pair of cockatrices who had already turned each other into stone. In no time at all, bored by the inaction and lack of blood, the rabble of spectators started to disperse. Selma was close to tears. *"Bırak Suleyman. Bu erkek benim arkadaşım.* He is friend. A teacher at Vefbi Bey's school."

This last piece of information had seemed to bring about a calming effect on the eponymous Suleyman. Maybe he was the one heading for trouble. He left the scene shaking his fist and with a parting threat.

"My uncle will hear about this!"

Once Suleyman was gone, Selma began to explain, as calmly as she could, the reasons why Pete had been subjected to that thoroughly embarrassing incident. As Lysander so aptly remarked in "A Midsummer Night's Dream", "The course of true love never did run smooth." And so it proved on reflection of the foregoing calamitous series of events. It remained a matter for conjecture whether or not Pete took any comfort from Selma's explanation. Apparently, her sister's husband mentioned to his nephew Suleyman that Selma would be a good match for him when he decided to marry, and that he would speak to her father on his behalf. Naturally, she had not taken this proposition seriously, and she fully believed that her father would never give his consent. Of course, if he ever found out what was going on between her and a certain Englishman, a possible punitive marriage may have been on the cards.

Mecidiyeköy

During the month of March that year, some notable events were taking place outside the Turkish Republic. The white government of Rhodesia had declared itself a republic; the Supreme court in the USA had ruled that draft evaders could not be penalised after five years; the first flight of a Boeing 747 had taken place and the Nuclear Non-Proliferation Treaty came into effect. However, as Pete made his way towards the Parisiennes for another assignation with Selma, those events would have been as completely lost on him as the surrounding streets and buildings that he was passing en route. This was due to a quite different version of the real world that now assailed him.

Yet again, he had been robbed!

Since well before Christmas, he had been squirrelling away cash left over from his weekly expenditure. The Turkish banknotes of several denominations were kept in a zip up money belt buried in his rucksack. Recently, through the agency of his good friend Kemal who it seemed had limitless contacts in the city, he had managed to exchange the cash for American dollars. Kemal knew a dealer and shop owner in the Grand Bazaar who could give Pete a favourable exchange rate. After his experiences with Izzet back in October, Pete was apprehensive about taking up the offer but Kemal assured him that the dealer could be trusted – or at least as far as Kemal was concerned. Pete met the dealer, whose name was Mo, in the Grand Bazaar and the exchange took place. Pete walked away with around forty dollars. This would go towards his flight back to England which he planned to undertake at the end of April.

He had not checked the stash of money since his move from

Beyoğlu, but the previous day he had managed to exchange more lira that he had been carrying around with him and now had another ten dollars which would make his planned departure date more of a possibility. When he arrived at Fikret's, he went to his rucksack, removed the money belt, and then, to his utter bewilderment and vexation discovered that it was as empty as the day he had bought it. He scrabbled through all the other contents of the rucksack and all the spare pockets on the side, but the plain fact of the matter was, the money he had been saving had been stolen. But by whom?

It did not take long to work out the answer. It must have been Masood. Sadly, he realised that there was no way that the money could ever be recovered and he would not be able to replace it before the summer. What was he going to tell Selma? She would probably upbraid him for his foolishness in not keeping the money in a safer place. He considered that she might be pleased as he would be staying in Istanbul for longer. He had actually planned to return to her in July. He also sensed that she would be most concerned about him having to wait to see his family again. However, events earlier on that Thursday morning had somehow put a new perspective on his situation. He had received requests for private lessons outside the auspices of Vefbi's school which would bring extra income. All he could think of now was not only how to make up the amount he had lost, but also where he was going to keep it. As the day wore on, the concerns rushed back in and he almost walked past his rendezvous In fact, he only realised he had arrived when he heard Selma's honeyed voice calling to him. Now to tell her all!

As it turned out, he need not have experienced that deep flush of embarrassment, that dread of being exposed once again as inadequate and gullible. This was because Selma could not have been more sympathetic and supportive, at least until after her initial reaction.

"Why you trust that bastard Masood? You know he's not a nice kind of person!"

"To be honest, I never really trusted him, but then again, he did not live with us in Beyoğlu. Though I heard he had visited the flat, but with Roger, who would definitely not have let him look in my bag, let alone steal from me. He may not like me much but he has always said he hates thieving."

"And you believe him. Huh! Well never mind. How much money you have now?"

Pete informed Selma that he had ten dollars on him as well as fifty Turkish lira. She was adamant that he should find a safe place to keep his savings. Then to his surprise, and more than a little relief, she said that in future she would look after the money for him. As far as he knew, Masood was still in prison but it was better to be safe than sorry.

A new travel plan was now needed. He handed over the dollars and continued to do so for the next few weeks, until he calculated that by the end of May he would have enough to catch a train to Munich, hitch hike to Calais and get a Cross - Channel ferry back to England. Then there would just be his train fare to nis home town.

Selma had more good news for her lover. Another of her cousins, through her brother in law, also related to Hüseyin, was a student at the Teknik University. His name was Turgut, and he had started attending evening classes at Vefbi bey's school. In fact, he was in Pete's group. She had asked him if he and his fellow tenants would be prepared for Pete to go and live with them. After consulting with the others, he had agreed to Selma's proposition and said that Pete could move in at the weekend if he wanted to. Naturally, she had told Turgut nothing of her relationship with his teacher, which allayed some of Pete's fears. What a conflict of emotions he now felt. He may have lost his savings, but now had somewhere permanent to live, seven days a week, until he was ready to leave Istanbul. Better still, Turgut could turn out to be an ally, as by all accounts he did not get on very well with cousin Hüseyin. The latter person's volatile nature did not chime with his own more taciturn approach to life. Turgut picked his battles very carefully, as Pete was to find out.

By the following Saturday evening, Pete had installed himself in his new home, which was a one storey beige coloured flat roof building with a grassless rear garden situated in the village suburb of Mecidiyeköy. No more than a twenty minute dolmuş ride from Taksim Square, the whole area lay in the shadow of a road flyover and the Ali Sami Yen Stadium, which had been the home ground of Galatasary Football Club.

Mecidiyeköy, in those days, before it was transformed into a major financial district - with the imposing shopping mall of Cevahir and Trump Towers, was a sleepy suburb which was slowly growing out of its village identity. This was in common with a number of other locations bearing the *köy* appendage,(meaning village) and including places such as Feriköy, Ataköy, Bakirköy and Erenköy. The city itself seemed to be awakening from its long grey slumber and expanding into more of a metropolis. For the duration of Pete's stay there, however, this district retained a kind of village atmosphere, with cattle and horses on the streets, and all the accompanying livestock aromas; market stalls selling fruit, vegetables, hardware and drinks ranging from Coca Cola to *Kanyak*, the local brandy. Apart from the booming of traffic on the flyover heading towards the Bosphorus, where work had already started on a suspension bridge, there was a tranquil atmosphere. Pete soon found that the population consisted of friendly locals who appeared to have no problem in accepting this new foreigner. At least he was attempting to speak their language.

At this stage, certain individuals of Pete's acquaintance seemed to disappear out of his life. He continued to see his musician friends and attended the occasional jam with them. There was talk of forming a new band, but Pete was unable to commit to this, as he had his sights firmly set on a return to England. There was also the fact that he did not consider his musical ability to be anywhere near good enough to perform professionally in public. Somewhat significantly, he had seen nothing of Roger for over a fortnight and rumours abounded that he had gone back to London.

Brian, meanwhile, had been spending more and more time in Anatolia, especially after Vefbi had ordered a massive reprint of his evening class flyers, of which he had inexplicably run short.

Fortunately he never discovered where the missing ones had finished up.

The three Kurdish students - his new friends and co residents in Mecidiyeköy - were, at this time, intent on engaging themselves in a series of battles versus the Istanbul constabulary, or to be more precise, the riot police. This branch of the Turkish constabulary wore green uniforms with white helmets. Indeed their headgear caused them to be nicknamed *"Fruko"* as their helmets resembled the bottle tops of a popular Turkish brand of *gazoz* or fizzy lemonade. This band of law enforcers specialised in bringing down their riot sticks on the heads of unruly students, whenever there were confrontations in the city streets, or even on campus. In the prevailing political climate, these clashes were practically a daily occurrence. Turgut, who was the proud owner of a set of metal knuckle dusters, failed to return home one evening, much to everyone's consternation. However, he was able to present himself early the next morning, having spent the night in a police cell.

"My university teacher came to police station and spoke for me, so they let me go."

"Good thing he did," was Pete's response, "he must think highly of you. How did they react to your knuckle dusters."

"I did not take them last night." In truth, thought Pete, he probably never took them on any night.

The general unrest felt by young people, that had been sweeping across the western world, was now sowing its seeds among certain sections of the student body in high schools and higher education institutes across the nation. From Istanbul to Ankara, from Konya to Izmir and all points east. Turkey was not involved in the Vietnam War, but its armed forces formed part of NATO. In addition, the country was heavily involved in commerce with the United States, and this had fanned the flames of revolution which threatened daily to explode into deadly conflict. The would be revolutionaries accused the ruling administration of being "Nixon's arse lickers", the "running dogs" of America, and making Turkey its "fifty first state". That is if the graffiti springing up daily on a number of walls in the city was anything to go by.

Protests, as covered by the far from neutral Turkish media, usually involved hundreds of participants, many of whom were students and disgruntled workers. This uneasy alliance turned out to be a potent force, whose members tended to embrace the egalitarian teachings of Karl Marx rather than aligning themselves with Moscow or Beijing. Nevertheless, such was the fury of their demonstrations, that on some occasions, in addition to water cannon and tear gas, live rounds had been fired by the police. Indeed, some of the demonstrators had been killed as a result of escalating violence. And there had been casualties among the police.

Meanwhile, Sunday afternoons at the Mecidiyeköy residence had been set aside by the students for combat training, which took place in the rear garden. Although the whole event was intended for them to indulge in the art of boxing, it soon descended into a free for all, in which they all piled into each other just for the sake of it. Two of the lads were Syrian Kurds, while Turgut hailed from near Diyarbakir in South East Turkey. One of the Syrians, Abdul, initiated the proceedings.

"I think we will to fighting now!" And that was also to include their English guest.

Now Pete, in all honesty, was not much into pugilistic activities of any kind. The only times he had ever used what few skills he possessed in fighting had been utilised to defend himself against fellow male aggressors, intent at the time, on punching his lights out for one reason or another. That Sunday afternoon, through a combination of pulled punches and mutual cheating using wrestling holds, he managed to win one contest, draw one and lose the other. The pattern tended to be repeated on subsequent occasions, but he could never beat Turgut, Selma's cousin in law, who was a formidable scrapper. It was with some relief that Pete reflected that he knew nothing of her relationship with him. It was also true to say that Turgut was fast becoming a worthy and dependable friend.

The Kurdish students were always good natured in their banter with the Englishman, even when they touched on his country's cosy relations with the United States, and about Great Britain's imperial past. To counter this, Pete was quick to point out that his country had not allied themselves with America in the Vietnam War and that the former British Empire had never been a particular source of pride for him. He informed them that his greatest pride in the UK was its Welfare State, the NHS and free education.

As a general rule, in the evenings, they all ate well, with meals typically consisting of salami, *pastırma* (pastrami), huge salads and fresh fruit such as apples, pears, orange and quince. Quantities of orange juice, peach juice and *vişne* (black cherry juice) were consumed, and sometimes, beer. Indeed, life was becoming much easier for Pete as the month of March drew towards its midpoint. After all, he was continuing to meet Selma discreetly. Also, his work at the school was going well, with Vefbi expressing much satisfaction with his efforts. Another promising prospect had come to his attention, via one of his evening class students, concerning a secondary school which catered for less affluent pupils and was looking for teachers with an English speaking background. He had decided to apply and with any luck, he would have a permanent, well paid post to return to.

These were longer, warmer days. Trees were in bud, daffodils were sprouting. A general feeling of optimism pervaded with the anticipated arrival of spring. There was still the hint of a chill in the air which may have threatened the nascent green buds of the fig trees, hiding their pretty white flowers as if they were reticent brides to be. The filberts and aspens confidently displayed their blooming progeny in certain quiet streets, and sheltered parkland was bringing ever expanding splashes of colour to the grey city.

The date which proved to be of great significance to Pete and in Middle Eastern history was March the eleventh 1970, even though the events of that day were ultimately to turn into one of the supreme betrayals of modern times. And there have been ample contenders for such an accolade. Suffice it to say that a few days later, when Pete returned to the bungalow after work, he detected a hubbub of male voices surging on the other side of the front door, rising in volume as if they were about to burst through the very walls. On opening the door, he beheld a crowd of young men milling around the front room in earnest and animated conflab. Behind them, the table was loaded with various kinds of food and drink. A party was about to start, but they had shown the good grace to wait for Pete's arrival. He was handed an opened bottle of beer, then the eating and drinking began. It was some time before he was able to adapt to the situation and speak.

"This is something else Turgut. Wow, what's it all about?" Pete enquired, delighted at the sight of the plentiful food and drink on offer. The quarter tones of Middle Eastern folk music began to ring out from a small stereo system perched on a cabinet near the table. Turgut was just about able to respond, as his utter elation was plain to see.

"It's Iraq, the Ba'athists have given independence to Kurdistan and now the Iraqis recognise our identity and language too!"

To say that this news was momentous would be something of an understatement. After decades of persecution and subjugation to successive regimes – the mostly Kurdish city of Suleymaniye was even bombed by the RAF in 1924 – the Kurds were informed that the Iraqi government was going to recognise their language, and the same accord stated that the land of Iraq now consisted of two nationalities: Iraqi and Kurdish. This in itself would have been cause enough for celebration, and the future looked bright for Turgut et al. However, Kurdistan happened to be a word as opposed to an entity. It existed in the minds of a people who could trace their lineage back to pre history; recall with pride the victories of their ancestor Selahattin (or Saladin as he is known in the west) over the Crusaders in medieval times. Kurdistan, in theory, stretched eastwards from Diyarbakır, all through northern Syria to Irbil in Iraq.

Only one thing wrong with this party, thought Pete; no women! Nevertheless, he was soon caught up in a veritable tidal wave of joy, celebration and pure, raw emotion. In their youthful optimism the revellers could see before them a changed world; Kurdistan's identity on the global stage, lit up by the unquenchable fires of cultural and national recognition and representation in the United Nations. Indeed they looked forward to enjoying all the usual trappings of a nascent republic in the not too distant future.

At this point, the shadows of dark deeds that would fall upon them in the years to come remained a dismal and distant prospect, blissfully absent from the imaginings of the young men, who were noisily chanting what must have been their national anthem. After all, this day promised to be the start of better times for their homeland. Following Iraq' declaration on March the eleventh 1970, negative thoughts were set aside. However, there existed some inescapable facts: Turkey did not recognise the concept of Kurdistan as a nation, at least not in Turkish territory, nor did it acknowledge the Kurdish identity, referring to Kurds as "mountain Turks". Speaking the Kurdish language was proscribed. In addition, similar conditions existed in both Syria and Iran. As the party proceeded and various toasts were drunk to someone whose name sounded like "Bar zarny", Pete found himself musing on information he had gleaned from various sources. Nonetheless, many people of his acquaintance, including the more liberally minded Turks, tended to remain comparatively tight lipped on the subject of Kurds, as one could never be quite sure who might be listening in.

Then the young men started their dance, as the cassette player started belting out folk music from Eastern Turkey. Linking hands together, side by side, and forming a line much in the manner that Pete had seen in Greece, they began crossing their feet from left to right repeatedly, then bending their knees left and right in a near perfectly synchronised manner. How did they manage that? Pete was about to find out. After completing their first dance, they grabbed him and placed him in the middle of their line, where he only just stopped himself from going into a Tiller girls routine. Turgut gave the instructions. Apparently, the dancer at the end would squeeze the hand of the person next to him, and that signal would be swiftly passed down the line to bend their knees and half rotate them on the spot. With the added music, he found the whole experience highly exhilarating. A couple of beers beforehand helped remove any inhibitions he might have felt.

After what seemed an eternity of eating, drinking, dancing and cheering for Mustafa Barzani, the party finally broke up with the revellers on an all time high. Pete and his pals certainly slept soundly enough during what was left of the night. Indeed, the combination of food, alcohol and increasingly frantic, energetic dancing ensured that Pete enjoyed the kind of slumber that was not assailed by the usual surrealistic dreams, with improbable, anarchic plot lines. The following day was a Thursday and it was work as usual. At least he would only have to teach during the morning, then there would be the afternoon to follow. And Selma.

The first lesson on the following day at the European Languages school was delivered by a young Englishman still quite unsteady on his feet, with a mouth that felt like used sandpaper and the kind of headache that makes one nostalgic for a medieval executioner. Unsurprisingly, no mention was made in the class of Kurdistan, independent or otherwise. Pete thought it judicious not to bring up the subject. Somehow, the session on active and passive verbs seemed to drag on, and in his ragged mind, he started questioning the usefulness of his students learning utterances such as "Susan was asked by Jim if she would be free next week," as opposed to "Jim asked Susan if she was free... etc."

Later that afternoon, he found himself relating to Selma details of the previous night's events. She showed little interest. Even though she was related to some Kurds by marriage and had a soft spot for Turgut, her apathy towards them and their striving towards autonomy was most apparent.

"You know that Turgut is very good hearted boy. But that Huseyin, my God he is prick!"

Pete was taken aback, somewhat, by her frankness but thought her feelings towards Huseyin were justified. There was also her sister's husband. "Your brother in law sounds like a nice guy. You always said he was generous and fun."

"When he is in good mood, yes. But he also told my sister if she is unfaithful, some men will take her in mountains and leave her there."

Pete felt a light hearted, sarcastic response was called for. "I like his style."

"Oh but he goes with other women."

"So he's a hypocrite. Anyway, you don't know that for certain."

She was right about Turgut, though. He had been only too pleased to accept Pete into the Mecidiyeköy household and the others had made him feel very much at home.

The foregoing conversation was taking place as they were strolling along İnönü Caddesi, past the German Consulate and the Teknik Universite downhill towards Dolmabahçe. They were taking a walk because Pete had discovered that the key to their love nest was missing from its usual hook in the school office and on this occasion Hassan must have been making use of the facilities. Their route took them towards the Ismet İnönü Stadium, where they paused for a moment to gaze at the vista before them. The Golden Horn glittered in the fading sunlight as its waters joined those of the Bosphorus and the wider stretch of the Marmara Sea. A car ferry, almost as broad as it was long, was leaving Kabataş, its white wake trailing back towards the harbour. Even further in the distance, the Princes Islands appeared as spectral grey shapes in a gathering sea mist.

Pete was familiar with this spot, on an outcrop of scruffy ground bereft of any grass, about twenty yards from the stadium perimeter. In between, a sheer twenty foot drop ended on litter strewn waste ground. On two occasions, he had been here at night when a football match had been in progress. This free vantage point was packed with many of the city's poorer element who were no less fanatical about their team than the paying customers inside the stadium. They could not afford the admission price but could view from afar the action taking place in one half of the pitch. Pete had been able to make out the colours of Galatasaray as their red and orange shirts were just about discernible.

The mighty stadium lay silent, as a yellowing sun slid dejectedly towards the sea, as if, in common with the couple standing together on the promontory, it did not wish for the day to end. The noiseless terraces and stands, which on match days would be reverberating with the crescendo roars of fans chanting *"Cim bom bom!"* - creating a cauldron of passion for themselves and the players on the pitch - seemed almost ghostly and uninvitingly cold.

This was in contrast with the lovers, as they stole warm embraces in their limited time of isolation, free from prying eyes. The moment was poignant but they needed to set off back to Taksim. Suddenly, Pete glimpsed a movement at the edge of his range of vision. They had not been free from prying eyes, it seemed, and a less welcome sight could not possibly have appeared at that moment than the one that met their anxious gaze. Selma's cousin, Huseyin and a tough looking friend were striding purposefully towards them.

"Mob handed, I see," Pete muttered involuntarily. Although Selma was not familiar with that example of the English vernacular, she nevertheless voiced her concern.

"Oh my God. What does he want now?"

Huseyin's eyes narrowed perceptibly as he approached the couple. Both young men came to a halt not two yards from them.

"So we are meeting again." His voice positively dripped with menace.

Pete realised with some alarm that he was at that moment standing rather too close to the path's edge for comfort. The drop seemed to go on forever, as did this somewhat tension filled pause in proceedings. He began to imagine himself as a pathetic heap of broken bones, lying on top of the filthy, fly ridden garbage below. Then Huseyin continued, while his companion remained silent, eyes fixed on Pete.

"You made some trouble with my uncle you know. I don't like that."

Selma was incensed, but in glancing towards her, Pete noticed she was actually looking quite scared. This threw him somewhat. Then she looked straight at her cousin.

"What do you want from us? Come on Peter, let's go."

However, as she stepped forward, pulling Pete with her, the young Kurd barred their progress. To his left the gap and the sheer drop yawned like the very jaws of hell. He was trapped and was wondering how, or if at all, he was going to survive the fall that was now inevitable. In that same moment, he began to look more closely at Huseyin's accomplice. Just how useful would Martin's six week karate course prove to be? Not at all, he suspected. Suddenly he realised he had seen that fellow before, somewhere. Yes, he realised, with very mixed emotions, he had been at the party in Mecidiyeköy the previous night. The young man was also staring at Pete, his eyes narrowing, not with hostility but with recognition. Much to Huseyin's surprise, he began to address Pete very clearly, in English.

"I remember you. I saw you at Turgut's last night!"

Pete's potential nemesis postponed his intended actions. which were definitely aimed at pushing him over the edge. He turned to his companion then back to Pete.

"Do you know Turgut then?"

"Yes I do. I live at his house and he is a good friend."

The other would be assailant now put in a word.

"Yes it's true. He is a friend of Turgut."

Huseyin gave one withering glance towards the couple, then he and his friend strode off, the latter stealing a furtive parting smile towards them, which Pete returned. They headed swiftly towards the road leading back up to Taksim. Pete turned to Selma, feeling calmer now. She was still shaken.

"I don't think he fancied upsetting me again, as Turgut would definitely have sorted him out, and he knew it."

"I tell Turgut and he will beat him."

"Ah well, I did mention what happened in the street the other day and he offered to 'speak' with Huseyin. I thanked him but said he needn't bother. Better leave it as we don't want your father hearing about all this."

Pete had been careful not to give Turgut the impression that he was seeing Selma, but he had no clue as to how many of her family knew about their true relationship. Besides, Turgut had probably guessed, as he was no fool. He now quivered with dread as he pondered on how that encounter with Huseyin & co may have turned out. Bearing in mind all the scrapes he had been in from a very young age, perhaps his mother had been right about a guardian angel watching over him. Even though whoever that may have been had evidently not been paying full attention on a couple of occasions during the past five months. Anyway, he anticipated no more problems from his love rival.

Strange as life is, and no more strange than what had happened to him up to this particular point in time, it transpired that a few years later, Pete found himself in the company of his former foe at a party in Istanbul. His first words to Pete at that gathering were,

"I think we had some problems in the past."

To which both young men laughed at the memory and were soon chatting, drinking and reminiscing together in the manner of old friends. Such is humanity and its many faceted enigmas. Such is the healing power of time, and as far as Pete was concerned, of eventually becoming part of Selma's family.

The month of March in Western Turkey is one of increasing sunshine and rising temperatures, although the evenings remained chilly until well into April. The situation regarding the love nest in Harbiye was becoming more and more problematic. This was due to the fact that a third friend had moved in with Hassan, and the flat itself was rarely empty. It was then that Selma suggested crossing to the Asian side where she knew of a remote spot where they were highly unlikely to be disturbed. It was quite near to Erenköy and only a short walk from the railway station. Fortunately, with the warmer weather they would be able to spend a fair amount of time outside without fear of catching a chill. The journey to this spot involved a dolmuş ride to Karaköy, crossing the Bosphorus on the ferry, then a train trip to Erenköy. Total time, about one hour. A five minute walk, and they were in a quiet wood with grassy banks amid the heady aroma of linden blossom from the tall trees which screened them from voyeuristic eyes.

"The flowers on these trees make *ıhlamur*. Very good for you if you get ill"

Selma's casual but informative remark caused Pete to smile inwardly. He had drunk some glasses of linden tea which was of a similar hue to sage tea but did not taste to him quite so revolting. Several Turkish men of his acquaintance had slyly informed him that the tea was very good for…then they would raise their index finger, simulating an erection. They also tended to make the same observations about pistachio nuts, hazelnuts and *ayran*. Pete thought that they would probably say the same about apples or potatoes, given the chance.

The Trouble with offal

Pete's Tuesday and Thursday evenings were taken up with teaching private students, but one day he received a very strange request from a colleague at Vefbi bey's school. Cengiz Göktepe was a mid ranking administrator with Turkish airlines, THY, who assisted at the school in the evenings. His English grammar was near flawless and his accent was more American than Turkish. This made him a valuable asset to the school where, like Pete, he taught for two hours three nights per week. He was slight in build, standing no more than five foot four inches in his plain but expensive black shoes. At work, he tended to wear the grey suits, white cotton shirts and Italian silk ties of the growing Turkish middle classes.

His gleaming bald pate was skirted on either side by strong dark brown short cut hair. His small boned faced often exuded a ready smile and Cengiz's round eyes at once showed earnest interest and inquisitiveness when participating in conversation. His dialogues with Pete mostly took place in the break between lessons and sometimes after school. Although they rarely touched on politics, whenever they did, Pete detected in Cengiz a suppressed desire to be honest about his country, rather than reel off the platitudes that glossed over the facts, like others tended to do. However, the patriotic fervour instilled in him during his education and military service always prevented him from overstepping the mark. Pete could see that he was certainly well regarded by Vefbi bey..

It just so happened that THY, which was the chief source of his income, published a financial report each year at the end of March. This fine example of an international conveyor of persons and commodities across the air lanes of the world, had established such a reputation, in terms of punctuality, that its aircraft had, the previous year, been banned from landing at some airports abroad, including Heathrow. The "Top Airline" awards that were to accrue to THY, were to come thirty years later. Meanwhile, Turkey's retaliation for these humiliating prohibitions had been swift, and subsequently BEA's flights were no longer welcome in any Turkish airport, at least not for the time being.

The aforementioned request made by Cengiz, involved Pete's assistance in the translation of THY's financial report into English. As chance would have it, Pete had been applying himself more diligently to the task of learning Turkish. A favourite pastime of his was to sit in tea houses, listening to the various conversations that were in progress, and watching games of *tavla* or backgammon being played by earnest, chain smoking participants. As he sipped black tea from small bulb shaped glasses, or coffee – *orta şekerli* – from espresso sized cups, he made mental notes of frequently recurring words and phrases. He also carried out the same process at restaurants and gatherings of Turkish friends, so gradually a pattern of familiar sounds began to emerge from which meanings could be made and communicated. Naturally, his accent at first was laughable, but his listeners turned out to be most forgiving and helpful in this respect. After all, how many English people had ever taken the trouble to learn their language? He found that he could also distinguish words and their spellings from street signs, hoardings, shops and buses.

However, the prospect of attempting to comprehend what would obviously be a highly complex document daunted him to such an extent that he had begun to phrase a polite refusal. In the event, Cengiz seemed to anticipate this reaction and his tone was reassuring.

"You can check over my English translation for mistakes as I go through, so it looks right, like correct my English, then I treat you to some dinner and drinks."

"It's a deal, Cengiz."

The first session on the THY financial report took place two nights later at Cengiz's office, with the next session proceeding in the more relaxed atmosphere of his apartment. For the initial meeting, the other office staff had long since gone home. Only the *kapıcı* remained, so there were no prying eyes, no snooping enquiries as to why a foreigner was being made privy to the company's documents, before they were released to the world's business community. The original report, in Turkish, lay on a desk, alongside several foolscap sheets containing Cengiz's scribbled notes. Pete, for his part, sat opposite Cengiz like an interview candidate, but under no pressure, sipping tea, poring over notes and pointing out errors which were mostly in grammar, meaning and tense.

Many Turkish publications in English that Pete had managed to peruse during his sojourn in Istanbul, were poorly translated from the original Turkish, as exemplified by the Istanbul Tourist guide for 1969 which contained passages such as:

"For every age of them is a pleasure to help all visitors..... noone (sic) stranger ever met difficulties to be understood."

Charming in its way and just about intelligible with a little effort. However, that standard of English expression would not pass muster in the international business community. Cengiz's efforts had in fact been far more accurate. Thus, for two nights only, Pete became a proof reader who was tasked with untangling literal translations, reorganising some of the syntax and polishing up the text, with the result that it actually appeared to have been written by an English person.

With the translated document completed and ready for typing, Pete felt that it was a job well done. Thus, brimming with satisfaction and feeling more than a little fatigued, he left Cengiz's apartment at around ten pm for the short *dolmuş* ride to Mecidiyeköy. Cengiz had promised to take him out for drinks and a meal the following evening. As he stood on the pavement, scouring the street for a dolmuş, he could hear from afar the honking of a couple of ships as they passed through the Bosphorus. The sound was like and old man groaning in the night, indignant at the childish hoots of cars, vans and buses which were still crowding the streets of a benighted city. Even as late as this, the straits glittered on both sides with multi coloured neon signs and fairy lights of the scores of clubs and restaurants stretching from Beşiktaş to Bebek and points north and east.

A lone taxi chugged towards him, and as it passed, Pete yelled out, "Mecidiyeköy!". The car stopped and he joined two passengers who were sitting behind the driver. It took only ten minutes or so to reach his stop, and as he disembarked, he noticed the make of the car. It was an Anadol. He was aware of these Turkish made vehicles, consisting of a Ford engine and gearbox, Italian tyres and seats and a Reliant fibre glass body, but had not seen a four door model before. He felt overall as if he had been riding in a large pram. However, it made a pleasant enough change from the usual Desoto or Chevrolet.

*****

Istanbul is one of many major continental cities justly famed for a number of popular meeting places, dependant, of course, on the purpose of each gathering. East of the Golden Horn, in the modern city, the favoured meeting places for lunch might be The *Altın Tabak* (Golden Plate) restaurant near Taksim, or the *Bab Kafeterya* in Yeşilcam Sokak. Afternoon trysts may be held in the *Atlantik* on Istiklal or *Cennet Bahçhesi* (Heaven Garden). In the evening, *Istanbulluler* (Istanbulites) like to gather in the outdoors along the Bebek shoreline, or make their way to the *Çiçek Pasajı* in Pera as they still do to this day.

It was towards the latter named venue that Pete found himself walking, beside Cengiz, on a mild April Friday evening. They were strolling along Istiklal Caddesi in the direction of Galatasaray.

The Çiçek Pasajı turned out to be a long, wide, covered arcade, leading at right angles to Istiklal towards the edge of the Beyoğlu district. Its name was taken originally from the flower shops inside which were opened by Russian women, who had escaped the communist regime in their home country. By coincidence, this haven for topers and gourmandisers was situated very close to the British Consulate. As Pete and Cengiz entered, the delightful aroma of kebabs cooking over charcoal pervaded the air, mingling with cigarette smoke and stale sweat. In fact, several eating places had superseded the flower shops in the 1940s, and were crowded into this centuries old complex, but as the erstwhile traveller entered, they would first encounter pop up bars serving draught beer. They made one of these bars their first port of call, where the THY's translation assistant was treated to two pints of local beer. Pete noticed that the barman was pouring the fairly lively beer too quickly and was removing the inevitable two inch head with a far from hygienic looking flat piece of wood. (If he did that in Essex, he'd get a beefing, mused Pete.) Still, the taste was most agreeable.

As they sat down to enjoy their second drinks, Cengiz suggested an appetizer. "We should start with some *kokoreç*. They are making it over there."

"OK, I'll try that, Cengiz. What is it, by the way?"

"It is Armenian dish made of sheep's intestine, covered in spices and cooked over charcoal."

Pete could hardly believe what he had just heard and even less imagine that he was actually going to consume such a revolting sounding dish. However, after another pint, he had changed his outlook. The evening was warming up, rather agreeably, and he was beginning to feel mellow. Ready for anything, in fact.

Five minutes later, Pete found himself munching on Kokoreç which was served in a bread roll with some black pepper and onions. The additional herbs and spices added during cooking rendered the taste pleasant enough, even for offal, which he usually despised. He looked up momentarily and noticed Cengiz, who had finished his meal. His face was rendering a fair impression of a Cheshire Cat. He concluded that he must rank sheep gut as among his favourite foods. Or was there another explanation? There was.

"The company accepted my draft translation and were very pleased. Maybe I get promotion. Who knows?"

"I'll drink to that," replied Pete, growing steadily more cheery – until he noticed his near empty glass. Cengiz soon put that right. Only then was he able to voice the Turkish for "Cheers".

"*Şerefe!*", he almost shouted.

Having finished their snacks and beers, they decamped to a nearby table and ordered kebabs, salads with *pide* and *pilaki* (pitta bread and cold beans in tomato sauce). Cengiz also ordered a bottle of white wine which had been produced in the western area of Turkey known as Trakya, or Thrace. The waiter placed an array of *meze* on their table, consisting of the customary hot and cold starters. Then just as Cengiz was starting to pour the first glasses of wine, a wave of wild eastern music assailed Pete's ears, and from around the corner, a trio of musicians was approaching, playing *saz*, *ne* and *tabla*. Pete's thought were summoned back to the evening in Karaköy at the government brothels.

Somehow, this present location was much more exotic. Then, as if by some sophistry, a belly dancer hove into view, all swaying hips and clicking fingers. However, much to Pete's astonishment, the dancer was not a woman. At that moment, a kind of realisation dawned on him. Looking around him, he perceived that in the entire confines of the Flower Passage, there was not one woman. Even the belly dancer was a male.

Now the ancient art of belly dancing has its historical roots in the very depths of civilisation. However, the particular form of the dance commonly seen in Turkey, was evident during the Osmanlı period in the harems and households of sultans and the nobility. Since those times, it has been on view in various places of entertainment across the Middle East and North Africa. This particular iteration in the Çiçek Pasajı was Pete's second experience of the dance which was, of course, dripping with eroticism. Indeed, in the era of the sultans, the dancer's lithe gyrating body enabled the sultan to remain in a supine position whilst the woman performed her movements with his penis firmly inside her. All highly desirable, if you were able to afford it.

As far as this male dancer was concerned, the slightly built young man was amicably received by the diners and he seemed a familiar figure in those surroundings. He was dressed in a billowy white blouse and tight blue jeans. Pete concluded that he must be gay but then again, there seemed to be more of an acceptance of homosexual men and transexuals in Istanbul than in his own country. Differing cultures, he mused. Cengiz, in common with many members of the audience, slid a five lira note down the front of the dancer's blouse. As the young man and his band moved off towards another part of the passage, Pete and Cengiz resumed their meal and then ordered some fruit.

"We must have *rakı* now, " asserted Pete's companion, shortly after they had drained the last of the wine from their second bottle. Accordingly, a bottle, with its distinctive gold label, containing a clear liquid was brought to them, along with two tumblers and a jug of water. Cengiz poured out two generous measures and added the same amount of water. As Pete regarded the milky substance he was about to drink, he could not help reflecting on the fact that ninety five percent of the Turkish population was Moslem, but the national drink was forty percent proof. Despite imbibing rakı on a few occasions since his arrival in the city, he had never really accustomed himself to the bitter aniseed tang that lingered in his palate. However, after three pints of beer and a bottle of wine, the taste seemed irrelevant. It was agreeable almost, even though the spirit scorched his throat and almost stripped away the roof of his mouth.

By this time it could be said of Pete that he was very drunk; launched into a vale of numbness in which he felt nothing and seemed to be on the outside looking in, regarding himself, as it were, through an alcoholic haze. It was in this state that his usual reserve all but disappeared, leaving him to respond to drunken perceptions of his new environment and the stimuli it generated. On this occasion, something quite bizarre happened. Bereft, of any inhibitions, he began blurting out words and phrases in fluent Turkish. Cengiz reacted with both amazement and delight. It seemed that his English colleague had absorbed more than he had hitherto considered during his six months or so in Istanbul. It must have been by a form of osmosis or something. If only a technique like that could be employed in Vefbi Bey's school in the teaching of English. For Pete's part, he had listened to so much of the language being spoken around him that the phonemes and lexical structures

265

of Turkish must have somehow stuck in his subconscious. Or alternatively, he had just learned a third language and its release had been precipitated by an over consumption of alcohol.

Obviously Cengiz was also tipsy but he continued to converse with Pete in English.

"I think we are both very drunk. We should eat something to make us sober."

Pete did not really believe that such a food existed. Then he was reminded of a night during his first year in college, when he had been in a similar condition. A kindly, tolerant girlfriend had prepared him a hot laxative beef curry which he had consumed quite rapidly, just after the bar had closed. Oddly enough, he was unable ever to recall how well the curry had actually worked for him. Cengiz had evidently made up his mind as to their next port of call. He suggested they should sober up by visiting an *İşkembici* – a tripe restaurant!

Pete was not at all sure about this. *"İşkembe demek, 'tripe' demek. Onu hiç bir zaman yemedim!"*

Despite Pete's slurred speech, Cengiz was able to deduce from his accurate Turkish that he had never eaten tripe before. He too reverted to Turkish.

"Oh burada işkembe çorbası çok iyi. Lezzetli" (The tripe soup here is very good. Tasty.)

So according to Cengiz, tripe soup was ok. Pete remembered the waiters who shared their accommodation in Beyoğlu. They used to serve tripe soup until one in the morning in this very district. No harm in trying it, he supposed. Although he disliked the taste of offal generally, this evening's introduction to barbecued sheep's intestine had been agreeable enough. After Cengiz had settled the bill for dinner, they crossed the street together and entered the premises of a dimly lit tripe restaurant, which nevertheless was packed with late night diners. It was said that the ethnic Greek citizens of Istanbul were the greatest consumers of this type of food, but looking around, Pete could see just as many Turks seated at the formica topped tables, obviously enjoying this fare. Perhaps they were all pissed as well.

Years later, Pete would regale anyone who cared to listen with his account of "what arrived and was placed in front of me". This would probably revive much discomfort in any offal hater who had shared a similar experience. Suffice it to say that Pete, in his inebriated condition, eyed with concern the blanched tubes and lumps from a cow's digestive system which were floating around in a glutinous grey liquid. The lemon juice and olive oil he added hardly disguised the taste, but he struggled on gamefully, managing to consume half of his meal, the consistency of which reminded him of some whelks he had once eaten at a seafood stall in London's East End. The shellfish were also tough, slippery and hard to swallow. He feared that this very substance was almost certain to make a return appearance a few hours later. They left the *İşkembeci* with Pete feeling no more drunk or indeed sober than he had felt beforehand. Except for the fact that he was continually gabbling in Turkish the length of Istiklal. Once they reached Taksim Square, he thanked his companion for a most entertaining evening and bade him farewell.

The *dolmuş* ride home was uneventful. Pete somehow resisted the temptation to engage the driver in conversation, despite his new found fluency in the native language. Due to there being comparatively light traffic in the streets after midnight, the journey was a short one. His Kurdish housemates were still up but about to retire. Much to their delight, their mad English companion proceeded to relate to them the evening's events in near fluent (and more or less correct) Turkish. Evidently their teaching had not been in vain. Suddenly a great tiredness came over him and he made his way wearily to his bed. In fact he was so fatigued that he felt he could drop off to sleep in an instant.

However, there was something that he had forgotten: the whirling pit. He was presently reminded of it. As soon as he closed his eyes it hit him. It seemed as though his head was being corkscrewed into a veritable maelstrom of nausea from which the only escape was to open his eyes again and focus on the ceiling. Obviously, as far as sleep was concerned, this proved to be counter productive. Was this some kind of Hell he was entering every time he shut his eyes? Eventually, those diabolical agents responsible for torments such as the whirling pit, decided their victim had had enough. and somehow Pete managed to fall into a deep and resonant slumber.

The fact remained though that at the moment he fell asleep there was still a certain amount of turmoil going on in his digestive system. Animal intestines and other offal, vied with kebabs, pitta bread, rice and salad, not to mention a heady concoction of alcoholic beverages. In truth, though, Pete had a proud record of hardly ever throwing up after getting drunk. Indeed, he hated being sick so much that he would always fight off the surge of vomit until he had driven it away, or more usually, when he actually had to submit to a mighty choking hurl.

Indeed, there had been one instance during his sojourn in higher education when he had supped rather too heavily at a party in one of the hostels, but in addition had scoffed a number of fishy tasting vol-au-vents. At the time he had been dating a girl three years older than him. and after the party they had repaired to her room where doubtless both had been anticipating a night of pleasure. They had just begun kissing, when he felt something like a large boot kicking him in the guts. Breaking off suddenly from his astonished partner's grasp, he rushed out of the room and into the corridor toilet. He felt he had made it just in time as he sat down expectantly on the lavatory seat. Unfortunately, the waste products inside him had decided on taking a different exit. Too late, he swung himself round as a cascade of dark yellow vomit formed a perfect arc on the cubicle walls. He had of course returned the next day to apologise to the female occupants of the said corridor. After all, they were the ones who had had to clean up the mess he had made. He always insisted that it was the vol-au-vents that had made him throw up, rather than the drink.

The scene now switches back to a bedroom in a small bungalow, in a sleepy suburb of Istanbul. No girl this time. Observe the prone figure of a drunken Englishman lying stretched out under the covers, blissfully unaware of the disaster about to unfold. Once more, a vomit volcano was preparing to erupt, and when it did, grey-green and dark yellow magma shot into the air and spread itself all over Pete's sleeping form. He found himself choking a couple of times, and a warm sticky mass spurted out of his mouth, over his head, and splattering on to the wall behind his pillow. Pete, for his part, was barely conscious and, believing it all to be just a dream, fell asleep once more. All he knew about this was that something had caused him to wake up with a start. His guardian angel perchance, as there had been multiple cases of people drowning in their own sick. Indeed, within a few months of this episode, the world was to lose a major rock star from the very same cause.

The next morning, Pete awoke at around seven thirty but as his usual morning drowsiness melted away, he felt that something was distinctly awry. For a start, he was unable to open his eyes. Furthermore, his nose was blocked and there was a diabolical taste in his mouth. Gingerly he tried to prise apart his eyelashes, only to discover that they were stuck together with his own dry vomit. He desperately needed to get to the bathroom, not only to relieve himself but to clean up somehow. It was at that moment he noticed, to his horror, that a disgusting yellow mass had coagulated on his *yorgan*, the thin Turkish duvet that covered him. It got worse. Glancing behind him, he was now able to discern what had splashed on the wall. Indeed, if the excellent curators of the Tate Modern had been present, the multi coloured mess on that wall with its dried up rivulets running down from it (caught in an irridescent stasis) might well have been of great interest as an exhibit. As his

nose gradually cleared, the acrid stench of offal and stale aniseed was starting to tamper with his olfactory functions in a far from pleasant manner.

This was an unmitigated disaster writ large, and it was not over yet. He found himself negotiating his way to the toilet past his Kurdish housemates, who were not displaying too many signs of amusement or admiration. As they were usually such jovial fellows, this did not augur well.

For his part, however, the cleaning bill for the bedclothes was going to set him back a few lira and he would, of course, have to wash the wall down. For future reference, it would be a very long time before he would re-acquaint himself with that chalky concoction of rakı and water. It would be fair to say that he was to avoid any close contact with that drink for a good ten years or so. From this time forward, every time rakı was introduced to a meal table - not infrequently in Turkey of course – that same sick feeling came over him that he was now experiencing, having at last reached the WC. The whole episode, however, did make a thoroughly entertaining anecdote to recount to friends back home in England, whose responses were invariably uproarious.

Part Three

Sulemaniye

April, with its fine, clear days, was drawing to a close. Pete could never have imagined that springtime would be so warm and sunny. Back home in Eastern England, recovery of the land from harsh, bleak winters could be slow, and the stark terrain would reflect little greenery for some weeks to come. Meanwhile, all around the Bosphorus, migrating birds that had followed the sun southwards were returning north, with many of them set to make landfall in England before the onset of summer.

Perched on the rear seat of a *dolmuş*, wedged between two portly Turkish women who both gave off an aroma of lemon cologne and stale sweat, he wondered how much longer this journey would take, across the city to Sulemaniye Mosque, which he had been determined to visit before leaving for the UK. He also pondered on how his own body odour must have smelt to the two women on his flanks

The time had arrived for Pete to return to the homeland he had been missing so much of late. However, despite the desire to set off as soon as he could – and he had by now saved up enough money to do so – he wanted to visit Sulemaniye Cami before he departed. His Turkish acquaintances were constantly telling him that it was the largest mosque in the world and well worth a visit.

The actual intent of his journey was to purchase a train ticket for Munich at Sirkeci Station but he found he could make a diversion, and the dolmuş ride would take him to a point just outside the mosque, on the Third Hill, with a view overlooking the old city and across the Golden Horn to Galata. It was lunch time when he arrived, and opposite the entrance to the mosque was a restaurant with indoor and outdoor seating. The most popular dish appeared to be a white bean stew in a tomato sauce served with *pilav* rice. At three lira a portion, how could he resist? He also ordered a glass of *ayran* to wash it down with.

Seated alone at an exterior table, quite unnoticed now, it seemed, Pete was able to take in the forefront of the mighty Islamic edifice.

"I live here, well, over there…"

He came close to actually voicing these sentiments. Parting from Istanbul would be something of a wrench, in more ways than one. As expected, lunch tasted very much better than it looked. Finishing his *ayran*, he began to feel a tiredness spreading over him that always made him vulnerable to negative images and thoughts. These now came rushing into his mind, dispelling the mood of contentment he had previously been feeling. Inevitably, caught like this on the borders of depression, he began to recall all that had happened to him over the past six months or so. How much had he changed as a person during this time? Quite considerably, one might argue, as he had gone to bed one night and woken up next morning virtually penniless in a foreign city. He had worked and earned money there and had lived among its people. He had, in effect become a tiny part of the fabric of this enigmatic, fabulous metropolis. The city, for its part, had taken him to its bosom, but now he had to leave. Would he definitely be returning? Or might he revert back to his old persona, once he had made contact with his family and former acquaintances?

Slowly but purposefully, he rose to his feet and headed towards the mosque of Suleyman the Magnificent. Its vastness of grey stone and marble, its sheer height and span, was designed to represent the pre-eminence of that lost Osmanlı Empire. Indeed, the empire that the Sultan ruled over had dominated the Balkans, the Middle East and washed against the very borders of powerful western domains. The intention of Sinan, architect of the Sulemaniye Mosque, had been to represent his sultan as a (self proclaimed) second Solomon. Perhaps some of Solomon's wisdom may not have gone amiss when Suleyman embarked on his ultimately failed attempt to capture Vienna.

Pete marvelled at the many smaller domed buildings surrounding the main construction which itself appeared almost like a corpulent mother figure gathering her children around her. It was certainly the case, as he discovered, that the whole religious complex included the provision of food, bed and board for the poorer citizens, and education centres or *madrasas*. His mind began to reflect once more on the nurturing nature of this city, and how it once presented itself as the principal purveyor and guardian of Islamic values. He turned to inspect the *"Qibla"* Wall. On the Qibla wall, there were majestic tiled displays in vivid colours of red, blue green and purple, proclaiming the names of Allah, the Prophet Muhammed, and the caliphs. Near the western portal, he saw a stained-glass window, which at first he felt was somewhat incongruous in a mosque, especially with their inverted shield-like ecclesiastical shapes. On closer inspection, there were panes, again in different and vibrant colours, displaying Arabic script and golden flower patterns.

After inspecting the mausolea of Suleyman and his wife Hurrem, or Roxelana, Pete made for the exit, somewhat overwhelmed by the vastness, the opulence, but at the same time tranquility that constituted the main features and atmosphere of this sanctified construction. Just outside the mosque walls, he noticed yet another tomb; that of Sinan, the greatest architect of the Osmanli classical period, who had overseen the design and construction of no fewer than three hundred mosques and hundreds of other buildings all over the empire. Busy guy, thought Pete. Must have suited him though, as he lived to the age of ninety four. Not everyone dies of overwork! He began his journey of a mile or so, on foot, to Sirkeci Station.

Spreading out in all directions, was a plethora of streets, alleys and pathways, like the arteries, veins and capillaries all flowing into and out of the "Dome of the Rock". The hill he was now descending and its mosque had been named after the location, in Jerusalem, of Solomon's Temple. All of these thoroughfares were crammed with vendors of multifarious commodities. In each street or alleyway, there were different shops and stalls, all selling the same wares, but each street boasting its own different set of products. All were in opposition to each other, yet there still existed a spirit of bonhomie among the sellers.

Continuing in what he surmised to be the direction of Sirkeci, Pete manoeuvred his way through crowds of locals and visitors alike, some affecting disinterest and some inspecting and negotiating over the goods on offer. In this street there were items essential to ordinary family life, such as kitchenware, as evidenced by the clanging of pots, pans, metal teapots, Turkish coffee makers and large metal tureens. They hung from the walls, inside and outside of vending places, smallest items at the top. They were the fruits of labour from the same factories, offered at the same (but negotiable) prices, but with the same hopes of each different trader pinned on one or more customers choosing to buy from them and not the others. The alley Pete was walking along squeezed itself between rows of mouldering, grey buildings, typical of the non-style of post republican architecture. Back up the hill, Sinan was still turning in his tomb.

Providing some old world eastern charm and character to these drab residential blocks were ancient Osmanli timber houses, which he came upon every fifty yards or so. Peering past the bustling, noisy proceedings, he decided to turn left along another street, then down some stone steps, flanked by stalls purveying modern plastic children's toys. Further along, as he made his way towards Sirkeci, the beckoning banners of cheap embroidered fabrics, hung out proudly in their massed ranks, but they failed to tempt him into parting with his cash.

The old city streets were now broadening out and becoming choked once more with afternoon traffic. With every stride he was progressing nearer to the station. He and his three friends had travelled into this terminus on that fateful day last October when he had been swindled so pathetically out of his last twenty pounds. The rest was history, as far as he was concerned. He sidled past a couple of stalls, where oranges and pomegranates were being sliced in two by hand and crushed in large appliances with black handled levers at an industrial rate. The juices were mixed together and he noticed that queues had formed, due no doubt to the rising afternoon temperature. He resisted the temptation to purchase what had, in fact, become his favourite non alcoholic drink. Passing the now familiar post office, he proceeded along a busier, noisier street, at the confluence of several others, where the cries of milk sellers, shoe shine boys and men carrying *simit* rings threaded on wooden poles, mingled with the honking and buzzing of Istanbul's perpetual traffic.

As his strides took him ever nearer the terminus, he mused to himself on how fortunate it was that he had remained in contact with one of his college girlfriends. In his last letter to her, he had asked her to send him a Student Union card, as he had lost his. Due to her still being at the college and a union rep. to boot, this did not prove to be a problem. Besides, to the best of his knowledge, Pete was entitled to membership a year after leaving higher education anyway. The aforementioned card had arrived a few days ago, together with an invitation to visit the sender at the college on his return. This, he certainly intended to do and was quite looking forward to thanking her for her kindness.

Making their way through a broad, grubby street, filled, it seemed, with every conceivable form of road transport, Pete observed two Türkmen porters, carrying between them a huge white refrigerator, suspended by thick broad leather straps. At some point they would need to take their chances with the traffic and cross the road. Good luck to them, he thought. As he diverted his gaze from the two men, Sirkeci Station came into his range of vision, just across the street from where he stood. The European terminus itself, unlike the Germano-Gothic style edifice that was Haydarpaşa on the Asian side, was an ugly, smelly railway station, hardly basking in its former glory of the days when the great and rich of the world passed under its portals to board or disembark from the Orient Express.. As far as Pete was concerned, its destinations were far less exotic than those to be reached from Haydarpaşa. For him, Sofia, Bucharest, Munich, Paris, did not compare with Damascus, Amman, Baghdad and Teheran.

Nevertheless, this was his way out of the clutches (or was it the

277

loving embrace?) of Istanbul. He would be away from the city for two months at least. Then he planned to return, to continue with more private tuition work, and by September he would be ready to take up a teaching post at Darüşşafaka High School. At least that was what he was hoping to do, even though he had not as yet been called for interview.

Purchasing his ticket at Sirkeci Station proved to be much less problematic than he had anticipated. The process involved showing his student card and passport before handing over the twenty five dollars for his fare to Munich. Clutching the ticket, which resembled a chequebook with only three cheques left in it, he felt a frisson of excitement which took hold of him momentarily, then he spotted a bus bound for Taksim and hopped on board. He managed to get a seat for once, and as the bus made its bumbling way through the old city, he started to examine his travel document. It was inside a two page cover, the front of which displayed the TCDD (Turkish Railways) motif and a picture of a fast diesel train. A thin paper rectangle proclaimed the date, time and price. The trip would transport him from Istanbul to Munich for a mere twenty five dollars and was scheduled to last almost three days.

At least the train would take him on a different route through Trakya from the one which they had travelled on their way to Istanbul the previous autumn. That way, he would get to see more of the country. The train would be crossing into Greece at Uzunköprü - the long bridge. The road route took travellers from Greece via Ipsala with its endless queues and waiting times. Hopefully, when the train passed through Edirne, it would not be too dark, as that would enable him to catch a glimpse of another Sinan masterpiece; the Selimiye Mosque. A glance outside the dust caked bus window showed him the Taksim bus stop for this service, as it hove into view, attended by what could be described as a queue, but was in fact a rabble of noisy impatient commuters, anxious to be homeward bound. Pete managed to manoeuvre his way through the central exit, past the besieging mass of humanity, and made his way to the ranks of dolmuş cars for Mecidiyeköy and beyond.

Crammed into the rear seats of an ageing Desoto Suburban, and having paid his fare, he started to take in the oh so familiar scenes either side of the Hürriyet Caddesi. As the *dolmuş* crawled through the congested thoroughfare towards Harbiye he pondered on whether this would be his final farewell. Even though this area was not part of the legendary Byzantium or Constantinople, the historic and at times magical ambiance of the ancient city seemed to have spread itself across the Golden Horn, even as far as Kurtuluş and Mecidiyeköy. Further on still, were the districts of Şişli, Levent and Nişantaşı, but they were the more modernistic and affluent areas.

Suddenly Pete was awakened from his reflections, as he caught sight of something, or rather someone, through the corner of his eye, standing on the pavement, not fifty yards from the road leading to the Hilton Hotel. The shock of what he saw, almost caused him to scream out his thoughts aloud.

It's Izzet! That thieving, lying bastard!

The mayhem he had caused to Pete, the expedition and the lives of his friends was inestimable. If it had not been for him, who knows what they could have gone on to achieve? In the brief glimpse he had caught of him, he had discerned that he was not alone, but in conversation with another individual.

"Musaid bir yer de inebilirmiyim?"

Pete made his usual, well practised request to the driver to put him down at a permitted stop. Meanwhile, his mind started churning over past events. How many times had he returned mentally to that moment when he had handed over almost all of his cash to that trickster? If only. Well, the other three members of the expedition had virtually run out of cash themselves. He wondered what story they would be telling others back in England. Now he had the chance to make amends. Adrenaline-charged by the prospect of confronting Izzet and exacting revenge, he left the dolmuş and glanced along the kerbside to where he had seen his nemesis. Who was he talking to? To his amazement and consternation, it turned out to be Mo, his friend from the Grand Bazaar. But then why not? Mo was in more or less the same business as Izzet, except that in Pete's case he had exchanged his lira for dollars at a very favourable rate. At least he had come back with the money. Indeed, without Mo's help, he would have found it much more problematic obtaining the currency for his return journey.

If Pete were to confront Izzet now, how would Mo react? Indeed, he was a friend, introduced to him by Kemal, but how close was the relationship between him and Izzet? Perhaps they were in the same gang together. He was also sure that the young Turkish con man, on spotting Pete approaching him, would very quickly take to his heels, as on the previous two occasions. Pete was by now in a situation of stasis; a freeze frame of both mind and body.

On the one hand, he dearly wanted to thump the living daylights out of this sneaky con artist, then demand his money back. But then how would Mo react to this, once he had recovered from the shock of seeing his English friend behaving so outrageously? Perhaps he could dispense with the violence and plead with Mo to persuade Izzet (or whatever his name was) to pay up. On the other hand, there were still further matters for consideration. Following the loss of his money, he had, after all found gainful employment relevant to his training; he had met a beautiful person with whom he felt he could spend the rest of his life; he had made a number of good friends; he had lived in and enjoyed the sights of a truly exotic, enigmatic eastern city.

As these troubling and conflicting thoughts raced through his mind, he looked once more towards the two men. They were engaged in an animated, not altogether unfriendly conversation. All in all, he concluded, he had been a prize chump. Firstly, for trusting Izzet and secondly for leaving cash in his rucksack lying on the floor in the Beyoğlu flat so that Masood, that other scoundrel, could help himself. When would he ever learn? As for Masood, he was now a guest of the governor of Sağmacılar Prison. And Izzet? Apparently, he was still living on his wits on Istanbul's unforgiving streets, where every day he faced imminent arrest by the police, or death at the hands of other criminals..

In the final analysis, Pete considered that he had come out of this unplanned chapter of his life somewhat the better for his experiences. Besides, what was twenty pounds? He had saved up four times that amount with very little difficulty – even though he had lost some of that money too. He still had fifty dollars for the journey back to England. So who were the winners here? Life had to go on. Pete took one more brief fleeting look at Mo and Izzet. It was, after all, their city, their manor. He

turned his back on them and took a few steps towards the bustling street where another dolmuş was approaching.

"Mecediyeköy!" he shouted.

Homeward Bound

The city is a cage.
No other places, always this
Your earthly landfall, and no ship exists
To take you from yourself.

Cavafy, writing about Alexandria. Translated by Lawrence Durrell

It was time now for goodbyes, or rather au revoirs, as Pete fully intended to come back to Istanbul some time in July. There was a tearful parting with Selma who had risked discovery by her family when she embraced him passionately in Taksim Square. She had also handed over the rest of the cash she had been looking after for him. They would be writing. He had also bidden farewell to his friends, including the lads whose band he had been invited to join on his return. Vefbi had been so emotional, as had Hassan but Pete had promised to continue teaching at the school in the evenings during the next academic year. It would be true to say that many were sorry to see him leave, but he now had to set his mind not only on the journey home, but also to reuniting with his family and friends. There was, in addition, the necessity of earning some money to finance his return journey to Istanbul. He had high hopes of being re-employed by the security firm where once again he would be donning helmet and goggles, girding his loins with a riot stick, delivering money to banks across Essex, and guarding commercial properties.

He would be among his own people again. How was he going to readapt? It was said, and not without some justification, that the English were taciturn, cool, some may say cold by nature. Did that describe his family? His acquaintances? Not really. However, he had after all, spent more than half a year among people who were hospitable, friendly, volatile and at times aggressive. How much had this engagement with them affected his own personality? He felt, as the time for his departure grew closer, that he may have to readjust, switch himself back to factory settings, as it were. That was not going to be an easy task.

These preoccupations were uppermost in Pete's mind as the bus carrying him to Sirkeci Station made its frustratingly sluggish progress through the customary melee of workers, vendors, and tourists. However, as he alighted at the station forecourt, he became elated and filled with excitement in anticipation of his impending journey. Making his way to his train which was waiting at Platform One, he observed, with a quiver of pure delight, that the locomotive at the front was steam powered. He had not travelled on a steam train since 1963, on a trip to Clacton on Sea, one sun - filled day in July. He located an empty compartment and was about to board when a shabbily attired boy, who could not have been more than ten years old, approached him and tried to sell him a bottle of water for five lira. Pete gave the standard response he always made to street sellers, when not wanting to buy their wares, *"Yok canım, istemiyorum,."* - No my dear, I don't want it. Despite this, the child persisted. *"Mikrob yok,"* he pleaded, indicating there were no harmful germs in the water. Pete was not convinced. He entered his chosen compartment and settled himself for the journey. Regarding accommodation on the train, he had taken the cheaper option by not booking a couchette. Consequently he was faced with spending the best part of three days, including two nights, in the same seat.

In choosing this compartment, he had failed to notice the luggage in the rack above the seat opposite. In all honesty, he had hardly expected to be the sole occupant of this compartment. Sure enough, the owner of the aforementioned luggage – from the Indian sub-continent by all appearances - strode into the compartment clutching a plastic litre bottle full of water.

"I just bought this bottle from little boy on platform. Five lira.

Very cheap," he declared. "Hello sir, I am Sadeeq."

"Pleased to meet you. Are you going all the way to Munich?"

"I have travelled by train all the way from Karachi. I go to work in Germany. Are you British?"

"Yes I am English," Pete replied, with some trepidation. He was half expecting to hear a tirade against the greed and cruelty of the British raj, but instead, Sadeeq replied,

" Ah, England. It's the guardian nation of the world, you know"

Pete wondered at that moment whether two World Wars, the Korean War and the Suez crisis had escaped this man's attention. The UK had been caught off guard in so many ways by those events. However, he did feel a fleeting frisson of pride as a result of Sadeeq's comment.

The Munich train departed from Sirkeci Station half an hour late. This, according to regular users, was a distinct improvement compared to other occasions. Soon, it was thundering across Thrace towards the city of Edirne. As they left behind the suburbs of Istanbul and threaded through sylvan scenes of farms and small settlements, plus a number of sleepy looking townships, Pete found himself listening, with bated breath and some envy, as Sadeeq related the details of his journey across Western Pakistan, Iran and Eastern Turkey. That had certainly been some trek.

At Edirne, Pete was rewarded with the sight of Selimiye Mosque away to his left, as he sat facing the rear of the train. Even from a distance of some miles, the building looked impressive. Four tall, slim minarets pointed heavenward and at their centre, a domed edifice; Sinan's signature. And to think, in 1574, when the mosque was completed, the best works of this gifted architect still lay ahead of him. But now they were progressing ever closer to the Greek border and the moment he had been dreading all along was fast approaching. The visa check.

Hardly had this thought crossed his mind, when a figure appeared in the darkening corridor. He was dressed in a green uniform with a green peaked cap and he loomed large in the doorway window. A border policeman entered the compartment and asked the two occupants for their passports. Once he had carefully perused Sadeeq's documents, it was Pete's turn. Unfortunately, the game was up. He looked at Pete's passport and, devoid of any expression, he declared, *"Visa bitti. Türkiyede dört ay fazla kaldınız."* Pete understood perfectly well what he meant, as he had spotted the fact that Pete had overstayed his welcome by four months. As calmly as he could but with no real sense of the seriousness of this situation Pete replied,

"Kusura bakmayınız efendi. Iki ay sonra Istanbul a geni geleceğim, Türk liseside çalışmak için. Ben Ingilizce öğretmenim".

It was clear the policeman spoke no English but Pete had made himself understood. After apologising, he had explained that in two months' time, he would be returning to Istanbul to teach at a Turkish high school. He had been advised to mention the name of the school, but decided not to name drop after all. How glad he was that he had persisted in his learning of the language, ignoring Selma's giggles every time he started to speak it. However, he was not so ingenuous as to mention that he had been in gainful employment in the city all this time. The officer, displaying no apparent signs of annoyance, told Pete to wait a minute while he left to consult his chief. No doubt he needed a decision on how much of a bribe he could demand from the English *salak*[7].

Five minutes later, the man in green returned. Sadeeq had remained silent all this time. All his experiences as an artisan in his own country had taught him that the least you had to say, the less likely you were to end up in a police cell, or worse. He had been warned that a Turkish prison cell awaited problematic travellers. He wondered if he should counsel the Englishman to say as little as possible. In actual fact, Pete, although he had truly dreaded this encounter, now that it was happening, it did not seem so traumatic after all. Such was the innocence of youth. He just needed to somehow come out of the other side of this. So far was he removed mentally from the implications of his visa infringement, that he never once thought that a pair of handcuffs could be summarily produced, resulting in his removal from the train, and into

7. idiot

odiferous accommodation consisting of four walls and iron bars.

The border guard stared at Pete, his countenance still devoid of emotion. Pete awkwardly managed a half smile which he immediately suppressed, in case he was seen as displaying frivolity. He sensed that something unpleasant was about to happen to him. However, as it turned out, he was going to be allowed to continue his journey.

"Yirmi Dolar, twenty dollars," declared the officer, regarding Pete as if he were a wayward child.

With an air of resignation, Pete reached inside his jacket, drew out his wallet and produced two ten dollar bills, making sure he maintained his expressionless demeanour. To his surprise, a receipt was duly issued. So it was a fine, not a bribe after all. To his great relief, Pete's third encounter with Turkish law enforcement was at an end.

The journey continued towards Uzunköprü and the Greek border with the train hardly breaking any speed records for railway travel, even though this very collection of carriages had been termed "the Munich Express". The conversation between Pete and Sadeeq also continued. The Pakistani was interested in the possibility of seeking work in the UK, and he showed Pete his impressive CV. Pete informed him he could possibly get him a job at the factory where his dad worked. This caused Sadeeq much excitement, and reaching in one of his travel bags he took out and pressed on Pete a photostat of the aforementioned document.

It did not take long to cross the sliver of Greece situated beyond western Turkey, and soon they reached Bulgaria. Whist traversing the border, they were forced to stand in the corridor whilst a posse of grim faced, officious and heavily armed Bulgarian border police entered their compartment and started pulling up the seats. Apparently, they were searching for fellow countrymen who could well have been hiding under those seats, in attempting to escape from their glorious republic.

The blue uniformed police officers were morose, gruff and actually looked quite dangerous, as one or two were carrying sub machine guns. They obviously took their duties very seriously, so much so, that Pete could not help singing to himself a *sotto voce* rendition of "When you're smiling…" It was totally lost on those guys. Obviously not music buffs. Pete and Sadeeq were left with the task of replacing their overturned seats, first checking, of course to make sure there were no absconders still cowering in the depths of the carriage.

Somewhere between the Turkish border and Sofia, possibly Plovdiv, Pete started to feel peckish, as he had consumed the *börek* and *ayran* he had brought with him whilst they were still travelling through Turkey. He still resisted drinking from the water bottle when it was offered to him, even though Sadeeq had not as yet keeled over or even complained of stomach pains. The train seemed to linger at each stop for what seemed like an age. However, during one such hiatus, he noticed that on the platform where they were paused there was a small kiosk selling what looked like salami rolls and spiral shaped sweet pastries. Stepping down from the carriage, Pete was in a constant panic in case the train departed without him. There was no chance of that happening in the next ten minutes or so, but he was not to know that. He ordered the salami, called "Lukanka" and two pastries, which contained a lot of raisins and were topped with icing sugar. He returned to his seat clutching his meal, eagerly awaiting the new taste sensation, and he was not disappointed. He would have offered some to Sadeeq but he was asleep. Besides, the Lukanka was out of the question as it contained pork and Sadeeq, if his name was anything to go by, was a Moslem. The coffee he had purchased definitely gave him the required kick and it was the first one he had consumed that was not in a tiny cup with half a centimetre of grounds in the bottom. This one came in a plastic cup.

The train on which Pete was travelling actually retraced the route of the famed Orient Express. However, the term "express" would definitely have been a misnomer for this service, as it seemed to crawl between stations and he had observed at least four locomotive changes between Istanbul and Sofia. On the plus side, before it became too dark, Pete was able to appreciate the stunning

287

scenery on view. He was particularly enthralled when catching sight of the broad, brown Danube, as it swirled its way across the Balkan lands to the Black Sea beyond.

At Belgrade, they were joined by a boisterous group of workers, who filled the compartment not only with their bodies, but also their raucous chatter. Pete guessed they were speaking in Serbo-Croat. It was not long, however, before they were passing round a large bottle of Schnapps which, when offered to Pete, he gratefully accepted the two or three swigs he was urged to take. Surprisingly, Sadeeq also imbibed some of the strong spirit. These fellows were fun. They were a tonic for Pete and Sadeeq, after the dour atmosphere that had pervaded in the train, like a bad weather cloud, during their passage through Bulgaria. When the men eventually left them at Zagreb, shortly before dawn, a sepulchral quiet settled over the compartment and the two passengers left managed to catch up with some sleep.

They crossed the country known in those times as Yugoslavia during the hours of daylight, when the bright sunshine outside helped to lighten Pete's mood, despite his fatigue. Glancing out of the carriage windows, he became transfixed by the panoramic views that were opening up to him. He was allowed glimpses of a simpler, more primitive lifestyle. The usual road traffic occasionally came into view, although there were few cars and no motorways, but the most glaring contrast with anything in his experience was on the vast acres of farmland. Here, women could be seen, in white headscarves, toiling in the sun, while men drove carts and ploughs drawn by oxen. It was a scene from centuries before, as if the advent of modern farming methods had simply passed them by.

During the second night, the train progressed northwards through Ljubljana and then north west across the Austrian border. The landscape on either side was curtained off from view, save for the odd light here and there that glowed on either side of the tracks or twinkled in the distance. Signs of life in an otherwise Stygian darkness. As this darkness gradually gave way to the inevitable greying of dawn, the trackside shadows began to dissipate.

Then the sun's early rays caused Pete to awaken from his seated slumber. Glancing out of the window, he was totally unprepared for the panorama that greeted his gaze. They were, at this time, traversing the Austrian Alps. Prior to this moment, he had only seen mountains in Central Wales and Switzerland, all of which were unforgettable in their beauty and splendour, but somehow, these massive peaks, visible on both sides of the carriage, seemed to surpass all else. Sights that are pleasing to the eye, increase our inner feelings of pleasure and go a long way to relieving stress At this instant, Pete's endorphin levels were off the scale. Row upon row of gigantic, snow capped walls of orogenic rock stretched away as far as the eye could see. Rob later told him that on his way back to England, he had also witnessed these sights which he described as "orgasmic". Pete, for his part, could only gasp with appreciation as each new bend in the track brought forth fresh vistas of pure mountainous magnificence.

In due course, the Austrian Alps were left behind and as the train drew ever nearer to Munich, Pete, his thought processes alive and buzzing, began to contemplate and reflect upon some of the reasons that he and his companions had embarked upon that expedition in the first place. Leaving aside the calamitous lack of organisation inherent in the planning and glossing over the fact that they had not even reached Beirut, the third port on their itinerary, they had, nevertheless, shared a variety of experiences that they would not have encountered had they stayed at home. Was this the limit of

whatever they had wished to achieve before settling down in their respective careers? Or was this just the beginning? A broadening of horizons.

Having just passed through the Austrian Alps in all their glory, and, as far as he was concerned, at the optimum time of day, Pete concluded that, if nothing else, it was the sense of seeing that had been most rewarded. Events of the past seven months had certainly opened his eyes, literally and metaphorically. He had witnessed for himself sights to please the eye, such as the beauties of the Ardennes, the Swiss Lakes, Rome, Athens, the Adriatic and the marvel of Istanbul, to name but a few. The intrinsic joys of travel had also contributed to a feelgood factor, which all too often had governed his mental processes, leading him into situations which, through lack of clear thinking on his part, would catch him off guard.

In addition, he had experienced true pain, which had, at times, gnawed away at him; like parting from his family, the loss of his money, his sense of isolation in a foreign place, the trials and tribulations in both his work and in his love life. All had been soothed to a degree by the balm of the more positive occurrences and the sights he had witnessed. Thoughts and visions of the beautiful lie deep within the human soul and exercise a strange power over everything we do. Such were Pete's conclusions as he lapsed once more into a light sleep. And as for Sadeeq? He was still dozing in his seat amidst his dreams – of home, perhaps. The thought occurred to Pete, as he slipped into slumber, that maybe he should have woken him up to see the mountains.

When he opened his eyes again, the train was entering the outskirts of a large metropolis. It could only be Munich. He had made it. Soon afterwards, he was stepping on to the platform at Munich Station. After shaking hands with Sadeeq and exchanging mutual good wishes for the future, Pete made his way towards the exit. Strange how it seemed that he and the Pakistani had become close friends over three days, but were destined never to see each other again. Such is the nature of travel. Such is life. He found himself saddened by the loss of Sadeeq's acquaintance and his company. Now the truly hard part of the return journey was about to begin.

He knew he had to make for the north west of the city so he asked at the station information kiosk for directions to the Köln Autobahn. He was given the number of the bus he needed to catch and the relevant stop to look out for. To his amazement, he discerned that the buses in the Munich streets were in two segments, joined together by concertina - like connections. Some years later, the same models would be introduced to Great Britain as "Bendy Buses". He boarded the rear section and after about twenty minutes, he had reached his stop, within sight of a slip road to the motorway. Strangely enough, no-one had collected his fare so he was able to hang on to some of the German marks he had obtained from Mo, in addition to sterling and dollars. He had crossed the city in a kind of haze and later swore he remembered nothing of the Bavarian capital's great sights.

However, to say that his trek northwards passed without incident would be a plain untruth. He was lucky enough to be picked up quite soon and close to the motorway slip road by a young German named Hans, in a new looking Fiat 125 saloon. This was the second time Pete had travelled on one of the a German motorways which criss-crossed the whole country. The first time had been at night, so he was unable to appreciate the broad vistas of the multi-laned roadways and their fast moving traffic. The going was smooth and soon many miles had been covered.

Then catastrophe struck. They were involved in a collision somewhere between Stuttgart and Karlsruhe, when a truck, entering from a slip road, slammed into the side of the Fiat, knocking it sideways into the outside lane. Luckily, no other vehicle was overtaking at the time. All traffic came to a halt and within minutes the police arrived. Pete was naturally shaken but unhurt, as were Hans and the truck driver. To Pete's astonishment, he could see that the Polizei were wearing nazi style caps with the low slanting peaks. As if that was not alarming enough, one of the officers began to ask him questions. He could not speak or understand German, apart from a few words he had picked up elsewhere. A kindly explanation from his driver, *"Er spricht kein Deutsch"*, was enough for the traffic policeman to lose interest in him. Pete got the gist of what Hans had said, basically, that his passenger did not speak German. He turned to survey the off side of the shiny blue Italian saloon. It looked as though it had been raked with machine gun fire. An observation he was careful not to share with a group of Germans. Meanwhile, the motorway had been partially cleared and the traffic was beginning to move away from the incident. It was noticeable that during this whole episode, everyone seemed to remain so incredibly calm.

Once all the details had been recorded, the car still being driveable, Pete and Hans were able to continue towards Heidelburg. However, after about half an hour, the driver, who spoke very little English, and with whom Pete had hardly exchanged a word during the trip, mumbled something like

"Du must leave now."

He had been most kind to convey Pete all this way, and despite his taciturn approach to the accident, he must have been churning up inside, not only with the shock. but emotionally, due to the damage to his car. A good lad – Pete concluded.

He was on his own, once again, by the roadside at the Heidelburg turn off, thumbing for a lift that he hoped would take him in the direction of Köln. The nearby road sign confirmed that he was standing in the correct spot. It was only at that moment he realised that he had not eaten since consuming yet another salami sandwich in Yugoslavia the previous night. On the distant horizon, he spotted what looked very much like a burger van, complete with a queue of customers. Surely not, it must have been a mirage. Before he could make his way towards that glorious vision, a Citroen CV6 slowed down beside him. He was not going to miss this opportunity for the sake of his stomach. The driver, a student named Georg, was heading back home to Wiesbaden his from university. In addition to giving Pete a lift, on arrival in Wiesbaden, he took him to the apartment where he lived with his mother. He was given a very welcome dinner, a good night's sleep and breakfast the following morning that consisted of croissants and seemingly endless cups of strong coffee.

At just after ten am, on the fourth day of his return trip, Georg set Pete down at what he described as " a good hitch hiking spot" just outside Wiesbaden. On the way there, they passed the huge Federal German Police Headquarters and Pete's thoughts returned to the accident on the autobahn the previous day. He wondered how Hans had fared and whether he would soon be able to get his car fixed. Half an hour later, a gigantic articulated lorry drew up beside him and he was taken, eventually, as far as the turn off for

Utrecht. Before reaching it, the driver stopped for refreshments at a Dutch motorway services where Pete hungrily consumed *broodjes* which in this case consisted of white bread, processed meat and a mustard sauce. He drank a half litre of Amstel beer, coincidentally, the same brew as he had imbibed on the Ostend ferry when the group had first set out. He was also able to watch some of the European Cup Final between Celtic and Feyenoord on the television inside the diner. Just before he left, the score was one goal each, with extra time about to begin. He missed Feyenoord's winning goal, as the lorry driver, who had been listening to the game on his cab radio, left him by the roadside close to the central Dutch city of Utrecht.

Twelve hours after he had begun this stage of his trek, way back in Central Germany, Pete was left, a solitary figure in a bleak, nocturnal landscape, devoid of any life, or, more importantly, devoid of traffic. Rows of lustrous motorway lighting could be seen snaking off in both directions towards a distant blur. Occasionally, he picked out twin headlights accompanied by the hum and clatter of internal combustion engines. The benighted motorists were carving out their own light trails above him as he stood, ignored and waiting anxiously by the slip road. The cold of a Northern European springtime was beginning creep through Pete's thin clothing. Then, sure enough, in the distance, a puttering sound could be heard, and yet another CV6 hove into view. The little grey vehicle which Pete liked to refer to as a "student car" (he did not own or drive any form of vehicle at this time), pulled up beside him, and a young Dutchman informed him he was travelling to Den Haag, the royal capital. A swift change of plan was formulated as Pete consulted his mental map. He could continue from the Hague to the Hook of Holland and catch a ferry to Harwich. The driver was also a student whose name was Willem and, as chance would have it, was also living with his mother. He kindly ran Pete to the Hook of Holland, a distance of some fifty miles, where enquiries were made about times and tickets for the ferry to Harwich. It transpired that the fare would cost Pete almost as much as he had in his possession. Willem had the solution.

"Tomorrow I take you to a place outside my city where you can thumb a lift to Ostend. The Cross Channel Ferry from there is much cheaper. You can stay with me tonight. Lets eat now."

They walked out of the ferry port and passed along a narrow street with dimly lit shop windows on either side, displaying prostitutes, sitting impassively, and resembling clothing shop dummies. They seemed to be staring into the middle distance, probably through and beyond the buildings opposite, back to the places of their origins, as they reflected on their lives to date. Who knows? Who even cared, for that matter? The occupants of those shop windows certainly brought back memories of that night in Karaköy, with Walter and Brian in the street of brothels. However, these women seemed to resemble maiden aunts waiting in their parlours for members of their family to visit. At that very moment, Pete caught a glimpse of one of them greeting her nephew. There would be more on offer than tea or cakes. More women, younger in appearance, wearing see through blouses with black leather mini skirts and black knee length boots, roamed the street, confidently expecting business to come their way.

Willem led Pete into a broader thoroughfare where several fast food stalls were surrounded by dozens of late night customers. The student treated Pete to a portion of chips with mayonnaise, then they entered a large wooden cabin inhabited by a number of hippies seated round wooden formica topped tables. There was an all pervading, cloying aroma of hashish. However, they merely ordered two beers. Amstel, of course.

That night, as a guest of Willem's family, Pete slept soundly again until nine am. He was given a breakfast of white sliced bread and strawberry jam with a cup of coffee. Later, Willem drove him into the city, past the royal palace, ready to embark on what he believed would be the final leg of his journey to the English Channel. Luckily, he was further conveyed through the outskirts of Ostend by a middle aged Turk who reminded him strangely of Hassan bey back in Istanbul. Could it be that feelings of nostalgia for that city were starting to creep over him?

Seated in the rear of the DAF 55 Coupé were two attractive

and nubile Dutch girls. Pete would not have said their dresses were short, but he knew the colour of their knickers within five minutes of joining them. There appeared to be some kind of a connection between these two and the driver, which Pete could not quite work out, mainly evident by a great deal of merriment and giggling. They were speaking in Dutch and seemed to be directing mischievous glances towards their English passenger, or so it seemed to him. Sadly, whatever hopes Pete had of getting a piece of the action, soon fizzled out, when the car stopped to drop the girls off somewhere between Rotterdam and the Belgian border. They both scampered off towards what looked like a small housing estate and disappeared from view.

The Turkish driver also spoke English, and was intrigued to learn that Pete had spent time in Istanbul. He informed his passenger that he had lived in the Levent district and after ten years away from his home, he was nostalgic about one day returning to that affluent suburb. In due course, they crossed the border into Belgium, and Pete left him shortly afterwards. A couple more lifts and he was by the quayside in Ostend. A kindly RAC man (what was he doing there?) noticing this somewhat bedraggled looking young traveller with a rucksack on his back, and clutching a khaki holdall, directed him to a café where he could get "a cup of English tea." Pete made his way to the dreary looking brick built eatery and tea house, where he ordered crisps, chocolate cake and a coffee. A healthy repast indeed!

The Channel crossing itself was uneventful. This time, Pete was aboard a British ferryboat and it was strange indeed to hear a babble of voices all around him mostly speaking his own language. Outside, the set of lights along one shoreline soon gave way to a distant sighting of another set of lights along the opposite coast. Except, of course that Pete was approaching his native land and getting nearer with each ticking of the watch on his wrist. Halfway across, whilst leaning against the rail on the starboard deck, and feeling quite seasick, despite the calm nature of the waters below him, he encountered a fellow passenger who was also feeling queasy.

He turned out to be an Italian button salesman, on his way, as he put it, to open up the market for his merchandise in the UK. They conversed for a while, and Pete felt that he just had to mention his journey across Italy. Naturally, he omitted most of the finer details regarding his experiences on the Italian railway network. The salesman was fluent in English and of a friendly disposition. He was delighted by Pete's reminiscences of places visited, especially his home city of Milan, to where he had not returned since childhood. So Pete had met yet another wanderer operating away from his homeland, for one reason or another. Were these guys happy in their present situations or would they prefer to be on their own native soil? The Italian generously purchased supper for them both and offered Pete a lift to London, where he could catch a night bus to Liverpool Street then travel onward by train to his home town.

Fortunately, in addition to his stash of dollars and marks, obtained of course through Mo, Pete also possessed enough sterling to buy the necessary bus and train tickets. However, how tempting, he thought, would it be to replicate the antics he had employed in his college days, thus saving himself a few pounds? Perhaps events in Italy had shown him that such practices had become a thing of the

past as far as he was concerned. Besides, he was by now feeling somewhat drained by fatigue as a result of his odyssey across Europe.

The Italian had dropped him off in a vicinity of London he neither knew nor recognised, and at an hour he did not altogether relish. Dawn was not yet stirring in the east, thus an eerie half light dimly illuminated a broad thoroughfare of large, grey-walled residences. He was standing beside a bus stop, where, he had been assured, a night bus would arrive in due course to convey him to Liverpool Street Station. He began reflecting on how boring it would be to have to wait for too long in this particular spot. As his eyes gradually grew accustomed to his surroundings, he was able to take in more details. He could make out low black railings on either side of the street that fronted the fairly substantial dwellings, with flights of stone steps leading up to their front entrances. It seemed that all of London was abed. Nothing moved on the road; not a light flickered on the street or in any window.

It was just then, and to his alarm, that he heard the sound of approaching footsteps which broke the silence with regular taps and an occasional scuffing on the pavement. A slightly crouched, shadowy figure drew near and began to address Pete in a voice that was elderly in tone and tinged with traces of a German accent.

"Aach, you wait for the night bus, I see." He consulted his pocket watch. " I can tell you, it is not due for more than an hour. You are welcome to join me in my humble abode for coffee while you are waiting."

There was a slight chill in the small hours of a mid May morning and even a hint of rain pervading the deserted street. The newcomer had reached Pete's side. He was a slight man, possibly sixty years of age, who walked with the aid of a stick. He was somewhat shorter than Pete. He repeated his invitation, and Pete, after considering the unattractive prospect of killing an hour or so in the cold and damp, replied,

"Thank you. That's most kind of you."

"My flat is just over there, across the road."

He pointed to one of the dull but stately buildings opposite and the pair crossed the road. He led Pete down some stone steps to a small basement flat, scantily furnished with a nondescript table and four matching chairs. Faded brown curtains covered windows that had grimy, beige painted wooden frames. The man had been right; it was a "humble abode". There were a few cheap looking ornaments adorning an old brown sideboard and Pete noticed some framed photographs of famous actors, together with some theatrical posters hanging on the walls. There was a strong smell of dog combined with some kind of odour that reminded him of school dinner cabbage. The man, whose name turned out to be Ben, busied himself with coffee cups and a jar of Nescafé. The kettle began to boil on a solitary gas ring. When he had made the coffee – black for himself and white for Pete – he handed the cup to his guest who had seated himself on a shabby and stained, light brown sofa. Next he sat down on the sofa, about a yard away from Pete.

Ben, it turned out, was an aging actor, close to retirement, in fact, with experience of stage, film and television. For the next half an hour, he regaled Pete with stories about Sir John Gielgud, Dame Edith Evans and the like. Pete, for his part, gave an account of his travels and rather humbly, it must be said, talked about his stage appearances at college and the times he had helped to pioneer innovative and ground breaking television programmes there, being one of the first of such colleges to work in this medium. They chatted in a convivial manner.

" I once made a televised speech imitating Harold Wilson," Pete declared. Gannex mac, pipe and a bottle of Wincarnis on the table."

" Sounds very amusing. I have been on television too. Recently I played a German officer in a BBC war drama. Perhaps you have seen it," was Ben's response.

Pete had not, as he was probably abroad at the time, but he was mightily impressed. However, he was not quite so struck when he noticed that Ben was now ensconced just a few inches from his left side. The actor continued,

"It was interesting you spent some time in Istanbul. It's a wicked city but wonderful too. Some of those eastern men, they'll have sex with anyone or anything; women, other men, dogs, donkeys. And why not! It all sounds like great fun to me."

Pete began to feel more than a little uneasy following that last piece of information. Not so much for its accuracy, or rather lack of, as he had never seen or heard of any evidence to support those observations, but it was more the way in which their conversation had suddenly been switched. He glanced across the dimly lit room to where a well nourished Jack Russell cross lay fast asleep in a basket, covered by a pink blanket. Ben seemed to read his thoughts and nodded an "Oh yes" towards his guest. This was getting somewhat surreal.

Pete was becoming less and less comfortable with each passing second but his host made no significant move. Perhaps he did not have to, Pete considered with alarm, and he started to regard his coffee cup which was now half full. Was that a strange drowsy feeling coming over him? Drinking more of this beverage could well work out to be a very risky business. Or was it too late? But no, this jovial, good natured old boy was surely not capable of such an evil act. Did he actually hint there that he was having sex with his own dog? Surely not! Appalled, Pete reflected that the man was obviously lonely and revelled in the company of others. What Ben came out with next made Pete shiver with trepidation.

"Myself, I especially like fair haired young men, but not boys. Have you ever had sex with another man?

It seemed he was not going to waste any more time. This prompted some inward searching from Pete. How was he feeling? - OK. Was he scared? – a bit, yes. Had his coffee been drugged? – unlikely. He now had to make his excuses and exit immediately. He replied as kindly as he could that he had never been tempted in that direction and actually he liked girls too much. Every word of which was perfectly true.

The actor seemed to take this statement rather more philosophically than anticipated. He subtly shifted slightly away from the object of his desires, and his initial look of disappointment was replaced by a thin smile of acceptance. His acting ability had not deserted him. Another time; another man, perhaps. Although Pete was experiencing some revulsion at what had just occurred, he had no wish to hurt his host, either physically or emotionally. He had to say something, though but all he could manage was,

"The night bus must be due very soon. Most interesting meeting you and thanks very much for the coffee."

As he showed Pete to the door, Ben, rather half heartedly tried to convince him that he should really try a range of sexual partners for optimum satisfaction and enjoyment. Pete acknowledged this advice with a nod and a farewell wave, then he stepped out into the still gloomy street. Soon he would be seated on the night bus and heading towards Liverpool Street.

The said night bus turned up at his stop just five minutes after he had made his way out of the elderly actor's flat. He was soon on an early train from Liverpool Street, arriving in Chelmsford half an hour later. On the way, he was able to experience again, on that beautiful sunlit early morning, the ecstasy he always felt when the train passed through the splendid vistas afforded by the Wid Valley. He was truly back home. A fifteen minute bus ride took him from the station to his familiar bus stop, and a ten minute walk through the silent, deserted landscape, saw him safely outside his family's home. It was six thirty am. He knocked on the front door.

Gel, gel, ne olursan ol yine gel,
İster kafir, ister mecusi, ister puta tapan ol yine gel,
Bizim dergahımız, umitsizlik dergahı değildir,
Yüz kere tövbeni bozmuş olsan da yine gel

Come, come again, whoever you are.
Wanderer, worshipper, lover of leaving — it doesn't matter,
Ours is not a caravan of despair.
Come, even if you have broken your vow a hundred times,
Come, come again, come

Mevlana Celaleddin Rumi

And Pete did go again. But that's another story, as they say.

About the Author – PJE Bailey

Peter spent forty five years in the teaching profession but is now retired and living in Leigh on Sea. He was Head of English in four schools. In studying for a Master's Degree in English at London University, Institute of Education, he was given a profound insight into linguistic aspects of the narrative form. That is to say it is not always the author speaking in literature, but language itself. There are also real events which are recounted in "The Way to Byzantium, but they serve as referents of the discourse regarding the historical period in which the novel is set.

In 1969, after training as a teacher at Bulmershe College, Reading, the author joined three colleagues on a gap year expedition, but ended up spending three years living and teaching in Istanbul. He feels this experience enriched his later literary output which has mainly been poetry. Some of his poems can be read in "Ten of the Best" (United Press Ltd.)

Raised in a beautiful part of Mid Essex, his writing is inspired by nature, scenery, the changing seasons and the influence of all these on the human psyche. Indeed, parts of this novel are set in and around Mid Essex as well as in more exotic locations. He states, "In my writing, I try to communicate my thoughts by directly addressing the reader, and augment this discourse with passages of description that attempt to evoke a sense of place."

The journey to Istanbul and certain life changing events, the traumas and delights of which occurred during his first seven month sojourn in the city, motivated him to write this first novel

"The Way to Byzantium". When asked why he wrote the novel, he replied that he felt he somehow had to make sense of what happened to him, and to consider the part Fate had to play in the unfolding of these events.

He is a guitarist and vocalist in two rock bands and has also performed his poems and his own songs for Southend and Colchester Poetry groups.

Printed in Great Britain
by Amazon